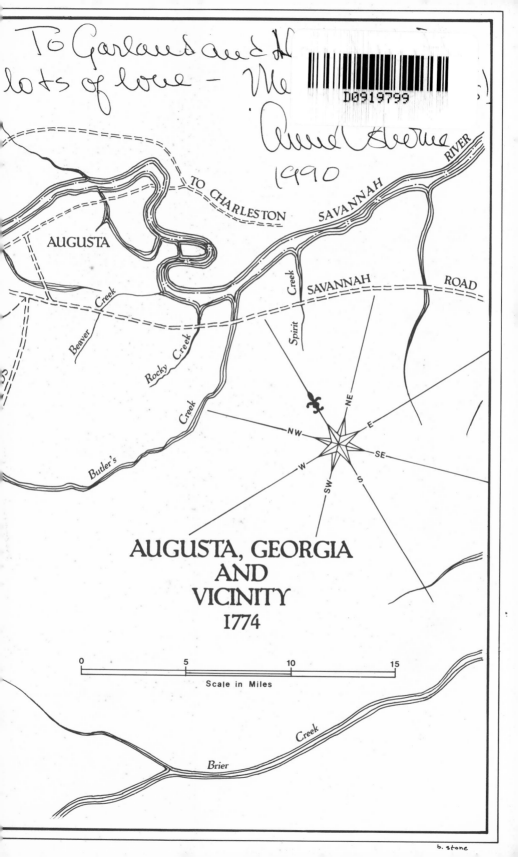

To Garland and H
lots of love — Me

1990

TO CHARLESTON

SAVANNAH RIVER

AUGUSTA

Creek

Beaver

Rocky Creek

Creek

Spirit Creek

SAVANNAH

ROAD

Butler's

Creek

NW W SW S SE E NE

AUGUSTA, GEORGIA
AND
VICINITY
1774

0 5 10 15

Scale in Miles

Brier

Creek

b. stone

REAP THE WHIRLWIND

Books by Anne Riggs Osborne

Fiction

Wind from the Main

Storm in the Backwoods

Nonfiction

Saluda, N.C.: 100 years, 1881-1981

The South Carolina Story

Dedicated to Jack Hagler and Pete Knox
who have done so much in their different ways
to preserve Augusta's heritage.

REAP THE WHIRLWIND

Augusta and the Revolution
A Novel

Anne Riggs Osborne

SANDLAPPER PUBLISHING, INC.
Orangeburg, South Carolina

Sandlapper Publishing, Inc.
P.O. Box 1932
Orangeburg, South Carolina 29116-1932

Library of Congress Cataloging-in-Publication Data
Osborne, Anne (Anne Riggs)
    Reap the whirlwind : Augusta and the Revolution : a novel / Anne
Riggs Osborne.
        p.   cm.
    ISBN 0-87844-087-9
    1. Augusta (Ga.)—History—Revolution, 1775-1783—Fiction.
2. Georgia—History—Revolution, 1775–1783—Fiction.   I. Title.
PS3565.S4R4   1989
813' .54—dc20   89-10334
                                                                                    CIP

Preface

Anne Osborne displays the courage of her Revolutionary War characters as she undertakes to tell the story of the American Revolution in the Augusta area. The history of the Revolution is so complex that few have dared to attempt to make it comprehensible. In fact, only William Gilmore Symms has used the Augusta locale as a setting for a Revolutionary War novel.

Reap the Whirlwind is a success because Anne Osborne has employed a clever literary device to provide a focus for the story and has introduced fictional characters to give it continuity and human interest. Angus MacLeod's tavern, The Sword and Thistle, is the imaginary meeting place for the main participants. There were several establishments in Augusta very much like the Sword and Thistle. Readers of Anne Osborne's first two books, *Wind from the Main* and *Storm in the Backwoods*, will be pleased to renew acquaintances with the indomitable Anne Bonny Seabright, aged but still sprightly, and John and Mary Anne Stanley. In *Reap the Whirlwind* they will meet Jamie Stratfield and Meg MacLeod, Bert Sheldon and Susan Merrill. But most of the participants in the story are real, historical individuals whose lives were fraught with such drama that they need no embellishment except the colorful language which the writer puts in their mouths. It is to her credit that the author portrays real persons and events, as accurately as possible, given the available records.

It is my hope that *Reap the Whirlwind* will introduce a new reading audience to the exciting events which form such an important part of Augusta's 250 years of history.

Edward J. Cashin
Chairman, Department of History
Augusta College

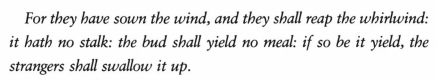

For they have sown the wind, and they shall reap the whirlwind: it hath no stalk: the bud shall yield no meal: if so be it yield, the strangers shall swallow it up.

HOSEA 8:7

Cast of Principal Characters

Angus MacLeod. A dedicated Scot who fought under Oglethorpe at the battle of Bloody Marsh where he lost his leg. He now is proprietor of the Sword and Thistle Inn in Augusta, Georgia.

Meg MacLeod. Angus' niece who came to live with him after her parents died now helps him in the taproom and is the real manager of the inn.

Jamie Stratfield. A young Maryland man who is fancy free but ready to find a way of life and somewhere to live it.

Bert Sheldon. A farmer's son who has joined the Georgia militia to earn money to buy a land grant for his family. His parents, Ben and Mary Sheldon, and their children, Francie and Benjy, plan to live in the Indian lands that are about to be opened to settlement.

Susan Merrill. A Charleston girl who has come to Augusta with her father and mother, Joseph and Jocelyn Merrill, and her two little sisters so that Joseph, a lawyer, can help the settlers register their claims.

John Stuart. The Superintendent of Indian Affairs for the South.

Thomas Brown. A Yorkshire squire who has bought a large land grant near Augusta, and is bringing indentured farmers over to till the land.

The Reverend Mr. James Seymour. Rector of St. Paul's Church who has been sent to Augusta by the Society for the Preservation of the Gospel.

The traders, Indians and settlers, the patriots and Tories introduce themselves as they enter the story. They and John Stuart, Thomas Brown and the Seymour family were real historical people while the MacLeods, Stratfields, Sheldons, and Merrills are purely fictional.

THE SWORD
AND
THISTLE

M eg finally had a chance to rest. The last guest had finished his noon meal and gone, and she had come to the tavern porch to shake the crumbs from the tablecloths so the birds could peck them from the path below. A steady hum of bees nuzzling the honeysuckle blossoms proclaimed that it was May. Winter was over and the hot days of summer were still a month away.

Nowhere in the world was nicer than Augusta, Georgia, in the spring. This May of 1773 seemed to be special for Meg. At seventeen she was not a dainty lass, giggling and cutting her eyes at the men as some girls did. She was too busy serving and clearing tables, dusting rooms, airing beds, beating carpets, and sweeping out the mud and sand brought in on heavy boots to pay much mind to the men who filled the common room at mealtime. A smile, a nod, or sometimes, an agile twirl and hop to avoid familiarities was all she could afford.

The purchase of black Desmond had made a change. With a man to stable horses, serve and clear tables, and help Amanda in the kitchen, Meg had more chance to act as hostess, stopping to chat or remembering the likes and dislikes of customers. For the first time she noticed admiring looks and listened to the stories of the Indian traders and men from the backwoods villages and farms. She suddenly was more than a busy pair of hands and two good legs to help her Uncle Angus.

Uncle Angus, bless him, did remarkably well on his wooden leg, but it was hard for him to carry trays without spilling. Lately, though, with money rolling in so steadily, they could afford extra help.

As she relaxed on the settle, legs stretched out in front and skirt still kilted up so that she could move in and out among the tables, a good six inches of ankle and bare leg showed below her dress. She'd shed her wool stockings as soon as it turned warm, and she never wore her one good pair of English shoes except for church. Soft doeskin moccasins for summer, with fur left inside for winter, were much more comfortable. Today even the summer moccasins seemed hot. She pushed them off and sat wiggling her toes in the sunshine, listening to the hum of the bees and the trill of a mockingbird in the sycamore tree.

"I beg your pardon, miss." The voice came from about the height of her knees.

Meg drew her bare toes back under the settle and tugged her skirt down to cover them. A man stood on the path beyond the steps, wide-brimmed hat in hand. He was obviously a gentleman, with good boots, whipcord breeches, and a fine cambric shirt. Over his arm he carried a jacket, and over his shoulder was a strap attached to a leather pouch.

"I'm sorry to interrupt you," he said. "I see that you enjoy the song of the catbird."

"It's a mockingbird," said Meg.

"I beg your pardon, miss. Mark Catesby made the same mistake, for he thought the catbird had only one note like a cat's cry. But he injured the bird's reputation. His song is not quite so sweet as the mock-bird, but he is a better mimic. And that is a catbird."

Meg just stared at him.

"Oh, I forget myself. I was told by John Stuart, the Superintendent of Indian Affairs, that I might find lodging here. I am to meet him for the conference."

"So you're Mr. Stuart's friend," said Meg. "He has engaged the big corner room overlooking Campbell's Gully, with a view of the river out of the side windows. We're going to be so crowded during the Indian Conference I'm afraid you'll have to share his room."

"That sounds delightful. After sleeping on the ground many nights or in settlers' huts with their entire family, I'll luxuriate in the privacy of only one roommate."

"Mr. Stuart hasn't come yet. You'll have the room to yourself till he does."

"Forgive me," said the young man, who had been conversing through the porch railing. Hurrying up the eight steps to the porch, he bowed in front of Meg. "I am William Bartram of Philadelphia."

"And I'm Margaret MacLeod of Augusta, niece of the proprietor Angus MacLeod."

Bartram took her outstretched hand and bowed low.

"I might have known you'd have found a pretty little bird," said a deep voice, again from the path. This man was taller than Bartram and wore buckskins. His hair, when he took off the wide-brimmed hat, was light brown and crinkled around the edges where the hat had made him sweat. Light blue eyes, set in a sun-browned face, were framed by laugh wrinkles. Brows and lashes were faded blonde by the sun.

"Miss MacLeod, may I present my friend, Jamie Stratfield," said Bartram as the newcomer climbed the steps and bowed to Meg. "He has accompanied me from Savannah as my guide. John MacIntosh had business to attend to before the conference."

Meg looked up and caught her breath. This was silly! She saw plenty of big, handsome men in the tavern every day. She'd learned to keep her mind and hands busy with tavern work and her heart under control.

"Did you need lodging, too?" she asked, trying to be business-like.

"No, thanks. John Stuart's arranged for me to stay at Grierson's fort where I can keep an eye on the trading goods for the conference. I'm sorry, though, as I would prefer present company to that of Grierson's militiamen."

"Then you'll have to excuse me. I must show Mr. Bartram to his room," she said, trying desperately to turn her moccasins around with her toes, under her skirt. She would hate to patter barefoot across the porch leaving the moccasins in front of the bench. Finally, sitting down and bending over, she hurriedly pulled them on.

Bartram and Stratfield were looking toward the river where Bartram pointed out a late-blooming iris on the bank.

"The steps are on the outside," said Meg, leading the way to the other end of the porch. "It's safer in case of fire, and it keeps guests from having to go through the taproom to get upstairs."

Jamie Stratfield started down the stairs to the hitching rail. "Would you like me to take your horse around to the stable?" he called to Bartram.

"Oh, I'm sorry," said Meg. "Desmond is in the kitchen. If you'll call him from the back yard, he'll take the horse."

Stratfield unhitched both horses and led them around the back of the inn. In a few moments his horse could be heard splashing through the gully.

The big corner room turned out to be bright and clean. A glass casement window opened onto the gallery formed by the porch roof, and another faced the side yard which sloped down to the river fifty yards away. Two beds, homemade but sanded and waxed to prevent splinters, were piled high with feather ticks and had netting looped up to a framework that could be lowered at night to keep out mosquitoes. One corner of the room was curtained to conceal clothes hung on wooden pegs. Two tables, one between the beds holding a tallow candle in a pewter holder, and one under the window with a crockery basin and pitcher, were all the furniture except for two handmade, three-legged stools. It was a luxurious room by frontier standards, and Meg was proud of it. The fur rug in front of the fireplace was soft and warm, and she herself had made the braided rag carpet between the beds. The sheets, brought from Scotland, were linen and were boiled in the black pot in the yard and dried in the sunshine after each guest.

Angus kept a good, clean tavern. On the edge of town toward the Cherokee Road, it was a favorite gathering place for traders. King's men all, they came to Augusta with pack trains loaded with thousands of pounds of hides and furs to store in warehouses for shipment down the river to Savannah or transport along the old trading path to Charlestown. In Augusta, they bartered the hides for beads and calico and guns sent from England to take back to the Indians as payment for the next load of skins.

The livelihood of the traders and of the white men who lived in the Indian lands and collected the skins depended on the English troops sent to regulate and protect the trade. Indians were friendly but likely to turn savage if they thought they were being cheated. The troops kept everyone honest, Indians and whites alike.

For the nearly forty years since Oglethorpe had ordered a fort built at the shoals of the Savannah, Augusta had been known to the Indians as the place to find a fair deal. It was their town, where they could come and camp on the Common, where people were friendly and gave them presents and smoked the peace pipe over tankards of rum.

Now there was fighting among the white men, and Indians were becoming involved. People were coming over the mountains from Virginia and Pennsylvania, wanting to settle and farm on Indian hunting lands. An agreement in 1763 had insured the Indians against fraud by forbidding any private sale of Indian lands to white men, but some were breaking the law as pioneers poured westward.

John Stuart, Superintendent of Indian Affairs for all the southern tribes, had finally persuaded the Creeks and Cherokees to sell to the Crown some of the lands on which they claimed hunting rights. These lands would then be sold to settlers, and the money received from their sale would be used to pay the traders for debts the Indians had run up over the years. It was to sign this agreement that Indians and traders and representatives of the King were flocking to Augusta. Meg and her uncle and every other innkeeper in town would be busy for the next few weeks.

Augusta, more now than just a frontier village, boasted over a hundred houses. Several inns like the Sword and Thistle catered to travelers. St. Paul's Church, near the hulk of the old fort, had been rebuilt and had a full-time rector, the Reverend James Seymour. A Methodist congregation met weekly across the river near Galphin's trading post, and a Baptist congregation had been formed on Kiokee Creek. Although Dr. Andrew Johnston and Dr. George Wells were the only physicians with proper medical degrees, several doctors of physic had practices in town. Married women with children were coming to live with their husbands, and squaws had been sent back to their villages and brothels pushed to the edge of town.

Meg checked through the other guest rooms to be sure there were towels and fresh water. She even provided small cakes of homemade soap, a real luxury. Turning back the covers, she searched for signs of lice and bedbugs that traders often brought on their clothes. The rooms would be full to the rafters soon. She'd have little time, then, for anything but serving food and drink.

As she passed the corner room, the door opened and William Bartram stepped into the hall. "Miss MacLeod," he called, "could you tell me what facilities there are for laundry in town? I'm wearing my last clean shirt. I do want to be tidy for the Indian Conference. Mr. Stuart has promised to introduce me to some of the chiefs so they may help me in my search for natural phenomena."

"Amanda can wash your shirts for you," said Meg. "If you'll give them to me along with your small clothes, she'll have them ready to iron tomorrow. She's boiling sheets now and can have your clothes drying in no time."

"Oh, dear me, I don't want to put you to any trouble."

"It's no trouble," said Meg.

"Miss MacLeod," said Bartram, "do you think it would be proper for you to sit with me on the front gallery and tell me about Augusta? I would not ask you to sit in the taproom, but I believe the settle where I first saw you would be perfectly proper. I am interested in the people here and their customs."

Meg smiled. What a droll wee gentleman. "I'll be glad to sit down," she said. "I'll only be a minute taking the clothes to Amanda."

A few minutes later she found him on the porch carefully examining a honeysuckle blossom.

"You know," she said, "if you pull the green bottom off the flower you can suck the honey through the hole. That's why it's called 'honeysuckle.' "

"Absolutely correct," said Bartram. "And that name is much prettier than the ones botanists use. But my job is to match the flowers with Greek names and put them down on paper."

"Do you mean that you're paid for looking at flowers?" asked Meg, amazed.

"It isn't so much a matter of pay," said Bartram, "as the satisfaction of adding to the scientific knowledge of the world. My father has spent most of his life studying nature."

Meg looked skeptical. Her Scottish blood rebelled at spending all that time and effort for nothing.

"What do you plan to do with all this writing about flowers?"

"Some day I plan to publish a book about what I find in my travels: plants and animals and native Indians and the people I've met and visited. I'll certainly write about Augusta because I'm sure it's going to be the most important city in Georgia some day."

They were interrupted by a flurry of hooves and a voice calling in a strong Scottish burr, "Come fetch my horse, Desmond, lad, I'm near famished for a cup o' good Scotch dew!"

In a moment John Stuart stomped up the front steps, pulling Meg to her feet and hugging her tight as he kissed her cheek. Not much taller than Meg, he was broad of shoulder and girth with a florid complexion that testified to his liking for strong drink.

"And where's your Uncle Angus, lass? I've been thinking of the bottle he keeps hidden for good Scottish clansmen these last ten miles. I've had naught but rum since I left Augusta a month ago. I do believe it's rum that causes my gout."

Turning from Meg, he noticed Bartram, who was watching a large black and yellow spider spin a web from the porch roof down to the railing.

"Well, by the Eternal, if it isn't Will Bartram! I was hoping you'd make it from Savannah in time for the conference."

"Yes, sir," said Bartram. "Since I saw you, I've been down the coast to the Florida border with John MacIntosh of Darien as guide. He'll be joining us here in a day or so."

"Have you seen a young lad by the name of Stratfield? He was to watch over the trading goods for the Cherokees."

"He is at Grierson's waiting for you," said Bartram. He guided me from Savannah when MacIntosh stayed on to do some business."

A hurried tap of a wooden leg on the pine flooring announced the arrival of Angus MacLeod.

"John, lad, welcome back to Augusta," said Angus, clapping Stuart on the shoulders. "I'm always glad to see you've not been scalped by the savages."

"Angus, you old curmudgeon. I feel a damn sight safer with my savages than with the bloody white men who are trying to drive them off their lands."

"In any case, you're here," said Angus. "Meg, lass, would you be kind enough to bring three glasses to the private dining room, and a pasty or two to fend off starvation until suppertime? Mr. Bartram may prefer ale or rum to ouisgebaugh."

"Oh, indeed I believe a bit of ale would be very refreshing," said Bartram as he followed the two Scotsmen through the taproom.

Meg filled a pewter tankard from the ale keg, then went out to the kitchen for a plate of cold pasties.

"I'm damned if I like the way things are going," said Stuart as the three men sat down at the table. "You'd best not plan to go into the Creek country any time soon," he said to Bartram. "This conference is a muddled-up affair, and the Creeks are as apt as not to go on the warpath before it's over."

"But I thought the Indians were happy with the proceedings."

"The Cherokees are," said Stuart. "They're not only getting credit for deeding their lands, but also for the land between Little River and the Broad that is claimed by the Creeks. The governor, damn his eyes, has wheeled and dealed with the Board of Trade till they've promised to buy the lands from both Cherokees and Creeks, with the Catawbas sitting in as neutrals. But the Board didn't send trading presents, and I've had to go into debt myself to gather up goods. That's what I've been doing in Charlestown."

"But I thought the Creek chiefs had agreed to come. Won't they sign the treaty?"

"Oh, Galphin and McGillivray have been out among the tribes, doing their damnedest to get their consent. But I'll be surprised if Oconestotah and The Mortar show up. They'd rather take Cherokee scalps than pass the peace pipe—and with good reason."

"Why are any of them selling land?" Angus asked. "I thought the government agreed ten years ago that settlers would stay east of the Ogeechee and south of Little River."

"They're all deep in debt to the traders, especially the Cherokees, and they're so used to white men's guns and rum and knives and kettles that they can't get along without them. Some of the traders who have half-Cherokee sons have been buying up land in their sons' names and selling it to settlers. The powers in England have hit upon the idea of buying the Indians' land, paying off the Indians' debts to the traders, and selling the land to settlers. That way everyone should be happy.

"But the Creeks were not in on the first deal. They had fought the Cherokees years ago over hunting rights on part of the land and had won. They think it's theirs, and they don't want to sell. We've been trying to talk them into taking payment for that land and more, but they're not happy with us or with the Cherokees. I'm making damned sure there's no ammunition among the presents."

"You think they may attack Augusta?" Angus asked.

"If Oconestotah stays away from the conference, God only knows what may happen. He and The Mortar can stir up the Creeks and the Chickasaws and Choctaws and have them killing every white man between here and the Mississippi."

"But the Creeks seem so peaceful and civilized," said Bartram. "I have had nothing but courtesy from them in my travels."

"You've been no threat to them," said Stuart. "They know you're not interested in land or money. Can you blame the poor devils for distrusting white men? I've spent years now trying to keep them from being cheated. They're no angels when it comes to bargaining, but they're no match for Scots and Englishmen. You've treated them as men, not animals, and they respect you."

"Men they may be," said Angus, "but when you've seen a body they've scalped and tortured, you'd not find a wild animal so cruel."

"As I say, they're not angels," said Stuart. "But white men can be pretty damned mean, too."

"Don't I know!" said Angus. "The Sword and Thistle takes a month to repair after spring trading season. I don't sell rum to Indians, and I wish sometimes I could refuse it to white traders. Indians are better behaved in Augusta than white men. We're becoming famous here for brawls and bloodshed."

"And now you've got the damned Virginians coming over the mountains spoiling for a fight."

"Virginians?" Bartram asked.

"The old timers here call all the rabble Virginians. They're the vagabonds from all the colonies. When law and order comes to their part of the country, they move on. To be 'free' they say. They talk treason and raise hell wherever they go."

Bartram was glad to see the door open and Meg come in followed by Jamie Stratfield. He didn't really like heated discussions, and John Stuart and Angus, though agreeing on their subject, were upset.

"Glad to see you made it, laddie," said Stuart, rising from the table and shaking Stratfield's hand.

Meg set a plate of pasties on the table, and Jamie Stratfield set down a tankard of ale while he drew up a chair.

"I understand you've met William Bartram," said Stuart, "but this is my old friend Angus MacLeod, late of the Highland Company of Rangers. He gave his leg for his king at Bloody Marsh, and now he keeps the best damned tavern in the colony of Georgia."

Stratfield shook the taverner's hand and nodded to Bartram. "You seem to have settled in already," he said, then turning to Stuart, "The Indian presents have arrived at Grierson's, sir. The ponies are ready to be unloaded. The drivers told me you'd be here. Colonel Grierson suggests we store the goods in one of the storehouses inside the palisade."

"They should be safe there," said Stuart. "Grierson's fort is better built than any of the fortified farms around here."

"Then I'll tell them to unload," said Jamie.

"Sit down, lad," said Stuart, "and finish your ale and eat one of Meg's good pasties. The pack men will do as Grierson tells them."

Jamie was glad for the chance to relax. The good ale and the crusty meat pie were the best food he'd had in weeks.

"This lad's looking for a piece of land," Stuart said to Angus. "I met him in Charlestown on his way to Savannah and persuaded him to come to Augusta before he decided on coastal land. There's money to be made in the Indian trade here, and we need honest men."

"Thank you, sir, for your confidence in my character," said Jamie. "I've lived in Tidewater Maryland since my family came over from Berkshire when I was a baby. I feel at home on the coast, but," as Meg came back to the table to refill his tankard, "there are attractions in the backwoods, too."

Meg blushed at his admiring gaze and hurried back to the taproom.

II

THE INDIAN
TREATY

In the next few days, as word sped along the Indian trails that Stuart had arrived with presents, Indians began to drift into town. On the broad Common where roads came together from Savannah, the Cherokee country and the Upper Creek lands, and from Charlestown by way of a ferry across the river, they set up cooking fires and spread their sleeping skins. Family units camped together and all of them, even the Creeks, were in high spirits with winter over and summer ahead, with a chance to talk to old friends and enemies on neutral ground, and with Superintendent Stuart there to keep the peace. To keep the mood jovial, Stuart broached a few barrels of rum, making sure that it was well watered before it was passed around the campfires.

Angus and the other innkeepers diluted the white men's drinks when they began to fill the taverns. It would never do to have them shoot up the town in their usual manner. They might kill an Indian by mistake.

Worse than the traders, who respected the Indians' rights in the city, were the frontiersmen, many of whom had already moved into the new lands in spite of the law. They had no dealings with Indians and resented Augusta's good treatment of them. With luck, the settlers would be on their good behavior in order to get legal title to their land. The Indians, however, thought Augusta was their town and resented the hostile frontiersmen here. Augusta residents crossed their fingers and kept careful watch.

One night John Stuart sat in the back room of the Sword and Thistle with George Galphin, Lachlan McGillivray, James Grierson, and Lachlan McIntosh, a farmer and fur trader from down near Darien who had come in during the day and joined the others to make plans.

"I don't think Chief Emistisiguo is coming," said Galphin, "and I know bloody well we won't get Otis here. My Creek brother-in-law has been around the villages, and he says Otis, or The Mortar as we call him, is in the Cherokee country conferring with Oconestotah. If those two old foxes can get together, God help the white men."

Lachlan McIntosh set his tankard down carefully. "I heard from up at Ninety-Six that emissaries from the Shawnees were seen at Keeowee last week. We could be in for a general uprising."

"We'd better get the conference over and get them the hell out of Augusta," said Colonel Grierson.

Stuart said, "I've been waiting in hopes Oconestotah could talk The Mortar into coming. Old Oconestotah really loves a party, and he's going to hate to miss this meeting. I believe, that instead of plotting massacres with The Mortar, he's trying to convince him to support the land sale."

"I hope you're right," said Grierson. "We're mighty vulnerable with the old fort in ruins."

"The governor should be on his way here by now. I've sent word that we've got representatives from the Creeks and Cherokees and Catawbas, even if they aren't big chiefs. We'll have to start the meeting tomorrow, however, and not wait for the governor."

"What are the Catawbas doing here?" McGillivray asked. "They're Carolina Indians."

"You're a Carolina trader," said Stuart, "and you're here in Georgia. They say they want the king to send them a missionary. I guess they mainly want to get in on the party and see what's going on."

At dawn the next day, a roll of drums and the squeal of a fife proclaimed the opening of the Second Congress of Augusta. Governor Wright had arrived in the night escorted by a militia company from Savannah—a show of strength to keep peace.

The Cherokees were ready to cede all the land Georgia wanted, but the Creeks were not. Speeches were made and pannikins of rum were passed. Galphin and McGillivray, both of whom had Creek wives and families, did their best to persuade their adopted kinsmen to sell the land to pay the debts they owed the traders. But the Creeks refused to cede more than the left bank of the Upper Ogeechee, and the governor was forced to accept the offer. Somehow in the discussion, the Cherokees offered some lands north and east of the Broad River that the Creeks thought were theirs, and the governor accepted them. In all, 2,100,000 acres would be opened to settlement and be known as the Ceded Lands or the New Purchase.

After the distribution of presents, the Indians packed their belongings and began to fade into the forests. Many of the frontiersmen hurried off to mark their claims, which were now legal. The traders stayed on to celebrate.

Governor Wright and John Stuart had repaired to the Sword and Thistle's back dining room to plan in private the best way to implement the treaty. A knock on the door announced Lachlan McGillivray.

"Governor," he said touching his forehead briefly, "I've just heard from one of my wife's brothers that all hell is about to break loose. The Upper Creeks think they've been tricked into ceding more land than they meant to."

"How long do we have?" Stuart asked.

"It should take them a few weeks to gather ammunition and food and send word throughout the Creek Nation."

"Then we'd better get the line surveyed right away," said Stuart, turning to Governor Wright.

"I plan," said the governor, "to put Colonel Barnard in charge of the escort for the surveyors who came with me from Savannah."

"What about letting Bartram go along," said Stuart. "He can live off the land like a trooper. I'd rather have him north in Cherokee country than with the Creeks. He's too trusting."

"What if they're ambushed?" the governor asked. "He and his father are much admired in London. We'd be hard put to explain if he came to harm."

"We'll send John MacIntosh along. He's been guiding Bartram in the south, and he knows the Cherokees. He'll take care of him."

"I guess it will be a big enough party to keep the Creeks from attacking," said the governor. "Besides, all the Indians will be curious about the line. They'll wait to see where it goes."

"That's what worries me," said Stuart. "I don't think the Creeks understood about that land. When they find it's been sold, too, they'll be ready to fight."

"What worries me," said McGillivray, "is that bunch of crackers already up there staking claims. They hate the Indians and want them out of the way. God help us if one of them gets liquored up and decides to protect his claim with bullets. Indians don't care about a man's politics when they go on the warpath. One white scalp looks like another."

At daybreak the next day the caravan passed the Sword and Thistle, headed for the Great Buffalo Lick on the ridge that separated the Savannah and the Ogeechee. Almost ninety men were in the company, most of them on horseback, and they were followed by twenty-five or thirty packhorses loaded with provisions. William Bartram and John

MacIntosh waved to Meg and her uncle who had walked down to the road to watch them pass. Jamie Stratfield hurried up from the rear where he was guarding the packhorses and swept off his hat to Meg.

"I'll be wanting a room and some more of that good cooking," he said to Meg, "when we come back. I want to see the country up in the hills, but I'll be back to Augusta."

"Take care, laddie, that you keep your scalp," said Angus, "and don't get in any discussions with the crackers who are moving into the land up there. They're worse than redskins."

"Good luck to you," said Meg.

Jamie wheeled his horse and hurried after the column.

III

MOONLIGHT
AND
HONEYSUCKLE

The survey was completed in record time with no bloodshed.
Meg was sitting on a big rock by Campbell's Gully with a cane
fishing pole beside her, the cork resting quietly on the water. She didn't
really want a fish to bite. It was cool and quiet as the red sky turned to
rose, then to gray.

Just as it grew too dark to see the cork, horses splashed through the
stream in the middle of the gully, and three horsemen turned up the
front path. Meg thought she recognized Bartram's precise manner of
speaking.

"Good evening, gentlemen," she called. "Welcome to Augusta."

"And a better welcome I can't imagine," came Jamie Stratfield's voice.

"Is it Miss MacLeod?" Bartram asked. "Have you been watching the
fish from the bank of the stream?"

"With luck," said John MacIntosh, "she's been catching them for the
kitchen pot."

"No fish," said Meg, "but we've a nice haunch of venison on the spit
and potatoes and greens from the garden. Come in and I'll draw you
some ale until supper's ready."

"Do you have beds for the night?" Bartram asked. "I plan to stay a
few days before going to Savannah."

"If you don't mind sharing a room again, we've one with a small cot
and a big bed that's been known to hold as many as four."

"I guess Jamie and I can share the big one and let Will have the small,"
said MacIntosh. "We've had naught but the ground for so long we'll be
grateful for goose down."

Meg sent Desmond to stable the horses, then drew three tankards of ale. The men were surrounded as soon as they entered the taproom. Everyone wanted to know about the survey and whether there had been signs of Indian trouble.

"The Cherokees won't start anything, and we saw few Creeks," said MacIntosh. "But the homesteaders don't know one Indian from another or how to deal with them."

"Only way to deal with 'em is to shoot 'em if they come on your land," said a tall man in homespun sitting at the table with two townsmen.

"And start an Indian war?" asked Colonel Grierson, who was sitting at the next table. "You are out of your mind, Bostick!"

"Maybe it wouldn't be a bad idea," said a nattily dressed man beside Bostick. "We'd have an excuse to chase them west for good."

"And you a physician dedicated to saving lives, Dr. Wells," said Grierson. "You would have every settlement burned and men, women, and children scalped and worse."

"Gentlemen," said Bartram worriedly, "surely you don't mean what you say."

"I say the only good Indian is a dead Indian," Bostick said thickly, pounding his tankard on the table. "Bring me ale, girl!"

Angus, hearing the noise came into the taproom as Meg left through the door behind the bar.

"Dr. Wells," said Angus, "I would be very much obliged if you would help Mr. Bostick home before he gets into trouble."

"Damned Tory Injun lovers," growled Bostick as Wells led him toward the door. "All they care about is making money from their filthy furs. Augusta's a damned Indian town, not fit for white men." He stumbled onto the front porch.

"Welcome to the peace and quiet of Augusta," said Angus as he joined Bartram, Stratfield, and MacIntosh at their table.

"You handled him well," said MacIntosh.

"I'd have pushed his face in for talking to Meg that way," said Stratfield.

"He seems to be lacking in manners as well as intellect," added William Bartram.

At their request, Angus joined them in an ale. "Superintendent Stuart's gone home to Charlestown," he said raising a tankard. "He left some money for Mr. Stratfield, to pay for riding gun on the pack train."

"Then drinks are on me," said Jamie.

"We'll move to the dining room," said Angus, "and I can furnish you with something better than ale or rum that I keep for Scotsmen. You and Mr. Bartram may not be Scots, but we won't hold that against you. I'll ask Meg to bring our supper there."

Later the men moved to the porch to take advantage of the breeze from the river. Meg checked to be sure Desmond and Amanda had washed the dishes and put away the food. In this climate, most food would spoil if kept more than a day, but flour, meal, lard, and bacon could be stored in the larder. Having checked, she locked the larder door and returned the key to the reticule that hung from her belt.

Going quietly to the front of the inn, she stepped down to the rock on the bank of the gully and watched the moon path that painted a silver arrow down the stream. With the spring rains over, Campbell's Gully was still. She could hear the tiny splash of fish coming to the surface to catch the insects that settled on the quiet water.

"May I climb down and share your moonlight?" came the voice of Jamie Stratfield.

"It doesn't belong to me," said Meg, moving over to leave space on the rock. "I've been sharing it with the fish and mosquitoes." Usually she stayed aloof from men who came to the inn, but Jamie seemed to be a gentleman, and Uncle Angus liked him.

Jamie sat on the rock and stretched his legs in front of him. The moonlight, reflected by the water, made his white cambric shirt gleam silver. Meg could barely see the side of his face and his neck where his hair was neatly clubbed and tied.

"I was afraid for a minute you were an Indian," she said, "you walked so softly."

"I'm sorry I scared you," he said. "Moccasins are comfortable after wearing boots all day."

"I'm usually not so jumpy," said Meg. "Do you think the Creeks are really going to attack Augusta? They've been our friends for so long."

"I don't know much about the Creeks," said Jamie. "We didn't have Indian trouble in Baltimore. The ones I have met were friendly."

"George Galphin and Lachlan McGillivray have traded with them for years," said Meg. "Indians like to trade in Augusta. They're treated well, especially the Creeks."

"I don't believe the Indians are angry with traders," said Jamie, "but men like those in the tavern tonight hate Indians. They are afraid of them and don't want them to come here or travel on the roads."

"But Indians don't bother travelers as much as white outlaws!"

"That's what they tell me," said Jamie. "I hear that all the scum run out of South Carolina by the Regulators have come across the river into Georgia."

"Uncle Angus hates to see them come into the inn," said Meg. "We had to board up the windows in the taproom after they were broken in the last brawl."

"I don't like to think of you mixed up in a brawl."

"Oh, I don't get into them," said Meg. "When I came to live with Uncle Angus, he taught me to watch for signs of trouble and duck out. If it gets too bad, I run over to Grierson's for help."

"How did you come to live with your uncle?" Jamie asked.

"My mother and father died of smallpox in Charlestown after we'd come from Scotland. Many people died that year. Uncle brought me here to the inn he'd built with money from his service at Bloody Marsh. I was nine years old."

"What a shock," Jamie exclaimed, putting his arm around her shoulders. "You poor child."

With no fuss, Meg slipped out from under his arm and off the rock.

"I'm not half as bad off as a lot of orphans," she said as she stood and faced him, the moonlight painting her face and neck silver above the dark blue of her dress.

"I'd best go in and see if Uncle Angus needs me in the taproom."

Two days later William Bartram left for Savannah. John Stuart had persuaded him that it would be foolish to go into Creek country with tribes stirred up over the survey, so he planned to send the packages of seeds and plants and pressed flowers to Europe, then go down the coast to the south of Florida to pick up more specimens.

When Governor Wright ordered Edward Barnard to raise a troop of Rangers to police the Ceded Lands, Jamie volunteered for the duty at Fort James, under construction where the Broad River met the Savannah. According to the governor's plan, lawless "crackers" were to be discouraged from settling and the land would be sold to industrious people from England, Ireland, and Germany. The governor was to visit the Ceded Lands to "deter the bad and encourage the good." How he was to tell the bad from good or enforce the plan, no one knew.

One day in the middle of June, Jamie found Meg alone again hanging clean tankards on their pegs in the taproom. He leaned his elbows on the bar, sure that if he went behind it, she would duck through the back door to escape him.

"I've come to say goodby," he said, "I've joined the Rangers."

Meg turned to the keg so that he wouldn't notice her concern. "Then this ale is on the house," she said, sliding it across the counter. "I hope you come back safely for another one."

"I'm hoping, when I come back, to find some land near Augusta to make a home," said Jamie.

Meg retreated from the warmth in his eyes. "We'll be glad to see you when you come," she said carefully, "and God grant you come back safely." She reached across the bar and squeezed his hand.

As Jamie swung onto his horse and rode out the Cherokee Road, he found that he was singing.

·IV·

THE

SHELDONS

By the end of July, summer had settled in with a vengeance. The springs in Cupboard Swamp that fed Campbell's Gully were almost dry, and the stream had narrowed to a trickle in the center of an expanse of mud.

Meg was glad to be out in the early morning sunshine. The inn had been busy with more and more people coming from Charlestown and Savannah on their way to the New Purchase and stopping to register their claims at the land office in Augusta. Travelers from the Carolina Low Country generally stayed at Thomas Goodale's inn on the Sand Bar Ferry Road, and those from the Ninety-Six District crossed on the Center Street Ferry and, along with Savannah people who cut off the River Road and came into the center of town, found lodgings with Mr. Fox and downtown innkeepers. The Sword and Thistle, at the other end of town, was not as crowded as the other inns, but, with the influx of strangers, its taproom became the refuge of upper-class Augustans.

James Grierson and Robert MacKay, having farms just down the road, were frequent visitors, while even town dwellers like Edward Barnard and Andrew McLean were found there most evenings now. John Rae came in occasionally from his farm on Stony Creek, and James Seymour, the rector of St. Paul's Church, stopped in on his parish rounds.

Thomas Brown, the young Yorkshireman who had bought five thousand acres of land in the New Purchase above Little River (definitely considered a "good" man by the governor) was becoming a frequent customer. Rather than ride back to Brownsborough, he often would stay overnight and join in the talk in the common room. Captain Manson, another wealthy English squire who had bought five thousand acres near Brown, sometimes came with him. Most of the customers, however, were Old Augustans, if a thirty-six-year-old town could be called old.

The real "aristocracy" of Augusta were the fur traders who had been living in the area before Oglethorpe sent men up the river to build Fort Augusta in the 1730s. Galphin and McGillivray still had their trading posts across the river in Carolina, but others had moved their warehouses into town.

Regular customers had their own tankards on pegs behind the bar, and they usually commandeered the two long tables at the back wall of the taproom. Now, with the influx of strangers, Angus reserved the dining room for the old timers, sending Meg to serve them. She stayed busier than ever, trying to help Desmond serve the taproom customers while she kept an eye on the dining room.

This morning there was a big basket of laundry to rinse in the river. Even the Savannah had shrunk so that Meg and Amanda had to tuck up their skirts and wade into the stream to reach clear water. In spring at flood time, the river was muddy, but much of the year it was sparkling clear. Here below the rapids, clothes could be held in the stream to rinse away the soap, then spread on the bushes along the bank to dry.

"Beg pardon, miss," a voice called from the path. "Can you tell me where I can find Angus MacLeod?"

Meg left the last few sheets to Amanda and hurried up the slope.

"I think he's in the taproom," she answered. "I'll call Desmond to cool your horse and water him. You look as though you could use a cool drink, too."

"Thank you, miss," said the horseman, hardly more than a boy. His buckskins were sweat-soaked and his hair hung in points around his face. He almost staggered as he climbed the steps to the cool taproom.

Angus was nowhere to be seen. Meg drew the young man a pint of ale. She heard the tap of her uncle's crutch.

"I'm Angus MacLeod. Don't get up. You look as though you might not make it."

"I'm afraid I'm not in very good shape," the young man said, sinking back on the bench. "I'm Bert Sheldon, sir. Lieutenant Stratfield told me to ride like hell, beg pardon, miss, and not to stop till I found you."

"What has happened to Mr. Stratfield?" Meg asked, her heart suddenly pounding.

"He's all right," said the youth, "but he's worried about you. Some crazy back settler named Hezekiah Collins killed two Cherokees on their way home from the land survey. Now the Cherokees have killed a white man. Settlers have been coming into Fort James, and Jamie, I mean Lieutenant Stratfield, is afraid they'll come down on Augusta, since the fort's tumbled down and the town is full of trading goods."

"Why did he send you to me, lad?" Angus asked, puzzled.

"He said I'd be able to find the Sword and Thistle first thing. He wanted to be sure you and Miss Meg had time to go where it was safe. He wanted me to find Colonel Grierson and warn him to strengthen the palisade around his fort."

"I'll send Desmond with a note to colonel Grierson," said Angus. "You look as though you could do with a rest."

"Did you see any Indians on the way?" Meg asked.

"None who looked like they wanted to fight," said Bert Sheldon. "Some Cherokees were watering their horses at the Little River ford when I crossed, but they made signs of friendship."

"I don't believe Oconestotah and Attakullakulla will let them go on the warpath," said Angus, "but you can't be sure the young braves won't go on a killing spree."

"How is Mr. Stratfield?" Meg asked Bert.

"He's Lieutenant Stratfield now," said Bert, "and he's the best officer we have in the Rangers. He wanted to come himself, but he couldn't leave. My family are on their way from Ninety-Six to take up land in the New Purchase, and he gave me leave to find them and warn them to stay off the road until this thing blows over."

"You can't leave until you've had some rest," said Meg.

"Oh, I'm all right now. I'm a little worried about my horse, though," said Bert. "Do you have one I could rent?"

"Would you like to take my mare?" Meg asked. "I wouldn't rent her, but if you promise to be gentle, I'll entrust her to you. There's a camp on the town Common for people who have crossed on the ferry from Ninety-Six and are waiting to go north."

"I promise to take good care of her," Bert said, "and bring her back as soon as I find my folks."

Meg led him to the stable. "I don't often lend Delight," said Meg, as he saddled the horse, "but you've come so far to warn us."

The mare didn't like men, but Bert was light in the saddle and had good hands. She ducked her head and side-stepped onto the path, but Bert held her firmly and leaned forward to speak softly in her ear. Delight snorted once or twice, then settled to a steady singlefoot as they moved into the main street.

The town was alive with travelers. Wagons and small carts filled with household goods and children moved toward him slowly, heading for the New Purchase. Some had cows and goats tied to the back and some were followed by pigs, geese, and turkeys herded by older children and dogs.

Bert looked carefully at each group as it passed. Ma and Pa would probably be in an ox cart, since they'd given him the sorrel gelding to ride with the Rangers. They had said that they needed his pay more than Moonshine, and old Esau, the ox they'd brought from Pennsylvania, could do farm work better than the horse. They'd only been in Ninety-Six a little over a year when the New Purchase opened up. They decided to move there, and he'd picked them out a claim. They had to get the papers signed here in Augusta.

In the yards of the log warehouses along the broad main street, families had parked their wagons and were sitting around breakfast fires, the dogs and children scrambling in the sand, hiding under the wagon beds, squealing with delight at the chance to play after a long trek. Parents swapped yarns and shared their scant food supplies. This would be their last chance to stock up on staples to carry to the new lands.

Bert turned left at Center Street toward the Savannah River Ferry. His folks might have crossed farther upriver, but he guessed that Ma would have wanted to come right into the center of town. She was a city woman from Philadelphia and would be eager to see the biggest Indian-trading town in the country, and a river port to boot.

There was no sign of the ox cart or his family on the ferry that was just unloading on the river bank. On his left he could see a wooden building with a belfry and beyond it, the remains of the palisade of Fort Augusta. If Ma was in Augusta, she'd be sure to go to church. She was always fussing about not having a real English church in Ninety-Six.

As Bert dismounted in the churchyard, a tall man in black was standing on the steps talking to a stocky man in blue coat and light buckskin breeches.

"I've written the Society over and over, Mr. Fitch. Until they send Bibles and hymnals, we'll have to do with the few we have."

Fitch started to reply when they saw Bert.

"Can I help you, lad?" he asked.

"I don't think so. I'm looking for my family."

"What's your name? Perhaps I know them."

"I'm Bert Sheldon, sir, a private in Captain Waters' Rangers at Fort James. The Cherokees are about to go on the warpath, and I came down to meet Pa and tell him not to bring the family up to the New Purchase."

"On the warpath," exclaimed the Reverend Mr. Seymour. "I knew I should have left my family in Savannah."

"What are you talking about, boy?" Fitch asked. "We've heard the Creeks were stewing over the land settlement, not the Cherokees."

"Lieutenant Stratfield sent me to warn Colonel Grierson," said Bert.

"A backwoodsman killed two Cherokees, and the Cherokees killed a white man."

"Hell, boy—your pardon Mr. Seymour—don't you know there's always a few scalps lifted in the spring? They won't go on the warpath in summer. It's too hot. After harvest when it turns cool, then you have to watch out. Indians fight in the spring and fall."

"They're pretty worried up in the Purchase, sir," said Bert.

"Bunch of clodhoppers don't know anything about Indians," said Fitch.

"No, sir," said Bert, "But the settlers get pretty mad when the Indians keep coming back to the Ceded Lands. Some of them have vowed to shoot 'em if they don't stay off."

"Cherokees have hunted those lands for years," said Fitch. "They figure the good Lord lent it to them to use, only they call him the Great Spirit. White men may settle there, but Indians figure the land is for everybody's use. They don't understand selling land."

"That is an extraordinary doctrine," said Seymour.

"I don't know," said Fitch. "Genesis tells us God created the earth. Man may move off and on, then he dies and goes back as dust."

"But what has that to do with land ownership?" Seymour asked.

"Man belongs to the land, not the land to man," said Fitch.

Bert had been shifting from one foot to the other. "Excuse me, gentlemen, I'm so glad to have met you," and putting the reins over the mare's neck, swung into the saddle.

This time he rode across the main street to the Common. Wagons and stock were milling in all directions, some just arriving and looking for a spot to camp, others gathering family and animals to depart.

A shrill scream caused him to turn toward a canvas-covered cart as a small, freckle-faced blonde in a calico dress came barreling out and bumped into the mare's shoulder. Delight shied and would have bolted if Bert had not gathered the reins and calmed her.

"Watch out, Francie," he called. "You dern near spooked the horse."

Swinging from the mare's back, he gathered his sister in a bear hug.

"Where did you come from, Bertie? Oh, I'm glad you came," Francie bubbled. "Come on. Ma and Pa are resting. We just got in this morning."

A tall, lanky figure crawled from under the cart. Ben Sheldon, combing his tousled hair with his fingers, walked toward his son.

They were almost equal in height. Ben caught his son around the shoulders, not wanting to embarrass either of them by too much emotion. "Son," he said, "we didn't expect to see you till we got to Fort James."

"Where's Ma?" Bert asked.

"She's asleep under the cart. She and the baby were so hot and tired

I made a bed in the shade. We've been on the road since sunup."

"How's little Benjy?"

"Benjy's fine, but we'll all be better when we get to the Purchase."

"Pa, I don't think you and Ma should go up there now," said Bert. "There's trouble starting with the Cherokees; and Lieutenant Stratfield thinks they may go on the warpath."

Ben Sheldon's head snapped back. "Goshamighty, Bert, do you mean we've come all this way for nothing?"

"No, Pa. The King isn't going to let the Indians keep people from settling up there; not after they've paid for the land. But it just isn't safe till the troops get things sorted out. Fort James is full of people who have had to leave their claims and come in for protection."

"We can't go back to Ninety-Six," said Ben dispiritedly. "I've sold the land and cabin to George Tillman. Lord knows we can't afford to stay here in Augusta. I need to get up there and get a crop in and work on a cabin."

"I can do that, Pa," said Bert. "All I have to do is put up a shack, plant some corn, and harvest it to show our intent to settle."

"But your ma and Francie and the baby can't live here in the wagon indefinitely," said Ben.

"I promised to return this horse to Miss Meg as soon as I found you. Moonshine was tuckered out from galloping most of the way from Fort James."

"That's a good-looking mare," said his father, who had been too worried to notice before. "She was kind to trust you."

"Jamie Stratfield thinks the world of Miss Meg and her uncle," said Bert. "You can talk to Mr. MacLeod about what to do."

"Can I go with you?" Francie asked as Bert started to mount.

"We'll see how the mare feels about it," he said reaching behind the saddle and pressing in several places on her back. "She doesn't seem to have a funny spot. Some mares will buck if you touch them behind the saddle." He reached for Francie's hand as her father swung her up. The mare turned and walked onto the broad main street.

"How far are we going?" Francie asked holding tight to Bert's waist.

"Less than a mile," said Bert. "This isn't a big city like Philadelphia."

"It's bigger than Ninety-Six," said Francie, "and there are lots more people."

"They don't all live here," said Bert. "Most of them are on their way to the Purchase like you and the folks."

They turned into the path marked by a signboard painted with a big claymore entwined in a lavender thistle.

"That's so pretty," Francie said.

"I guess the inn got its name from the Scottish flower and the sword that hangs over the fireplace," Bert said.

Desmond, seeing the mare was back, came out of the kitchen to take her to the stable. "Will you be needing your horse now?" he asked.

"Not just yet, thank you," said Bert, "if I may have a few minutes with Mr. MacLeod. And don't bother saddling him. I can tack him up when I'm ready."

Francie's eyes sparkled as she stared around her. The innyard was a self-sufficient little kingdom. Behind the big inn building, a circular driveway was lined with small buildings. A kitchen, a smokehouse, a cabin for Desmond and one for Amanda faced the driveway near the house, while beyond them on the ground that sloped to the river bank and far enough away to keep flies from the inn, were the stable and cow barn and two privies screened by bushes. Behind the kitchen and smokehouse, stretching from the high road to the river, were vegetable gardens and a small orchard.

Francie pulled on Bert's arm. "Couldn't we stay here?"

Bert put his arm around her shoulders. "Honey, Ma and Pa have to save all their money to buy land in the New Purchase."

Meg appeared at the door and Bert introduced Francie.

"Have your folks decided to go on to Fort James?" Meg asked.

"Pa's not happy with the camp on the Common. He'd rather push on than stay in the heat and dirt. But he's about changed his mind since I told him about the Indian trouble. I thought you might know of a better place to camp, close enough to come into one of the palisades."

"We'll ask Uncle Angus. A lot of our customers have land along the Cherokee Road, and they might let them camp on one of their claims."

Angus came to the front door just then. "So you've found your family," he greeted Bert, "or is this bonnie lass a sweetheart you have met in town?"

Francie blushed with pleasure. "No, I'm really his sister, Francie Sheldon," she said, remembering to bob a curtsy.

"Bert's family is camping on the Common," said Meg, "and it's hot and dusty and crowded."

"Dreadful," said Angus. "The Indians camp there so the troops can protect them, and the backwoods traders do so they can be near the warehouses. The grass and weeds are kept down by the traffic, but there's mud in wet weather and dust in dry."

"Do you know of anyone who might let them camp on his land?" Meg asked.

"Right now with all the people coming through, that may be a problem.

Everybody's afraid they'll be overrun with squatters." He looked from Bert to Francie, then nodded his head as though making a decision. "If your parents plan to stay here for any length of time, we may be able to make a deal. I've a hundred-acre plot of land near Rae's Creek that's already partially cleared and planted in corn and barley. Desmond is supposed to work it, but we've been so busy he hasn't had time.

"Ask your Pa to come and talk to me. Maybe we can work something out."

Francie forgot all her grown-up airs. Holding tight to Bert's arm, she jumped up and down. "Oh, come on! Let's get him now."

"Why don't you make it late this afternoon," said Angus. "He can park his wagon behind the stables for tonight. We have every room full, but it will be quiet near the river."

"That's very kind of you, sir," said Bert.

"I can't let them stay but one night," said Angus, "or we'd be plagued with travelers wanting to camp. Tonight all of you come to supper as my guests, so we can talk about plans."

By sundown the Sheldon wagon had been moved behind the stables. With the sides of the wagon cover rolled up, the breeze from the river cooled Mary Sheldon as she combed her hair back in a knot, securing it with the tortoise-shell pins she had brought from Pennsylvania. Little Benjy, freshly bathed in the water Ben had carried from the well, kicked and cooed on his mat on the wagon floor.

They were looking forward to supper at the inn. In the Ninety-Six District, they'd had little but game and salt pork, wild greens and berries, and meal made from Indian corn. Ben and Bert had been too busy clearing land and building the cabin to care for a garden, and she'd had a hard pregnancy. It was all she could do to keep the clothes washed and the cabin clean.

She saw her reflection in the little looking glass she had fastened to the side of the wagon. She'd lost the puffy face and thick ankles, but white was creeping into the gold hair that Ben loved. She was thirty-five years old, almost an old woman.

It was sinful to take pride in your looks. She had heard that from her Quaker grandmother as a little girl. Her mother was Church of England, but her father's mother was Quaker like Ben. She knew, though, that Ben set a lot of store by her hair and her blue eyes—like cornflowers he'd say. She'd left home and family to go roving with Ben, first to Maryland and then down through Virginia and North Carolina, close to the frontier, looking for the ideal spot for a home. Bless his heart, he wanted to give her all the comforts she'd had as a little girl, but all she wanted was to settle down.

They'd had a hard winter in Long Canes near Ninety-Six. Francie had come down with the croup, and the cabin had been so cold when Benjy was born that Ben had been afraid they would all die before spring. When they'd heard of the new lands opening up farther south, Ben had sold his land for a claim near Fort James.

A loud clanging came from the direction of the inn. Bert had told her they'd ring a triangle when it was time for supper. Her good black dress with the Belgian lace collar was still wrinkled from the trunk, but it was clean and looked like a lady. She wrapped Benjy in his quilt and called to Francie, who came running up the river path in her clean pinafore with a bouquet of daisies, phlox, and Queen Anne's lace. "Do you think Miss Meg would like them?" she cried.

Mary almost scolded the child for her tumbled hair, then caught herself in time. Her bright eyes and happy smile made her beautiful, tangled hair and all. Mother and daughter walked together to the inn. Ben and Bert joined them at the top of the steps. Ben's eyes were alive with excitement as he guided Mary to the long table along the back wall where Meg had saved four places.

Great platters of roast pork and fried fish, Indian corn and potatoes were in the center of the table as well as bowls of greens, stewed apples, mashed turnips, and yellow squash. Francie could barely wait until Pa said the blessing and dishes passed along the table. Mother had told her about this kind of meal back in Philadelphia, but she had been too young to remember clearly.

"Just a little bit of everything," said Mary giving Francie the family eye.

"But I may never see so much food again," Francie complained.

"We may be coming often," said Ben turning to Mary, "I think we've found a place to stay for a while."

"Thank the Lord," said Mary. "I've been asking Him to help us." And He's found us a place near civilization, she thought to herself, not wanting Ben to know how tired she was of the wilds.

"Mr. MacLeod has offered me a chance to farm his land for at least the next year. He'll help us with building a cabin, give us nails and hardware, and send Desmond to help when he has time. He's got this idea of growing barley and fermenting it for malt to make his own Scotch whisky and wants me to help."

"But you know nothing about making whisky."

"I can learn," said Ben. "I've learned to do a lot of things I never thought I would."

Mary looked up to see Angus on the way to the table. "Good evening, Mrs. Sheldon," he said bowing. "'Tis a joy to have two such bonnie lasses brightening the Sword and Thistle."

"I can hardly believe our good fortune in meeting you," Mary said. "I must have time to digest your good food and your good news before I can believe it all."

"The good fortune is mine," said Angus. "I have talked to some of my Scots friends about making ouisguebaugh, but they are most of them bachelors and more interested in drinking than producing it. I've been looking for a man with enough learning and gumption and with a family to tie him to the land so he won't leave me.

"I'm not sure barley will thrive here, and I'm not sure the water would be as good as that from Highland burns. But with the number of Highland Scots who come through here complaining about rum, I think we'll have a gold mine if we can make a reasonable substitute."

"I'll certainly give it a try, sir," said Ben. "I'm English on my father's side, but my mother was a Kerr from the Highlands."

"That's the spirit!" Angus exclaimed gripping Ben's arm. "We'll make a good team. English blood will tame the wild Scottish heritage and keep us both on the straight and narrow.

"You and Mrs. Sheldon enjoy your supper and have a good night's sleep. I'll take you out to Rae's Creek tomorrow."

"We'll be up with the sun and ready to go," said Ben.

"Good. We'd better go early before it's too hot. It's in July and August that I miss my Highlands most."

By seven in the morning, the Sheldon family was ready to move. Angus would ride in the wagon with Mary and the children while Ben rode Angus's big hunter. Bert would ride with them as far as the farm and then go on to Fort James. The road was already crowded with wagons and livestock. Either these people hadn't heard of Indian troubles or they were so eager to get to the new land that they were willing to take a chance.

Ben had gone to the land office and procured a legal deed to the land Bert had found near Fort James. All that remained was for Bert to plant a crop and build a rough cabin which could be improved when they moved to the New Purchase.

The party passed Grierson's trading post, with its fortlike palisade to protect the family and their trading goods, then came to other "forts." One belonged to the firm of McCarten and Campbell, another to Edward Barnard, and still another to Robert MacKay. MacKay's house was built of stone and timber and painted white with storehouses and outbuildings behind it, surrounded by a high fence. Between the house and the road was a low fence protecting flower gardens.

Pointing out the house to Mary, Angus said, "Some call it Garden Hill, but most of the folks call it the White House."

Mary was ecstatic. She had not realized that Augusta would have fine houses with real glass windows and painted blinds. These men must have wives and families. There might even be a school.

"The MacKays haven't been here but a few years," said Angus. "He's the son of a Church of England minister from Jamaica. They've a lot of relatives from Scotland who came with Oglethorpe to fight the Spaniards. I served with Captain Hugh MacKay's Highlanders on the coast. Rob was a merchant in Beaufort before he moved here."

"Their house and gardens are beautiful," said Mary wistfully.

"Augusta is more civilized than you would think," said Angus. "Some of the merchants and traders have homes and warehouses in the Low Country, too. They've brought furniture and silver and fine china with them to furnish their country houses here in Augusta, so they can entertain as they do in Charleston and Savannah."

"Is there a dame's school in Augusta?" Mary asked Angus. "I taught little girls in Philadelphia for a year before Bert was born."

"Mr. Seymour, the rector of St. Paul's, teaches the sons of some of the merchants," said Angus. "I'm afraid you'll be too far out in the country to find little girls to teach."

"I'm sure I'll be too busy working on the house and garden to have time for such foolishness," said Mary. "I wasn't thinking."

They had finally reached the road that led up the hill into John Rae's land. One of the earliest and most successful of Augusta's traders, he had holdings all around the area. Angus had bought a hundred acres, with a creek running through, on the edge of Rae's land.

It was beautiful, with plenty of hardwood trees as well as pines, and hilly enough for good drainage without being too steep to plow. Desmond had cleared a few acres on each side of the creek, and the Indian corn was two feet high and looked healthy. The barley had sprouted, and the rows were filled with feathery plants about six inches tall.

"I had thought we could put a cabin on the little knoll at the turn of the creek with a barn beyond it, under those big trees. When the grain is harvested, we'll build another shed for sprouting the grain to make malt."

"The soil looks good," Ben said, picking up a handful and running it between his fingers. "It's sandy, but it seems to have good leaf mold in it."

"There's a base of clay, too," said Angus. "It isn't good black loam of the Highlands, but the corn and grain seem to thrive. The creek is fed by springs, so the water should be good for growing as well as making malt. I'll see if John Rae will lease me a couple of his hands to help build a cabin now and a barn and shed later. You can work with them and, if Mrs. Sheldon would like, they can plow a garden plot for her."

Mary had walked toward the knoll Angus had mentioned as a cabin site. "This big oak would keep the sun off the cabin," she called. "We don't want to cut it down."

"Seems like she's already made up her mind to stay," said Ben.

"You'll want to clear most of the woods," said Angus, "so you can keep watch for Indians, and build a good stout fence around the house and garden. But you're close enough to Rae's that you can get there if there's any real trouble."

"You think there'll be trouble?" Ben asked.

"Not if Augusta people can help it," Angus answered. "But it never hurts to be ready. All the outlying families with anything worth stealing have their homes set up to be defended, as much against lawless whites who cross the river as against Indians."

"Bring the wagon up here under the oak," called Mary. "We can camp in the shade."

Angus mounted the horse that Ben held for him, carefully swinging his peg leg so as not to hit the horse's rump. He shook Ben's hand, waved to Mary, and clucked to his horse.

·V·

THE FUR
TRADERS

Angus found Meg busy preparing the back corner room for John Stuart, who had sent word by one of Galphin's slaves that he would arrive for a fortnight's stay and would have a party of seven other men for supper. The slave had gone to invite James Grierson, Martin Campbell, and John Rae. Stuart, George Galphin, and Lachlan McGillivray were coming from Galphin's fort at Moore's Bluff, and Edward Barnard and Andrew McLean would come from town.

"I'd like to know what his news is," said Angus. "He's been in Charlestown for over a month now, and he'll have something on his mind if he's asked the most important men in town to supper."

"Have we plenty of ale?" Meg asked. "With that crowd in this hot weather, we'll need it."

"The Savannah boat brought me three kegs, and they're already cooling in the springhouse."

"Did the Sheldons like the barley land?"

"Mary could hardly wait to get settled. I hope I can get them both interested in making ouisguebaugh. Maybe they'll change their minds about moving altogether."

Meg went downstairs to consult with Amanda about a supper menu good enough for John Stuart's party. If the Chickasaws had brought mussels from their village at New Savannah, they could be steamed and served with melted butter; she'd need at least six chickens and the last joint of beef from the larder in the springhouse. She'd make a trifle for dessert with plenty of wine in it.

John Stuart was used to Charlestown cooking, and she'd prove Augusta could serve a supper as good as he'd find at the Ugly Club, the Beefsteak Club, or any of the other places he went in the Low Country. She'd use the good Spode plates in the private dining room and make sure the silver was polished. Angus kept the flatware and tea service locked in a chest in his office. Pewter was fine for most meals, but Meg liked to set her best table when they had special guests.

James Grierson and Martin Campbell arrived first, clomping up the front steps into the taproom, waving to friends at tables and stopping to chat along the way to the bar. John Rae came in a few minutes later and greeted Angus who was helping Meg at the bar.

"Did you know there's a family camping on your land?" he asked as Angus handed him a tankard of ale.

"They're my tenants," said Angus. "They're going to tend my corn and barley until they feel safe to move to the New Purchase."

"You didn't persuade them that the Purchase was dangerous, did you? I know you've been looking for someone to help with your crazy plan to make barley whisky."

"Whisht, mon, keep it to yourself," said Angus looking around the bar room. "I don't want everyone to know until I see if it can be done."

"What's to stop you?" Rae asked.

"The wrong water, a poor crop, or no peat to burn while the grain's drying for malt. It may taste like hogwash."

"Is this man a Scot?" Rae asked.

"His mother came from the Highlands."

"We've enough thirsty Scotsmen around Augusta to have a ready market."

"That's what I'm depending on. So little good Scotch whisky makes its way across the Atlantic, I never have enough for my best customers."

James Grierson and Martin Campbell moved from the other end of the bar. "What is this about Scotch whisky?"

"Only that I've not enough for my customers."

"Maybe Stuart will bring some from Charlestown."

"Here he comes," said Grierson. "We'll ask him."

"Welcome," said Campbell. "Did you happen to have a bottle of dew from the Highlands in your saddle bags?" he asked shaking Stuart's hand.

"I've come from Charlestown not Edinburgh," said Stuart. "What would I be doing with ouisguebaugh?" He looked at Angus and winked. "There's naught but clothes in my saddle bags."

George Galphin and Lachlan McGillivray were with him, and McGillivray said, "Do you think we'd have left a drop last night if he'd brought a bottle?"

"You gentlemen will have to be satisfied with ale and a drop of apple brandy," said Angus offering tankards, two at a time, filled with the foaming ale.

Edward Barnard and Andrew McLean came in to pick up the last two tankards and Angus said, "Would you like to take your ale into the dining room?"

The two townsmen were more formally dressed than those who had ridden in from the country. McLean had driven in his new Charlestown carriage and picked up Barnard at his town house. They both wore stockings and knee breeches, embroidered waistcoats, and full-bottomed velvet coats with silver buttons. Even McLean, known as Little Macaroni for his sartorial splendor, wore no wig in the July heat, but a beaver tricorne trimmed with silver braid covered his own hair which was neatly clubbed. Barnard, who had been in and out of the Assembly since the time of the first Royal Governor, and took his social position as seriously as his political life, was formally dressed, too.

The six countrymen wore boots with doeskin breeches and broadcloth coats, and their hat brims were wide to protect them from sun and rain. Their linen, however, was faultlessly white and edged with Mechlin lace as fine as that of the townsmen.

Stuart led the way into the private dining room where the table glittered with porcelain and silver set on a fine linen cloth. A breeze from the river, blowing through the open windows, made the candle flames dance in spite of their crystal shades.

Meg felt a glow of pride as the men took their places. She would have liked to use the Waterford wine goblets, but these men wanted ale. They brought their own tankards from the bar and set them at their places. Desmond would bring the food from the kitchen, but she'd stand by to see that it was correctly served.

By the time the mussels and the chicken and the beef courses had been finished, the bowls of trifle eaten, and the brandy decanter placed on the table, coats, waistcoats, and neckcloths had gradually joined the tricornes on pegs along the wall. Old friends could afford to relax, and only a damned fool would wear a coat in Augusta in July.

"Well, laddie," said Martin Campbell to Stuart, "it's been a fine meal you've fed us, but you'd best tell us now what bee has been buzzing in your bonnet."

"Ninety to one it's to do with the Indians," said Rae. "Johnny wouldn't call this lot of old Indian traders together unless there was some trouble brewing among the nations."

"You're right, of course," said Stuart. "It was too good to be true when the Creeks agreed to the New Purchase the way the Cherokees rigged it. They still say the land along the Oconee is theirs, and they're ready to fight to keep the settlers off."

"Be damned to 'em!" said George Galphin. "They knew what they were doing when they came here in May."

"Ay," said Lachlan McGillivray, his Scot's burr more evident after the ale and brandy. "But The Mortar didn't come. And I understand, from some of my contacts in the nation, that he's been conniving with the Shawnees to stir up a war against the British, since he didn't get anywhere with Oconestotah."

"Oconestotah has more sense," said Stuart. "He and Attakullakulla have kept the Cherokees out of more fights than you'd believe."

"I remember when Attakullakulla saved your skin back in 1760," said Rae.

"Ay, and he's been a good friend to all the English. But he's an old man, and Oconestotah's getting old, too. He'll hold the young firebrands down as long as he can, and the Creeks may wait for help from the Cherokees before setting the frontier alight."

"God knows I hope so," said Galphin. "If it weren't for these damnable squatters and settlers, I know I could talk turkey to the Creeks. Hell! I've got sons and grandsons among 'em, as most of you do, even if you won't acknowledge 'em."

"It won't take much to set off a war," said Stuart. "We've got to warn the men in our outposts to be extra careful and try to make the settlers understand the seriousness of the situation."

"Those crazy Virginians in the Purchase would like to stir up trouble and have the militia run the Indians out completely. They don't know they'd be massacred before the militia could be called up," said Rae.

"The Assembly isn't interested in Indian troubles," said Barnard. "They might not even bother to call up the militia. They're all stirred up about the duty on tea again and talking about boycotting all British goods until the tax is taken off."

"It doesn't make sense," said Grierson, coming into the conversation for the first time. "The Crown has to support the East India Company, or they'll go bankrupt."

"They say there's seventeen million pounds of tea going unsold because people refuse to buy it. God help us here in America if they ever stop buying beaver skins for hats," said Rae.

"I hear that tea's going to be cheaper than ever before, even with the tax," said Barnard. "But the damned Liberty Boys say it's a matter of principle. They're planning to turn away any ships loaded with tea."

"Charlestown's full of talk about the Liberty Boys," said Stuart. "Christopher Gadsden's a rabble rouser, organizing the craftsmen and mechanics and urging them to join committees to help the New Englanders."

"To hell with the New Englanders," said Grierson. "Damned bunch of treasonous pulpit pounders!"

"You're right," said Rae. "The Crown and Parliament have spent hundreds of thousands of pounds to found a colony in Georgia and help us build the Indian trade. Without the king's militia, we'd never be able to keep Indians and traders in line."

"This must be just a temporary frooferaw," said Barnard. "I know the men in the Georgia Assembly. They want to live peacefully and keep trade moving."

"You're right, Ned," said Grierson. "The men with property and trade at stake will not go along with the radical rabble."

"Word in Charlestown," said Stuart, "is that Noble Jones' son Wymberly is hand in glove with the dissidents as are a lot of the other young cocks. Their fathers are fit to be tied."

"Thank God we're in Augusta where people are too busy making a living to bother with such tommyrot," said Campbell. "We've enough to worry about keeping the Indians happy."

"Which brings us back to the reason for this meeting," said Stuart. "I want you all to find out if the Creeks and the Shawnees seem to be joining together. I'll see if I can get Oconestotah to lay the law down to the young Cherokees."

"God help us if the Indians hear rumors of this 'liberty' business and try to take advantage."

"We'll pass the word to keep the peace if they want to have all the good things from the Great White Father Over the Water," said George Galphin, as the men pushed back their chairs.

"Thank you, gentlemen, for coming," said Stuart.

"And thank you for an excellent meal and an interesting evening," said Edward Barnard, bowing as he left the room.

·VI·

THE
MERRILLS

In a new clapboard house at the other end of town from the Sword and Thistle, Susan Merrill was getting ready for bed. Her two little sisters were already tucked under the netting in the next room. Now that Susan was sixteen, she was allowed to have supper with her parents in the dining room and stay up until nine.

Pulling the lace-trimmed lawn nightgown over her underclothes, she untied her shift and let it fall to the floor, put her arms into the sleeves of her nightgown, then stepped out of the shift. Her years in Charlestown sharing a room with her little sisters had taught her to dress and undress with modesty.

A breeze from the river stirred the lace curtains at the window, moving shadows in the moonlight on the polished floor. It had been so hot all day it felt wonderful to take off her cap and let her hair down. Pulling the curtains back as far as they would go, she sat on the window seat to brush her hair, brightened by the moonlight to red waves falling over her shoulders. On the river a silvery moon path seemed to lead to their dock, cross the road, and come up the sandy walk to the door of the house.

If only she could take that path, sailing down the Savannah and up the coast to Charlestown and her friends. She was so homesick she could die. All her friends were to be presented next winter at the Saint Cecelia, while she sat in the wilds of Georgia with nothing to do but embroider samplers and twiddle her thumbs.

Father had practiced law for almost twenty years in Charlestown. Why had he let Mr. Stuart persuade him to come to Augusta? True, his practice was ten times what it had been in Charlestown with people registering land claims here. But why did he have to move his family?

She finished her two hundred strokes, put the brush on the seat beside her, and began to plait her hair into braids for the night.

She really did like the new house, as fine as any in Augusta.

Father had shipped their furniture and belongings up the river and had sent to Belgium for new carpets and lace curtains. They did have more room here, and the gallery went all around the house. In Charlestown their house was close to the street and had a gallery only on the garden side; but it was home, and her friends lived within walking distance.

A whippoorwill in the live oak called a mournful note that added to her resentment. Like everything else in Georgia, it was off-key. Her father was busy from morning till night helping people through the process of buying land. But what a motley crew they were, stirring up dust with their wagons and leaving their garbage on the Common.

Susan had no reason to stay up, but she wasn't sleepy. Stepping over the low sill to the gallery roof, she stood with the breeze blowing her gown. Light from the next window meant that her parents had brought their candles upstairs. Not wanting to be caught outside, she sat down on the flat roof and leaned against the wall out of sight. Her parents' voices came to her as they made ready for bed.

"We're in the safest place in the whole backcountry," Joseph said in a conciliatory tone. "The Creeks have always avoided any sort of violence in Augusta."

"Mrs. Seymour says the rector is worried and wishes he had never moved them here from Savannah."

"You and the girls are safer here than in Charlestown if what I hear about the political situation is true."

"Bother politics! You know very well that Charlestown gentlemen are quite different from Red Indians."

"I understand some of the best families are represented at the rowdy meetings under the Liberty Tree in Mazyck's meadow."

"You know they just want excitement," said Jocelyn. "It's a change from cock fighting and goose pulling."

"But Parliament won't tolerate such talk forever. I'm glad to get you out of the thick of it. And if you don't go to sleep soon, I'm going to forget I'm a Charlestown gentleman."

Susan heard a chuckle, then decided it was time to crawl in her window and into her bed.

·VII·

FORT
JAMES

As July drew to a close and the August sun burned into the sweltering southland, it became less and less probable that there would be a general Indian uprising. It was too hot for more exertion than was absolutely necessary.

More and more settlers were moving into the Ceded Lands. Families came from near the North Carolina border and hurried to build cabins and plant crops. Hannah and Elijah Clark, Susannah and John Dooly, Nancy Hart and her husband all moved south near Fort James. The soil was good, the weather moderate, and refuge was available in the fort if things got too rough.

Fort James, at the confluence of the Broad and Savannah rivers, housed militiamen with time on their hands. After early morning roll call and drill, there was little to do. Quarrels often ended in fist fights. The mess was well supplied with fish and small game from the soldiers who used their leisure to set traps or fish for hours under a shady tree on the river bank.

Jamie Stratfield and Bert Sheldon were watching corks bob gently as the current urged them downriver. Despite almost a ten-year difference in their ages and a wide gap in military rank, they had become good friends. Since Bert's return with word of Meg, Jamie had felt closer to him than any of the other militiamen, most of whom were from the Augusta area and had their own ties of friendship.

Bert was hopelessly in love with the angel who had lent him her mare and found a safe place for his family to live. He felt unworthy of anything beyond worshiping at her feet, but he enjoyed telling of his trip to Augusta and his meeting with Miss MacLeod whenever Jamie gave him a chance.

"When do you think we can get back down there?" he asked.

"When our six-month hitch is up, I guess," said Jamie. "Captain Waters is afraid to let any of the Augusta men go home for fear they won't come back."

"He sure doesn't need us all here," said Bert. "The Cherokees aren't about to fight."

"It's the Creeks he has to worry about. We're hoping they will stay peaceful while we're near the Cherokee lands and can get their help if Creeks go on the warpath."

"Do you think my folks should come up here now?"

"Captain Waters tells me," said Jamie, "that we can look for the Indians to attack when they get the corn harvest in and the weather turns cool. He says it's usually about Christmas before they feel like fighting."

"I guess the Captain's been around enough to know," said Bert, "but they sure seem friendly, even the Creeks."

"They know the militia's friendly to them and won't fight unless the homesteaders are attacked. Ten to one, it'll be one of the homesteaders who stirs them up. They're scared of the Indians and don't want to admit it."

"I'm so sick of sitting around here on my backside in the heat, I'd almost welcome a good fight," said Bert.

Jamie gave him a searching look, and Bert shook his head. "No, I don't really mean that," he said, "but I'm derned tired of doing nothing."

"Then you'd better see what's jerking your line," said Jamie. Bert jerked his pole up, pulling a big bass out of the water.

"We'll both be back in Augusta in time for Christmas," said Jamie. "That is, unless the Creeks go on the warpath."

"Pray God they wait 'till we're home and another bunch of recruits are out here," said Bert.

·VIII·

CHRISTMAS, 1773

Christmas at the Sword and Thistle was the high point of the whole year. For days, Desmond and Amanda had been decorating the taproom with holly and mistletoe, and Meg had made a long garland of smilax to weave through the railings of the front galleries and down the front steps.

The brass had been polished, and new candles had been put in holders on the mantels of the two big fireplaces, with holly and evergreen boughs behind them. All the bedrooms had their own decorations; fires were laid in the fireplaces and logs stacked in the wood boxes.

The larder shelves were full of apple, sweet potato, and mince pies laced with brandy. Meg had baked five Christmas cakes full of currants and raisins, and there were enough hams in the smokehouse to feed an army. Wild turkeys and geese hung with rabbits and partridges, ready to be roasted.

The militia at Fort James was due to be discharged, and their relief company had ridden up the Cherokee Road more than a week ago. The whole Sheldon family had been invited for Christmas dinner at the inn. Their own cabin on Rae's Creek was comfortable and cozy, and they planned a family Christmas when Bert came home. The corn crop had been a great success, filling the bins in their barn. The barley had not done as well as they'd hoped, but there had been enough to cover two of the big racks in the sprouting shed. Ben and Angus had decided to try hickory smoke instead of peat to keep the malt working.

Mary and Francie had tended the garden and put away carrots and turnips and salted down chopped cabbage to make kraut.

At the other end of town, the Merrill household was getting ready for their first Christmas in Augusta, homesick for the Low Country and the month-long season of festivities when everyone went from one plantation to another for houseparties or into the city for balls and concerts. This would have been Susan's first year to wear beautiful gowns and go to grown-up parties. Jocelyn had hoped earlier to persuade Joseph to take them to Charlestown, for the dwindling flow of settlers had lessened his law practice. But the persistent rumors of trouble among the Creeks made overland travel dangerous, and riverboats were not suitable for passenger travel. Though they could go downriver in the winter floods, it took weeks to row them upriver against the current, and the gangs of oarsmen were too rough for ladies to be near.

Jocelyn, planning an open house on Christmas afternoon for members of St. Paul's and any other presentable Augustans who were in town, had ordered benne seeds for traditional Charlestown Christmas cakes and presents for the children and slaves to be sent by wagon train. John Stuart was in Charlestown, as were many of the merchants who had homes and warehouses in both towns. The few who shipped their hides through Savannah, had gone there for the holidays.

Three days before Christmas, Jamie Stratfield rode into town. In his saddlebags were a pair of doeskin moccasins lined with beaver fur. They were long and narrow, made to his specifications by a Cherokee squaw who could not believe anyone would have such a narrow foot. He would have a devil of a time finding another female to fit them if Meg refused them. He knew it wasn't proper to give a lady clothing, but they were more like a souvenir. They were trimmed with porcupine quills, and the ankle laces were dyed red with berry juice.

The gully was nearly filled with water when he crossed it and saw the inn nestled in the trees above the bank, decorated with garlands, its windows shining rosy in the westering sun. Smoke climbed lazily from four of the eight tall chimney pots, and the hitching rail was full of horses. The whole scene exuded welcome and good fellowship.

Meg had watched the road, off and on, for the past three days. She knew she was foolish to put any store in Jamie's interest; he was used to sweet-talking Baltimore women, and there was no reason for him to think twice about a tavernkeeper's niece. But still she watched the road and tried to make her heart stop thumping when a horseman splashed across the gully.

Her back was to the door when she heard Angus call, "Welcome back, laddie! We'd decided you'd gone to live with the Cherokees."

Meg turned, and there he was, face red from the cold wind and hair rumpled from his fur cap. His eyes were only for Meg, as he absently returned Angus's handshake and made his way toward the bar.

Meg would have liked to whip off her apron and repin her hair. All she could do, with a room full of interested spectators, was reach across the bar to take his outstretched hands and look into those shining blue eyes that seemed to light a fire in her own. From their clasped hands, a warmth spread.

Angus was saying, "Meg, lass, fill a tankard for Jamie, or would you rather have a cup of hot punch from the bowl on the hearth? It's guaranteed to warm the coldest traveler."

Jamie released Meg's hands and turned to her uncle smiling. "I've thought of nothing but a warm welcome here since we left Fort James. I feel as though I'd come home." He was not looking at Meg, but she knew his words were meant for her.

"And happy we are to have you here," said Angus.

Jamie would have liked a cup of spicy mulled punch, but he asked for a tankard of ale, knowing that Meg would serve him and he'd have a reason to stand with her at the bar.

"We were afraid you men would not make it for Christmas," said Angus. "Some families here in Augusta have been anxious."

"We'd have been back sooner, but we stopped to help two families who were building stockades around their farm buildings. Word is that Big Elk and a band of young bucks from the Lower Creek nation are on the move, looking for trouble."

"God help the people in the Purchase," said Angus.

"They've been so anxious to get their farms established," said Jamie, "that they haven't built defenses. They'd be safe at the fort, but they won't leave their homes."

"Have you heard what the trouble is this time?"

"One of the Lower Creeks was killed last week, up near the head of the Ogeechee. Big Elk claims a white man did it, and the Indians want him executed."

A group had gathered around the bar, avid for news.

"Who do they say killed the Creek?" a man in buckskins asked.

"They say it was a settler named William White, who was miles away from the place and had witnesses to prove it."

"I'd get my family into the fort, if I was White," said another. "Injuns don't care nothin' for white man's law."

"There's a company of Rangers at Fort James now besides two militia companies. Captain Few from here in Augusta has taken command. People would be safe enough in the fort," Jamie repeated.

"The Quakers up at Wrightsboro got chased out once," said a gray-bearded frontiersman. "They ought to know better."

"They've got a good stockade there now," said Jamie, "and they've built their houses close together. The Indians may leave them alone and go for the outlying farms."

Meg had been listening but, with all hope of a private conversation gone, she filled a pitcher from the ale keg and went among the tables to replenish empty mugs. It wasn't until supper was over and the crowd had thinned to the serious drinkers and overnight guests that she was able to sit in front of the fireplace and stretch her feet toward the fire.

Jamie, still the center of a group around the fireplace at the other end of the room, had been drained of every bit of information he had about the trouble in the Purchase. Most of the men in the group were old-timers who blamed the settlers for stirring up the Creeks. Some blamed the King for bringing in the ignorant clodhoppers and trouble-making vagabonds. Voices rose louder, tongues grew thicker as the spicy rum and cider punch warmed tempers. Slipping quietly from the group, Jamie moved to the other fireplace.

Meg had taken off her apron, redone her hair, put on a frilly new cap, and exchanged the plain kerchief she had worn for a sheer scarf of lawn trimmed with fine lace. The firelight added color to the tendrils of hair around the edges of her cap and tinted her cheeks and lips a deeper rose.

"I've been dreaming of you by a fireplace," said Jamie sitting down beside her.

Meg looked down to hide the happiness in her eyes. There was no reason to think Jamie meant more than to dally with a tavern maid.

"I've worried for fear you'd been hurt or killed," she said.

"I told you I'd be back," he said. "I hope to buy a plot in town and build a house. There's plenty of work for a surveyor with the land office here."

Meg leaned back and looked into his eyes, her hands on the bench. Jamie covered her right hand with his left, hidden between them from the eyes of any who might look their way.

"You may think I'm brash, but I've had six months to think of you. I keep seeing you in my home sharing my life."

Meg felt as though she'd fallen into the fire. Not one for megrims and vapors and fainting spells, she couldn't comprehend his words in the room full of drinkers and high-pitched argument. Freeing her hand, she hurried out to the winter cold of the front porch.

The front door closed again and Jamie gathered her into his arms. "I'm sorry I was so abrupt," he said. "I'm a damned, blundering fool."

"Oh, no." Meg cried. "It was just that I've been waiting and hoping, and all those loudmouthed men . . ."

Jamie tipped her head back and his lips came down on hers, first gently, then with gathering ardor until she felt her fears and inhibitions melt away and her hands go behind his head to press him closer.

The winter wind blowing across the river, carrying a sprinkle of snow, finally brought them back to earth. Meg settled her ruffled cap on her hair, then walked with Jamie into the taproom.

Argument was still raging around the punch bowl. Only Angus, standing behind the bar with his heavy brows drawn together, seemed interested in the young couple.

Jamie led Meg to her uncle. "Sir, I'd like your permission to ask for Margaret MacLeod's hand in marriage."

The frown changing to a smile, Angus hurried around the bar to shake his hand. "God bless you, laddie," he beamed. "The lass would be a dommed fool to turn you down."

Meg moved closer to Jamie and looked up into his eyes. "I'll not turn him down," she said.

His peg leg pounding the floor, Angus hurried toward the group at the punch bowl. "Stop all that fashing and come drink a toast. Lieutenant James Stratfield has persuaded my niece to be his wife."

"And a bonnie bride she'll be," called one of the traders.

"Ye'r not dolin' out real Highland ouisguebaugh?" called another trader. "I'd o' asked ye for her hand myself if I'd thought ye had Scotch whisky to offer."

"Nay," said Angus, "but I've plenty of rum, and there'll be no water in it."

Their argument forgotten, the men gathered around Jamie and Meg with ribald congratulations. Reared in the tavern, Meg was not easily shocked. Smiling and moving closer under Jamie's arm, she returned their banter, as she'd learned to do, with good humor.

Angus poured a measure of good Jamaica rum into each tankard, then raising his own to Meg and Jamie, he said, "Here's to the bonniest niece an old Highlander ever had. May she and Jamie live happily ever after."

Jamie, his left arm still around Meg, raised his tankard to Angus. "To you, Angus, with my thanks for taking such loving care of my Meg and sharing her love with me."

"When's the wedding to be?" asked a bearded trader.

"I'd like to have it at Hogmanay," said Meg.

"A braw plan," said Angus. "All good Scots will come to celebrate the New Year with a new marriage, and we'll even allow some English to help us."

* * *

Christmas Eve morning dawned bright and clear with a gentle south wind blowing away the clouds. That was the wonder of Augusta. You might have cold, frosty weather and even a bit of snow, but you knew it wouldn't last. The sun would come out, the south-flying birds would stay for a day or so to peck in the sun-warmed earth, and you could wash the clothes and hang them in the sun to dry.

Mary Sheldon had been awake for over an hour and had brought Benjy from his cradle to be suckled and cuddled back to sleep under the eiderdown, when Ben and Bert left to feed the stock and carry in the wood.

She could hear them talking now, as Ben showed Bert the full corn cribs and the shed with the floor of flat stones where the barley was spread to make malt for the whisky. Although the barley crop, with sheaves sparsely filled, had been a disappointment, there was enough of the grain to make a good batch or two of malt.

Angus had sent to Charlestown a month ago for the copper container and tubing that would be used to boil the malt and mash and cool the steam as it was forced through the *worm*, as the tubing was called. He'd built a fireplace of stone with a small opening at the front and a chimney to carry the smoke away from the shed. When the boiler arrived, it would fit over a hole in the top of the fireplace, and the copper pipe was already installed beside the hearth in a big wooden tub that could be filled with cold creek water. Ben proudly showed Bert the system of wooden pipes he had rigged from the creek behind the shed to direct the water into a barrel and the drain in the floor that would let it run out.

"Angus says he'll not waste the malt on experiments," Ben explained. "We'll first try the still with mash made of Indian corn. They've been making sour mash liquor in the hill settlements for years."

"Do you think you'll leave here," Bert asked. "You and Ma are so well settled."

"I don't know," said Ben. "Your Ma is happier than I've seen her since we left Pennsylvania. This sandy soil is better than it looks, and she and Francie loved having a vegetable garden and even a flower garden of plants Miss Meg sent her."

Bert blushed at the mention of Meg and turned his head so his father wouldn't notice. He didn't have a snowball's chance in hell with Meg, but he'd been thinking of her all the time he'd been in Cherokee country.

"Your land up in the Purchase is mighty fertile, too. The corn I harvested was sweet, and the ears were filled out. You've got a good spring right where I built the lean-to, and some nice families are moving in near the fort."

"I know, son. You told me last night. But your Ma looks so dejected when we talk about leaving, I think we'll stay for a while to see how things go. That land will be yours some day anyhow, and it's not going to run away. We have a title, and you've harvested a crop to show good intent. We'll let it lay for a while."

Francie hurried from the house. "Ma says to come to breakfast. We've got ham and cornbread and new-laid eggs fried in drippings."

Bert ruffled her blonde curls, not yet braided for the day. "It's a wonder you're not fatter than a pig."

"We don't eat this way all the time. We're celebrating you coming home and Christmas Eve. Miss Meg sent us the ham from the inn. She's the nicest lady in the whole world and lets me ride her horse. She even puts Benjy up on the saddle with me sometimes."

Entering the cabin, Francie led Bert to the table set with pewter plates and cutlery. "We are blessed," Mary said as she sat on the bench beside Bert, her hand on his arm. "We have our son home safe, and we have a fine, warm hearth and plenty of good food. It is going to be a wonderful Christmas."

* * *

In the Merrill house on The Bay, Christmas preparations had been going on for weeks. Since they weren't able to go to Charlestown, Jocelyn was determined to have a Christmas party in Augusta to equal any she had given in their Tradd Street house. Her "At Home" cards were delivered by the butler to all their neighbors along The Bay, on Broad Street, and on Back Street as well. She'd even sent an invitation to Brownsborough for Mr. Thomas Brown and to his friend Captain Manson. Rumor had it that Brown's father was an immensely wealthy merchant of Yorkshire. With Susan getting on to marriageable age, it didn't hurt to know young and eligible men.

Joseph thought she was presumptuous to invite people she hardly knew, but she'd met many of them in Charlestown and she'd talked to them after church at St. Paul's.

Robert MacKay and his wife Mary had accepted and planned to stay the night in the guest room with baby Robert, so Mary could suckle him. George Galphin had declined, but the Griersons and the Goodgions were driving together from beyond Hawk's Gully. The Raes were coming if Mrs. Rae was well enough to travel. A guest room was ready for them.

Most of the families who had homes in town as well as in the country had accepted. Both Dr. Wells and Dr. Johnston were coming, which could be a problem because they disagreed on everything from medicine to politics. Andrew McLean was always an addition to a party with his modish manners and clothes. He was a good friend to Thomas Brown and Manson and would see that they were introduced to anyone they didn't already know.

Thank heavens the Barnards had accepted. They were one of the oldest families. Edward Barnard was a pillar of St. Paul's and had been elected to the legislature for so many years he knew everybody in Georgia politics. He had raised the Ranger company and gone with Jamie and Bert to Fort James, but he had had to turn his command over to Captain Waters because of health problems.

The silver was polished, the punch bowl ready for the gentlemen, and a bowl set out for the ladies' ratafia. The Wedgewood tea cups and plates awaited anyone wanting tea, though its supply was getting to be a bother. Even some of the Charlestown gentry were making a stand against the tea tax. Actually very little tea was drunk in Augusta, even before the tax was levied. Most Georgians drank coffee from the West Indies.

Jocelyn took a last look around the drawing room, stopped to replace a sprig of holly that had fallen from the mantel, and hurried upstairs to check on Susan's dress. Unable to be in Charlestown for the social season, Susan's first formal introduction to society would be this party.

By three o'clock, the wind had shifted, and the temperature had dropped. If only it didn't rain, it would be more festive with the fireplaces lit. Susan stood with her mother to await the first guests. Her auburn hair had been brushed up high and caught in a pearl clasp, and Selena, the black maid, had used a curling iron to form it into long curls that fell in a cascade down her back. Her white lawn gown was much lower over the bosom than any she'd ever worn, and the panniers of her pale blue satin overgown were padded over the hips like ladies in the French fashion book. She found it hard to keep from pulling up her bodice or patting her hips to be sure they were in line.

As the first carriage wheels crunched on the drive, her father came into the drawing room. "I can hardly believe this beautiful young lady is my Susan," he said, taking her hand and bowing as she dipped a curtsy.

Samson announced the arrival of Dr. and Mrs. Andrew Johnston and, immediately after, Mr. and Mrs. MacKay. In no time, the drawing room and dining room were buzzing with people dressed in their best Sunday clothes and impressed with themselves and their behavior. Augusta might be one hundred miles beyond the frontier, but Augustans knew how to act like gentry.

Thomas Brown and his friend were late, because they'd stopped at the Sword and Thistle to engage rooms and change into their formal clothes after the ride from Brownsborough. "My abject apologies," Brown said, bending over his hostess's hand. "We lost almost half an hour at the Greenbrier Creek ferry."

"I'm so glad you were able to come," said Jocelyn. "It has been a long time since we met at the Manigaults' in Charlestown."

"Much too long," said Brown, noticing Susan out of the corner of his eye.

"I'd like you to know our daughter Susan," said Jocelyn. "Do take Mr. Brown to the punch bowl."

Brown placed Susan's gloved hand on his arm as they started toward the dining room. After a few steps, they were stopped by Martin Weatherford, who bowed to Susan, then grasped Brown's hand and said, "I've been waiting to talk to you."

"You must excuse me, Mr. Brown," Susan said, removing her hand from his arm. She had seen two curly heads duck behind the stair rail. Hurrying into the dining room, she picked up a small plate of cakes and, putting her finger to her lips, passed it over the railing to her two little sisters. By the time she returned to the dining room, Brown and Weatherford were deep in conversation.

"Jamie Stratfield was at the Sword and Thistle," said Brown. "Had you heard about the murder of a Creek up near the head of the Ogeechee?"

"George Galphin sent word to Colonel Grierson the day after it happened," said Weatherford. "The Creeks are claiming a white man killed him, but Galphin's source says it was another Creek."

Dr. George Wells, standing nearby, overheard Weatherford. "They're nothing but a lot of scrapping dogs," he said. "You're not going to be safe in Brownsborough until the whole bunch is chased out of this part of the country."

Brown raised his quizzing glass and stared at Wells. "I've found the Indians to be friendly when they are treated fairly," he said. "I am told it's when they're cheated or their women are molested that they kill."

Wells, after several cups of the hot punch, was a little unsteady on his feet. He caught himself by grabbing Brown's arm. "When you've been in this country a little longer, you'll learn that they've got to be treated like wild beasts," he said. "The wolves have been killed off or chased out west so they don't kill settlers anymore. We've got to do the same with the Indians."

Edward Barnard moved to the doctor's side, as Brown pulled his arm away and brushed his sleeve as if to remove filth. "Come off your high horse, George," he said, taking the doctor's arm. "You've had to patch up the results of Indian attacks, but there are many of us who owe our wealth to those Indian wolves you're talking about."

"Maybe it would be better if you traders moved west, too," said Wells.

Barnard had taken insults in the Assembly for too many years to be easily riled. "Perhaps we will some day, George, and leave it all to you young firebrands. But you'd best be prepared for a holocaust like nothing you've ever imagined if you stir up the tribes."

"Sometimes a forest must be burned to clear a field for planting," said Wells darkly. "Once we're rid of all the savages and all the wealthy hogs who get richer by trafficking with them, the poor pioneer settlers will be allowed to farm in peace."

Barnard, who had started as a baker's apprentice and had amassed a fortune by trading in furs, should have been the first to take offense. But it was Christmas Eve, and this was a civilized party. "Come along, George," he said. "Let this wealthy hog pour you a stirrup cup of punch, then my coachman will take you home."

"You're very kind, sir," said William Glascock, knowing that it was time to get his friend out of trouble. "Wells has promised to come home with us for supper. I'll see him safely home afterward."

About to protest, Wells remembered the generous table Mrs. Glascock set and allowed himself to be led to the door.

James Grierson, watching from the sidelines, approached Barnard, punch cup in hand. "You've more patience than I have, Ned," he said.

"He was in his cups," said Barnard. "I've run into worse than George in Savannah. Damned dewy-eyed radicals."

"Have you heard what's happened in Boston? One of the clerks from my Charlestown office rode in today to spend Christmas with his parents. It is all over Charlestown that the people in Boston refused to unload three ships full of East India tea. They said they were being tricked into paying the tax by reducing the tea price. Men dressed up as Indians, so the government agents wouldn't know who they were, boarded the ships at night and dumped all the tea in the harbor."

"My God, that's rebellion!" said Barnard.

"They say a crowd in Annapolis burned a ship carrying a cargo of tea, and Charlestown is just waiting to see if they send any there."

Mr. Seymour and Robert MacKay joined the group. The ladies, sensing a political discussion, retired to the dining room. They could hear from the parlor Mr. Seymour's pulpit voice raised to denounce the treasonous acts of the colonists.

"Treason be damned," said James Rae. "It's wanton destruction of private property. What if they decide to burn our warehouses because we're still trading with England?"

"I can't believe the Georgia Assembly will countenance a trade boycott," said MacKay. "Charlestown has always been full of rich addlepates, but Savannah people have more sense. They're still dependent on the Crown to keep them solvent."

"I hope they know which side their bread's buttered on," said Rae. "If they turn King and Parliament against us, I don't know how we'll deal with the Indians. Where would we get presents for treaty making?"

"Isn't this a tempest in a teapot, to make a terrible pun?" asked Thomas Brown. "Surely the gentlemen of Georgia will not condone the actions of that rabble in Boston."

"Georgia gentlemen with land and wealth are not the ones to worry about," said Grierson. "But we have a whole town full of New Englanders just south of Savannah and settlers coming to the New Purchase from all over the colonies. Most of them are malcontents who left their former homes because they didn't get along there."

"I've run into some in the Assembly," said Barnard, "like that doctor, Lyman Hall I think his name is, who taught at Yale before he moved to Sunbury. He's been preaching sedition ever since he came south."

"We have a few around here, like Wells and his friends, but most of them keep their mouths shut except when they're drunk."

Thomas Brown nodded agreement. "I've talked to some of the new settlers who have moved in beyond Brownsborough. They're hard-working yeomen, but some have said things that came close to being treasonous."

"You're right," said Rae, "the frontiersmen are hard workers, and most of them care nothing about politics. But they're all worried about taxes. They think we ought to be able to make our own laws and collect our own taxes over here."

"Gentlemen, the punch bowl is being neglected," said Joseph Merrill, "and I'm afraid the ladies feel they are being neglected, too."

The men, who had become so engrossed in conversation that they had forgotten they were at a Christmas party, moved sheepishly to rejoin their wives and daughters in the dining room.

By Boxing Day, the day after Christmas, everyone had forgotten the Boston Tea Party. Word had come that William White, the settler who had been falsely accused of killing a Creek, had been killed, along with his whole family, by a Creek war party. It looked as though the Indian uprising was finally a reality.

·IX·

INDIAN

TROUBLES

By New Year's Day, 1774, settlers from the Purchase began to drift into town, bringing wives and children to a safe place. Those who remained in the land above Little River hurried to fortify their farms or moved in with neighbors who had palisades and blockhouses. Settlers from the Purchase formed their own Ranger company and set out to find and kill the guilty Indians. When Edward Barnard called out the militia and Rangers from the Augusta area, Meg and Jamie's wedding was postponed indefinitely, and he and Bert returned to Fort James.

On January 14 a group of settlers on land west of Wrightsboro were attacked by a band of Creeks from Coweta, while they were working to fortify William Sherrill's farm. Sherrill and two others were killed by the first surprise volley. One of Sherrill's black slaves shot an Indian through the eye, then, with the rest of the group, retreated to a farm building, as the Indians paused to reload. Neighbors, hearing the gunshots, were able to escape and went galloping toward Fort James for help. Late in the afternoon Captain Barnard and his men arrived in time to relieve the weary frontiersmen.

During an all day siege, seven of the settlers had been killed, five wounded, and the Indians had set the farm buildings on fire three times, only to be put out by the defenders. The bodies of five dead Indians were found, but the wounded Indians had been carried off by the war party.

A few days later, Meg was serving bar when two militiamen came into the tavern on their way to town to ask for more help. She recognized one of them as Luke Johnson, a frontiersman who had shared the rum on Christmas Eve to toast her betrothal.

"Your Jamie has his hands full, and we could do with a hundred more like him," said Luke. A group began to gather at the bar, willing to pay for unlimited ale for the men in exchange for a first-hand account of the Sherrill massacre.

"Colonel Barnard sent us to help recruit more men," said Luke when he'd finished telling the story, drinking deep and wiping the foam from his beard with the back of his hand. "He wants his son-in-law Will Goodgion to organize another company and bring them on up to Fort James."

"I could use the pay," said a young redhead who had joined the group. "My Molly's going to have a baby soon, and I'd like to have money to buy a cow."

"The King's shilling is the best pay you can get!" said Luke, "and you'd only have to serve till we settle this Injun trouble."

"I reckon we'll all be fightin' for our lives," said another man, "and our wives and children will be in danger in Augusta if we don't get out and stop 'em."

"That's right," said Luke. "Come on to town with us and talk to Captain Goodgion."

"I don't have nothin' against Injuns if they're peaceful," said a gray-bearded trapper, "but I've seen what they done in white settlements when they're on the warpath. I'll go along with you."

When the two militiamen finished their third mug of ale and turned to leave, six men followed them through the door.

The following day a Ranger company was also commissioned to be filled by volunteers from the countryside as it accompanied Captain Goodgion's Augusta militia into the New Purchase. The two companies would reinforce troops from Fort James who were scouring the forest above Wrightsboro.

Governor Wright had sent a request to General Howe in Massachusetts for British Regulars to fight in Georgia and had ordered the Augusta traders to withhold all supplies from the Creeks until peace could be made. But, for the present, it would be a matter of the settlers and the militia looking after themselves.

There was little time to train the new recruits in the Ranger company, although the older traders and the men who had fought Indians before tried to indoctrinate the new men as they hurried north. At Wrightsboro they set up camp for the night, and the next morning split into two units, the Rangers under Lieutenant Grant going on toward Fort James and the militia under Captain Goodgion scouting the land around Wrightsboro.

An hour or so north of Wrightsboro, the graybearded trapper who had been at the Sword and Thistle moved his horse over close to the young redheaded recruit. "I don't like the looks of things, Sonny," he said. "This here would be a helluva place to be caught by Injuns."

The redhead looked around, but could see nothing but pine trees. "What do you see?" he asked worriedly.

"Not a damned thing!" said the graybeard. "But there's Injuns out there. I can tell by the crawlin' in the back o' my neck. If you see me duck an' run, you duck too. Lay down flat on your horse's neck, and kick him after mine. We're like ducks settin' on a pond."

They'd not long to wait. As Lieutenant Grant rounded the next curve, his horse suddenly reared and screamed, its neck and withers bristling with arrows. Grant clutched at his throat trying to pull out the arrow that was already cutting off his life's breath.

For a few minutes it was bedlam, horses and men milling in the pathway, a few experienced men sighting into the dusky pine forest and shooting at painted bodies seen slipping from tree to tree. Grant and his horse were both down, but one of his men dismounted long enough to throw the Lieutenant across his own horse's withers and remount, holding Grant with one hand while he wheeled his horse with the other. Arrows were flying from the forest and a few musket shots. The ammunition shortage had made the Indians turn back to old methods. Weatherford, Hammond, and Ayres were all down; several others with arrow wounds were still sitting on their horses in pain.

"Let's get the hell out of here, Sonny," said the graybeard. "We ain't got a chance, twenty-five of us against a couple o' hundred Injuns." He turned his horse and, bending low in the saddle, raced off down the path toward Wrightsboro. His red-haired friend kicked his own mount into a gallop behind him, and soon the whole troop was in retreat. The officers, unable to rally the men, stopped long enough to throw the dead and wounded into the baggage wagon, keeping up a steady gunfire to cover their rout.

All along their path, settlers had abandoned their homes at the time of the Sherrill massacre and had either moved into Wrightsboro or were on their way to Augusta. The Indians stopped to loot and burn the deserted farmhouses and destroy the crops, allowing the surviving recruits to escape. Smoke from the fires drifted over the forest as they fled back toward camp, the only remaining officer and two sergeants escorting the wagon carrying the bodies of the slain and wounded.

Riding into camp, the remaining lieutenant dismounted wearily and tramped across to the headquarters tent, his jaw set and his lips drawn thin. Captain William Goodgion came to meet him and gripped his hand as he swallowed hard to keep back the tears.

"The Goddamned red bastards jumped us and killed Grant and Williams before they could draw their guns," he said. "Hammond and Weatherford were killed before we could rally the men, and then the rest of the troop turned and ran. We picked up the dead and brought them back in the wagon." Goodgion had reached into a pack beside him and now opened a brandy flask and handed it to the lieutenant.

"Go on, drink it. That's an order," he said. "And sit down on that bale of hay before you fall down."

The young officer turned up the flask and drank deeply, coughing as he handed it back to his commander.

"Sir, I ain't excusing the men," he said, "but they'd none of 'em had any training. And there must have been more than a hundred Indians, and us caught bare assed on that path."

"They're new volunteers, Sam," said Goodgion. "They don't know anything about army tactics and discipline. I'm surprised so many volunteered."

"They've got families, and they want to stop the Indians before they go really wild and hit around Augusta."

The tramp of boots announced the return of Captain William Few and Zachariah Williams, who had been scouting the Wrightsboro area.

"My God! What happened?" Few exclaimed as he rushed into the tent. "That looks like a slaughterhouse wagon!"

"Grant's troop was ambushed up near the head of the Ogeechee," said Goodgion. "Sam was the only officer left, and the volunteers bolted. He and two of his sergeants loaded the dead in the wagon and brought them in."

"My men from the Purchase are ready to head for home, too," said Few. "They saw a few burned farms and began to think about getting back to protect their own homes."

"They know nothing about Indian warfare," said Goodgion. "They thought they'd shoot a few Indians and chase the rest back into the wilderness."

A shuffling of feet and a nervous cough outside the tent brought the officers out in a hurry. A young Ranger sergeant, backed by seven or eight other Rangers, saluted and cleared his throat, then said resolutely, "Sir, me and the boys volunteered to come up here to clear out the Injuns that attacked Sherrill's Fort. But them was a bunch of renegades. Now it looks like the whole dern Creek Nation's on the warpath, and we don't know where they'll hit next. We've all got wives and kids that are mighty dear to us, and they ain't got nobody to protect them. We're respectfully submitting our resignations."

"You understand that you can be shot for deserting?" Captain Goodgion asked.

"Yes, sir," answered the sergeant. "But I'd rather take my chances with a court-martial than let my wife be raped and my kids murdered."

Goodgion shook his head sadly. "I have no intention of forcing the volunteers to stay. I probably would not be able to if I tried. All I can do is order my Augusta militia company to stay here to help bury the dead and to try to find the Indians who ambushed and killed Grant and the others. Those militiamen who disobey my order are subject to courts-martial when I get back to Augusta.

"Now, you Ranger volunteers who have changed your minds, get the hell out of my sight and back to your bloody farms!"

Most of the Rangers walked quietly to the picket line, mounted, and set off in a body southward. The men of Goodgion's Augusta company looked at each other and, though a few of them joined the deserters, most of them stepped up and formed a double line, facing their commander. A few of the Rangers, including the graybeard and the redhead, fell in with the militiamen.

"Thank you, men," said Goodgion. "New, Captain Few, if you will form a burial detail, we'll get on with it."

·X·

THE
MAD TURKEY
MURDER

Rae, McGillivray, Galphin, and Barnard met at the Sword and Thistle. John Stuart in Charlestown had sent orders to try to cool things until he could work on some sort of alliance of the Cherokees, Chickasaws, and Choctaws against the Creeks. His cousin Charles had been sent to West Florida to deal with the Choctaws, and Alexander Cameron, another cousin, had been sent to the Cherokees.

"From what I can gather from my friends in the Creek Nation," said Galphin, as they sat around the table in the back dining room, "this is a group of young renegade bucks under Big Elk who are raising hell and trying to stir up the rest of the Creeks to attack the settlements. The Upper Creeks want to stay out of it; so do most of the Lower Creeks."

"The Cherokees would love to see the Creeks start a war," said Barnard. "They're sitting up there egging Big Elk on, hoping the British troops will come in and burn out the Creeks the way they did the Cherokees in 1760."

"If we can just keep the settlers from taking punishment into their own hands," said Rae, "we may be able to keep the fire contained till Stuart can call the Creeks together for a powwow."

"I've given orders that the militiamen are to bring in prisoners to be tried," said Barnard, "instead of shooting them."

"That's the big thing," said Galphin. "We can't expect the Creeks to act civilized if we act like savages."

"Most of the Creek chiefs want peace," said McGillivray. "I hear that Emistisiguo and Mad Turkey have been helping get the white traders out of the villages safely, and they've been going around the Nation talking peace."

"If Cameron can just keep the Cherokees from stirring up the young Creek bucks!" said Barnard. "Attakullakulla and Oconestotah don't want a Creek war. They know the Cherokees are bound to be involved. They remember the winter we burned them out, but the young bucks were babies then."

"Oconestotah's in Charlestown now with Stuart, talking peace," said Barnard.

"Talking peace, hell!" said McGillivray. "Drinking good Scotch whisky and gambling on the horse races, I heard from one of the wagoneers from Charlestown."

"I hear the old bugger's going to start wearing a kilt," said Barnard. "They tell me Stuart's had him made a member of the Saint Andrews Society."

"God bless us!" said McGillivray. "There may be plenty of Indians with Scots blood, but I never heard that of Oconestotah."

"Stuart's no fool," said Barnard. "Both Creeks and Cherokee count him as their friend because he really likes them. Augusta and all of Georgia would have been burned and plundered years ago, if it hadn't been for Stuart."

"God knows what we'd do without him on our side," agreed Galphin.

"If we can only keep these damnable Crackers in line!" said Rae. "Augusta's a tinderbox. They've been pouring into town for safety, filling the taverns, and shouting about what they'd do to any Indians who came their way. They're brave as hell as long as they're safe in a crowd."

"This is about the only place in town that isn't overrun," said McGillivray. "Angus won't give credit to the rabble, and I've seen him use his crutch on a few who wouldn't leave when asked."

"Speak of the Old Nick," said Rae, as Angus came through the door carrying a big pitcher of ale. "What do you think of Oconestotah as a member of the Saint Andrew's Society?"

"I'd prefer him to many young troublemakers with the names and faces and bony knees of Highlanders, who are ready to get us into a war," said Angus. "And you know I have no love for Indians."

"That's the trouble," said Galphin. "Indians have different ideas of right and wrong. We can like an Indian and respect him as a man without approving of his ways."

"Plenty of hardworking, peaceful pioneer families get along with the Creeks. They only want to be left alone to till the soil," said Rae. "It's the bloody Crackers who are stirring up trouble, but they'll all get hurt."

"God help us if the Crackers ever get the upper hand," said Barnard. "They'd bring the nations down on all of us. All white scalps are the same, hung on a lodge pole."

"God give us more leaders like John Stuart," said McGillivray.

"Amen," said Angus. "Can I fill your cups again before I close the bar?"
"Give us all one more for the road," said Rae.

* * *

It wasn't long before Rae's fears were realized. The Creek chiefs, Emistisiguo and Neathlacco, were in Savannah to talk peace with Governor Wright and John Stuart. Mad Turkey, an Oakfuskie Creek chief, stopped in Augusta on his way to join them in Savannah. William Goodgion, knowing the temper of the settlers, asked him to stay at his home, but Mad Turkey remembered the good days when an Indian was welcome in Augusta and wanted to enjoy a day on the town.

In a tavern on Broad Street, a blacksmith, Thomas Fee, asked him to have a drink. Mad Turkey, having spent the past months traveling through the villages and meeting traders, talking peace, was filled with benevolence toward the white race. Fee, however, had had relatives butchered by Indians and he hated all of them. When Mad Turkey tipped up the bottle to drink, Fee swung an iron bar up over his head and brought it whistling down to crush the Indian's skull.

In the old days, Fee would have been arrested immediately, tried, and executed. But now Augusta was filled with Indian haters. Friends of Fee helped him to escape across the river into South Carolina before the forces of law and order could act.

Old Augustans were sick at heart and terrified of Creek reprisal. Doors and shutters were kept tightly closed; prized belongings were packed for a quiet flight to the nearest palisade. Governor Wright offered a reward of one hundred pounds for Fee's capture, and John Stuart alerted the South Carolina militia. Fee was captured and jailed in the Ninety-Six district, but a crowd of frontiersmen broke into the jail and released him before he could be tried.

Jamie Stratfield was still at Fort James. He had ridden back to Augusta twice with messages and stayed overnight at the Sword and Thistle, and he and Meg had agreed to wait until summer to be married, when the Indians had settled down and they could build a life together.

Orders in April cut off all trade between the Creeks and the British settlements and established a watch on the Cherokee towns. The Creeks had lacked ammunition for their muskets since the Augusta treaty. Now they would have to forgo all the other white man's goods they had become dependent upon. The militia was assigned to watch the white trading posts in Cherokee country as well as the Indian villages and trails.

However, old friendships and trading partnerships could not be broken up by an order from Savannah. Fur and hide traders in the backwoods, furious that the enmity of the settlers had cut off their livelihood, traded with the Indians despite the embargo.

John Stuart had been careful at the Charlestown and Savannah conferences to cement his personal friendship with both Cherokee and Creek chiefs.

Emistisiguo agreed that the Creeks must be punished for the massacre at Sherrill's and the ambush of Clark and his men. One Creek must die for each of the murdered white men. But the Creeks, according to Indian law, wanted the life of a prominent white as atonement for Mad Turkey's murder, since Fee had escaped. Three Creeks, including the ringleader in the ambush, were caught and executed by the Lower Creeks. Four more were captured, and negotiations went on through the spring and early summer about their punishment.

Although there was no further outbreak of hostility, Governor Wright sent one appeal after another to General Gage in Massachusetts for Regular troops to keep peace. Gage was too occupied with a rebellious rabble in Boston to send his troops to the Georgia frontier to be "exposed to Indian attacks brought on by the activities of land speculators and the lawless conduct of American frontiersmen."

As the weather grew hotter, the Indians were less anxious to fight. Summer was the time to sit in the shade. In June, a Ranger company of settlers from the Purchase was officially commissioned, and Bert was discharged to go back to Augusta. Jamie would leave as soon as Lieutenant Dooly came to replace him. The ambush had left spaces in the officer ranks that were hard to fill.

Riding up the path to the house on Rae's Creek, Bert could see that the corn was beginning to tassel. The barley was green, and the rows were well filled, though it remained to be seen how the sheaves would develop.

The deep, mellow notes of a hound's alarm sang out from the shade of the tree in front of the cabin. Running and barking, Bo started toward Bert, stopping now and again to put his head back and bay.

"Hello, the house!" Bert called. "Anybody home?"

Bo stopped, then came wagging up to Bert's horse, yipping an excited greeting, his whole body swinging from side to side. Bert dismounted and leaned down to scratch Bo's ears, then led his horse to the cabin.

Mary had come to the door, and was brushing her hands together to get rid of the flour as she hurried to meet her son.

"Where's Pa and Francie?" Bert asked, after hugging his mother until he picked her feet up off the ground.

"They've gone off looking for blackberries," said Mary. "Ben promised he'd take her after she finished weeding the garden. I don't like her to go off by herself."

Bo bayed again—this time a definite greeting, not an alarm—as Francie came running along the edge of the field from the woods, her father striding close behind her. Ben gave his son a bear hug, then stepped back as Francie climbed up into Bert's arms and hugged him around the neck.

"Have you really come home for good?" she asked as he set her back down on her feet.

"For as good as I can make it," Bert said. "They've sent Rangers to replace us. They don't belong to Georgia or Carolina, so they can go anywhere they're needed. Militia has to stop at borders."

"Thank the good Lord," said Mary. "We are proud of you for doing your duty, but I've been so worried."

Bert put his arm around his mother and led her toward the house. "Now all you have to worry about is feeding a no-good son who's starving for your cooking," he said.

Next morning, full of fresh eggs and ham and cornbread, he started for town to give Colonel Barnard dispatches from Fort James.

As he sloshed through Campbell's Gully, his eyes searched the inn yard for a glimpse of Meg's lithe figure. He couldn't stop now or he'd never get the dispatches to Colonel Barnard, but he'd stop on the way home.

There were many more shacks along the road now, thrown together by settlers who had been frightened into leaving their New Purchase claims. It was too bad to see Augusta looking so ramshackle! Only when he reached the center of town, near Saint Paul's and the old fort, did the town begin to look like the prosperous center of commerce General Oglethorpe had planned.

Though the fort was no longer garrisoned, some dilapidated buildings were still used by militia and ranger units when they were not in the field. Edward Barnard, seated behind a fine mahogany desk in one of them, motioned Bert to a chair.

"Glad to see you back, sergeant."

"I've brought you some papers from Fort James," said Bert slipping the strap of a dispatch case from his shoulder and handing the pouch to the colonel. "Sir, Lieutenant Stratfield sends his regards."

Barnard put the case near him on the desk, but left it closed. "They can wait," he said. "I'd rather you told me how things stand at Fort

James. Help yourself to some grog and pour me a glass, too. My rheumatism is giving me trouble today."

Bert took the glasses to the earthen jug hanging in the window, and poured them full of the cool rum and lime mixture, then returned to his chair.

"Everything seems to be quiet in the Creek villages, sir," he said. "The Indians have accepted the governor's embargo better than the white traders. The traders are furious, with pelts and skins stacked up and not being allowed to sell them. They hate the settlers more than ever."

"Sitting here in Augusta," said Barnard, "you can see both sides. The landowners feel trade brings the Indians into the area, and they're afraid of them. They'd like to keep the embargo on. But Augusta's living is built on trade, and the settlers just don't have enough cash to keep the city going without the traders."

"I've heard some of the settlers say we ought to burn the Indians out for good, and send them out west in the wilderness where they belong," said Bert.

"We've had that sort of talk, even in the Assembly," said Barnard. "But the British government will spike their guns! King George has put too many thousands of pounds into Georgia not to want some return. The coastal people haven't been successful with silk or any of their other projects. We traders are the only ones who've paid our own way. The governor's going to have to lift the embargo soon."

"It would be easier on the Rangers not to have to enforce the embargo. The people up there are afraid to put in crops knowing the Indians may come down on them any time," said Bert.

"How it will end, God only knows," said Barnard. Let's hope the militia won't have to be called up again soon. Have a good time while it lasts."

"Thank you, sir," said Bert, touching his hand to his forehead in a sketchy salute and leaving the room.

Outside on Center Street, people were coming and going. On the left, stretched along The Bay, facing the river, were fine houses of brick and timber. The sound of hammers and saws told of more building. Bert turned his horse and rode toward the sound.

Suddenly his horse shied as a feisty mongrel charged across the street in hot pursuit of a fluffy gray kitten, closely followed by a small blonde girl, hair flying, eyes streaming with tears, and shrieking at the top of her lungs. The kitten scrambled up a tree on the river bank, while the dog stood on his hind legs yipping excitedly. The child stumbled over a rock and tumbled helter skelter, coming to a stop near the foot of the tree.

It all happened so fast that Bert had scarcely quieted his horse before it was over. Dismounting and winding his reins around a bush, he hurried toward the river bank to find the child sitting up and rubbing an elbow.

"Are you all right?" he asked, squatting down beside her.

"I'm all right, but please make that terrible dog leave my kitty alone."

Bert picked up a stick and walked purposefully toward the mongrel who turned tail and ran back up to the street. Then he went back to give the little girl his hand and help her to her feet. Except for the scraped elbow, she seemed to be all right.

"Thank you," she said. "Now could you get Dusty out of that tree?"

The kitten had climbed up into the higher branches and now sat howling for help. Bert tried putting a fallen branch up, but the kitten only climbed higher. Finally he sat down, took off his boots, and started up the tree, suddenly noticing a hole in his sock.

The higher branches were so small that he was afraid they would crack under his weight; he was barely able to reach the kitten and grasp it by the back of its neck so that it couldn't struggle. But how was he to climb down with only one hand?

"If you can reach the kitten down, I'll take her," said a voice, much lower and sweeter than that of the little girl.

Bert looked down at a pair of laughing brown eyes in a face framed by dark red tendrils of hair. The kitten squirmed, her four paws beating the air, her mouth drawn back by Bert's hold on the scruff of her neck.

"Careful or she'll scratch," said Bert as he leaned down, holding tightly to a limb with his other hand. The girl took the kitten carefully around its chest, and Bert let go of its neck, then climbed down, terribly conscious of his stocking feet with his big toe showing through the hole.

The girl had given the kitten to the child, who sat cuddling the small gray ball of fluff and crooning to it reassuringly.

"I'm Susan Merrill," she said offering her hand. "I do thank you so much for rescuing Dusty. Betsy and Kate would just die if anything happened to her."

Bert took the small white hand and would have liked to kiss it, as Europeans did. He'd been dreaming all these months of returning to Augusta to worship Meg from afar, knowing she belonged to Jamie. But this girl was tiny and pretty and must be barely sixteen. This girl was wearing a dainty, flowered dimity gown like a doll.

"I'm Bert Sheldon," he said, bowing ever so slightly and holding her hand as long as he dared. "I've just come from Fort James. Our militia company's being mustered out."

The little girl, carrying the kitten, started toward home, and Susan called, "Wait for me at the road," then turned back to Bert. He was wearing his new fringed buckskins and wide-brimmed hat with militia insignia to report to Colonel Barnard. If he'd only worn good socks!

"I'd better put my boots back on," he said. Luckily they were big for him, and he could pull them on without making an awkward fool of himself.

Susan started toward the house, and Bert clumped up the hill behind her, working his feet into his boots as he walked. They both stopped where Betsy was waiting at the road for a wagon to pass. Moonshine had pulled his reins loose and now stood contentedly cropping grass beside the road.

Bert thought desperately for something to say to keep this vision of loveliness from walking out of his life. "Your little sister hurt her elbow," he said. "It should be cleaned and bandaged."

"I'll tell Mama," said Susan, then, "Won't you come up to the house and let her thank you for saving Dusty?"

"Let me just catch my horse," said Bert, picking up the dragging reins and leading Moonshine across the road to the hitching post in front of the big, galleried house.

Betsy ran ahead, and they could hear her voice talking excitedly to her mother as they went up the steps to the front gallery. Jocelyn Merrill came out, glancing quickly at Bert's frontier buckskins as she held out her hand.

"I'm Betsy's mother, Jocelyn Merrill," she said, "and I'm so grateful to you for taking care of her and getting the kitten out of the tree."

"I'm glad she wasn't hurt bad," said Bert. "She really tumbled down that hill."

Betsy had put the kitten down and was trying to see her wounded elbow, puckering up for another cry as she saw blood.

"I'm sorry, but I must go and tend to her," said Jocelyn. "Susan, will you ask Mindy to bring me a basin of water and a clean cloth? And, thank you again for your kindness, young man."

Bert was dismissed. He unhitched Moonshine and rode back toward the Sword and Thistle.

·XI·

JUNE
WEDDING

Meg was setting tables for lunch when she saw Bert in the doorway. Putting down her box of flatware, she hurried to meet him, looking hopefully behind him. An hour before, Bert would have resented her looking for Jamie. Now, the whole world had changed, and he had trouble concentrating on her questions. When he had finally reassured her that Jamie was not dead or wounded and would be coming to Augusta as soon as an officer could be found to replace him, she walked to the bar and filled a tankard.

"The first one's on the house," she said, then frustratedly, "If only I knew when he was coming, I could plan for our wedding. The banns were ready long ago, and Mrs. Seymour says we can be married as soon as he comes."

Now Bert could wish them well with a light heart. Susan's mother might have sent him packing, but he had the whole summer to prove to the Merrills that he was a sober, sensible young man.

"Do you know anything about some people named Merrill who live on The Bay?" he asked.

Meg, deep in her own thoughts of white dresses and flowers, dragged her mind back to Bert's question.

"Merrill? Oh, yes. He's the lawyer from Charlestown who has built the fine, big house with galleries."

"I rescued their cat," said Bert.

With important things like Jamie's health and the time for their wedding to discuss, Meg had trouble focusing on the Merrill's cat.

"Susan Merrill came out when her sister rolled down the hill, and I handed her the cat."

Meg looked as though he'd gone daft, then light dawned.

"She's a pretty girl," said Meg. "Her folks seem to be looking for a wealthy husband. They've been entertaining all the bachelors with land and money in Augusta." Might as well warn Bert now. He hadn't the chance of an icicle in the bad place.

"I don't think she's the kind of girl who'd marry a rich old man," said Bert. "You should have seen how she handled that scared kitten and her little sister."

"They say her mother's got her eye on Thomas Brown for her, with all his money and land here and an estate in England."

"He must be over thirty years old!" said Bert.

"I don't think Thomas Brown has any idea of marrying," she said, "and he's too much of a gentleman to encourage the Merrills."

Bert brightened noticeably.

"But don't get your hopes too high," warned Meg. "They'll not let a young frontiersman get in the way of a good marriage!"

The tap room was beginning to fill with customers for the noon meal. Meg excused herself, and Bert drained his tankard and left the inn to ride thoughtfully out of town.

* * *

When Jamie rode in from the north the next week, Meg had her wedding dress ready and had asked Francie to be her only attendant. The ceremony was to be at Saint Paul's at high noon, with a wedding breakfast at the Sword and Thistle. Plans had been made for months, and now the date could be set for the last Saturday in June.

The inn's good customers and their wives had been invited. Meg, who didn't expect many wives at the wedding of a tavern wench, was surprised and touched to find the church crowded with ladies in their best lawns and muslins as well as gentlemen in fine broadcloth with snowy neck-cloths and wrist ruffles. Some even wore wigs in spite of the heat. The Raes, the Griersons, the Barnards, the Goodgions, the Jacksons, the McLeans, Robert and Mary MacKay, and Dr. and Mrs. Johnston had come from the town, and Thomas Brown and William Manson had come all the way from Brownsborough. The Galphins and Lachlan McGillivray had ridden in from Silver Bluff to show their affection for Angus and his niece. Most of them had met James Stratfield and knew that he was proving to be a responsible officer and probably a good husband. It was, however, for Angus and Meg, whom they loved, that they took the time and trouble to dress up and be present this hot June day.

Meg wore a creamy white lutestring dress with small panniers trimmed with matching braid and a veil, her mother's, of mechlin lace. Jamie had sent to Savannah for the trunk he had stored there, and wore knee breeches with mother-of-pearl buckles and a dark green velvet coat over a brocaded waistcoat. There were silver buttons on his coat and silver buckles on his shoes.

Angus had offered the bride and groom the corner guest room of the inn until they could move into a house of their own. With Jamie subject to be called for militia duty and the Creeks still on the prowl, it seemed foolish to buy or rent a house. Meg would go on helping Angus, and Jamie could do any surveying that came his way and lend a hand in the tap room.

When the vows had been made, the blessing given, and the young couple pelted with rice and driven away in a borrowed carriage, Bert mounted his horse but left the procession as it turned through town; turning down The Bay, he passed the house with the galleries. Betsy and another slightly older girl child were playing with a kitten on the front path under the watchful eye of a black nursemaid, but there was no sign of Susan.

The Merrills had not been invited to the wedding, as Joseph Merrill rarely came to the inn and Meg knew Susan and her mother only by sight. Joseph had been drawn into a group, new to Augusta, of relatively young, educated men who were considered upstarts by the old timers and snobs by the uneducated frontiersmen.

Mary, Ben, and Francie Sheldon had been invited to ride in with the Raes in their carriage and had already reached the inn when Bert arrived.

"Wasn't it beautiful, Bert?" Francie cried when she saw her big brother. "Can I be a bridesmaid when you get married?"

"You may have to wait forever for that," Bert said.

"But I did look pretty in my new dress, didn't I? And I didn't get in Meg's way when I threw the rose petals."

"You were perfect!" said Bert. "I'm going to recommend you to all my friends' brides."

"Silly!" said Francie, catching his hand in both of hers and walking proudly with him through the crowd to the refreshment table.

Normally the wedding would have been the talk of Augusta for weeks. A few days later, however, news came from the north that banished everything else from the minds of Augustans. Parliament had passed an act closing the port of Boston.

Georgians didn't care much about Massachusetts, but they did care about rights. The fur traders had felt the pinch when their trade was cut off, and even the settlers knew they could be ruined if the blockade of the coast was extended to Georgia. What would Parliament do next?

Every tavern was filled with arguing, gesticulating men. Women talked in parlors and over back fences, though, of course, not to the men, who thought women's minds were not suited to political discussion.

Men from Augusta took the river boat down to Savannah or rode to Charlestown to find out what other colonists were planning to do. Colonies were forming committees of interested citizens to meet and discuss the actions of Parliament and to keep in touch with each other. The Charlestown committee felt so sorry for the hungry Bostonians that they sent a whole shipload of rice to Massachusetts.

In Savannah, the talk led to organized protests. George Walton, who had met with Noble W. Jones, Archibald Bullock, and John Houston at Tondee's Tavern in Savannah, brought word of a meeting to be held on August 10 at the same tavern to organize opposition to the Parliamentary acts.

The Sword and Thistle was more crowded than ever most nights, and the back dining room was the meeting place of the traders, who were still more worried about the Indian uprising than about the troubles of the New Englanders. John Stuart was in town for a few days to talk to McGillivray and Galphin about the Creeks, and Thomas Brown, whose outlying lands were in danger, had come to learn what he could about the Indians' state of mind.

"It looks now as though we'll have a peace treaty before the summer's over," said Stuart. "The Creeks have caught most of the renegades and executed them. It's just as well. With all this trouble in Massachusetts, General Gage couldn't afford to send any troops, even in a general uprising."

"What about our trade?" Galphin asked. "Will the governor lift the embargo on skins?"

"I believe so. The Indians are all hurting for supplies and ammunition. They'll be more than ready to make peace if they know they'll be able to sell their pelts."

Edward Barnard had been listening. "The anti-Indian faction is not going to be happy," he said. "They have been supporting Governor Wright in the Assembly ever since he stopped the trade. Now they're liable to join the radicals in opposing the government."

"I can just imagine how our friend, Dr. Wells, will scream," said Brown. "I have heard him haranguing the rabble about the way the governor pampers the Indians." He looked at Stuart. "He is no friend of yours."

"He's trying to build up a following," said Stuart. "He plays on the fears of the ignorant Crackers. Some things he says border on treason."

"Not all the settlers go along with Wells. I have a lot of respect for Daniel Marshall and his Baptist congregation on Kiokee Creek and the Quakers at Wrightsboro. They only ask to be left alone. But there are too many shiftless, low-life drifters who are ready to join any cause that means a chance for plunder. Those are the ones Wells is encouraging."

"What worries me," said Stuart, "is the way the rabble are flocking to the meetings in the Low Country. The artisans and mechanics, meeting under a big oak tree in Isaac Mazyck's pasture in Charlestown, shout against the government taxes. It's beginning to get out of hand! They're calling themselves Liberty Boys, and talking about liberty for the colonies."

"It's spread to Savannah, too," said Barnard. "Some of the reputable landowners are joining in the meetings against taxes there and bringing their ideas into the Assembly."

"They should be horse whipped," exclaimed Brown.

"Well, Tom," said Stuart, "you haven't been over here long enough to get used to Americans. They holler a lot, but they don't usually do much about it unless somebody tries to shut them up."

"The Bostonians did something about it," said Galphin, "and I don't much blame them, dumping that tea in the harbor. They didn't want Parliament telling them they had to buy it."

"That's it!" said McGillivray. "Don't try to force an American to do something against his principles."

"As long as they keep the law, that's all right," said Brown. "But lawbreakers should be punished."

"You're right, sir," said McGillivray, "But it's better to look the other way sometimes, when the law's unjust. In the backwoods, you're liable to have a barn fire or lose your livestock if you don't temper your justice with common sense."

The other men nodded and Stuart said, "It's best to let them rant and rave and get it out of their system. They're sticking up for their rights as Englishmen."

There was a murmur of assent, as Meg came in with a pitcher of ale to refill their tankards. Soon talk turned to the drought and the chance of the river's being too low for navigation soon, and eventually to the time of night and the need to go home.

In other Augusta inns and taverns, the talk was more of Boston and less of Indians. George Walton was besieged by worried Augustans every time he entered a public place and made to describe the meeting in Savannah. Everyone wanted to be a delegate to the meeting in August, though only twenty-six delegates from the different parishes were to be admitted. The governor had heard of the plans and had declared any such meeting to be "unconstitutional, illegal and punishable by law." This only added tinder to the fire.

·XII·

TONDEE'S
TAVERN

One morning, as Robert MacKay was walking in the garden in front
of his home, he saw six Indians on horseback riding in the Cherokee
Road. When they turned into his front path, he recognized them as
Creeks who had done business with him. Walking out to greet them, he
invited them in to the trading post behind the house for refreshment.

It was obviously a delegation of some sort, since they had no furs to
be traded, and after they had accepted tobacco for their pipes and cups
of well-watered rum, the leader turned to MacKay.

"We come to talk for our people of friendship and peace with the
white man," he said, looking to his companions for grunts of assent.
"Before the coming of the Virginians to our lands, we had happy thoughts
and good feelings for the people in Augusta. We brought many, many
packhorses with fine skins and pelts and we traded for the knives and
pots and guns of the white man. We came to Augusta to feast and dance
and drink with our brothers.

"Now we are afraid to walk in the streets. Our people are insulted
and even killed, and nowhere do we find welcome except with our old
friends, the traders. That is why we come to your home on the edge of
the town to bring a message.

"Our people need calico for their clothes, steel knives and iron pots,
bullets and powder for their guns. We no longer follow the old ways of
our fathers to hunt and cook and sew.

"Your Governor Wright has put a stop to our trade because of the
crimes of our young and foolish braves against the white man. We have
caught and killed those we could find. We will kill any others we catch
and do anything the governor wants to turn away his anger."

MacKay moved to fill their cups and invited them to stay until he
could send word to John Stuart, but the leader shook his head.

"We have come here because we know you would not hurt us," he said. "But you and James Grierson and Edward Barnard are now among the few. If the many new Virginia people know we are here, they may come to kill us all and burn your home." He rose and his companions rose with him, filed out of the trading post door, mounted their horses and rode away, raising their hands in the gesture of peace.

Word of the delegation spread like wildfire. Those along the trading path who had seen the six Indians ride to MacKay's could hardly wait to hear what they had talked about. When it was learned that the Creeks were asking for peace and resumed trade, many of the displaced settlers from the Purchase began to make plans to return to their land holdings to plant a late crop.

The Sheldons were not interested in moving. They liked Augusta. Most Sundays the whole family rose early and rode in the wagon to Saint Paul's to church, then to a big dinner at the Sword and Thistle. Angus insisted that this weekly meal was a business meeting to discuss plans for the farm and distillery and would not hear of their paying. Now that the vegetables were plentiful in the garden, however, Mary and Francie usually had baskets full of squash and beans to bring as a present to Meg.

One Sunday morning late in July, they had started early to avoid heat and dust while the road was still damp with dew. When they reached the churchyard, Ben helped Mary and Francie down, and Bert drove the wagon to the fort where the horse could stand in the shade.

"Can't we walk around a little bit?" Francie asked. "We never get a chance to see things in town."

"I don't see why not," Ben answered, looking to Mary for final approval.

"We'll get our Sunday shoes full of sand," Mary laughed, "But I think it would be fun."

Bert came striding from behind the little wooden church, and they set off on the footpath along the edge of Center Street toward Broad Street. When Oglethorpe had sent men to build Fort Augusta in 1738, he had given them a carefully drawn plan with streets running in a grid with squared corners where they crossed. A broad parade ground for troops which was to be bordered by Government buildings was located where Center Street crossed the main road from the Sand Bar Ferry to the Cherokee lands. Augusta, however, seemed to have a mind of its own.

Where government buildings were supposed to be, there were inns, taverns, and coffee houses which Augustans found more convenient and convivial for doing government business. Blacksmiths, greengrocers, butchers, and drapers had built along the lanes and alleys between The Bay and Broad Street and along the sandy cross streets. Warehouses, built near the river, had been expanded so that they jutted into the streets.

Compared with Philadelphia, Augusta was a village, but Mary had been in the backwoods for so long that she considered this river town a metropolis. Although the shops were closed, she looked in the multipaned windows of the more prosperous ones and smelled the Sunday dinners being cooked by black slaves in the kitchen buildings behind the inns and private homes. However much she might love her house and garden on Rae's Creek, this glimpse of civilization made her long for her parents' home.

"Mama," Francie asked, pointing toward an inn on the corner set back from the street and shaded by two big oak trees, "Can I go sit on the bench under that tree and dump the sand out of my shoes?"

A black woman in a calico dress and turban was sweeping sand from the steps that led up to the inn porch, but there was no one else around this early. Already the cool shade was a welcome sight in the river-valley heat.

"Do you suppose it would be all right?" Mary asked Ben. "We have almost an hour till church time."

"I don't see why we shouldn't go in if they're open," said Ben.

A stout man with gray hair clubbed tightly and wearing a black apron over his open-necked white shirt and knee breeches came out on the front porch. "Welcome to Fox's," he said, smiling and rubbing his hands together. "Won't you come in for a cup of coffee before church?"

"Good morning," said Ben, "Mary, I'd like you to meet Mr. James Fox who is host to most of the important men of Georgia here at his inn. And my sons Bert and, on his shoulders, Benjy and my daughter Francie."

"We've buns warm from the oven and real coffee from the Indies if I can tempt you," said the innkeeper. "Most of my customers come after church, but you've plenty of time before church and you can hear the bell of Saint Paul's from here."

Francie looked up at her father with shining eyes, and even Mary gave him a pleading look.

"I reckon we can spare the time and the money," said Ben. "We get to town so seldom."

This inn, like the Sword and Thistle, had a big common room with a bar at one end, but the ceiling was much lower and the huge oak beams had turned black with smoke from the big walk-in fireplace.

"We used to do all the cooking in here," Fox explained, seating Mary at the table in the bay window. "We've added rooms above and behind and now the kitchen is out back. We still have big roaring fires here, though, in the winter."

"It is a lovely room," said Mary. "No wonder you have important customers."

A black woman in a full calico skirt, white apron, and turban came in through the back door carrying a tray laden with cinnamon sprinkled buns on a Delft plate and five matching cups and saucers. Two steaming jugs with wooden handles held hot coffee and hot milk. Setting the cups and jugs in front of Mary with a bowl of rock sugar lumps, she passed the buns around the table, then set the plate down in the center of the table.

"This reminds me of home," said Mary, placing a lump of sugar in each cup and holding the milk and coffee pots on either side so that they poured together mixing a light tan, foaming, delicious-smelling brew.

"And where is home?" asked Fox, whom Ben had invited to join them at the table.

"My parents live in Philadelphia," Mary said, "but we've been homesteading in Virginia and then in Carolina since Francie was a baby."

"And now we've a lovely house with a garden that belongs to Mr. McLeod, and I hope we stay here forever and ever," said Francie.

Mary put her finger to her lips to remind Francie that children should be seen and not heard, but Mr. Fox smiled at her and nodded. "That's the way my nephew feels about Augusta," he said. "But his mother and father wanted him to go to school in England, so I've sent him to Winchester. He's nearly eleven years old. His mother and father died of a fever in New Providence last year, and he's been living with me here."

"It seems a shame for him to be so far away," said Mary. "Does he have any family in England?"

"No close relatives," said Fox. "But he wants to go in the army, and that means Winchester and then Sandhurst, unless there's money to buy a commission."

"Regulars aren't too popular in the Purchase where I've been," said Bert. "The militiamen and Rangers laugh at them out there in white breeches and crossbelts and red coats fighting Indians."

"Red coats aren't too popular even in Augusta these days," said Fox. "Some of the arguments in this room at night come close to treason."

"I hope it's all talk," said Ben.

"Most of my customers are loyal subjects of the King, but they're ready to stand up for their rights as Englishmen," said Fox.

"I guess we all feel that way," said Ben. "I'd hate to see Savannah and Charlestown closed."

"That's what's going to happen if we don't watch out," said the innkeeper." John Walton and Robert MacKay were in here talking last night about the meeting that's been called in Savannah next month to decide how we can help the people of Boston."

"What do we have to do with the Boston yankees?" Bert asked.

"We're a long way from London," said Fox, "and we have to depend on help from other Americans. Here in Georgia it hasn't been the King's soldiers that have kept the Indians in line; it's been militia, like you."

Just then the bell in the steeple of Saint Paul's began to peal, and the Sheldons said a quick goodbye.

The little clapboard church was filled to overflowing, the windows opened wide to catch any breeze from the river. The worshippers gave their time-honored responses to the prayers and supplications, joined in the general confession and were pardoned, gave thanks for the blessings of their lives, and settled down in pools of perspiration on the hard wooden benches. The Reverend Mr. Seymour, sweltering under shirt, trousers, gown, and chasuble, cut his sermon blessedly short. The hymns were all familiar ones, and had to be sung from memory as hymnals still had not been shipped from England. With the final "Amen," the congregation hurried out into the churchyard under the oak trees where they could breathe.

Although families came out together and met other families to talk, the gathering soon split into groups of women discussing children, births, deaths, and courtships and groups of men who had heard the news of the meeting to be held in Savannah.

Meg and Jamie had come from the Sword and Thistle, arriving late and standing in the back of the church through the service. Angus had stayed to supervise breakfast, but had asked Jamie to listen in on any talk. Meg was left to chat with Mary and Francie as Ben and Jamie joined the men's discussion group. Francie wandered off toward the cemetery, holding Benjy firmly by the hand.

Two little girls in straw bonnets tied with ribbons to match the ribbons on their dimity dresses were watching a fuzzy orange caterpillar with black horns climb up the trunk of a big oak.

"I dare you to pick it off," said the older girl.

"I won't!" said the little one.

"Don't either of you!" said Francie, hurrying up. "Some of them sting like blazes!"

The two children turned around, big brown eyes staring, and looked Francie and Benjy up and down.

"How do you know?" asked the littlest.

"Cause one stung me, and my arm swelled up and got hot."

All four children backed away from the tree.

"What's your name?" the older sister asked.

"Francie Sheldon. What's yours?"

"I'm Kate Merrill, and that's Betsy. Is Bert Sheldon your big brother?"

"Yes," said Francie, "and Benjy's my little brother."

Jocelyn Merrill hurried over, having caught sight of the little girls at the edge of the crowd.

"Mama," said Kate, "this is Francie Sheldon. Her brother rescued Dusty. And she knows all about caterpillars."

Francie was glad she was dressed in her checked-gingham Sunday-go-to-meetin' dress and that Benjy hadn't dirtied his clothes yet. This lady was real dressed up with her hair all pretty and curly under her hat.

She could see her own mother looking distractedly around her, searching for them. "I beg your pardon, ma'am," she said to Kate and Betsy's mother, "Could you please hold Benjy's hand while I go tell my mama where we are?" and she ducked off, leaving Benjy staring up at the stranger. Just as Benjy had decided to yell for help, Francie and Mary came to rescue him.

"Oh, thank you so much," Mary said as she picked him up and held him close to keep him from screaming. "Francie shouldn't have bothered you."

"It was no trouble," said Jocelyn, "and she didn't want you to worry. She is a very thoughtful little girl."

Francie basked in the praise. "Kate and Betsy nearly got stung by a caterpillar," she said, hoping for more.

"I'm Jocelyn Merrill, and I believe you must be the mother of the young man who was sweet to Betsy when she hurt her arm."

Betsy turned her elbow around, but could find no scar to show off. "He saved Dusty," she said.

"Bert didn't tell us," said Francie. "I'll tell him I saved you from a caterpillar."

"Jocelyn and Mary smiled over the children's heads and herded their progeny back to the front of the church.

Bert stood with his father and Jamie in a group near the gate of the old fort, glancing around the crowd, hoping for a chance to talk to Susan. He'd only seen her once, though her mother and the girls were in church every Sunday.

All the men knew that Sunday after church was a good time for political talk; there was less chance of an argument's ending in a brawl with everybody sober.

Robert MacKay, James Grierson, John Howell, and Dr. Andrew

Johnston were gathered around George Walton, whose brother had been at the meeting in Savannah on the twentieth of July.

"John says people in Savannah are all het up about this Boston thing," said George.

"Well, by gum, I'd fit up a sloop and sneak by the bulldogs if I was up there," said John Howell. "I'm willing to bet there are fishermen up north carrying in supplies!"

"You're probably right," said MacKay, "but it isn't right for British subjects to have to break the law that way. The fleet is supposed to protect the colonists, not starve them."

"They broke the law in Boston by destroying that tea," said James Grierson. "The King can't let people get away with rebellious behavior."

"What about this meeting we've heard they're going to have in Savannah on August tenth?"

"John says they want representatives from all the parishes to be there," said George Walton. "They're going to form a committee to keep in touch with the other colonies, so we can all act together."

"I don't see why Georgia should have anything to do with this irresponsible mob in Massachusetts. We have never received anything but help from England."

"Have you heard whether anyone plans to go to the meeting from here?" MacKay asked. "I was planning to be in Savannah for a few weeks, and I'd like to see what's going on."

"I know George Wells wants to go," said Andrew Johnston. "I'll have his patients as well as mine to care for."

"I'd like to go," said Grierson. "I don't believe Georgia should get into this mess without a lot of thought."

"You'll have to be ready to fight it out with Wymberly Jones and Edward Telfair and all that crew of young dandies," said MacKay.

"I'd be willing to bet that bunch of radicals down in Medway are behind all this," said Howell. "Lyman Hall's tried his hand at preaching and doctoring and teaching. Now he's going to help his damned Massachusetts yankees defy the king!"

"You're right," said MacKay. "I've heard he's in Savannah now in the thick of it."

Ben was beginning to worry about Mary. She had passed by the group heading back for the wagon carrying Benjy. He knew the baby was probably wet and cranky.

"We'd better be going," he said motioning to Bert. "Come out and let us know what goes on, Jamie."

"I'll send you word if I decide to go to Savannah," Jamie said. "Have Mary make a list of what you both need, and I'll pick it up."

In the next few days, the road to Savannah was crowded with groups of men on horseback and in wagons and carriages. A letter had come from John Glen, who had been appointed chairman of a correspondence committee formed in July, calling for delegates from all parishes to meet at Tondee's Tavern on the tenth of August.

Inns and taverns in Savannah were full, and Robert MacKay, who had a home there as well as in Augusta, invited Jamie and some of his other friends to stay with him. Much good ale was consumed, and MacKay's black servants were kept busy killing and roasting chickens and netting shrimp and crab to feed the guests until the meeting day.

The night before the meeting, after errands had been run and calls made on old friends, Jamie Stratfield found MacKay, Andrew McLean, and Edward Barnard sitting in the garden hoping for a breeze to stir the moss hanging from the live oaks.

"I hate to think how hot it will be at the tavern tomorrow," said MacKay.

"Have you heard anything more about the plans?" Jamie asked.

"The committee formed in July has drafted a lot of resolutions," said McLean. "I think they plan to read them and let us vote on them."

"Will there be a chance to discuss them and make changes?"

"I don't know," said McLean. "That's why it's so important for us to be there. I know Bulloch and Houstoun have mighty radical ideas. And you all know Wells. He's a troublemaker, and his friend Button Gwinnett is worse. We've got to have some level heads there to see that we don't find ourselves in the same mess as Massachusetts."

Barnard had been silent, but he now began to unfold a paper he had been holding. "I won't say how I obtained this," he said, "but I have friends. It's a summary of the ideas in their resolutions."

Everyone was quiet as he adjusted his spectacles and stood beside the torch stuck in the ground near the refreshment table to read: "The committee feels that Americans should have the same rights as Englishmen in Britain; that they should be able to petition the King directly in any emergency; that the blockade of Boston is unconstitutional; that the charter of Massachusetts cannot be revoked without the consent of the people; that Parliament has no right to tax Americans without American representation in Parliament; that Americans should not be taken to England to be tried; that we in Georgia align ourselves with the other colonies to protest our wrongs; that a committee of correspondence be set up to give and receive help from other colonies."

There was silence as he finished reading, folded the paper and sat down.

"My God!" said MacKay, finally, "What will Parliament say to that?"

"I guess we've all felt these wrongs need righting," said Barnard, "but not by defying authority."

"What good has it done to petition and protest legally?" MacKay asked. "Maybe if the king sees we're all together in protesting, he'll see that Parliament treats us better."

"Not German George," said Jamie irreverently. "He expects unquestioning obedience."

"Jamie's right," said Barnard. "Defiance is the worst possible policy. We have plenty of good friends in Parliament now who will desert us if we defy their authority."

"And, God forbid, if it comes to armed conflict," said McLean, "how can we expect to fight the King's troops and the Indians with no arms and armies of our own?"

"Gentlemen," said MacKay, "We'll have to talk some sense into that committee tomorrow."

"Hear! Hear!" said the others raising their glasses.

The next evening the four friends set out in Robert MacKay's carriage for Tondee's. Barnard and McLean had spent the morning drafting a speech against any precipitant action, and Barnard now carried a copy to present to the committee. As they approached the meeting place, they found the streets crowded with men of all ages and stations of life. Tradesmen and laborers predominated, though there were some gentlemen in wigs and broadcloth coats and a good number of backwoodsmen in buckskins. A few red-coated soldiers stood at ease, their guns handy, as the crowd eddied about the squares where the streets crossed, talking, laughing, ogling anything in petticoats that came near. As the carriage drew up to the door of the tavern, Jamie recognized three men in buckskins from the Fort James area.

"Hey, Lieutenant," one of them called, "maybe they'll let you in, since you're an officer."

"Hello, John Dooly," Jamie cried, jumping from the carriage and shaking the man's hand. "Are you the delegation from Saint George's?"

"We thought we were," said Dooly. "We damn well left our wives and bairns to take care of themselves and came here thinking we'd speak for the New Purchase. But they won't let us in."

Jamie saw the Augustans going up the steps, so he waved to Dooly and followed them. At the door, they were met by a self-important individual with a high, whining voice and a long, pointed nose.

"There's no more room," he said, barring the door with his arm.

"But we've come from Saint Paul's Parish in answer to the call for delegates."

"Then you'll just have to go back there," said long nose.

"My good man," said Barnard, "we have brought a protest to the committee, and we insist on being allowed to present it."

"Insist and be damned!" said the man. "Every man jack on the streets has som'at he wants to say to the committee. I've got my orders to turn anybody away not already in the tavern. All the men on the list are in already."

Robert MacKay pulled a pound note from his pocket and slipped it toward the doorkeeper who eyed it covetously but shook his head. "If you ain't on the list, you can't come in. Those are my orders," he said.

MacKay's jaw set and his fists clenched, but Edward Barnard put a restraining hand on his arm. "There's no sense in starting a disturbance," he said. "The man is acting on orders."

The four men turned and walked down the tavern steps, Barnard waving to his driver to bring the carriage around.

"They turned you away, too," said Dooly at Jamie's side. "What are we going to do about it?"

"There's not much we can do right now," Jamie answered, "but we've got to let the King know we're not defying government rule."

Edward Barnard, who was standing beside him, turned to Dooly. "I guess our only recourse is to send statements to the *Gazette* signed by all the responsible Upcountry people we can find, telling the world we were not party to any treasonous resolutions they may make."

"You're right, sir," said Jamie. "Governor Wright controls the newspaper, and he'll see they are published."

"By the Eternal, I'll ride all over the Ceded Lands and get people to sign," said Dooly, "but who's going to write the protests?"

"Why don't you drop by my house tonight, and we'll have something ready for you," said MacKay.

"I'll be there," said Dooly. "And when I get back home, I'll get Elijah Clark and Stephen Heard and Sherwood Bugg to help me carry copies around to get signatures or marks from everybody in the Purchase."

"Good man," said Andrew McLean. "We've just persuaded the Creeks to settle down and trade again. We sure as hell don't want them to think we're against the King who sends them presents!"

"Amen," said Jamie. "We'll see you tonight, John."

The next morning handbills were circulating all over Savannah, citing eight resolutions that had been approved at the meeting. The friends found that they encompassed the ideas Barnard had read two nights before. Copies were to be sent to the committees of correspondence of all the other colonies, and a collection committee was set up to gather supplies and money to be sent to the people of Boston.

Casks of ale and rum were broached in the squares, and the streets were filled with shouting, laughing, singing crowds ready to fill their cups and drink damnation to Parliament and freedom for all good Americans. Countrymen drank with mechanics, merchants, and planters. Boxes and trash were piled in the squares, ready to be lighted into bonfires to keep the merrymaking going far into the night. Only the older, wiser generation of Savannahans stayed behind closed and guarded doors. Many, like James Habersham and Noble Jones, whose sons were in the thick of the crowd of radicals, foresaw the terrible struggle ahead and remained steadfastly loyal to their King.

Governor Wright, who had threatened to arrest anyone attending the meeting, found it impossible to do so. Instead, meeting with his friends Habersham and Jones, he planned a campaign to write and talk with responsible conservative citizens all over Georgia, reminding them of England's goodness to the colony and of the danger of Indian uprisings if civil strife should become widespread.

Robert MacKay and Andrew McLean, who had warehouses on the waterfront filled with pelts and trading goods, had trouble finding guards. At any minute the crowds might turn ugly and decide to burn and loot. Both men decided to stay in Savannah to protect their property. Jamie Stratfield and Edward Barnard left in Barnard's carriage as soon as they had obtained copies of the statements renouncing complicity in the Tondee's resolution. They were anxious to get to Augusta before firebrands like Wells had a chance to stir crowds there to frenzy.

"The hell of it is," said Jamie as they drove up the road along the river, "there is right and wrong on both sides."

"There always is," said Barnard. "I've been in the Assembly, off and on, since the very beginning, and I've seldom heard a proposal that was all good or all bad."

"God knows I feel sorry for the poor people of Boston," Jamie said, "but they were damned fools if they thought they could defy the King and the East India Company and get away with it."

"And it isn't the young radicals who dumped the tea that are hurt," said Barnard. "It's the little householders living on the edge of poverty who will starve."

"I guess if the tons of rice and ammunition get through to them, I'll be glad," said Jamie, "but I sure as hell don't want to cut off all trade between here and England."

"I don't think they signed that yesterday," said Barnard, "and I don't think they agreed on sending delegates to Philadelphia to the Continental Congress. Maybe they realize that could cause the Upcountrymen to leave the movement altogether."

"I hear they're calling a meeting of a Georgia Provincial Congress in January," said Jamie, "but the delegates are to be the same bunch of radicals that met at Tondee's."

"All we can do is talk to the people of Saint Paul's Parish and let Dooly and his friends pass around the papers in Saint George's, so the King will know we mean no treason.

"And pray to God," said Jamie, "that the Creeks and Cherokees don't decide we're against the Great White Father who sends them presents."

They were on the road to Augusta for four days, stopping in the early afternoons and staying overnight in crowded inns along the way. In the August heat, there was very little sleep for anyone in the inns, and the taprooms rang with drunken arguments far into the night. Jamie stayed up most nights until dawn, talking about the meeting in Savannah to the people who had gathered from the countryside. Whenever he could, he convinced his audience that the best policy was to keep the peace, then suggested that they sign the protest to the meeting where they had not been represented and ask that a proper and respectful application be made to Parliament for any grievances as loyal subjects of the King.

Names and marks were usually forthcoming. The Creeks were about to sign a treaty of friendship with the Crown. For God's sake don't stir them up now.

Edward Barnard, feeling his age, went to bed early thankful for the space made by Jamie's absence. Talking in the taproom until daybreak, Jamie crawled into the coach in the early morning and napped when potholes allowed.

A little after noon on August 15, they pulled up at Barnard's house on Back Street, where Jamie dismounted stiffly and gave Edward Barnard his arm and shoulder to help him out of the coach and up the steps to the gallery of his house.

"If you don't mind, I'll go along to the Sword and Thistle," Jamie said in answer to Barnard's invitation to stop for refreshment. "You've no need to send your horses another mile. It will feel good to stretch my legs."

"I'll not hear of it," said Barnard.

Rather than argue, Jamie climbed on the seat with the driver. Although the horses were reluctant to turn back into the road, the driver cracked his whip and started them toward Broad Street.

Meg, watching from the front porch, hurried down the steps when she heard the coach turn in. Jamie jumped down and caught her in his arms, kissing her until Meg struggled away, knowing that guests were watching from the porch. The coachman took Jamie's valise out of the boot, then drove toward the road. The horses, headed for home, stepped out smartly without need of a whip.

Jamie picked up his bag in his left hand and, with his other arm around Meg, turned into the back door hoping to avoid a crowd in the common room. As they slipped through the back hallway, Angus greeted them.

"We've been waiting for you, laddie," he said, clapping his arm about Jamie's shoulder. "We want to hear all about it firsthand."

Jamie looked hopelessly at Meg, who smiled and took his bag, giving him a little push toward the door of the back dining room.

Seated around the table were John Stuart, James Grierson, John Rae, and Thomas Brown. They rose as Angus and Jamie came in, and Grierson came forward holding a tankard of ale which he had poured from the pitcher on the table.

"Welcome, lad. Come slake your thirst and tell us about the meeting," he said.

"We couldn't get into the meeting," said Jamie. "They only let hand-picked radical representatives in."

"Have you heard what was decided?"

Jamie unfolded a handbill from his pocket and handed it to Grierson, then excused himself while the paper was being read aloud. "I've read it so many times in the last few days, I'll clean up the road dust while you gentlemen look it over."

Hurrying to the outside stairway, he took the steps two at a time and caught Meg as she was hanging up his shirts. Sweeping her off her feet and dumping her on the bed, he resumed where he had left off in the innyard, kissing her lips and eyes and throat and the spot where her breasts parted at the top of her bodice. Meg ruffled his hair and ran her hands over the muscles in his back and shoulders, glorying in his strength. After the first joyous welcome, she gave him a push and moved across the counterpane.

"Get away with you," she laughed. "You will have me so mussed I can't serve the customers."

"And who has a better right to be served than your husband?" he asked, sitting up on the side of the bed, then bending over to kiss her again.

"You must wait for tonight," said Meg as he started to push her gown from her shoulder. "We'll be the laughingstock of Augusta if you don't go back down to your friends. After all, we're no longer bride and groom."

Jamie sat back and regarded her seriously. "Has anything happened?" he asked.

Meg turned pink and her eyes twinkled. "No, and it's been two weeks now. I've never been that late before."

"Great jumping Jehosephat! I'm going to be a father," he crowed.

"Hush. Everybody in Augusta will know it," said Meg. "Now you go down and talk to your cronies and don't you say a word about me. It isn't decent."

"But I'm proud of you," said Jamie, then seeing her face, "all right, I'll not tell yet. But you can't keep it a secret forever." Patting her on the stomach, he ducked her slap and went chuckling toward the stairs.

The dining room was in an uproar when he entered. John Stuart was walking the floor waving the handbill. "I can't believe James Wright let them get away with this," he exclaimed as he saw Jamie.

"I guess he hadn't much choice," Jamie answered. "If you'd seen that drunken crowd around Tondee's, you'd have known there was no stopping them short of shooting them."

"And we'd have had another 'massacre' like that scrap in Boston," said Grierson.

"I can't believe that some of the men whose names are on these papers could condone such imprudence. Some of them are gentlemen," said Thomas Brown.

"Some of them are friends of mine," said Jamie. "Wymberly Jones invited me out to his plantation last year when I first came south. Habersham and Telfair and Bulloch were there. We all were high on rum and did a lot of talking about taxes and the rights of Englishmen. They're all loyal to the King. They're just mad as hell at being treated like foreigners."

"Perhaps we've become foreigners," said Grierson. "We've had our own way over here for so long we don't want to be told how to act."

"I can see how ignorant bondsmen and backwoodsmen might want to rebel from paying taxes," said Brown, "but surely, educated Englishmen must feel obligated to the King."

"Well, lad, I've taken the 'King's shilling' and have this stump to show I've fought for him. I'd hate to see this argument turn into a war. But

Parliament almost seems to be daring us to revolt," said Angus.

"It was the King who kept the tea tax when Parliament would have dropped it," said Jamie.

"And he was right," said Grierson. "You can't let a horse get the bit in his teeth or a lad defy his father. You lose all authority."

"But have we not come of age?" Jamie asked. He could see Thomas Brown's fists clenching as his face turned red.

"Don't fash yourself, sir," said Angus hurriedly. "Jamie is only acting the devil's advocate. We're all of us good British subjects."

"True," said Grierson. "And it will behoove us all to try to keep the peace. If those young hotheads from the Tidewater want to put their necks in a noose for treason, let them. I only hope it doesn't spread."

"I'll see that my tenants are peaceful," said Brown, "and the Quakers of Wrightsboro will be no problem."

"Some of the New Purchase settlers were in Savannah," said Jamie. "They were anxious as we are to keep peace. They're carrying petitions around to protest the meeting, too."

"Have you one of those petitions?" Grierson asked. "I'd like to sign it."

Jamie reached for his coat hanging on the peg by the door and drew a paper from the pocket.

"Sir, I'd be much obliged if you'd take this around to your friends. You know everybody in Augusta and they respect your opinion. As newcomers, Squire Brown and I have less clout."

"I'll be gone, then," said Grierson, rising. "I can have this printed in the *Gazette*, with a list of signers. The rest of the good people will follow the lead."

Jamie was glad to see the gathering breaking up and pleased to have passed the responsibility for the petition along to Grierson. He and Angus waved to the three men from the front gallery as they rode off toward Grierson's stockade on the bank of Hawk's Gully, a quarter of a mile farther out the Cherokee Road.

·XIII·

THE STANLEY
FAMILY

The end of August came, and with it news that the Creeks had promised to keep the peace. It looked as though autumn might come without fear of massacres. Elijah Clark had formed a militia company made up of settlers from Saint George's Parish in the Purchase and promised support to Fort James, so the Augusta militia had not been called up.

Every few days Bert rode in to the Sword and Thistle with baskets of vegetables tied on either side of his saddle, then on into town on any errand he could fabricate. But there was no sign of the pretty girl from Charlestown. His mother had talked to her mother after church, but nothing had been said of Susan. Sometimes he'd see her two little sisters with their black nurse walking on the river path or playing in their flower garden. He was afraid to make a fool of himself by stopping to ask about her.

This morning was cooler. There was almost a hint of autumn in the air, and the sun was beginning to lose its deep gold and shine with a whiter light on the sandy road. He had carried a crock of spiced crab apples to the church to leave with the vicar for Mrs. Seymour and was turning to leave when the two little girls came running up the steps and grabbed him around the knees.

"Susan's home," said Betsy, "and she hasn't got herself begaged!"

"She's going to be an old maid!" said Kate. "She says she doesn't love nobody."

Mr. Seymour had followed Bert to the door and now clucked disapprovingly as he disentangled Bert from their clutches.

"Your sister should have no fear of spinsterhood," he said, "and certainly won't be happy if she knows you're talking that way."

Betsy put her hands on her hips as she had seen the maids do when they were arguing and looked up at the parson.

"But Mama told Papa that Susan should go to Charlestown for the summer so she could meet people of her own class and find a suitable husband."

"Men wear suits in Augusta, too," said Katie, "not just in Charlestown." She turned to Bert. "Would you be suitable if you took off buckskins and put on a wool coat and knee breeches?"

Bert, blushing furiously, held Kate by one pigtail and answered, "If I wore a wool coat in this weather, I'd be a blamed fool."

"But I like you because you saved Dusty. And now she's grown up and she's a mother cat."

"Do you want to see her kittens?" Betsy asked. "She had them under the house." She and Kate each took one of Bert's hands and started pulling him down the church steps.

James Seymour smiled and thanked Bert again for the crab apples, then turned back into the church. Sheldon was a fine lad, and his mother was a good churchwoman.

Black Lissy was on her way up the path. "What you chillun' mean, runnin' away like that?" she scolded. "You had me plum scared silly."

"This is the man who saved Dusty from that dog," said Betsy, "and we're going to show him the kittens."

"And we want to ask Susan if he's suitable," said Kate.

Bert stopped dead in the path and pulled the girls to a stop on either side. "Now just a minute. You won't say anything about this suitable business to your sister, or I'll turn you both over my knee, you hear?" he said seriously.

Both little girls looked as though they might cry, but they stood their ground.

"Will you come see Dusty's kittens if we don't talk to Susan?" Betsy asked.

"All right, but you both have to promise."

The little girls traced an X over their hearts. "We promise," they chorused.

Lissy took one child's hand in each of hers and started across The Bay toward the Merrill's house while Bert unhitched his horse and followed.

Susan was in her room when she heard Lissy calling the girls. They weren't allowed to leave the front yard with all the traffic along The Bay: wagons carrying building materials and pack horses loaded with furs and trading goods for the warehouses on the river bank. From the window, she could see a boat loading at McCarten and Campbell's wharf. Last week's rain had raised the river, and river traffic had started again with less danger of being caught on a mudbank.

Why couldn't she get on the boat and go back down to the Low Country? She'd had a wonderful summer in Charlestown. Everybody was in town for the season, away from the fever-ridden rice fields, and there was the excitement of the Liberty Boys. Aunt and Uncle Seabright thought they were dangerous radicals, but even the young plantation crowd were going to the meetings in Mazyck's pasture. They said it was more fun than cockfights and horse racing.

Mother had wanted her to find herself a beau, but they were all so het up about this liberty foolishness, they just stood around at parties and talked politics. Mother said the Liberty Boys must be riffraff, but Edward Rutledge, just back from studying law in London, was one of the biggest protestors. He and his brother John and Henry Middleton and Christopher Gadsden were planning to go to Philadelphia next month for a congress of all the colonies. You couldn't call them riffraff.

Things were so dull here in Augusta. She looked up the street toward the church and could see Lissy hurrying home, pulling a little girl in each of her hands. That Sheldon boy was leading his horse behind them. It might be fun to go down and talk to him. He was countrified, but Mother couldn't complain about his manners.

She looked in the mirror, ran a brush through her curls, then rubbed her cheeks and bit her lips to make them pink. She could hear Betsy calling "Kitty! Kitty! Kitty!" and Kate saying, "Be quiet! You'll scare her," and Lissy fussing with them both for going under the house in their good clothes.

By the time she reached the front door, Bert was sitting on the grass with two kittens in his lap while a worried Dusty walked around him meowing, and Kate and Betsy crowded as close as they could get on either side.

"You'll get grass stain on your skirts, sure as sure," said Lissy. "I just finished getting them clean from last time."

"Oh, bother the grass stain," said Kate.

"Shame on you, Kate," said Susan, "talking back to Lissy. And the kittens are too little to play with."

Bert picked up the kittens carefully and struggled to his feet, trying not to step on Dusty or bump Betsy or Kate. Why did he always seem to have his hands full of cats when he saw Susan?

Each little girl put a kitten in the skirt of her pinafore and carried it to the flower bed at the edge of the porch. The mother cat picked up one kitten by the nape of the neck and hurried under the porch, then returned for the other. Lissy herded the little girls in to have their hands washed, and Susan invited Bert to sit in a rocker on the porch and have a glass of lemonade.

"I haven't seen you in church, or anywhere," said Bert as they waited for the butler to bring the lemonade. "Betsy says you've been away."

"I've been in Charlestown all summer," said Susan.

"I bet you hate coming back out here," said Bert.

"I do miss my friends," Susan answered. "We had parties and concerts, and we went to the races and sailed and rode. There was always something to do."

"You won't find much of that in Augusta," said Bert. "Everybody's too busy trying to make a living, and they're scattered all over the countryside on farms."

"I never even get out to the country," said Susan, "but now my cousin's here, maybe Mama will let us ride. Mary Anne's a matron with a baby, but she's lots of fun. She used to live in the mountains and she loves to ride."

"I could show you the country," said Bert. "Do you think your mother would let you and your cousin ride out with me?"

"Mama and Mary Anne have gone to call on Mrs. Seymour," said Susan, "but I'll ask her when she comes home."

"Maybe we could ride out some morning to my folks' farm, and Ma could fix us a picnic by the creek. There are some good places to canter over the hills if you really like to ride."

"I'll ask Mama," said Susan.

Bert could think of nothing more to say. "I'd better be getting home now," he said finally, his lemonade glass empty and no excuse to linger.

"Maybe I'll see you in church," said Susan.

Bert unhitched Moonshine and started toward the Cherokee path, forgetting completely the spool of thread he had promised to buy.

He was hardly out of sight when the Merrill carriage brought Jocelyn Merrill and Mary Anne Stanley home from their call on the rector's wife. Betsy and Kate met them at the top of the steps.

"You missed Bert," said Kate, "but we showed him the kittens."

"And Susan gave him lemonade on the front porch," said Betsy.

Just then a young black girl came to the door carrying a baby wrapped in a soft wool shawl. Seeing his mother, he reached out, and Mary Anne hurried to take him from his nurse and cuddle him close.

"He's been so good, ma'am. He don't ever cry," said the girl. "Just laughs and smiles all the time."

"Ain't nothin' like his little girl cousins," said Lissy, who had followed the children to the porch where Kate was pulling on Betsy's pinafore sash, and Betsy had snatched a handful of Kate's curls. "You all is de baddest girls," and she put a competent black hand on each little white neck as she herded them into the house. Mary Anne followed with little Johnny, and Jocelyn had a chance to talk to Susan as they followed.

"I don't know that I approve of your entertaining a man when I'm not at home," said Jocelyn.

"Oh, Mama, he's not a man," said Susan. "He's just a freckle-faced country boy who was nice to Betsy and Kate."

"I suppose you had to be polite," said her mother. "His mother seems to be a pleasant little woman. They go to Saint Paul's, and her family is from Philadelphia."

"Mama, I don't see why you have to act as though I'm going to marry everybody I meet," said Susan. "I'll leave Bert for Betsy. He may have grown up by the time she's ready to marry, but he's too young and awkward for me."

They had reached the central stairway, and Susan ascended with her head held high, while her mother turned into the parlor where Mary Anne held Johnny on her knees, crooning to him and tickling him under the chin.

"I wish his daddy could see him," said Mary Anne. "When John came down to Charlestown in July, Johnny was just six weeks old. He's learned to laugh and be a real person, now."

"Did John say when he might come?"

"Just that he had to go to Ninety-Six to carry word back about the General Meeting. You know, there were delegates in Charlestown from all over Carolina, even the backwoods."

Jocelyn had been in Charlestown three years ago when Mary Anne and John had come to live with her parents on Tradd Street after a horrifying experience in the backwoods. Mary Anne had miscarried her first baby during a terror-ridden kidnapping by an outlaw band, and had come home to try to recover her health. John had tried to fit into Charlestown ways but had finally left her to go back to the mountains. Mary Anne had moved out to her grandmother's plantation. Everyone had thought that she'd live and die there, but she had packed up suddenly and, with peculiar old Charles Woodmason, a backwoods parson, for a protector, had headed back for Saluda Mountain. The next thing Charlestown knew, Woodmason had brought word that she and John were together again, happy as clams.

Mary Anne sat on the horsehair sofa with Johnny lying in a cradle made by her skirt. "John says we can't go back to the mountain," she said. "When we settled up there, the Cherokee had been whipped into poverty and submission and the ones we saw were friendly and eager to trade. John and I had friends among them. Now, he says, they're all stirred up over the land purchase, and with white men squabbling among themselves, they're likely to go on the warpath."

"I hope you'll stay with us for a long visit," said Jocelyn. "Susan always worshipped you, and you're enough older than she that she respects your opinions."

"After a season in Charlestown," Mary Anne said, "it's hard for her to come to the back country again. I can sympathize."

"I thought you loved the back country," said Jocelyn. "Heaven knows there are times when I hate Augusta with the coarse, brawling people here. All the trash and outlaws who've been thrown out of the other colonies have come here."

Mary Anne nodded. "I know all about trash and outlaws."

"But Augusta was becoming such a civilized town before all the New Purchase people came. The Griersons and the MacKays and the Barnards and the other merchants are as nice as Charlestown people. Dr. Johnston and the Seymours are well educated. But, now, you can hardly walk down Broad Street without an escort for fear of being insulted."

Mary Anne thought of the way she had looked down on her Saluda Mountain neighbors as trash and how she had grown to love them. But they could never mix with Charlestown society, nor would they want to.

"I guess you'd better just stay away from Broad Street then," she said. "Augusta's a wide open town. I've heard there was always liquor here even though Oglethorpe made laws against it. Men have to have somewhere to celebrate after months in the woods."

"But it used to be so safe here. The Indians were free to come and trade, and the white men's fights were kept out of town for fear an Indian might be hurt. Now you hardly ever see a Creek, and even the friendly Indians from New Savannah are afraid to bring in fish and mussels. These Virginia people don't know one Indian from another, and hate them all. We had a good old Creek chief murdered in a Broad Street tavern."

"The settlers have reason for being afraid," Mary Anne said. "After all the massacres in the ceded lands almost everyone has had a brother or sister or good friend scalped and tortured. There's bound to be hatred."

"Our friendly Indians are more civilized than the backwoodsmen," Jocelyn insisted.

"Then let's stay in our part of town and enjoy the pretty houses along the river," said Mary Anne. "I'm hoping you can teach me to do needlepoint while I'm here. I've never had time to learn."

And pray John will come soon, she thought. He was looking for a house in Ninety-Six. It was not a big town like Augusta, but there were enough people to stand off an Indian attack. She loved Jocelyn, but she'd forgotten how silly and shallow city women could be.

John rode in the next day. Ninety-Six was peaceful for the time being, with the Cherokees busy with the autumn harvest and the Creeks anxious to trade now that the embargo was lifted. All this talk of the Association in Charlestown was causing ripples, however, in the back country. At the General Meeting there in July, delegates had been chosen to go to a Continental Congress in Philadelphia. Now the colonies were going to associate to boycott all trade with England. Gadsden, Middleton, and Lynch, the Carolina delegates, were determined to take Carolina in with the other colonies.

"I'd rather know that you and Johnny are here," said John as he and Mary Anne dressed for bed. "Joseph and Jocelyn are anxious for you to stay. Jocelyn says she needs you to keep Susan happy."

"What a lot of foolishness," said Mary Anne. "I'd be just as safe in Ninety-Six, and we have lots of friends there. Will Wofford and Andy Williamson, the Cunninghams and the Kirklands!"

"But Jocelyn is family. And that crowd in Ninety-Six are all at each other's throats. Most of them are against the Association, and ready to fight anyone in favor of it. And the Cherokees are waiting and watching."

"But, John, what do Upcountry people have to do with this Association thing? They don't trade with England. Anything they buy comes from Charlestown or Augusta. They grow most of their own food and flax and shoot their game and trap their furs."

"It's a matter of principle," said John. "There's beginning to be talk, too, about the English stirring up the Indians to make Americans toe the line. I talked to John Stuart when he was in Ninety-Six, but he swears it's a lie. He says he'll refuse to have anything to do with any such order."

"Then why can't I come to Ninety-Six?"

"Because, my darling, I don't want anything to happen to you or little Johnny. I'll never forgive myself for leaving you before to be dragged off by outlaws."

Mary Anne looked over at the cradle where she could see soft red curls and a little pink hand reaching out beyond the quilt.

"Besides," said John, "I'll probably be in Augusta more than I am in Ninety-Six. Stuart gave me a letter to a man named Thomas Brown who needs some land surveyed, near Brownsborough. Brown's brought a whole slew of bondsmen over here from Yorkshire, and he plans to put them all on plots of land that they'll own when they work out their indentures. He needs a lot of surveying done, and I'd like the job."

"Oh, John, that would be perfect."

"Well, I'd be close enough to get back to see you often, but it's a good thirty miles up in the wilds. he has five thousand acres to survey and divide, and I'll have to camp out up there."

"If it weren't for Johnny, I'd camp out with you."

"I'd rather camp in that handsome four-poster tonight," said John, "if you will just stop all the talk and come to bed."

"I thought you'd forgotten all about going to bed," she said.

"I'll show you how much I've forgotten," said John, picking her up and tossing her into the center of the feather puff and taking her into his arms.

·XIV·

BROWNSBOROUGH

The next morning, John Stanley and Joseph Merrill walked over to Fox's coffee house. Thomas Brown didn't come in often, but someone there would probably know where he was.

Dr. Andrew Johnston and William Goodgion, sitting at the table in the bay window, beckoned to Joseph to join them. Joseph introduced John, who bowed. "I believe I know your father-in-law," he said to William Goodgion. "Isn't your wife Edward Barnard's daughter?"

"You're right," said Goodgion. "Her father has told me about your exploits together with the Regulators."

"Thank the Lord that's all over," said John.

"I think you chased most of the scum into Georgia," said Goodgion. "We have been overrun here by vagabonds."

"They're not all bad," said the doctor, "but they keep me busy patching up knife and gunshot wounds."

The door opened, and Martin Weatherford and James Grierson joined the table.

"What are you doing in town?" Johnston asked as Grierson took a chair beside him. "I thought you patronized the Scotsman's tavern out on the gully."

"I came in to talk to Barnard about a bale of pelts the Creeks brought in for him. They don't like to come into town if they can help it these days."

"Damned shame," said Weatherford.

"Are you still shipping pelts to England?" John asked, surprised. "I didn't think they were going to let them through Charlestown."

"We're shipping them downriver," said Grierson. "Governor Wright has played it smart and ignored most of the agitators. Georgia people know which side their bread is buttered on. Why should we side with a bunch of treasonous New Englanders?"

"South Carolina is all set to join the Association," said John. "The Liberty Boys in Charlestown have even tarred and feathered a few conservatives who opposed it."

"Damn bunch of hotheads," said Weatherford, "ready to fight at the drop of a hat."

John turned to Grierson, "Do you happen to know, sir, where I can find Thomas Brown? I understand he lives out beyond your post."

"I'm to meet him at the Sword and Thistle for lunch," said Grierson. "Would you like to join us?"

"I would like to very much," said John. "I have a letter to him from Superintendent Stuart recommending me as a surveyor. Do you know whether he's found one yet?"

"Jamie Stratfield from the Sword and Thistle has been working for him, but he needs two men working together. I know he'll be glad to talk to you."

Joseph had gone over to the fireplace to choose a long-stemmed pipe from the mantel and now held one up. "Would you like a pipe?" Two of the men nodded, and he brought three back to the table where they skillfully broke a small piece from the end of each stem, then filled the bowls with tobacco from their pouches and lighted up.

As soon as Grierson had contacted Edward Barnard, he and John Stanley rode to the Sword and Thistle.

"I'm mighty glad to see you," said Jamie who was bartending when Grierson introduced John and explained his mission. "Squire Brown should be in soon for lunch, and I'll put in my tuppenny's worth. It gets lonesome out there in the forest when you imagine an Indian in warpaint behind every tree. We could get the job done together in one-fourth the time."

"Mr. Grierson tells me you're from Tidewater Maryland," said John. "I was born in Williamsburg, Virginia, not too far away. We should have a lot in common."

A clatter of hoofs in the inn yard signaled the arrival of Squire Brown. Dressed in dark green ratcatcher and hunt boots, a typical English gentleman, he doffed a beaver hat, as he came through the door, then strode up to the bar.

Grierson made room for him while Angus took Brown's tankard from its peg to fill with ale.

"I've brought this young man to meet you," said Grierson, nodding to John. "May I introduce John Stanley, who has a letter for you from Superintendent Stuart?"

Brown shook John's hand. "Stuart told me about you," he said. "He was very complimentary. Says you've surveyed most of the land between the Saluda Gap and Ninety-Six. His recommendation is all I need."

"He exaggerates the mileage," said John smiling, "but I've done my share."

"Could you ride out to Brownborough in the next few days, so we can come to terms?"

"Yes, sir," said John. "The sooner the better, before the winter rains begin."

Brown insisted that they all have another ale with him and some lunch, and John rode back to the Merrills full of good news and good food and drink.

John and Jamie started out together for Brownsborough two days later. After a stop at the plantation house to agree on terms and to pick up copies of the land grants to be surveyed, they were ready by afternoon to begin charting the five-thousand acres of New Purchase that Brown planned to develop along Little River.

Acres of land around his manor house had already been cleared and planted in crops. Barns, stables, and storehouses had been built and a mill was already in operation on the banks of a creek, grinding corn and wheat. Small tenant farmhouses were springing up as quickly as trees could be felled and land cleared on the thirty-six plots assigned to the immigrant families from Yorkshire and the Orkneys.

John and Jamie stopped at sunset at one of the new log houses on the edge of the uncharted land. As they dismounted, the farmer came down the steps, bobbing his head and pulling his forelock while his wife curtseyed.

John stepped forward, hand outstretched. "I'm John Stanley and this is my friend James Stratfield," he said.

The farmer hesitated a moment, then held out his own hand. "Jeremy Potter," he said, "and my wife Anne."

"Could we roll up in our blankets by your fire tonight?" John asked, in the manner of the frontier. "Those black clouds look like rain."

Potter hesitated. Noticing their well-bred horses, he was sure they must be gentlemen in spite of their buckskins. "I be proud to welcome you," he said, "but you must take the bed and let us sleep by the hearth."

"We'll do nothing of the sort," said Jamie. "We welcome the hearthside when we might be sleeping on the ground."

The Potters insisted that they share their supper of fresh-laid eggs and corn pone with wild grape jam. "Likely you're out to survey the lands," said Potter as they sat at the trestle table. "I seen your gear when you untacked your horses."

"You're right," said Jamie. "Squire Brown has hired us to finish charting this claim. He says he has another seventy-odd people coming from England."

"Oh, ay," said Potter. "Squire will have a town here soon. He's givin' poor men a chance to make a livin'."

"This is the country where they can do it," said John. "Any man with two good hands and a will to work can make his fortune."

"It's hard, think me, to learn the ways," said Potter. "Our country people from home knows nothin' when they comes here. They be like new black slaves from Africky that comes out o' the ships. Americans are smart and hardy, and they ain't afeard o' nothin'. Some o' the lads from the Purchase tells us we're all fools to do Squire's bidding."

"Do you think it's foolish?" Jamie asked.

"Nay, but some does. I think Squire will make the passage money and more from us before we're done clearing his fields; but think me, we'd o' never had the chance without him."

"This is some of the best crop land in the colony," said John.

"Some say they'd rather break their bond than have to bow to Squire. They'd not ha' thought that way at home. It's all these big talkin' lads they call Crackers that turn their heads. They talk about 'liberty' and 'rights' and shoot their guns and drink their liquor. Anne and I plan to bide here at home."

As soon as the stock had been fed and the shutters closed for the night, Jeremy banked the fire and repaired to the bedroom, while John and Jamie fell asleep in their blankets near the hearth.

*　*　*

As Indian summer turned to autumn and the woods and fields turned to crimson and gold, Augustans tried to ignore the rumors that came with every traveler from the Low Country.

In Savannah Governor Wright was doing his best to keep the peace, with the fur trade once more booming and merchants able to ship as many hides and furs as the traders could bring in. Charlestown trade had nearly dried up under the Association's embargo, and merchants were taking advantage of the shift to Savannah, since Georgia had not formally joined.

In Augusta's Broad Street taverns, visitors from the coast were plied with ale and surrounded by backwoodsmen wanting news. Most of the backcountry settlers had been enthusiastic supporters of Governor Wright when he tamed the Creeks by restricting trade in furs. Now that trade had resumed and the Indians were getting uppity again, they had nothing good to say about him. They wanted the Indians out of the country!

Dr. George Wells had been to Savannah and had met Button Gwinnett, a young man who had tried his hand as a storekeeper and as a planter and was now in the thick of the liberty movement. Wells and his friend Chesley Bostick had a table at Fox's where they could face the room and were well into their third round of rum.

"It's a bloody shame," said Wells, "that Georgia's not a member of the Association. The damned greedy merchants don't give a hoot in hell for the other Americans who are ready to die for liberty. All they care about is their bloody pounds and shillings, while other colonies are being starved!"

"Hear! Hear!" said Bostick, pounding his tankard on the table.

"I ain't never seen no Massachusetts yankee I'd take the trouble to spit on," said a countryman at the bar. "As long as the King gives us land and keeps the Indians quiet, I don't give a damn about the Bostoners."

"Governor Wright's been fair and square," said another farmer. "He got the Indians to cede us the land so we could settle it."

"But he didn't make 'em give up the land on the Oconee," said Bostick. "There's settlers already livin' there that could be scalped and burned out."

"Word's going around Savannah that Wright and John Stuart are planning to set the Indians on the warpath if Georgia joins the Association," said Wells.

A shock wave ran through the room, and all conversation ceased.

"Where did you get that word, Doctor?" asked John Dooly, who had been sitting at the next table.

"At a meeting of the Liberty Boys," said Wells.

Dooly stood up and faced the tavern group. "Men, Dr. Wells has brought fearful news from Savannah. It could mean the end of all the progress we have made in the new land. But until it is proved true, I suggest that we bide our time."

"It may be too late when the war whoops sound and our women and children are massacred," said Wells.

John Wereat who had been sitting with Dooly, now stood up and turned to Wells. "As I understand it, Dr. Wells, John Stuart is a man of peace and has always had a deep regard for the Indians as well as for the white settlers. I don't believe he would stir up the tribes against white men. He knows they'd kill friends as well as foes."

"I, for one, don't want to take a chance," said Wells.

"Then quit talking about the bloody Association before you have us all massacred," said a big frontiersman at the bar.

A murmur of assent swept over the room, and the barman came around with a pitcher of ale.

* * *

As autumn became winter, Jocelyn Merrill decided not to have a Christmas party this year. It was hard to know whom to invite, with all this liberty talk and good manners forgotten when an argument began. The Seymours, however, planned a small gathering at the parsonage on Christmas Eve afternoon.

They lived on the plot of land assigned to the pastor of Saint Paul's, out toward New Savannah. The parsonage, built reluctantly by the townspeople for the unpopular former pastor, left a lot to be desired. Mrs. Seymour, however, had brought curtains and linens and family silver from England, and the house was bright with holly, mistletoe, and candles. The Seymour children were dressed in their best suits and pinafores, their eyes sparkling with excitement as they helped their mother greet guests at the door.

Like many of the farmhouses around Augusta, the rectory was really two buildings with a covered walkway between. The larger main house was built up high, over an air space, with a large parlor across the front and two bedrooms behind. At the end of the walkway was the kitchen, with storeroom tacked behind, and outbuildings for feed and seed and stabling on beyond.

The parlor was heated by a fireplace where a Yule log lay on the hearth, ready to be pushed into the flames of the small fire. It had been cold and frosty early in the morning, but the Georgia sun, even in December, now made it too warm to keep windows closed.

The windows and doors were roughly finished, and the floor boards needed sanding. Ben Sheldon pulled his hand away from the railing along the front steps for fear of splinters. This was no way for a clergyman to live. You could tell he didn't know anything about carpentry or cabinet making.

"Bert, you and I are going to have to come back after Christmas and work on this house," he said.

Mary beamed at him, "How lovely, Ben. Mr. Seymour spends so much time riding around the parish, he has none to spend on his own home."

"Likely he doesn't get enough of a living to hire anyone," said Ben. "I can't give money to the church, but I can give some time."

They had reached the door where Margaret Seymour stood with the children. "Mary Sheldon," she said, grasping both of Mary's hands, "and Francie, so tall I hardly knew her. Sally's putting sandwiches on the tray; would you like to help her?" Francie hurried back down the steps and around to the kitchen building.

The sound of wheels on gravel announced the arrival of the Merrills and the Stanleys. John, here for Christmas, was riding his bay gelding beside the carriage, while Mary Anne rode inside with Jocelyn, Joseph, and Susan.

"I was hoping you'd bring the little girls," said the rector's wife at the door. "Jane and Beth have been waiting for them."

"They both have runny noses," said their mother. "Besides, they are so excited about Christmas they are driving us all mad. We left them with their nurse and their little cousin."

Mary Anne introduced John to their hostess.

"We're so glad you can be here," Margaret Seymour said. "We all love Mary Anne."

Susan had worn her new green velvet coat and bonnet trimmed in fur, and carried a matching muff of mink. She knew that they made her eyes look greener as she gave Bert Sheldon a smile and looked up at him from under her lashes.

Bert nearly fell over the porch rail, where he had been standing.

"Good afternoon, Mr. Sheldon," Susan said, twinkling. "This is the first time I've seen you without a handful of cats."

"That's because you didn't bring your little sisters," said Bert recovering. "They'd have found me a cat somewhere."

James Seymour had come to the door beside his wife, smiling benignly. "I see you two young people have met," he said. "Do come in and have a cup of tea."

John and Mary Anne were standing at the tea table when Susan walked in with Bert. "This is Betsy and Kate's friend, Bert Sheldon," said Susan to her cousin. "He's fond of cats."

Mary Anne looked puzzled, but held out her hand.

"Well, Sheldon," John exclaimed, turning around, "I didn't know you were in Augusta. I haven't seen you since that little Indian skirmish at Fort James."

"Yes, sir. My parents live out on Rae's Creek. I'm staying with them 'till I'm called up again."

"Mary Anne, this lad was one of our best scouts up in the Ceded Lands. Didn't I hear you'd made sergeant?"

"Yes, sir. That was after Jones was killed."

"I heard about that fight and how you held them off till they could carry his body in. Good work."

"Thank you, sir."

Susan's eyes had opened wide. This boy was a friend of John's? And a soldier, promoted for bravery in action? It was hard to believe.

There was a bustle of new arrivals, and the MacKays came to the doorway, followed by Squire Brown.

"I knew you'd want us to bring Mr. Brown," said Mary MacKay. "He was going to be by himself on Christmas Eve."

"Welcome and Merry Christmas!" said the parson. "We would certainly have invited you had we known you were in from the country."

"I'm to have Christmas tomorrow at Brownsborough for all my farmers," said Brown, "but it is very pleasant to have a real English tea with gentlefolk today."

Susan turned from Bert and the Stanleys as Mr. Seymour led the squire to the tea table.

"Miss Susan Merrill," Brown said, taking her hand and bowing. "I enjoyed talking to you at your parents' party last Christmas. A year is too long between meetings."

How he stood out in this country crowd. His velvet coat and brocade waistcoat were tailored to perfection. His knee breeches fit him with no need for the padding that some men wore, and were fastened with knee buckles of mother-of-pearl over stockings of white silk. His silver-buckled shoes were polished to perfection.

"May I bring you a cup of tea?" he asked, then noticed Bert.

"Sheldon, isn't it?" he asked holding out his hand.

"Yes, sir," Bert answered, grasping it.

"We've met at the Sword and Thistle," Brown explained to Susan. "You've been with the militia at Fort James, have you not?"

"Yes, sir, but I hope I won't have to serve again soon."

"It's good to know you men are ready to protect us in the Ceded Lands."

"Thank you, sir," said Bert, bowing slightly and leaving him with Susan. What was the use of dreaming when there was a rich, highborn gentleman for her to talk to?

After tea and cake when everyone had found a seat or a good place to stand, Mr. Seymour suggested that they sing carols. He had a good, true baritone voice strengthened by hours in the pulpit and his wife, a sweet soprano, so that they needed no accompaniment. After the first few verses, the whole party joined in. The old English carols conjured up memories of different times and different places, creating a warm glow of peace and good fellowship. Let the Low Country fret about liberty and taxation. In Augusta this Christmas, the Indians were docile, the fur trade flourishing, and all was right with the world.

·XV·

WINDS OF WAR

In February of the new year, 1775, a call came to another meeting in Savannah to elect delegates to the Second Continental Congress, which was to be held in May in Philadelphia. A few of the firebrands like Wells and Bostick planned to go, but the weather turned bitter with cold sleety rain and a gale whipping up waves on the river. Influenza and pneumonia and all the other ailments of winter kept both Augusta doctors so busy there was no question of Wells' making the trip. Dr. Johnston was loved for his willingness to visit sickbeds in any sort of weather, and Dr. Wells could not afford to lose his already dwindling practice by leaving town. Other Augustans, remembering the way they had been turned away from the meeting at Tondee's, decided to stay at home. Let the Low Country hotheads put their necks in the noose.

When the Second Continental Congress met in May, Georgia was still not represented. Archibald Bulloch, Noble Wymberly Jones, and John Houstoun had been elected as delegates in February, but refused to go to Philadelphia. Like Saint Paul's, the rest of the Upcountry parishes had stayed home from the February meeting, so that only four out of twelve parishes had been present. Bulloch, Jones, and Houstoun felt that they lacked the backing they needed to speak for the colony. By April 1775, the document known as the Association which proclaimed a boycott of all British trade by the colonies represented in the Congress, had been disseminated up and down the coast from Maine to the Savannah River. Copies of the proclamation were sent throughout the colonies to be signed by those who supported the measure.

Parliament had rejected the petitions of the Continental Congress, and British commanders in America were ordered to crack down on protesters. On April eighteenth, British troops were sent from Boston to nearby Lexington and Concord to seize stores of gunpowder hoarded by the townspeople and to arrest the troublemakers, Samuel Adams and

John Hancock. In Lexington, armed patriots met the troops. Shots were fired which killed eight Americans and wounded several more, and the British pushed on toward Concord.

In Concord, however, the Americans, shocked and furious over the action in Lexington, met the red-coated formation with deadly rifle fire from behind thick stone walls. The disciplined British soldiers, unused to such tactics, continued to advance until their lines were so decimated that they were forced to retreat to Boston.

There could be no answer to such open rebellion but war. The rebellious acts of the colonists had become the American Revolution.

When the Liberty Boys of Savannah received news of Lexington and Concord on May tenth, all hell broke loose. A mob, led by Noble Wymberly Jones, Edward Telfair, Joseph Habersham, and John Milledge, raided the powder magazine and sent part of the militia's gunpowder and a shipload of rice and money to Massachusetts. When the governor ordered the raiders arrested, no one paid any attention even though a reward of one hundred and fifty pounds was offered. By June fourth when the King's birthday was to be celebrated by a salute of cannon fire, it was found that the guns had been spiked and rolled over the bluff. The next day the Liberty Boys erected a pole in one of the squares as an official rallying point and proclaimed the birth of liberty in Georgia.

The news was several days in reaching Augusta. Edward Barnard had been in poor health for months, worried about the fur trade but more worried about the strife among his friends. Always loyal to his King, he was torn by the news that Englishmen were killing Englishmen. On June thirteenth, he died, leaving Augustans to grieve for his wisdom and justice in making decisions.

Even the Sword and Thistle was loud with talk of liberty. Angus filled the tankards and held his peace. The idea of British Regulars being mowed down by Yankee farmers was hard to endure, and he had heard there was a Highland regiment involved. He had to make a living, however, and all this talk certainly promoted the sale of ale.

Robert MacKay had gone to Savannah to send his young son off to school in Edinburgh and had stayed on to watch over his mercantile interests. His wife Mary received letters by nearly every post telling of the goings on in the Provincial Assembly, so that her parlor became a gathering place for old friends who wanted to hear the news.

One evening late in June, Meg carried a tray with small glasses back to a table in the dining room of the inn where six men were sitting over cups of coffee, with a dark bottle of French brandy open and waiting to be poured.

"Don't ask me where the brandy came from, gentlemen," said George Galphin. "Let's just say that some of my Creek relatives have more to do with the Spanish than they like to admit. But who am I to look a gift horse in the mouth?"

"God forbid!" said Andrew McLean, breathing in the scent of the now-forbidden elixir.

"It's as good a cognac as I have ever tasted," said Thomas Brown, who had been accepted as a regular member of the backroom fellowship. "But don't the Indians drink brandy?"

"They'd rather have rum, and they know the value of good cognac. This is worth more than a whole packload of pelts."

"Amen!" said James Grierson.

"I'm surprised sometimes," said Brown, "at the wisdom shown by some of the Indians. One would expect savages to think only of the appetite of the moment."

"Don't believe for a moment that some Indians aren't wise," said Galphin. "Their customs are different, but they aren't lacking in brains."

"I've found the Indians who have come into Brownsborough to be fine fellows, if you treat them well. My tenants are deathly afraid of them, but I've had no trouble."

"Don't be too quick to trust them," Galphin advised. "What an Englishman considers dishonorable may seem good tactics to a Creek. We don't have the same ideals."

"Have you heard the canard that Superintendent Stuart is stirring up the Indians against the colonies?" Brown asked. "Surely no Englishman would turn them against his own kind."

"Stuart talked to me about that rumor when I saw him in Savannah," said McLean. "Apparently Drayton and Timothy in Charlestown are out for Stuart's blood. He was opposed to Drayton for the Council, and Drayton thinks Stuart kept him from being elected. And Timothy's newspaper has been so radical that Stuart has given all his news about Indian affairs to Robert Wells for his journal. Stuart thinks Timothy is spreading the rumor that he's stirring up both the Indians and the black slaves."

"You might know they'd add the slaves," said Galphin. "Ricebirds don't have to worry about the Indians any more, but they're scared as hell of a slave uprising."

"Why don't the British take Indians into the army?" Brown asked. "Surely they'd be good fighters against these rebels."

"Don't even mention it," Galphin exclaimed. "Noble as the savages may seem, they're still just that. Take it from a Squaw Man. They hate the white men who have swarmed over their land, and they'll kill them all, good and bad, if given the chance."

On the way out through the tap room, Thomas Brown stopped to talk to Jamie Stratfield, who was serving at the bar.

"I haven't had a chance to thank you properly for the excellent job you and Stanley did, surveying my land," he said. "It should make the division into tenant plots simple."

"Are you expecting more tenants soon?"

"As soon as this bloody rebellion is cleared up," said Brown. "They tell me even Savannah is closed to shipping now, though I may be able to get my people in through Florida."

"The tenants you have now are fine people," said Jamie. "It was cold as sin out there in the woods last winter, but they were always ready to welcome us to their hearths."

"I've tried to bring good yeoman stock from Yorkshire and the Orkney Islands," said Brown, "but some are picking up the American idea of equality. They're my bondsmen, but many of them are barely civil these days. Hardly a man doffs his hat to me."

"Jeremy Potter and his wife Anne are certainly loyal to you," said Jamie. "We stayed in their cottage several different nights."

"Oh, they're fine people," said Brown. "Anne's mother was my mother's maid in our home near Hull. Potter's ancestors have been tenants of my family for generations. If they were all like the Potters, the riffraff would never turn their heads."

McLean and Grierson came through the tap room. "I'm heading out for Savannah tomorrow," McLean said. "I'm on my way now to MacKay's to pick up some shirts Mary wanted me to take to Rob with a letter. I wish she'd stay in town until he comes back."

"I've been trying to keep an eye on her," said Grierson. "It's a short ride over there."

"I hear you're not the only one going to Savannah, Andrew," said Angus, who had come up behind the bar beside Jamie. "They tell me there's a regular delegation going down to the Provincial Congress on July twelfth."

"Two of my neighbors are going as delegates," said Grierson. "James Rae and Andrew Moore are both good, sound thinkers. John Walton is a little liberal in his ideas, but Burns and Burney and Marbury can talk sense to him. Maybe they'll talk sense into the Low Country radicals, too."

"Do you think anything can keep us out of war, now?" Jamie asked. "It seems to me that we're already in it."

"Not until Georgia signs the Association," said Grierson.

Before the delegation reached Savannah, however, word came of a battle fought at Breed's Hill in Massachusetts, where an American force of sharpshooters held out against a British force twice its size, mowing them down as they made a frontal attack on the strongly entrenched countrymen. Although the Americans finally ran out of ammunition and were forced to abandon the hill, the British force was cut to pieces. Jubilant Americans filled every tavern on the Atlantic seaboard.

In Augusta the news was received with mixed emotions. Nobody wanted to see Americans, even New Englanders, pushed around by British troops. It was good to know that the colonists could fight back and win. But could the Americans really win once the British Lion was loosed to fight? So far, his tail had been twisted and sticks had been poked through the bars, but now that the cage door was open, it was too late to retreat. Georgians would have to join the Association or be considered cowards.

Wasn't discretion the better part of valor, though? Couldn't the Upcountry stay out of the whole mess? Let the hotheads get involved and pay the price of treason.

Toward the end of July, word came through from Charlestown that John Stuart had gone to Florida to live, accused by the Liberty Boys of plotting to incite the Indians and slaves against white people in the South. Sick at heart and unable to convince people of his innocence, he moved to Saint Augustine, where the British colonists remained loyal to the Crown. He had been the mainstay of all Indian affairs for so long that both Indians and white traders were afraid of what might happen now.

George Galphin sent word to Lachlan McGillivray and James Grierson to come to his post at Silver Bluff to talk. McGillivray had represented Stuart in several boundary disputes and was trusted and respected by Cherokees and Creeks alike, as was Grierson.

The three men sat on the porch of the trading post looking down on the open ground where Indians had so often met in peace to trade and talk. The summer sunlight filtered through the pines, the heat so intense that all three had stripped to the waist and taken off their boots to put bare feet on the porch rail.

"Thank God for this heat," said Galphin. "It's too bloody hot for the tribes to go on the warpath."

"They're as stunned as we are," said McGillivray, "but God knows who the powers in London will send in Stuart's place."

"Word came through yesterday," said Galphin, "that he's going to try to carry on his work from Saint Augustine, but my nephew talked to one of the guides who helped carry him there. The Indians say he has a lung fever and he'll never get well."

"Is that just Indian medicine talk?" McGillivray wanted to know.

"It's hard to tell, but for the time being he's out of it. And Alexander Cameron is in charge of Cherokee affairs."

"God help us," said McGillivray. "He's about as hard-nosed a hater of the white settlers as anyone I know. He's more Indian than the Indians."

"Nevertheless he has a commission from the King. And where Stuart would have done his best to keep the Cherokees in order, Cameron will encourage destruction."

"Surely the King won't encourage massacres," said Grierson.

"The King is in London," said Galphin. "It is up to the ones of us with Indian ties to keep their trust and try to avoid bloodshed."

"My son Alexander by my Creek wife has become a minor chief," said McGillivray. "I'll have him talk to the elders and chiefs. They all think of Augusta as a peaceful town, even though times have changed. They believe that you two and John Rae and Andrew McLean are their friends. Some of them have dealt with Thomas Brown in the Ceded Lands, and they trust him. He has been honest in his dealings with them and with the Cherokees up there."

"Maybe we should talk to him," said Grierson. "He's certainly vulnerable out there on Little River. He'd do well to let them know he's a friend."

"For the time being," said Galphin, "the Creeks seem to be quiet. They're still poor from the trade embargo and afraid to anger any white man. As long as we can keep the trade goods coming, they'll keep the peace. But if the Cherokees come down on the frontier, the Creeks just may join in."

"Do you think all this liberty talk will stir them up?" Grierson asked.

"I don't think they understand it," said McGillivray. "One white man looks very much like another to them, and as long as the presents are forthcoming and the settlers stay away from their squaws and horses, they won't fight."

"I want us to keep in touch," said Galphin. "Grierson, you know what's going on in Augusta. You'd get word of any political move. McGillivray and I will have ears out among the tribes. With God's help, we can keep the Indians peaceful while the white men fight among themselves.

* * *

Although most of the old inhabitants of Augusta were ready to sit tight and hope for peace, a Liberty Pole had been set up on the common land on Broad Street. Agitators like Wells and Bostick met there in the evenings after the sun had gone down and the taverns were too hot for a crowd. Usually a keg of ale or one of rum was set on a big flat boulder under the trees, and men could fill their drinking cups. Settlers from the New Purchase, with little farm work to do in the late July heat, rode into town to join in discussions.

Thomas Brown's tenants had begun to leave their cottages and their work early in the afternoon, returning late at night drunk from rum and the heady talk of liberty and equality. When he had restricted them to the estate and threatened punishment—for they were still in bond to him for their passage money—some of them left Brownsborough with word that he could sing for his money.

One sweltering afternoon, Brown saddled his horse and rode into town to find his bondsmen. As he crossed the nearly dry bed of Campbell's Gully, he reined in to talk to Meg and Jamie Stratfield in the inn yard.

"The damnable rabble-rousers have stirred up my people," he explained. "I don't want to call the law down upon the poor fools, but I'm going to see if I can't put some sense into the spellbinders who rant about liberty."

"I'd be careful, sir," said Jamie. "I don't go into town in the evenings myself, if I can help it. Their meetings get pretty wild sometimes, with all the rum."

"They'd better be careful!" Brown answered, his face red in the setting sun. "They're talking treason and sedition, and they could be hanged for it!"

"We're a mighty long way from a British magistrate," said Jamie. "The local lawmen are afraid to tangle with the Liberty Boys, and some of them are Liberty Boys themselves."

"I don't need a backwoods sheriff to discipline my bondsmen," said Brown.

"No, sir," said Jamie, "but it would be a good idea to talk to Colonel Grierson. He's in charge of the militia company since Colonel Barnard died."

"I'll need no militia to warn the rogues to leave my people alone," said Brown as he touched his whip to his horse's rump and cantered off toward town.

Jamie and Meg went inside where a few guests were already gathering in the tap room. Dr. Johnston and Martin Weatherford were seated near the bar.

"I hope you won't be patching up bodies," Jamie said. "Squire Brown is headed into town to tell the Liberty Boys off. He's liable to start a riot."

"No doubt my colleague, Wells, will be in the thick of it," said Johnston. "I wonder sometimes if he doesn't provoke fights just to drum up business."

Weatherford looked at him sharply.

"No, Martin, I'm joking, of course."

"I'd hate to be in Brown's shoes if they turn nasty," said Weatherford. "I find the best thing to do is put up with their rantings and keep my head low."

"Do you think we'd better ride over and alert Colonel Grierson?" Jamie asked, "or just be ready to help Brown if he needs us?"

"Lord willing, they aren't really drunk yet," said Johnston. "It's early in the afternoon."

"Better keep out of it," said Weatherford.

Jamie went over to the bar to speak quietly to Angus. "I think I'll ride in to see John Stanley at the Merrills," he said. "Mr. Brown was very kind to us when we surveyed his land. I'd hate to see him get into bad trouble with that mob."

"Be careful, laddie," said Angus. "The mobs in Savannah have been pouring hot tar and feathers on the people who disagree with them."

"We've still enough good, sensible men in the militia that we could handle a mob," said Jamie.

Meg was helping Angus at the bar. "I don't want my baby's father killed or crippled in a drunken brawl."

"But you'd not have me desert a friend," said Jamie as he kissed her gently and walked toward the door.

Just then he heard hoofbeats and saw Thomas Brown galloping out the road to Brownsborough. Brown didn't stop or look, and his face was bright red.

"Brown seems to have concluded his business," Jamie said, returning to the tap room. "He looks madder than hell, but he seems safe if he doesn't die of apoplexy."

The next morning, Thomas Brown set out for the Ninety-Six District in South Carolina, where he knew the settlers had shown little affection for the cause of liberty. Thomas Fletchall, whom he had met in the Purchase, was a colonel of the militia regiment of the Upper Saluda and was as vehement in his denunciation of the Liberty Boys as anyone he had met. His friends, Moses Kirkland and the Cunningham brothers, had saved a pack train loaded with gunpowder from Fort Charlotte that had been seized by James Mayson for the Provincial Congress and had jailed Mayson in Ninety-Six, keeping the powder in the name of the Lord William Campbell, Royal Governor of South Carolina.

Riding into Ninety-Six two mornings later, Brown was greeted by Fletchall, who invited him to stay nearby at his farm in Fair Forest. By nightfall Fletchall had sent word to most of the men of influence in the district to meet there the next day.

"This matter of the Association is raising hell among old friends," said Fletchall as they waited on his front porch for the group to gather. "James Mayson and Will Wofford were neighbors and good friends of mine until they signed the paper. But I'm resolved and do utterly refuse to take up arms against my King and am determined to oppose anyone who tries to make me do so."

"Are there many like Mayson and Wofford here?" Brown asked.

"Not right now," said Fletchall, "but God knows when they'll change their minds. I hear that Judge William Drayton and the Reverend William Tennent are on their way through the back country trying to drum up recruits for the Association."

"I'm thoroughly disgusted," said Brown. "I have spent a fortune bringing bondsmen over to America to colonize the country for the King. I've given them a promise of land and have furnished them with all they need for their families to start farms. And now they are joining this damnable Association against the King.

"I didn't think Georgia had joined the Association," said Fletchall.

"It's only a matter of time before the Georgia Congress signs," said Brown. "Individuals are signing right and left, or making their marks, because most of them are too ignorant to write their names."

Men on horseback began to arrive, and Brown and Fletchall moved down the steps to greet them and offer them cider from a keg that had been cooled in the creek. Horses were turned into the paddock behind the house, and men sat on the front steps and on log seats in the front yard. Thomas Fletchall rose to his feet and went to the center of the circle on the lawn.

"I think most of you have met Squire Brown of Brownsborough, near Augusta. He's settled some thirty-six families on his land in the New Purchase and now he's afraid of losing them. They're jumping bond and joining the Association. He's protested to the ringleaders in Augusta, and they've threatened his life if he tries to force his bondsmen to work."

"I'm bloody damned furious," said Brown, joining Fletchall in the center ring. "No one in Augusta will move against them. You people saved the King's powder from the rebels. Thank God we still have a few men who are loyal to their King!"

"Hear! Hear!" said Moses Kirkland, and was answered by cheers from the other men.

"I understand that the Carolina Upcountry is full of German settlers," said Brown. "Do you think they will sign the Association?"

"Nein!" said a squarely built farmer. "Ve haf much to be thankful for to King George. He is a Hanoverian. Ve vill not fight against his vishes."

"Can I hope for help from you people?" Brown asked the gathering, "if I oppose the Augusta Liberty Boys?"

"What kind of help?" Patrick Cunningham asked.

"Will you talk to the people in the Purchase on the Georgia side of the river? Let them know that not all Carolinians are rebels. There are more loyal Georgians than rebels, but most of the people don't want to take sides at all."

"We'll do what we can," said several of the men.

"While you're here," said Fletchall, "I'd like to announce a muster of my militia regiment for next week. I suggest that you officers from other regiments do the same. Most of the Low Country militia have gone over to the Congress."

"The treasonous dogs!" exclaimed Moses Kirkland.

"Talk to your men," Fletchall continued. "We want to be ready for Drayton and Tennent when they come to the Upper Saluda."

"I'm glad to know we have so many good Englishmen in Carolina who will not desert their King," said Brown as the meeting broke up.

Thomas Brown crossed the river near Fort James to talk to the Georgia militiamen there. As he travelled down through the Purchase he talked to settlers in each hamlet and trading post, hinting that they'd be wiser to stay with the King who had the Indians as allies. By the time he arrived in Brownsborough, word had spread back to Augusta that Brown was enlisting Loyalists against the Association and threatening Indian massacres to those who joined.

·XVI·

TAR AND
FEATHERS

O n the evening of August first, the crowd gathered at the Liberty
Pole on the Common had grown to almost two hundred. Backwoodsmen from the Purchase, local barflies, a scattering of black slaves
and freedmen out to watch the excitement, and a few militiamen with
orders to report to Colonel Grierson if the meeting became too rowdy,
stood around the pole to listen to the speeches. The day had been
sweltering and hardly a breeze stirred the oak leaves. Lightning played
across the sky in the west and thunder rumbled, but there was no let up
in the heat. A big tub of grog sat on a boulder under the trees, the sugar
and lime juice disguising the potency of the rum as the thirsty crowd
filled their cups.

The Merrills had invited the Griersons and Dr. and Mrs. Johnston to
supper. John Stanley had come in from the Ninety-Six District the day
before, after a trip to his property in the mountains.

Pleasantly full of fried chicken and rice with field peas, hot biscuits,
and suppernong preserves, the men had adjourned to the porch overlooking the river in hopes of an evening breeze.

"Tell us about he Carolinians," said Joseph Merrill. "Are the men in
Ninety-Six stirred up as they are here?"

Drum rattles could be heard from the direction of the Common and
occasional shouts and loud laughter.

"They're as mixed in their feelings as everyone else," said John. "Some
of my friends from Regulator days are leaning toward the Association,
and others are standing up for the King. Jim Mayson, Will Wofford, and
Tom Woodward, three of my best friends, were representatives at the
South Carolina Provincial Congress, and Jim's being held in the jail in
Ninety-Six village now for trying to confiscate the powder and shot from
Fort Charlotte."

"I thought the Upper Saluda people were loyal," said Grierson. "Their militia companies refused to sign the Association."

"None of them likes the rumor that the Indians are to be turned loose on the frontier. That powder and shot that Jim tried to steal was going to be sent to the Cherokees by the rebels to try to bring them around against the King."

"But I thought the rebels were against giving anything to the Indians."

"Stuart had been keeping their supplies of powder low to discourage their going on the warpath," said John. "Congress thought they could bribe them into fighting on the side of the settlers."

"It doesn't make sense," exclaimed the doctor.

"Does any of this rebellion?" Grierson asked.

Just then there was a flurry of footsteps on the front walk, and a young man in buckskins came running up the steps. From the Common the noise of shouting had grown louder. Drums were beating and horses whinnying.

The militiamen came to attention in front of Colonel Grierson, who had risen with the rest.

"Sir, you asked me to report any sign of riot. They're all drunk as billy goats, and they're going out to tar and feather Squire Brown if he won't sign the Association."

"My God!" exclaimed Joseph Merrill.

"We'll call up the militia immediately, Corporal," said Grierson.

"Sir, they're most of them in the crowd," said the corporal, "or they've gone home drunk."

"Take my horse," said Grierson, "the gray down at the hitching rail, and ride around to any members of the outfit who may be sober. Give them the order to alert anyone else they can find and report to Fort Grierson."

"Sir, I don't want a coat of tar, myself!"

"Stay away from the crowd, but call on anyone in the regiment you think may have guts enough to help."

"Yes, sir," said the corporal, saluting and hurrying down the steps.

John turned to Joseph Merrill. "I think we'd better follow the crowd and help Brown if we can. But if it's the mob it sounds to be, we'd better stay at a distance till the militia or other help comes. I've seen innocent bystanders shot or beaten during the Regulator troubles when the mob was drunk."

"I have medicines in my saddlebags," said Dr. Johnston. "I'll come with you. I'm afraid my services will be needed before the night is over."

It took a few minutes for Merrill and Stanley to get into breeches and boots and to check their pistols and ammunition belts. Joseph had no experience with mobs, but knew John to be a seasoned frontier fighter. Surely with the help of Brown's people, they could stop the mob.

By the time the three were mounted and had started down Broad Street, there was no sign of the Liberty Boys except a few drunks who had fallen by the wayside and were peacefully sleeping in the ditches.

As they came to Campbell's Gully and the Sword and Thistle, Angus was standing out beside the road, resting on his crutch, looking north.

"Ho, there!" he called, "Jamie Stratfield's gone on. You should meet him at Rae's Creek. He's going to get Sheldon to help."

"Did you get a look at the mob?" Joseph Merrill asked, reining in his horse.

"Saw and heard them, and they bode no good," Angus exclaimed. "I was afraid they'd turn into the inn yard and ransack the place; but they were yelling and carrying on about Thomas Brown. They had a wagon loaded with old featherbeds and barrels of tar."

"How many are there?" John asked.

"Well over a hundred, I'd guess," said Angus, "and most of them are armed with staves and cudgels. Some had pistols in their belts."

"Maybe they'll sober up before they get out to Brownsborough," Merrill said hopefully.

"Little chance," said Angus. "There's liquor in one of those barrels in the wagon. I saw a man filling tankards and passing them down. Chesley Bostick was driving the wagon and cheering them on."

"That son of a bitch," said Merrill. "He's pushed himself up to the top of the very worst element in town."

"Let's get on with it," said John spurring his horse, "if we want to join Jamie and Bert." They put their horses to a canter, then an extended gallop toward Rae's Creek, but then saw the glow in the sky.

"That's the Sheldon's farm," said John. "It must be the still, from the way those flames are shooting."

They whipped their horses on and turned into the farm road. The house seemed safe, though the woods behind it were blazing. They could see figures silhouetted against the flames chopping at the brush behind the house. Nothing remained of the shed where Ben had his still except the stone chimney and a few upright posts that had held the roof.

The horses plunged and reared as they approached the fire, and Stanley and Johnston dismounted, giving their reins to Merrill who led the horses back to tether at the edge of an open field. Johnston slung his saddlebags over his shoulder as he hurried to the house.

"Thank God!" said Mary from the door. "Ben's been shot, and Bert's had a blow on the head."

The two men found Ben lying on the bed, his right shoulder wrapped in bloodsoaked cloths. Bert was nowhere to be seen, and Francie sat sobbing on the hearth holding a white-and-black hound in her arms.

"Bert's with Jamie trying to put out the fire," said Mary.

"I'll leave Dr. Johnston with you," said John. "Have you an axe?"

"No, Bert has it, but there's a blanket by the bed you can soak in the creek."

John grabbed the blanket and ran to the door. They heard him calling Merrill to help, too.

Ben was weak from loss of blood, but the wound was clean. The bullet had broken his collarbone and exited through his shoulder muscle. In a short time, the doctor had stopped the bleeding and dressed the wound.

"The drunken ruffians came barreling in here," said Ben, "ten or twelve of them wanting whisky. Said they had orders from Chesley Bostick to confiscate the drink in the name of liberty. When I told them to go to hell, they started for the still, and when I tried to slam the door, one of them shot me in the shoulder. Bert interfered, and they hit him over the head with a club. By the time Bert had come to and he and Mary had dragged me inside, the rebels had stolen God knows how much whisky and set the shed afire."

"Why did they have to hurt Bo?" Francie sobbed. "He was just barking."

"Let me see," said Johnston squatting beside the girl on the hearth rug.

The hound rolled its eyes in misery as the doctor gently felt the gash on its head then ran his fingers along its body. When he touched its hind leg, Bo ky-yied in pain.

"Do you have any whisky here in the house?" the doctor asked.

"There's a jug in the larder," Mary answered.

"Pour a cup for Ben and one for me, please," said Johnston. "We can both use a sip, and I'll give some to Bo so he won't bite me when I sew up his head." Pouring the whisky on a piece of rag, he held it over the wounded dog's muzzle until it stopped struggling, then quickly stitched up the gash in its head. With a piece of kindling from the hearth basket, he aligned the injured leg, wrapping them together so the leg was kept straight.

"Try to keep him down, even when he feels better," he said to Francie, "and keep cool, wet rags on his leg tonight. He may limp, the rest of his life, but I believe he'll live to a happy old age."

Francie was too choked-up to talk, but she put her arms around the doctor's neck and sobbed into his shoulder.

Mary turned from the door. "They've put out the fire," she said.

Bert came in first, his head tied in a bloody kerchief, his eyelashes and hair singed.

"I'll shoot those bloody bastards if they ever come near here again," he said, "I'm sorry, Mother. Close your ears, too, Francie."

"Let me see that head," said the doctor. Feeling Bert's bloodsoaked crown gently, he said, "You'll have a big lump there tomorrow, lad, but the skull doesn't seem to be cracked."

"It would take more than a drunken bum to crack that hard head," said Ben, feeling much better after his shot of whisky. "Thank you, doctor, for taking care of all three of us, and if you'll keep it to yourself, I've several barrels of corn whisky aging where I hope no one will find it, as well as Angus's ouisgebaugh. I haven't much in the way of money, but I'll see you don't go thirsty."

"Thank you, Ben," said the doctor. "I'll gladly wait for the drink to mellow. I'll be back in a day or so to see you, in case the wound festers. I've left a wick to drain it, but send Bert for me if you get a fever."

"Let's get on to Brownsborough," said John.

"Oh, Lord!" said Jamie. "I'd forgotten. Squire Brown is no match for that crowd of ruffians, even with his bondsmen to back him up. He'll never sign the Association."

"God grant they've sobered up some," said Ben, "or there'll be more for Doctor to patch up tonight."

"Bert, you stay here," said Johnston. "Sometimes a head blow makes a man weak, and I don't want to worry about you. Give them both plenty of water, Mrs. Sheldon. Francie, you keep your dog's leg cool." Closing his saddlebags and donning his tricorne, he hurried after the three young men.

Long before they reached Brownsborough, they knew they were too late. They could hear the banging of drums and shouts and catcalls before they saw the torches that lighted the procession. Moving into a clump of trees, the four men dismounted. With all the noise, there was little chance of their being heard.

At the head of the procession was a small cart drawn by a mule, with what looked like a large white bird slumped on a bench, wings tied together behind its back.

"God have mercy!" exclaimed the doctor, starting forward.

"You can't go now," said John Stanley catching him around the shoulders and chest. "They wouldn't let you near him."

The procession straggled on with several carts and wagons loaded with furniture and food, oil paintings in gold frames, and a crystal chandelier. In one of the carts a man lay with his leg bandaged, and several of the other men had bandaged heads.

"We'll have to stay hidden and watch for a chance to help," said Jamie.

"You know the country and the militiamen, Jamie," said John. "We'll stay with the mob and watch for a chance to get to him. You ride ahead and see if you can bring help from town."

Jamie nodded and remounted, looking for the path that led along the river, parallel to the road to Augusta. He could hear the crowd and see the glow of their torches as he pushed through the undergrowth under the tall pines. He thanked God he had learned the way during Brown's survey.

John and Joseph and the doctor were ready to mount when they saw a lone horseman riding close to the trees in the direction of town. Riding out onto the road, John called, "Who goes there?"

The horseman quickly spurred his mount into the woods, snatching his rifle from the boot on his saddle as he rode.

"We're not highwaymen," shouted John. "It's John Stanley, Dr. Johnston, and Joseph Merrill." They stood in the roadway lighted by the moon.

"Thank the Lord it's you, Mr. Stanley," a voice called, and Jeremy Potter rode out of the trees, his head wrapped in a stained white cloth and his clothes mottled with dried blood.

"They've taken Squire, sir," said Jeremy, tears streaming down his cheeks. "Them bloody bastards is worse than Indians!"

"We saw him in the cart," said John.

"How badly is he hurt?" Andrew Johnston asked. "I saw a bandage on his head, and I know he must be burned from the tar."

"Aye, he is sore wounded," said Jeremy. "They come howling up to the manor like a pack of wolves with that man Bostick at the head. Squire come out on the front stoop and ordered them off his property, and Bostick called out, 'We've no use for King's spies in Georgia. Sign the Association or get out of the country.'"

" 'That would be treason,' said Squire. 'I'll not betray my King.'

" 'Get 'im men!' Bostick yelled, and they started up the stairs in a crowd.

" 'Stop right there,' calls Squire, an' when they come on, takes 'is sword and pistols down from the wall an' shoots Bostick in the leg. That stopped 'em for a minute, but then they swarmed like ants in treacle. I'd come up to the big house when I heard the noise an' I'd a cudgel, but some whoreson caught me a clout from behind before I'd more 'n started splitting heads.

"I couldn't ha' been out more 'n a few seconds. Squire were holding 'em off wi' his sword, backing into the house. Then some bloody ruffian sneaked around through a window an' hit Squire in back o' his head with a rifle. You could hear his skull crack."

"The bloody murdering savages!" said John.

"Savages they be," said Potter. "One o' them took out his knife an' started to scalp Squire, like an Injun.

"Someone in the crowd grabbed that man, an' others yelled, 'Save 'im for his tar bath!'

"I tried to crawl to him, but they hit me again an' that time, I stayed out. When I came to, the crowd was all out in the yard, an' squire were tied in a cart, all covered wi' tar an' feathers, an' the ruffians were stealing everything in the house an' barns. I kept low an' crawled back toward our cottage, but Anne called from the bushes. She'd hidden when they came to our door an' watched 'em. But we had naught they wanted."

"What of the rest of Brown's men?" Joseph asked. "We had hoped they would stand up to the crowd."

"Many o' them were in the crowd," said Jeremy, "the ungrateful scoundrels. An' many lived too far back in the woods to get there in time. They're stayin' wi' Anne, while I follow Squire."

"Mr. Stratfield's ridden in to try to raise the militia," said John.

"And we'd better be getting on," said Dr. Johnston. "Brown's going to need me."

"God grant he lives that long," said Jeremy.

The torch light was no longer red in the sky, and the four men set off at a gallop.

Meanwhile Jamie had reached Grierson's Fort. There had been stretches where he could gallop along the river path, and he had cut through the woods to the main road when he was sure he had passed the mob. Now he found the fort empty, except for a sleeping militia man who reeked of rum, so he rode on to the Sword and Thistle.

"Has anyone seen Colonel Grierson?" he called to the few men at the bar. "They've tarred and feathered Squire Brown, and they're bringing him to town."

"We heard the crowd going out the road, but we hoped they were so drunk they'd fall out before they got far," said Martin Weatherford, who had come to the door from the bar.

"Grierson wasn't at the fort," said Jamie. "What's happened to the militia?"

"Lying low," said Angus.

"I've been riding all over town," said Weatherford, "but most of the company have either joined that drunken crowd or refuse to help. They say they'll fight Indians but won't fight the Liberty Boys."

"Damn the treasonous scoundrels," said Angus. "Grierson came by almost an hour ago looking for militiamen, but he's gone into town to try to rally any he can find at the old fort."

"If we can find out what they plan when they get Brown to town, maybe we can help," said Weatherford.

"They're so drunk they probably don't have a plan," said Jamie.

"I've been to their meetings and they trust me," Weatherford said. "I'll admit I think their fight for liberty has merit. But Squire Brown's liberty is important, too. I'll do my best to see him freed."

The distant sounds of drums and shouting could now be heard from the Cherokee Road.

"Could you join the crowd when they come? Maybe you could talk some sense into them?"

"You'd better not be seen at the Sword and Thistle," said Angus. "The Liberty Boys know we're friends of the Squire."

"I'll ride in and see if Colonel Grierson has had any luck," said Jamie. "I'll talk to any men he's collected and see if we can figure a way to help Brown escape."

"I'll go along the road with you a bit and join the crowd as they come into town," said Weatherford.

Jamie found James Grierson on the Common with three sleepy young militiamen, standing under an oak tree, listening to the approaching mob.

"Godamighty," said one of the men. "I ain't gonna try to stop that crowd."

"They should all be horsewhipped or hanged," said Grierson.

"There's no way the five of us can do it," Jamie said. "Martin Weatherford has a plan to help Brown, but he will need to be able to find you. Will you wait at the old fort and send your militiamen to help us carry Brown if we get the chance?"

"What is Martin's plan?" Grierson asked.

"To try to turn them toward his farm at the end of town. They should all be tired and, with the help of more liquor, may be persuaded to give up for the night."

"Brown will need medical care," said Grierson. "Dr. Johnston is not at home."

"He and John Stanley are with Joseph Merrill and are to meet me at Merrill's house. They're following the crowd hoping for a chance to help Brown."

Martin Weatherford had worked his way into the crowd surrounding the mule-pulled cart.

"Hey, Weatherford, where you been?" a bearded ruffian asked. "We're goin' to make the damn King lover sign the 'Sociation where everybody in town can see."

"I just came in from the country," said Weatherford. "He doesn't look like he could sign anything!"

"Oh, he'll perk up once we get him out of the cart an' warm his feet a bit," said the man.

Brown was slumped forward, his head touching his knees, his hands still tied behind him. Blood from his head wound had run down over his knees, staining the feathers that were stuck all over his legs.

"What do you mean, warm him?" Weatherford asked.

"Back in the days before the Regulators put us out of business," said the man, "we used lightwood kindlin' to persuade miserly storekeepers to give up their money. We figger Brown will sign anything once his toes begin to sizzle."

Weatherford suppressed a shudder. "Where are you going with him?" he asked.

"Somewhere near the end of town. We want everybody in Augusta to have a chance to see the high and mighty nabob put in his place."

"Why not take him to my farm?" Weatherford asked. "I've a barrel of rum hidden away."

"Hey lads!" the man shouted. "Weatherford has a keg of rum at his farm. Let's go!"

Cheers from voices now grown hoarse greeted the suggestion, and the driver of the cart cracked his whip to hurry the mule. The prisoner, jolted out of position, sat up and braced his feet on the floor of the cart, his eyes staring feverishly at those around him.

The cart came to a halt in Weatherford's field and Brown was dragged out between two backwoodsmen. He was hardly able to walk, and his arms had lost all feeling. The men half carried him to a tree at the edge of the field and stood him against it, wrapping him with ropes to keep him from slipping down. A bonfire was lighted nearby.

One of the men who, with Chesley Bostick, had led the pack at Brownsboro brandished a sheet of paper and a pen. "Thomas Brown," he said, "will you sign the Association paper?"

Brown raised his head and spat on the paper.

The man slapped Brown across the face with all his strength, and he slumped in the ropes.

"God damn you, I'll make you sign," said the man snatching a burning piece of pitch pine from the bonfire. Carrying it back to the tree, he leaned down and thrust it into the tar and feathers that covered Brown's feet. The tar bubbled and caught fire, and the semiconscious prisoner shrieked in pain, then reached for the paper.

Martin Weatherford, watching but afraid to intervene, hurried to sluice the flames with a bucket of water, stopping the fire from spreading up Brown's legs.

The crowd had grown suddenly quiet. Brown reached for the pen, which he could hardly hold, and marked an X on the paper.

"Make him denounce the King," shouted one of the ruffians.

"He's passed out," said Weatherford. "Why not leave him till tomorrow? There's a barrel of rum in my barn."

The crowd, distracted and some secretly ashamed of the night's work, staggered off toward the barn with Weatherford leading the way. The man holding the paper watched the mob retreat, then called to two men in buckskins standing nearby.

"Carry the prisoner to the shed over there," he said, "and watch him till we're ready for him. Mind you don't let him get away."

"He's passed out again," said one of the men.

"I reckon he couldn't get far on those feet, but you keep an eye on him till we get back." and he hurried off to get a drink before the rum was gone.

The two men, who had been sent by James Grierson, carefully untied the ropes and lowered the unconscious man to the ground, then taking him under the arms and legs, hurried toward the shed. The moon had gone down.

* * *

Thomas Brown lay in Jocelyn Merrill's guestroom bed, swathed in bandages soaked in goose grease. They had slipped his tar-covered clothes from him in Weatherford's shed, leaving them wrapped around a sack of feed and covered with a blanket in case someone came to check on him. There were a few hours before sunrise.

Fortunately the mob had not taken the time to strip him before dousing him in tar. He was young and physically fit and, with the help of his two guards, could be put on a horse and led to the house on the river.

Andrew Johnston closed his bag and came to sit beside the bed. "You'll not be able to wear boots for a long time," he said, "and you may lose some toes, but you'll live," he said.

"I'll live to make every bloody rebel sorry," said Brown.

"It's your safety we're worried about now," said John Stanley, coming to the bedside. "Last night they were threatening to force you to denounce the King. We've got to get you out of here before they find you're not in that shed."

"I've been thinking about it while Johnston was bandaging my feet. Thank God the tar didn't reach the insides of my legs or my arse. I think I can ride. I'll go to Fair Forest to Thomas Fletchall. The loyal militia there will help me."

"I'll ride with you," said John Stanley, "and we can stop along the way if you are too weak. I have friends among the farmers who will take you in and say nothing about it."

Brown sat up on the side of the bed, but turned pale with pain as the blood rushed into his feet.

"Don't try to put them to the floor," said the doctor. "Stanley and Stratfield can make a seat with their hands and carry you down. You'll stay off your feet for at least two weeks if you want them to heal."

Jeremy Potter was waiting with the horses saddled.

"I'd like to come with you, sir," he said.

"You're a loyal friend," said Brown, "but I'd rather you stay at Brownsborough. "Your cottage and garden plot are in your name on the books of the colony. No one can take them from you. I may need your help later."

"Thank you, sir," said Jeremy.

Jamie and John Stanley heaved Brown onto the horse, with his bandaged legs hanging free. Jeremy opened the stable door, and they rode at a walk along the edge of the road, grass muffling the noise of the hoofs, then turned down the riverbank behind the church. The river was so low from the August drought that they walked their horses for a long distance, then swam them across the narrow channel, and clambered up the bank on the Carolina side. Waving to Jeremy and Jamie, who were watching from a clump of trees behind the church, Brown and Stanley started along the road to Ninety-Six.

Three nights later, they arrived at Thomas Fletchall's farm. Brown was bone weary, the burns on his feet terribly swollen and beginning to fester, but his head wounds were nearly healed. They had ridden at night, sleeping during the daylight hours in the cabins of John's trusted friends and sharing their corn and greens and salt pork, letting the horses graze in their fields.

"It's better not to tell them your name or the way you were wounded," John had told Brown on the first morning when they had ridden up to Stuart's fort. "They are kindly people who care nothing for politics and will forget we have been here, if I ask them to. But the less they know, the less likely they are to talk."

"Surely they'll be curious about these bandages," Brown exclaimed.

"Frontiersmen don't ask questions," John answered. "Everyone has something he wants to keep hidden."

As John had expected, the Stuarts and the Walkers, who took them in the next day, accepted without comment John's story that Brown had been in a fire and that they were riding at night to avoid the August heat. Both men had ridden with John during the Regulator troubles and knew him to be a man of honor.

When they rode up Fletchall's driveway in the early hours of the morning, they were met by a pack of hounds. Thomas Fletchall came out on the front gallery in his nightshirt, then hurried down the steps, shouting the dogs to silence, flailing about him with his hunting whip till they settled down and retreated under the house.

Brown, near exhaustion, stayed in his saddle while John dismounted and hitched his horse to the rail.

"My God!" exclaimed Fletchall, hurrying toward Brown, "what's happened to you?"

"He was tarred and feathered and damned near scalped by a mob in Augusta," said John. "We slipped across the river before they could torture him to death."

Fletchall looked at the bandaged feet and at the scarf wrapped around his head under his tricorne.

"The damned bloodthirsty savages," he said grimly. "But you're safe now and welcome to stay and be healed among friends."

"We're going to have to carry him up the steps," said John. "His feet were badly burned when they used fat-wood torches to make him sign the Association."

"My poor friend," said Fletchall, tears in his eyes, gripping Brown's hand.

"Call Sam to help you get Squire down from his horse," he called to a black man who had materialized from the cabin at the side of the house. "You two can carry him up to the guest room."

In a few minutes, Thomas Brown was tucked into the big canopy bed with a glass of brandy on the bedside table, the linen sheets cool against his inflamed skin. Propped up on pillows with his chest and shoulders bare and blistered, he reached for the glass and raised it to the two men at his bedside.

"Confusion to the bloody rebels. May they rot in hell," he said, taking a long draught. "By the good God, I'll do everything in my power to put them there."

POLITICS IN
THE CAPITAL

The next morning John left for Augusta, riding openly on the main
roads in daylight and stopping only for a meal and to rest his horse.
Under a bright moon, he was ferried across the Savannah near midnight
and rode into the Merrill's stableyard without meeting anyone. Lord
willing, no one but the Merrills and the others who had helped Brown
knew where he had been.

Before he had the horse unsaddled and rubbed down, the latch clicked
and Mary Anne was in his arms.

"I've hardly slept since you left," she said snuggling her head into his
shoulder, her hair streaming down over the shoulders of her night wrap.
"I was sure that was you when I heard you come into the yard."

"Then come along to bed," said John dousing the lantern and unlatch-
ing the door.

He and Mary Anne tiptoed to the kitchen where she found a slice of
ham in the larder and a loaf of bread. Then, drawing two cups of cider
from the cask in the corner, they crept up the stairs.

"How is Squire?" Mary Anne asked as John stripped off his travel-
stained clothes and poured water into the basin to wash his face and
hands.

"Much better than I expected," he answered slipping on his nightshirt
and sinking onto the settle in front of the cold fireplace to eat his supper.
"His head was nearly healed by the time we got to Fair Forest, and most
of the burns on his arms and legs were beginning to dry up when I left
him. Fletchall's handyman whittled out a pair of crutches, and Brown
was planning to try them out. He's so determined to punish the ruffians
who hurt him he was already talking about gathering a force to arrest
them."

"Do you think he will?"

"Lord knows," said John. "Fletchall was planning to call up his militia, and Moses Kirkland and Pat Cunningham were hell bent to help."

He finished his bread and cider and stood up, brushing the crumbs from his hands then pulling Mary Anne into his arms.

"In any case he's not coming tonight, and I'm going to crawl into that bed and sleep the clock around. Are you coming with me?"

*   *   *

Less than a week later, word came that Brown was riding to Augusta with a force of a hundred and fifty South Carolinians to arrest and punish the people who had persecuted him.

Chesley Bostick, still crippled by the shot from Brown's pistol, sent a messenger to George Wells in Savannah. John Wilson, the secretary of the Augusta Committee of Safety just organized by the Liberty Boys, confronted Colonel James Grierson in the bar at the Sword and Thistle and asked him to call out the militia for the defense of the town against Brown and his South Carolinians.

"I'll do no such thing," said Grierson. "I've had no official word of any attacking force, and as an officer of the Crown, I'll not call up the Georgia troops against South Carolina militia."

"But, sir," said Wilson, "they say that Brown has sworn to avenge his injuries by burning the town."

"Balderdash!" said Grierson. "Thomas Brown is an English gentleman, and Thomas Fletchall is in command of British militia. I have every confidence that they will treat any miscreants according to British law. As to burning the town, it is more likely that drunken Liberty Party people will burn it down with their torchlight parades."

Wilson looked around him at the interested barroom spectators, then turned and stamped down the steps to his horse.

Behind the bar, Angus and Jamie had been quiet. Now Colonel Grierson turned to Jamie. "Lieutenant," he said, "will you be so good as to ready yourself for a journey to Savannah as a messenger of the Crown? You'll be given full pay and rations as a militiaman."

"Yes, sir," said Jamie. "Must I go in uniform, sir?"

Grierson thought for a moment. If the man went in uniform, he could not be treated as a spy. On the other hand, if he went as a civilian, there was no reason for anyone to think he was on anything but personal business. It was dreadful to have to worry now about Americans mistreating other Americans.

"Dress as you like," he said finally. "I'll give you a letter for the governor which you may carry with your own possessions. It will be a request for instructions about the present situation and need not be hidden."

"Yes, sir," said Jamie starting to salute. Grierson caught his arm. "There's no use calling the attention of everyone in the tavern to the fact you're traveling under orders."

"No, sir," said Jamie going around the end of the bar to collect tankards from an empty table. Removing his apron, he went out through the back door.

He and Chesley Bostick's messenger both spent the night at a wayside tavern on the Savannah road, sitting amicably on the front porch, in the cool of the evening and leaving early the next morning. As far as either of them knew or cared, the other was going south on business.

Jamie rode through the pine barrens and into the swampland before dark. Camping on high ground for the night, he rode into Savannah at noon the third day.

Savannah was an anthill of activity. Men and boys were marching in the moss-hung squares to the sound of fife and drum. Some wore militia uniforms but more were in the everyday clothes of clerks, stableboys, carpenters, or fishmongers and carried everything from muskets to cudgels.

As he rode along the waterfront toward Robert MacKay's warehouse on Bay Street, Jamie could hardly believe this was the same port he had visited the year before. The docks were deserted except for a few men standing watch on the ships tied at the piers. Gulls and pelicans roosted in the rigging or flapped lazily over the garbage-strewn water searching for tidbits. He had heard that the Continental Congress had ordered the port closed, even to the export of rice, but remembering the smuggling that had gone on after Parliament's orders, he had expected Savannah to ignore congressional orders as well.

MacKay greeted him at the warehouse door, calling the office boy to run down to the bakery for buns to go with the coffee brewing in the copper pot on the hearth.

"God only knows what we'll do for coffee when this last shipment is gone," said MacKay, handing Jamie a cup and offering him a chair beside the empty hearth.

"I can't believe it is Savannah," Jamie said. "Are merchants so fired up for liberty that they forget their empty pocketbooks?"

"Liberty, nothing," said MacKay. "They're afraid of a coat of tar and feathers, of being beaten to a pulp, or having their ships sunk. The King's ships won't allow trade with New England, and Congress won't allow trade with old England or the islands. I'm tired of sitting here on my backside with nothing to do, but I'm afraid to go back to Augusta for fear this warehouse will go up in flames.

"Have you seen Mary? She writes as often as she can find someone to carry her letters."

"I'm sorry I hadn't time to contact her before I left," Jamie said. "Colonel Grierson sent me here on militia business. I have to talk to Governor Wright, but I thought I'd check with you first to see how things stand between the governor and the council."

"At the present moment there are two councils, the Royal Council and the Council of Safety, and Sir James Wright is walking a tightrope between them.

"It is a farce. Half of the Royal Council members are members of the Liberty Party, too. The militia companies have all been taken over by the Liberty Party. About the only power left to the governor is the Chancery Court. They let him prove wills and grant letters of administration. I'm afraid it's only a matter of time until they throw him out altogether."

Jamie sipped his coffee silently, then leaned forward to look MacKay full in the face. "And where do you stand, sir?"

"God only knows," MacKay answered, slowly shaking his head. "I haven't any use for the rabble who are shouting 'liberty' and using it as an excuse to bully and burn and rob. But I have talked to Glascock and Habersham and Walton; they're all intelligent, educated men. They see a chance to make America into a well-governed, prosperous country without any of the old, worn-out prejudices of England. Many of the young bloods here and in Charlestown have gone to school and read law in England. They say the old establishment is rotten to the core. They've almost persuaded me we can do better alone."

"I'm afraid," said Jamie, "that my impression of the Liberty Party comes from people like George Wells and Chesley Bostick. I suppose you could say they're educated, but they're poison. You know, don't you, what has happened to Thomas Brown?"

"I haven't seen him since he was here in January," said MacKay.

"Chesley Bostick and his henchmen tarred and feathered him and damned near scalped him," said Jamie. "The drunken mob sacked his house and dragged him back to Augusta in a cart, then burned his feet with pine splinters to make him sign the Association."

"Lord God Almighty!" exclaimed MacKay, jumping up from his chair and striding up and down the room waving his arms. "Of all the men in

Georgia he's least deserving of that sort of treatment. Those bloody ruffians! Where is he now?"

"That's why I've come to talk to Governor Wright," said Jamie. "He was able to escape to South Carolina to recuperate. Now the word is that he is about to attack Augusta with the aid of loyal South Carolina militiamen to take vengeance on his tormentors."

"Attack Augusta?" MacKay asked incredulously. "Carolina militia attacking Georgians?"

"The Augusta Liberty Party is trying to make Colonel Grierson call up Saint Paul's militia to defend the city, but he refuses. He's asked me to get the governor's approval. That's why I'm here. And it's time I was on my way to Government House."

"Come to my house when you've seen the governor," MacKay said. "I have a cook who can make shrimp and rice taste like nectar and ambrosia."

"Thank you, sir," said Jamie. "I was hoping your invitation was still good. And I'd rather you didn't mention why I'm here, although I'm going openly to the governor's office. The less comment, the better."

Governor Wright, hearing that Jamie had official news from Colonel Grierson, had him shown in ahead of some twenty-five or thirty grumbling citizens waiting in the anteroom. He waved Jamie to a chair, received Grierson's letter, quickly scratched an answer, sanded, folded it, and affixed his seal.

"I'm giving Colonel Grierson authority to do as he thinks best," said the governor. "He's a loyal Englishman and has shown discretion in the past."

"I'm afraid most of the militiamen are not so loyal," said Jamie. "They'll serve against an Indian attack, but I wouldn't trust them not to attack the King's forces under Thomas Brown."

"God help us," said the governor. "I don't see how we can help ourselves now. This rebellion is getting out of hand."

That night after supper, Jamie smoked a cigar in the MacKay garden watching silver moss sway in the breeze.

"Would you mind taking a note to Mary for me?" MacKay asked. "I'm worried about her being there without me. I had thought to keep her away from the strife here in Savannah, but it seems to be getting almost as bad there.

"Thomas Brown used to stop in on his way to and from Brownsborough to check on the store and cheer Mary up. He's been a good friend. Now I'm afraid the mob may turn on Mary."

"I'll be glad to help any way I can," Jamie said.

"If you'll give her my letter and tell her to be ready to move, I'll be eternally grateful. I think I'll write to George Galphin by the next post and see if she can stay with them out at Moore's Bluff."

"Perhaps things will settle down in Augusta," said Jamie.

"Not bloody likely," said MacKay. "I dropped into Tondee's this afternoon and heard that Habersham's calling up the Congress militia to fight the South Carolinians if Brown attacks in Augusta. They are to march to Augusta as soon as they're ready."

"I'm leaving at sunup," said Jamie. "I'll try to get word to Brown somehow. Maybe we can avoid bloodshed."

"It should take several days for the militia to get moving," said MacKay. "They've had little practice getting supplies and transportation organized. They're not like our backwoods Indian fighters. You should be there well ahead of them."

"Then I'd better get to bed now, so I can push through tomorrow."

The next two days were bone wearying. Galloping much of the way, slowing to a walk only when he and the bay were winded, he made it to Augusta in two days.

Meg, watching from the front porch, hurried to the steps. Jamie swung from the saddle, knotted the reins, and swatted the gelding's rump to hurry him toward the stable, calling to Desmond to rub him down and feed him. Striding to meet Meg, he pulled her gently into his arms and held her close.

"I'm so glad you're here," she sighed. "I think this is going to be the day. Mary Sheldon's here and says the way my back's been aching low down, it has to be soon."

"I hurried all the way," said Jamie. "But now I have to get in touch with Squire Brown fast. I'll just have to grab a bite and climb on a fresh horse."

"Oh, no, Jamie," Meg said, clinging to him.

"I have to warn the squire that Savannah is sending militia to stop him."

Entering the tavern through the back door, Jamie saw Bert Sheldon standing at the bar talking to Angus.

"You don't know how glad we are to see you," he said, gripping Jamie's arm. "The whole town is in an uproar about the South Carolina Loyalists, and Mother's sure Meg's going to have her baby, and Colonel Grierson's trying to keep the peace with half the boys wanting to help Brown and half of them wanting to shoot him."

"Where is Brown?" Jamie asked.

"We've heard he's camped over across the river waiting to burn the town, but I think that's a lot of hogwash."

"Do you think you could find him?"

"I have the feeling that Jeremy Potter may know where he is. He's out in the tap room at a table by himself."

"I'm going in the back dining room," said Jamie. "Meg, you wait a minute or two, then offer to fill Potter's glass and tell him to go out the front door, then come in the back when no one's looking." Gripping Bert's arm and talking casually, he strolled to the dining room. In a few minutes, Potter joined them there.

Stratfield rose from the table and shook Jeremy Potter's hand. "Thank you for coming," he said to the Yorkshireman. "I was hoping you might know of Squire Brown's whereabouts. I have to get a message to him right away."

"I learned in Savannah that the Council of Safety is sending a large force from Savannah to confront the South Carolina militia. I think Brown should know what he is up against."

Bert added, "The Liberty Party here in Augusta is gathering recruits from the old militia company, too. They tried to get me to join up."

Potter looked from one to the other, then nodded his head. "I believe I can get the message through," he said. "Squire told me to come here and listen for news. I am to ride out to his camp late tonight."

"Then do as he told you. That's soon enough. You can't tell about the politics of the men out in that tap room. Go on home now, and be careful tonight." Jamie shook his hand again, and Potter put on his hat and left.

Meg was waiting in their room on the second floor, her feet propped on a stool, the breeze from the river billowing the curtains and cooling the perspiration on her forehead. Mary Sheldon rose from the settle by the hearth when she heard Jamie's steps outside the door, but Meg asked her to stay.

Jamie bent over Meg's chair and kissed her forehead, then squatted on the floor beside her.

"How're you feeling?" he asked, noticing the swollen ankles, the flushed cheeks, the wet tendrils of hair on her brow.

"I'm getting these funny pressing feelings in my back, and I feel as though I'm going to pop wide open. Mary says things should start for real pretty soon."

"Don't you want me to get Dr. Johnston?" he asked worriedly.

"Of course not," said Meg. "I don't want a man mixing in woman's work. Mary has had three babies, and she's helped women birth their babies in the wilderness. This is the job that the Lord made me for. You can stay till I tell you to go and then you can wait downstairs."

"Maybe I'd better go now," said Jamie. "You don't seem to need me here." Meg leaned toward him to be kissed, then sent him on his way.

Going downstairs to the tap room, he wasn't sure whether to be annoyed or relieved.

Angus and Bert were talking at the bar. "She's going to be all right, laddie," said her uncle. "She's of good, tough Highland stock who've birthed their bairns for hundreds of years without help."

Jamie turned to Bert. "Would you do me a big favor? Ride into town to Dr. Andrew Johnston's and invite him to supper. God willing, he'll never have to leave the table, but I'll know he's here."

"Aye, lad," said Angus, nodding to Bert, "tell him I've smoked some fish he'll never know from Scottish salmon, and we can wash it down with real Scotch whisky, brought over before this damnable blockade."

Bert emptied his tankard and left by the back door.

Later that night, as Jamie and Angus and Bert sat with Andrew Johnston over their coffee and brandy, Amanda came bustling into the dining room wreathed in smiles. "Miss Meg, she tole me to send up the daddy of her new little boy," she said. "She kinda tired but mighty happy."

Jamie jumped from his chair and ran out onto the porch, taking the outdoor staircase two steps at a time. Andrew Johnston picked up the bag he had left on a chair by the door and turned to Angus. "Give your niece my best wishes," he said, "and accept my thanks for a real feast."

Angus reached into the pocket of his coat and handed the doctor a small leather sack that clinked as he dropped it into his hand. "You'll please take this," he said. "Even though you never saw the lass tonight. You've done more to ease my mind and Jamie's than you'll ever know."

The doctor started to return the sack, then thought better of it, dropping it unopened into his bag.

"When a Scot turns loose his money," he said, "I know he has given it thought. I'll not insult you by refusing, but hope I may be of service to you in the future."

Bert and Angus went back to the table to toast the father and his newborn son.

"We're naming him Angus," said Jamie when he finally returned, "and we want you and Bert to be godfathers."

"How's the lass feeling?" Angus asked.

"She's sound asleep now, with the little fellow in his cradle beside the bed," Jamie said proudly. "She says she had an easy time, and Mary said so, too."

"We need never tell her Dr. Johnston was here," said Angus. "It would fash her to know we worried."

Bert and Jamie nodded agreement as they filled their glasses for one more toast, "To Meg!"

The next morning word was brought by a traveler that the South Carolina militia had broken camp and were on the road back to Ninety-Six. One more alarm had proven false, and Augusta could settle down again to daily routine, with only the new Continental militia companies drilling on the Common to show that the city was feeling the swing toward liberty.

After the definite threat by the Carolinians, the Liberty Boys spent their time organizing defenses, strengthening stockades around the already fortified trading post, digging ditches, and throwing up walls to protect riflemen.

Bonfires and speeches became a thing of the past. The *Georgia Gazette* reported that William Davis of Augusta had been drummed around the Liberty Tree three times as a person "inimical to the rights and liberties of America," but there was no more mention of tar-and-feather episodes. People seemed to realize that battle lines were finally being drawn; there would be serious war, not drunken debauchery.

·XVIII·

RIVERSIDE
RENDEZVOUS

Late in August, rumors spread that George Galphin had been chosen as Superintendent of Indian Affairs for the Continental Congress. James Grierson and Lachlan McGillivray met him in the back dining room at the Sword and Thistle to talk it over.

"I'm going to accept," said Galphin, sticking out his jaw and looking defiantly from one to the other.

"But what of Stuart?" McGillivray asked. "He still holds the King's appointment."

"And he's banished to Florida, his wife and children held captive by the Congress to assure his cooperation," said Galphin. "Cameron's in the Cherokee country, and there's no one to watch over the Creeks."

"But, hell, George, you can't go over to the rebels," said McGillivray.

Galphin took a long swig of ale, then set his tankard on the table. "It looks to me," he said, "as though the rebels have the upper hand around here now. The Creeks know that, and they also know I'm their friend. If I can avoid bloodshed between Indians and whites, I'll take any sort of commission that anyone wants to give me."

"Even if it means committing treason?" Grierson asked.

"Treason be damned!" said Galphin, "You can't turn around these days that someone isn't hollering traitor or treason on one side or the other. I plan to sit tight and try to keep the peace."

"God help you," said Grierson, "when the King's troops put down this rebellion."

"God help us all," said Galphin. "I don't plan to stir up trouble for either loyalists or rebels. Pray God we can keep Augusta quiet."

"From the looks of those militiamen drilling on the Common, it will take the Almighty to keep the peace," said Grierson.

"As a Scot, I've no love for King George," said McGillivray, "but I'll not join the rebels, either."

"I'm still your friend," said Grierson, holding out his hand to Galphin, "but I'll not embrace your politics."

"So be it," said Galphin, rising and shaking both their hands. "You're always welcome at Moore's Bluff as long as you come in peace." Taking his hat from a peg and his riding whip from the bench, he strode out the door and rode off toward the river.

A few days later, Susan was sitting on the front porch with her mother and Mary Anne as Jocelyn bemoaned the fact that Henry Drayton, an old Charlestown friend, had not come to join the Reverend William Tennent, as planned. Tennent had been staying at Fox's tavern and making speeches on the Common while waiting for Drayton to join him in recruiting new signers for the Association. Jocelyn had made elaborate plans for a dinner party, with invitations waiting for the date to be penned in. Even though Drayton and Tennent were Association members, they were gentlemen of distinction. A hurried note from William Tennent this morning had said that he was on his way to Fort Charlotte where Drayton was calling up the Continental militia to fight Moses Kirkland's troops from Ninety-Six.

"I just can't believe all this is happening," said Jocelyn. "Why should the militias be fighting?"

Mary Anne shook her head and smiled. "You just can't seem to understand that things have changed. Moses Kirkland and the men around Ninety-Six don't want people to sign the Association, and Drayton and Tennent have been signing people up all over South Carolina."

"All this liberty business is so aggravating," said Jocelyn. "With Henry Drayton in favor of the Association, there must be some good in it."

Susan, disappointed about the party, was in a foul mood. "You've all thought I was being difficult when I told you what my friends in Charlestown were saying about wanting a chance to live a new life without having to bow down to the English. We can have our own gentry here and run our country without paying to keep the dirty old English lords in their castles."

Mary Anne counted the stitches in the sweater she was knitting. "I am afraid the backcountry people aren't anxious to have the coastal planters running their country," she said to Susan. "They would rather bow down to the King than to the planters, though I really can't see backwoodsmen bowing to anyone."

Jocelyn looked up from her needlepoint. "Mr. Tennent told us that a lot of John's friends had signed the Association, didn't he?"

"More than I would have believed," said Mary Anne, "but even John can see both sides. Most of them read Timothy's Charlestown paper. He writes whatever he pleases and he's a radical Whig. The *Georgia Gazette* is controlled by the governor, so the people who can read in Georgia see only the Tory side."

Susan made a mental note to lend some of her father's papers to Bert Sheldon. She and Mary Anne had gone riding with him once or twice and had found him quite intelligent. Now and then, when she took Betsy and Kate for a walk along the riverbank or strolled over to Saint Paul's to talk to Mr. Seymour, Bert would materialize from the old fort, where he was helping Colonel Grierson straighten out the papers left in the office there.

Bert was a Tory. He was devoted to Colonel Grierson and admired Thomas Brown. He'd like to see the Liberty Boys whipped and pilloried for shooting his father and burning his barn. But those were drunken ruffians. In Charlestown it would be different. Gentlemen planters wouldn't act that way.

Jocelyn and Mary Anne had changed the subject to knitting stitches and the advantages of wrapping babies loosely and letting them kick their legs over the old method of swaddling. The country people had thought they'd grow up crooked if their backs were not held rigid.

Susan excused herself and left them rocking on the porch. Running upstairs, she changed from her house slippers to her walking shoes and tied the yellow straw bonnet trimmed in daisies over her curls. Mother and Mary Anne would sit and chat for hours after that big dinner. She'd take a basket of stale bread to feed the ducks on the river or the pigeons in the trees along the bank.

As she had hoped, she was barely seated on the river bank when Bert appeared. He had found that he could watch the front porch of the Merrill house from an upper window in the fort and had seen Susan start for the river bank. For once she seemed to be by herself.

"Miss Merrill," he called, so as not to scare her coming up from behind. Her bonnet had fallen back, and her coppery curls fell around her face and onto her shoulders. The breeze from the water ruffled her hair and the lace on her dress. Looking back and up at him, her green eyes alive with mischief under the long dark lashes, she taunted, "No cats or children to save this time! How did you happen to come?"

"I saw you come by yourself and couldn't believe my good luck," said Bert. "Do you mind if I sit down?"

"And what would you do if I said I would mind?" Her smile and the light in her eyes belied any such intention.

"I'd not believe you," Bert answered, sitting on the grass beside her. A thicket behind him shielded them from view from the road.

It might be another year before he was alone with her again. Bert put his arm around her waist and drew her toward him ready to let her go if she seemed to object. Susan leaned forward, eyes closed, lips parted, and he gathered her into his arms.

Susan had been kissed in the garden in Charlestown while promenading with a planter's son and behind the palms in a ballroom, by another. It was the thing to do. But she had never felt the explosion that struck her now. From her lips down through her whole body, she was washed with liquid fire. Arching her back, she put her arms around Bert's neck and pressed herself against him, drawing him closer and parting her lips under his.

Bert leaned over her, his hand slipping up to the lace of her bodice, feeling the swelling of her breast, the softness of her throat. She didn't seem to mind.

He'd had his face slapped by tavern wenches or tumbled them in bed when they were willing, but this was the first time he had ever been this bold with a lady, except in dreams. But she was a lady, and, God willing, some day he'd have the right to love her. His body told him to bury his lips under the bodice, to kiss the soft white throat and eyes and all the unthinkable softnesses under her dimity dress. But it was broad daylight, and a boat might come along the river at any minute.

Susan had finally come to her senses, too. They drew apart at the same time, then looked deeply into each other's eyes and clung together again, this time without the driving passion of a kiss. Bert relaxed his arms, and Susan pushed gently against his chest, then moved over so she sat without touching him. They stared at the river in silence.

"I love you, Susan," Bert said, finally. "I know I haven't the right to ask for your love, but I want to spend my life loving you."

Susan looked at the sunlight on the river, avoiding his eyes. "My parents will never approve," she said, hating to hurt him. "My mother has talked of a good marriage for me since I was old enough to listen. I just don't see any hope."

"I've known that all along," said Bert. "But I've land up in the Purchase near Fort James. If I can make a success as a planter there, maybe they'll accept me."

Susan knew that a red clay farmer would never be the same as a rice planter to her mother. But John Stanley was an Upcountry farmer, and Mary Anne's family were Old Charlestown. Maybe she'd help.

"I'd better go back home before Mother sends Lissy to look for me," she said, standing and straightening her dress, tying her bonnet strings.

Bert drew her into his arms again, kissing her on the lips, but gently this time.

"I'm not going to give up," he said. "The whole world's in a turmoil now. Something is bound to happen to help us."

"There's no one else in this world I want to love," said Susan. "If I can't have you, I'll be unhappy all my life."

Tears in her eyes, she walked slowly up the bank toward home.

Mary Anne had been watching from the porch. She could knit without watching while Jocelyn had to look at her needlepoint. She had seen Susan go down to the river bank and had watched young Sheldon's approach from the direction of the fort. Now Susan was coming home looking dazed and starry eyed. God help the youngsters! Jocelyn would raise the roof if she realized.

"Susan," she called before the girl reached the steps, "Would you give a message to Saul for me? I want Star to have an extra ration of grain today, and it's almost feeding time."

Susan looked up at the porch as though coming out of a fog, then waved to Mary Anne and changed direction toward the back yard. By the time she had found Saul, she should be back in the real world. Mary Anne would have a cousin-to-cousin talk with her later.

* * *

Word trickled into Augusta the next week of a false alarm at Fort Charlotte.

Drayton had called in Provincial militia units from all over the Carolinas to prevent a takeover of the fort by Moses Kirkland's Loyalists only to find that Kirkland's troops had been disbanded. Furious at having been fooled, Drayton then ordered the arrest of Kirkland, Robert Cunningham, and Thomas Brown as ringleaders of the plot to discredit him. Knowing Thomas Fletchall to be more peaceful than the others, he sent him a message inviting the Loyalist leaders of the district to come in and negotiate.

Brown and Cunningham wanted to fight and tried to incite Fletchall and his men to send a strong reply to the rebels. Fletchall fortified himself with rum and, taking six officers from his command, rode into

Drayton's camp. A treaty was finally signed in which Loyalists agreed not to assist British troops that might be sent in, and Drayton promised to punish any Association signer who molested a non-signer.

Most lukewarm Loyalists in the area went home to sit out the war, but Thomas Brown was furious. When he found that he had little support among his South Carolina friends, he went to Florida which had become a strongly loyal British colony and joined the Royalist militia forces under Governor Tonyn. Robert Cunningham was accused of sedition and sent to prison in Charlestown. For the time being, Upcountry South Carolina was ruled by the Association.

·XIX·

POLITICS
AND PISTOLS

Harvest time and Christmas of 1775 passed in the Upcountry without
Indian alarms. Settlers in the New Purchase gathered in their crops,
and traders in Augusta filled their warehouses with pelts. Many citizens,
ashamed of the drunken brawl that had led to the torture of Thomas
Brown, avoided the meetings at the Liberty Pole. Local agitators like
Chesley Bostick and George Wells, finding that their following had
dwindled, spent much of their time in Savannah where the action was.

The Revolutionary Council in Savannah was expecting an attack by
British forces at any moment, so the Council of Safety ordered the arrest
of Governor Wright and members of the Royal Council. Major James
Habersham and twenty men of the Grenadier Company of the Savannah
militia broke into a meeting in the governor's residence and took all the
officials into custody, allowing the governor, who was well liked and
respected in spite of his politics, to remain in his home under guard. In
early February, the governor slipped past his guards and was spirited
away by boat to Tybee where he was welcomed aboard a British
battleship.

The rebels were finally in complete control and set about enforcing
rules and regulations for governing the province. Membership in the new
Provincial Congress had been apportioned to all the parishes and the
right to vote given to all who had paid taxes the year before. Now
munitions began to be brought into Georgia to arm the province for war.

One morning in early March, a group was gathered at Fox's Tavern
in Augusta. George Walton, just back from Savannah, was the center of
attention.

"Savannah people swore they'd burn the city and the rice vessels rather
than let them fall into British hands," Walton was saying.

"What rice vessels?" Joseph Merrill asked as he and John Stanley walked into the room. The barman drew two ales, and everyone began to explain at once.

Walton held up his hand for quiet, then filled in the newcomers. "The two British warships and the troopship anchored off Tybee that we heard about last month hadn't been able to get provisions. There were eight ships full of rice at the wharves in Savannah; so one night the warships sailed up the river, slipped by Hutchinson's Island, and seized several of the rice boats. Lachlan McIntosh and a group of Georgians and South Carolinians boarded the rest of them and set them afire. The British got away with two, and the Georgia boys dismantled the six that were left to keep them from getting away."

"Were there any casualties?" John Stanley asked.

"There was a lot of small-arms fire," said Walton, "and I heard there were a few people killed on both sides and some wounded. But the big news is that the whole adventure scared hell out of the Provincial Congress. They're planning to move to Augusta."

"To Augusta!" Merrill exclaimed. "Where in the name of Goshen will we put them?"

"Business will really boom," said Fox, going behind the bar to slake the crowd's thirst. "I will have to add rooms at the back."

Merrill and Stanley left the tavern and rode hurriedly home.

"How marvelous!" Jocelyn exclaimed when she had heard the news. "We'll be right in the center of things with all the Georgia statesmen here in Augusta."

"I thought you were against all this liberty talk," said Mary Anne.

"Of course, I don't want a crowd of ruffians ruling the country," said Jocelyn, "but men like Joseph Habersham and Noble Wymberly Jones are gentlemen. They'll keep the rabble in order."

"I guess there'll be a lot of Augusta people who agree with you," said her husband. "But we'd better learn to keep our mouths closed about rabble and ruffians."

On March first, the Provincial Congress convened in Augusta and elected John Wereat their Speaker. All the inns were jammed. Delegates who had friends in Augusta moved into guest rooms. Barns, sheds, and even haylofts became dormitories for families and servants who had come along.

As there were no public buildings large enough to hold general meetings, they were held in warehouses or out on the Common. Meetings of delegates, however, were held in the taverns on Broad Street with room for only a handful of spectators.

Fox's tavern was one of the several where they met. Joseph Merrill, an old customer and good friend of the innkeeper, was able to bring home bits of information.

"They've been working on a sort of constitution for Georgia," he told the family at supper one night. "Of course, we are still Englishmen with allegiance to the King, but there must be rules and regulations to insure such rights as being able to elect our own governor."

On April fifteenth, it was announced that the Rules and Regulations had been passed, and that Archibald Bulloch, president of the Congress, had been elected President and Commander in Chief of the new state of Georgia.

Susan Merrill was tired of all the talk of politics and resented the crowds in town. Before the government moved to Augusta, she had been free to walk on the river bank and along The Bay near home. Now she was not allowed to leave the house without Lissy or one of her parents as chaperone. Girls were being insulted, and even physically molested, on the streets.

Bert Sheldon still met her occasionally when she and the little girls walked with Lissy, but they never had a minute alone. Though Bert would certainly be able to protect her, she knew her mother would never approve of her seeing him alone.

It had just been fun to flirt with Bert until that day on the river bank. Now she woke in the morning hoping for even a glimpse of him, afraid to let her mother know.

With Augusta as the Provincial capital, there were no more Royal Militia companies in town. Most of the militiamen had joined the new Provincial militia to protect the city from Indian attack. Colonel Grierson, refusing to be involved in the new company, had closed the office in the old fort, and Bert had lost that excuse for being near the Merrill house. Besides, it was time to plow and plant the new crops on the farm at Rae's Creek.

Susan was recalled from her wool-gathering when she realized that the political discussion had stopped and that her mother must have asked her a question.

"I'm sorry, Mother, I wasn't listening," she said.

"I thought you'd be excited," said Jocelyn. "Your father suggests that we spend the summer in Charlestown."

"In Charlestown!" Susan exclaimed.

"Your father will drive us all down there when he goes on business. We'll take Lissy with us and stay with Grandmother Seabright on the Ashley River."

Susan was torn. Her Charlestown flirtations seemed shallow now that she'd found a real man. But all the fun of parties and picnics and oyster roasts under moss-hung trees came back in a flash. After all, it would only be a few months.

"When are we going?" she asked, beginning to plan the wardrobe she would take along.

"Your father plans to leave a week from Monday," said Jocelyn. "We'll take the carriage and the wagon to carry trunks and boxes. We should be there by the following Friday."

"Maybe I'll take my new sprigged muslin," Susan said. She had worn it to church on Sunday in case Bert was there. Now she'd be able to show it off to all her Charlestown friends.

Hearing the delight in Susan's voice, Mary Anne thought: "She's still a child at heart. The Sheldon boy will be crushed, but it may be for the best."

In May, George Galphin and the other Indian commissioners arranged for a meeting of the Creeks and Cherokees in Augusta. It was known that Thomas Brown was organizing a Loyalist force in Florida with Indians as auxiliary troops. Galphin hoped to convince the Indians that Augusta was still friendly under the Provincial Congress. Settlers from the Purchase were encouraged to remain at home, and taverns were ordered to curtail the sale of rum in town, in hopes there would be no anti-Indian incidents.

The Indians had already begun to drift into town when the Merrills crossed the river on the Sandbar Ferry. Small bands of Creeks were camped near Galphin's station at Moore's Bluff, and more family groups tramped along the Charlestown road. As the carriage and wagon approached, they moved to the side, and some even raised their hands in the sign for peace.

The Augusta conference was inconclusive. Greetings were exchanged, presents given, and promises of friendship made; but neither Creeks or Cherokees offered to fight against the British. Having learned the scorched-earth tactics of the English under Colonel Grant only fourteen years before, they were afraid to anger the British Lion. Their friend George Galphin said the Provincials were friends. They would wait and see.

Early in June, a merchant from Charlestown brought distressing news. A British fleet of warships and troop transports was headed for Charlestown to attack and occupy the city. General Charles Lee had been ordered there by George Washington to take command of Continental forces in the South. Builders were working night and day to complete a fort on Sullivan's Island across the harbor from Fort Johnson on James Island, so that artillery could catch any enemy vessel in a crossfire. There had been rumors that a fleet under Admiral Howe would sail south in April to attack North Carolina. Now the fleet was heading for Charlestown instead.

In two weeks, Joseph Merrill came back to Augusta leaving his family in Charlestown. The city was agog for news from the Low Country. Word had come over trading paths of a victory at Charlestown, but no one had details. Merrill had hardly washed the dust of the road from his hands and face before friends and acquaintances began to arrive.

Members of the Congress and Augusta merchants crowded onto the front porch, forgetting political differences in their eagerness to hear the news firsthand. The porch soon became a stage with Merrill the only speaker.

"I'll tell you," he said, standing by the porch railing with a drink in his hand, "everybody in Charlestown thought the jig was up. Admiral Howe knew about the unfinished fort on Sullivan's Island.

"A colonel named Moultrie was in command there, with some militia troops led by a Huguenot lieutenant from the swamps named Marion. General Lee took a look at the unfinished palisade built of green palmetto trunks and the inner quadrangle filled with nothing but sand and sent word to President Rutledge to abandon it. Rutledge had enough faith in Moultrie and Marion to veto the order.

"The English warships planned to sail to the back of the fort and bombard Moultrie's men through the unfinished palisade. But they didn't know about a reef there, and several ships ran aground. When they tried a frontal assault, the cannonballs bounced off the green palmetto logs, or, if the balls went into the fort, they buried themselves in the sand."

"Godamighty," said a man in buckskins who had come up the path. "I bet the English were furious."

"Not only furious, but badly hurt," said Joseph. "The guns of the fort blew hell out of the ships, and those militiamen from the swamps picked sailors out of the rigging like shooting squirrels out of pine trees.

"Then the British troops from the transports, who had been landed over on Long Island, were ordered to wade across the inlet to the other end of Sullivan's. The only trouble was that the fool Britisher who gave the order didn't think about the tide. It was so deep that some of them drowned, and the rest were turned back by fire from Colonel Thompson's backwoodsmen and Catawba Indians who were posted behind a low barricade on the point of Sullivan's."

"It sounds like a bloody massacre," said another bystander.

"I don't think King George's men are going to be anxious to fight

Carolinians again," said Joseph. "I have heard that they lost over one hundred men killed, and God knows how many wounded."

"How about the Carolinians?" John Walton asked.

"Only twelve Carolinians were killed and twenty-five wounded," Joseph answered.

"It almost seems like the good Lord is on our side," said a countryman from the Kiokee Creek settlement. "It's like David and Goliath."

Mr. Seymour, who had come from Saint Paul's, shook his head and said quietly to Colonel Grierson, "It's more likely the work of Satan when Englishmen turn their back on their King and slay his soldiers."

The new government continued to meet in the Broad Street taverns. Many of the hangers-on had returned to their homes, but the town was still so crowded that the sounds of hammer, saw, and pickaxe rang daily from the cross streets where houses were being built to accommodate the overflow.

George Walton had left to attend the Continental Congress in Philadelphia where, it was rumored, Thomas Jefferson of Virginia had framed a declaration breaking all ties with England. George Walton, like his brother John, had been part of the protest against tyranny, but had never been considered a radical fire eater like Wells and Bostick. The other two delegates, Button Gwinnett of Savannah and Dr. Lyman Hall of Medway, were expected to sign the paper without question. Everyone wondered what Walton would do.

It was early August before word finally arrived in Augusta that the Declaration of Independence had been signed by representatives of all thirteen colonies, including Georgia. The irreversible step had been taken. The lines would have to be drawn now. Augustans would find it impossible to remain neutral.

Through the rest of the summer and until the Provincial Congress adjourned for Christmas, delegates struggled to set up a sovereign government like those of the other twelve states. Men with Tory leanings were left completely out of the Congress, and even Whigs with conservative leanings were shouted down or ignored. George Wells, Button Gwinnett, and other radicals formed the majority on the committee to revise the old Rules and Regulations into a state constitution which created new counties from old parishes and gave the new House of Assembly power over the Governor and Council. Lachlan McIntosh, leader of the conservative faction, felt that the radicals were out for money and power, while Gwinnett and Wells accused McIntosh and his friends of Toryism.

In February 1777, the state constitution was finally adopted and Saint

Paul's Parish became Richmond County, named for the Duke of Richmond who had spoken for American liberties in Parliament. Ostensibly independent, Georgia still had spiritual ties with England.

Angus, Meg, and Jamie did their best to keep peace at the Sword and Thistle without taking sides in political discussions. Like most Augustans, their loyalties were split. Angus had fought for the King at Bloody Marsh but had little love for German George or his arrogant supporters. On the other hand, he felt that the Crackers who had taken over the government were irresponsible radicals.

He missed the gatherings in the back dining room, for only a few old friends were left in Augusta. Robert MacKay had died in Savannah last year, and Edward Barnard the year before. John Stuart and Thomas Brown were both in Florida, their lives devoted to the Loyalist cause, and Lachlan McGillivray, along with his half-breed son Alexander and the Loyalist-leaning Creek tribes in Florida, would have been in peril of his life if he had shown his face in Augusta.

James Grierson was still a regular customer and was living now at his fortified trading post on Hawk's Gully. He and Martin Weatherford and Andrew McLean were gathered at the bar one evening in April when Lachlan McIntosh came stomping up the steps and into the tap room.

"Those two sons-of-bitches!" he exploded as he joined the group. "They're going to start a conflagration in the backwoods that will have us all scalped and burned."

"Hush, laddie," said Angus, handing him a tankard of ale. "Wet your whistle and then come to the dining room before any more customers arrive. We don't want to start a riot here." He called to Meg, who was setting tables, to take over the bar and followed his friends to the back of the building.

"That crazy sawbones Wells and his friend Gwinnett are pushing the Congress into invading Florida," said McIntosh. "Gwinnett is so puffed up since he signed the Declaration and became president of the Executive Council that he thinks he's God Almighty."

"Doesn't he know the Tories in Florida have all the Lower Creeks as allies?" Grierson asked. "The Georgia troops wouldn't stand a chance against the British Regulars along with the Tories and Creeks."

"Oh, we have some damned good troops," said McIntosh, who had been made commanding general of the Georgia forces, "but they'll be outnumbered and bogged down in that swampy hellhole."

"I thought that was your country," McLean remarked.

"You're right," said McIntosh. "That's how I know it's a helluva place to fight. Lee and Moultrie tried to invade last year and had to give it up."

"Who will be in charge of the attack?" Angus asked.

"That's the bloody hell of it," said McIntosh. "As president of the Council, Gwinnett is commander-in-chief. He doesn't know beans about military tactics. He'll get the pants beaten off of him, and he'll stir up the tribes. If they see the militia and Continentals beaten, it will give them courage to attack the frontier. 'Burnfoot' Brown, as they're calling Thomas now, has been training the Indians as auxiliary troops. The young braves have learned fast, and they're armed with good English muskets instead of outdated trading pieces."

"You know how I feel about the whole thing," said Grierson. "If we'd remained a British province, we could have come to an agreement without all this bloodshed."

"I know, old friend," said McIntosh. "I guess all of us have doubts when we see the way this crowd of bloody fools is running the government. But as long as we're in this mess, we've got to swim or be caught in the undertow. I'd rather fight for my friends and neighbors than for that crowd of supercilious dandies in Parliament."

"Spoken like a good Scots Highlander," said Andrew McLean. "But I don't feel that this rabble in the Congress are my friends."

"At least we are friends in spite of politics," said Angus. "Let me fill your tankards so we can drink to old friendships."

The invasion of Florida turned out to be a disaster, as McIntosh had predicted. Baker's militia was to go by land, and Elbert's Continentals, by sea; they were to rendezvous at Sawpit Bluff on the Saint John's River. As could have been expected, they arrived at different times, and each force had to fight the Florida Loyalists separately. The expedition was a complete failure. Gwinnett came back to Savannah with his tail between his legs and was relieved not only as commander-in-chief but also as Council president. Adam Treutlen, a more conservative Salzburger, replaced him.

General McIntosh was ecstatic—not only was he proved right about the Florida expedition; he was also rid of an enemy in the Congress. In his usual brash manner, he made the air blue in the taverns of Savannah with his opinion of Gwinnett.

Incensed by the insults, Gwinnett challenged McIntosh to a duel. Both men were wounded in the leg.

George Wells returned to Augusta in sorrow and anger. As Gwinnett's second, he had removed the bullet from his leg at the duelling ground, then stayed by his sickbed as his fever rose. On the fourth day, Gwinnett had died in delirium. McIntosh had recovered from his wound.

Opinion in Augusta was split along political lines. Dr. Andrew Johnston stopped at the Sword and Thistle, on the way back from the Kiokee Creek settlement.

"All the people out there are blaming McIntosh for killing him," he said to James Grierson and Martin Weatherford. "I think Gwinnett was a damned fool to call him out."

"If McIntosh had been trying to kill him," said Grierson, "he wouldn't have shot him in the leg. He's been killing squirrels and partridges in the swamps since he was a child."

"How could a leg wound kill him?" Weatherford wanted to know. "I can't say much for Wells as a surgeon."

"I am not fond of George Wells, as you know," said Johnston, "but I'll have to admit that a leg wound can become putrid in spite of everything we do. Thank God Lachlan is recovering."

"Did you know that Wells and Lyman Hall are demanding that he be tried for murder?" Weatherford asked. "All the radicals are behind Wells."

"Murder, hell," said Grierson. "McIntosh had to accept his challenge. No gentleman could do otherwise. And he didn't shoot to kill."

When the case came to trial, McIntosh was acquitted. The verdict aroused so much bitter feeling, however, that General George Washington placed General McIntosh on his staff in the North, rather than expose him to the hostility of the Georgia radicals. So another of the old crowd left the Sword and Thistle.

Jamie, like Angus, stayed out of political discussions. The success of the inn depended upon keeping peace there. He had been as horrified as John Stanley and Joseph Merrill by mob rule and the torture of Brown, but now that the die was cast and the new government active, he had found that he agreed with many of the principles of the new constitution. All men should have a part in deciding their own destiny.

Stirring up an Indian war, however, was irrational. Wells was promoting a plan to attack the Indian tribes and drive them west of the Mississippi, but he didn't seem to realize how many innocent white scalps would have to be sacrificed. The settlers in the outlying lands, many of them new to Indian warfare, were backing the plan, anxious to be rid of the fear of raids. Old timers wanted peace and trade.

·XX·

BARN BURNING

B ert Sheldon had spent the summer working on the farm.
"Thank the Lord that little chit has gone back to the Low Country," said Ben one night as he and Mary prepared for bed. Since Bert was sleeping in the barn loft to guard the stock, they could talk without his hearing.

"Oh, Susan's a sweet little thing," said Mary. "All she needs is to grow up. But I can't see her as a frontier farmer's wife."

"Maybe she'll find herself a blue-blooded Charlestown husband this time," said Ben. "Her mother's doing her best, from what Bert let slip to me one day in the hayfield."

Bo, who was sleeping in front of the fireplace, raised his head and pricked his ears, then untangling his lame leg, ran to the door barking an alarm. A minute later, Bert was beating on the cabin door.

Ben pulled his trousers over his nightshirt and raised the bar on the door. Bert pushed by him and snatched the rifle from the pegs over the fireplace.

"Stay here, Mary," said Ben, "and dress yourself and the children as quick you can."

"It may be Indians," said Bert. "You'd all better go hide below the creekbank where we keep the butter."

"We'll look for you there," said Ben as Mary climbed up in the loft to wake Francie and Benjy, "and don't come out even if they fire the house and barn. You and the children are more important than the stock."

Bert had slipped out the door with his rifle ready.

Drawing near the barn he could hear the horses nickering and the ox roaring in fright. Ducking and running in a crouch, he burst into the barn in time to see in the moonlight a dusky form striped with warpaint fumbling at the latch of Moonshine's stall.

Swinging his rifle to his shoulder, he sighted briefly and squeezed the trigger. The Indian dropped, and Moonlight, frightened by the noise of the shot, plunged out of the stall over the fallen man and rushed out the open barn door.

Bert ducked behind the feed bin to reload his rifle, then he stared warily into the darkness of the barn. There was silence, until he heard a click and saw a spark in the hayloft where he had been asleep only minutes before. Aiming at the spot where he had seen the spark, he squeezed off another shot as the hay began to smolder and glow.

A grunt of pain and a scrambling sound in the hayloft told him that he had at least winged his target. When a man half crawled, half fell down the ladder from the loft, he knew that it was only a wound. Rushing to the ladder, he caught the man around the shoulders, jerking his right arm up behind his back. The man struggled but gave up as Bert forced his arm higher. His other arm hung useless, blood pouring from his sleeve.

No Indian, this one, but a white man in the green uniform of the King's Rangers.

A groan from the Indian told Bert that he was still alive, but how badly hurt was not known.

"You bloody, traitorous bastard," said Bert to his prisoner. "I'd have expected this of the rebels, but not of a ranger."

The man was losing a lot of blood, and Bert felt his body go limp against him. Grasping him under the arms, he dragged him to the door of the barn, calling softly "Pa."

Ben came out of the darkness near the cabin.

"I've got two of them," Bert said. "They're both alive, I think, but I'm afraid this bloody Tory set the hay on fire."

Smoke and a crackling from the loft told them he was correct.

"We'll have to get the rest of the stock out," said Ben hurrying into the thickening smoke.

Bert snatched a grooming rag from the stall door and smacked the new mare to hurry her out of the barn. Terrified, she tried to come back to the familiar stall, so Bert had to lash her with the rag to turn her out.

Ben had goaded the ox out of his stall and now was carrying an armful of mewing kittens from the harness room, the mother cat following frantically at his heels. Finally as the flames threatened to engulf them, they dragged the wounded Indian into the moonlight.

"The barn's as good as gone," said Ben. "I'll watch them while you check on Mary and the children. These men must have come alone. I didn't see anyone when I searched around the house."

The Indian was showing no signs of consciousness. Ben could see that his leg was wounded, and he had a great gash in his head where he had been struck by Moonlight's hoof.

The ranger's arm was still bleeding freely. Ben took the man's neckerchief and made a tourniquet to slow the bleeding.

"We'd better carry the two men out and leave them on the roadside," said Ben as Bert returned from scouting the territory. "There must be others around. I'd heard that Thomas Brown was coming toward Augusta to raid."

"But, damn it, Pa, we helped Squire Brown. He was our friend," said Bert.

"I'm sure these men had no idea who we were or what our politics," his father answered. "I'll do my best to keep them alive to get back to their command. They were only following orders."

Bert looked at his father in wonder. Pa really believed in his religion.

The ranger was stirring now, his eyes open watching them.

"Go hitch Moonshine to the wagon," said his father, "and we'll take them both out to the road. From the looks of the sky, they've set some of Rae's buildings afire. This man can call to his friends as they pass. I'll not wait to see if they come."

The Indian was beginning to move around and groan again as they left the two men on the roadside. Ben had bound his wounds and poured a good slug of corn whisky between his lips. The ranger was sitting, propped against a tree with a jug beside him.

"God bless you," he said as they started to leave. "You ain't like the bloody rebels we been told about. We both be thankin' you."

"Forget it," said Ben brusquely.

"You better be damn glad Pa's a Quaker," said Bert as he headed the wagon back up the hill.

All of Augusta was in a panic the day after the raid. Brown's Rangers had struck and hurried back to Florida, leaving burned barns and cabins and slaughtered livestock all around the outskirts of the town. There was no time to muster the militia before the Tories and Indians had faded into the swamps. Augustans were livid with rage.

At Fox's tavern, Joseph Merrill was standing with George Walton listening to a discussion at the bar.

"Damned savage!" said Chesley Bostick. "We should have hanged him when we had him instead of tar and feathering him."

"It seems to me that 'savage' is being applied to the wrong man," said a conservative at the next table. "You're lucky he didn't come into town and burn your feet."

"Brown's shown his treachery, leading Indians against his own people," said George Wells who was at the table with Bostick.

It was too much for Joseph. "Even when his own people scalped and tortured him?" he asked. "Loot from his home is scattered through Augusta and the Purchase, and all he did to deserve that was to refuse to sign a paper."

"I didn't take you for a bloody Tory," George Wells said, getting up and walking to the bar.

"I'm no more Tory than ninety percent of Georgians," Joseph answered, turning to face Wells, looking him straight in the eye, "but I know that Thomas Brown would not be harassing Augusta if he'd not been driven to vengeance by a drunken mob."

"We've no use for English nabobs who come lording it over Americans, setting up kingdoms on our soil," said Bostick, joining Wells at the bar.

"What's the matter, are you envious?" called a man at a table.

"Gentlemen, gentlemen!" called the tavern keeper, anticipating smashed crockery and windows. "Have a round on the house or settle your differences outside."

Joseph relaxed his hold on the heavy tankard he had picked up when he had seen Wells headed in his direction. Wells and Bostick returned to their table grumbling.

"Brown's going to be sorry," said Wells. "I've a commission now as a colonel, and I'm going to raise troops to wipe out that bunch of bloody savages."

"And all you Tories had better change your tune," said Bostick. "The Assembly's going to pass an act to get rid of you all and take your lands for the state."

"And I'll see that it's enforced," said Wells. He flung a handful of coins on the table and left, followed by Bostick.

Joseph had heard rumors of the plan for expulsion of Tories, and he could understand the need. An enemy within the walls was much more dangerous than a frontal attack. But who would decide a man's loyalty?

On September sixteenth, the Act for the Expulsion of the Internal Enemies of the State was passed, and committees were set up in each county to examine loyalties. Richmond County's committee was composed of twelve men, many of whom had been members of the original Liberty Boys.

One of the first Tories to be questioned was Dr. Andrew Johnston. The envy and hatred of George Wells made his conviction a foregone conclusion. He was given a week to leave Augusta and take his family and their household goods with him. His house and land would be confiscated by the Revolutionary Council.

As soon as word reached Angus, he sent Desmond to the doctor's home to ask the whole family to stay at the Sword and Thistle until they could make arrangements for the trip to Florida. Tories were being openly insulted on the streets, and some had been beaten and robbed.

As a innkeeper, Angus was expected to house anyone with the money to pay and could not be legally punished for housing Johnston until his week was up. The wagon full of his household goods could be locked in the tavern barn.

When Mrs. Johnston and the children were settled in one of the guest rooms, Andrew and his eldest son Andy came down to the tap room.

Martin Weatherford, Andrew McLean, Mr. Seymour, and James Grierson had come quietly through the back door to the dining room. Although many of the customers in the tap room were only lukewarm Whigs, there was no use calling attention to a gathering of known conservatives.

Young Andy Johnston, who had served in the King's Rangers with Jamie and Bert at Fort James, walked up to the bar with his father, where Meg and Jamie were filling tankards. Jamie hailed his friend, then said quietly, "Tell your father to wait a minute or two, then go to the private dining room. Some of his friends are there."

"God bless you, Andrew," said the vicar as Johnston entered the dining room. "The Crackers are fools to send you away. They'll realize it when their children have the croup, or someone needs a bullet removed in the middle of the night."

"We'll miss you here at the Sword and Thistle, too, laddie," said Angus. "I'll never forget the night that Meg had her bairn."

"Will you go to the islands?" Andrew McLean asked. "I hear the Bahamas and the other British territories are full of displaced Loyalists."

"I think we'll probably go to Saint Augustine," replied the doctor. "Andy plans to join the King's Rangers again and serve under Colonel Brown."

"If the time ever comes when I have to leave Augusta," said Weatherford, "I'll probably go to the islands. But I'm going to stay until they run me out."

"I hope to be able to remain in Augusta till this rebellion is over," said

Seymour. "Surely they wouldn't force a clergyman to leave his church. There are still plenty of Church of England men, even among the rebels."

"I didn't think they'd evict a physician," said Johnston. "My real sin was having a larger and more devoted practice than George Wells. I hear he is so busy now that he hasn't time for his own practice, much less mine. But he turned the Inquisition against me.

"I hope he doesn't do the same to Folliot and Taylor. They may not have studied many medical books, but they can set bones and prescribe physic, even if they lack degrees."

"A doctor's politics shouldn't matter unless, like Wells, he's more politician than physician," McLean remarked.

"God knows I've removed more bullets and set more bones for Whigs than for Tories," said Johnston. "I've treated Indians and blacks with as much care as white men."

"And they all love and respect you," said Angus. "God grant you'll be coming back when this madness is finished."

"Any time I can be of any help," said Grierson, rising and reaching for his hat, "send a message through the tribes. There are still runners on the trading paths, and the Indians know I'm their friend."

"Thank you, all of you," said the doctor, his eyes ashine with tears. "I hope some day to come back." Patting one man on the shoulder, grasping another by the arm, he made his way to the door.

"Those bloody, malicious blackguards," said Grierson, "are cutting their own throats, as they'll find when they need him."

The men slipped quietly out the back door and rode separately into the night.

After the expulsion of Andrew Johnston and several other well known Loyalists, the rougher element among the radical Whigs took delight in baiting the conservative shopkeepers and even setting fire to haystacks and stealing livestock from their neighbors in the name of liberty. "We were only doing what their friend Brown did," they would say when called to answer for their vandalism. Conservative householders, who had hoped to live and let live, picked up their belongings and moved south to Florida or the British islands in the Caribbean.

The Reverend James Seymour stood strong in the pulpit and denounced the hatred rampant in the state. Careful never to name names, he cautioned his parishioners to love their neighbors and avoid the temptations to rape and steal; fight against the forces of evil, serve God and not Mammon. Rites of the English Book of Common Prayer were followed at Saint Paul's Church, with prayers for the King and all others in authority, including the Continental Congress.

In early October, word arrived that George Washington and his Continental troops had been defeated in battle at Brandywine Creek by British General William Howe's Regulars and a force of Germans. The Continental Congress had been evacuated from Philadelphia, and the city had been taken by the English and Germans.

At the Sword and Thistle, the mood was brighter than in the taverns in town. No one would come out and toast the King for fear of retribution, but tankards clicked and eyes met with a smile and a wink.

Meg and Wee Angus were on the gully bank, catching crayfish scared up by the last night's rainstorm. The little boy was two now, with ginger-colored curls and a band of freckles across his nose. Meg had made a halter of soft leather to fasten around his chest and shoulders with a leash of stout hemp rope, now tied to a small tree near the top of the bank. He could follow his mother for ten feet in all directions but was kept a foot above water level.

"Hallooo," Bert Sheldon called from the path as he spurred his horse into the ford across the gully. "What kind of a beast is that you have tethered?"

"It's a long-legged beastie that goes bump in the night," Meg answered, transferring a fat crayfish from her dipper into a pail.

"We's catchin' crawdads!" said the child.

"Have you heard about the battle?" Bert asked as he dismounted on the path above them.

"I've heard of nothing else all day," said Meg. "Uncle Angus and Jamie are watching for arguments, but none of the Liberty crowd have shown their faces here."

"I guess the Continentals just can't stand up to trained troops," Bert said. "What does Jamie say?"

"Come in and talk to him yourself," said Meg. "I think we all feel a little let down and disappointed."

"It's funny," said Bert, taking Meg's pail in his free hand. "I never have thought I could be in favor of fighting against the King. I was just beginning to feel proud, though, of the way we had stuck up for our rights. And I'm mad as hell that the Rangers burned our barn."

"It was better when all we had to worry about was Indians," said Meg.

"I'm a injun," said Wee Angus, patting his mouth with his hand as he whooped.

"Hush, Wingus," said his mother. "That's what he calls himself now," she explained to Bert, "and it has stuck."

"We still have to worry about Indians," Bert answered. "Brown has set them on us all, Whig and Tory alike. It was an Indian that helped burn our barn."

Meg stopped before climbing the steps. "Don't start a discussion in the tap room please, Bert. I'll take over the bar and let you and Jamie talk in the back."

Bert smiled. "I'll hush, too," he said. "You see, Wingus, your mother keeps us all in line."

Jamie left the bar to sit at a corner table with Bert, afraid to leave the room with the chance of tempers flaming into a fight.

"What do you think about the Continental troops they're raising in Georgia?" Bert asked. "I'm wondering if I should join."

"After the beating Washington's Continentals took at Brandywine, I'm not impressed," Jamie answered.

"We've got to have protection," said Bert. "It looks like the Whigs are going to stay in power around here, and we've got to have some kind of army to keep outlaws and Indians in line. Ma and Pa have been attacked twice now by different sides, and there are plenty of others who've been murdered and had their homes gutted."

Jamie shook his head. "I was ready in a minute to join the King's Rangers back in '74. Now I don't know who I'd be fighting or why."

"I believe I'm going to join," said Bert. "The Continental Congress has authorized two battalions in Georgia and two troops of horse."

"I didn't think you'd be wanting to leave Augusta," said Jamie. "Did you know that the Merrills have finally come back from Charlestown?"

Bert blushed, but looked Jamie in the eye. "That's more reason to join," he said. "I've made enough of a fool of myself over her."

"You're no fool," said Jamie. "Love can do strange things to all of us. I'm glad you've gotten over her though."

"Let's just say that I'm going to like being on the move, trying to keep Georgia safe."

When word came, a few weeks later, that British and German troops under General Burgoyne were defeated at Saratoga by the Continentals of General Horatio Gates, Bert was already wearing that uniform and was given extra rations of rum to drink toasts with his fellow soldiers. The winter that Washington's Continental army spent starving and freezing at Valley Forge, Bert spent in Savannah drilling and learning the tactics of warfare.

Christmas and New Year's Day were quietly celebrated in Augusta with no Indian alarms. The Assemblymen, who had resumed meeting in Savannah, adjourned before Christmas and returned to their home counties, but they were recalled in April to meet in Augusta when rumors circulated that British forces in Florida were preparing to invade South Georgia. With no money to pay militia companies, the Assembly passed a bill proclaiming that anyone raising a company of at least fifteen volunteers would be entitled to a roving commission to plunder in Florida and keep any goods acquired from the Tories there. Augusta taverns lost large numbers of patrons as legitimate companies were formed. Unfortunately the old outlaw bands formed again, too, under the legal mask of Volunteers. Many of them headed south for the Florida border, but some stayed in Georgia and South Carolina using their commissions to rob and burn settlements in the backwoods there.

John Stanley, worried by reports of looting near the North Carolina border, headed Upcountry in the Ninety-Six District to talk to his old friend William Wofford. Will's blacksmith shop near the Tyger River had grown into an ironworks where he was making rifles and muskets for the Continental militia. He would know what was going on in the area, if anyone did.

The two old friends sat before the fire in Will's parlor after a supper served on fine china by a black butler.

"You've really become a country squire, Will," John said smiling in the firelight. "Do you remember the night Mary Anne and I rode here with you, when Govey Black and the outlaws were attacking the cabin and your family was inside? The cabin's grown to a mansion."

"The hell of it is," said Wofford, "that we're facing the same thing again from the same bunch of bloody outlaws."

"Not the Volunteers?" John asked. "You're making guns for them to shoot."

"Volunteers!" Will sneered. "They're a bunch of bloody rabble. But they're supposed to be on our side, so we can't keep them from having our guns. Now I guess it's your side too, isn't it?"

"God knows," said John. "I wish we could all go back about ten years. With the Tories stirring up the tribes against the countryside, I guess they're worse than the crowd of ruffians who are defying the King. I suppose you could say I'm on the Whig side."

"In this part of the country, most of the Tories are ruffians. You remember Joseph Cofell?"

"That illiterate chicken thief that we fought when we were Regulators?" John asked. "The last thing I heard of him was that he was sentenced to thirty-nine lashes for cattle stealing in Orangeburg."

"He left Orangeburg and came to Ninety-Six a year ago," said Wofford.

"Lately he's gathered up a group of his old outlaw cronies to organize the Tories around here to plunder and burn. We've had to fortify the ironworks, and my militiamen are guarding this whole area."

"You mean that son-of-a-bitch has got enough people with him to be a threat to you?"

"Damn right!" said Wofford. "There must be more than five hundred ragtag and bobtails ready to march with him."

"Have you heard anything about the country around Saluda Mountain?" John asked. "I'm on my way up to check on my farm."

"Old friend," said Wofford, "I'd advise against going up now. What the outlaws haven't ransacked, the Cherokees have burned. The Indians always claimed that country as hunting grounds, and they've taken advantage of the white men's fight to burn out the settlements."

"What about Page's trading post and our neighbors, the Moodys and the Slatterys?"

"I heard they all picked up and left when the Indians came in."

"God help them," said John. "They were just beginning to prosper. Do you think this mess will ever be straightened out?"

"If all the responsible men get together and fight for a good way of life," Wofford answered. "We fought as Regulators and won. Things quieted down for almost ten years."

"It's too bad we can't reorganize our old Regulator companies," said John, "but they're split between Loyalists and Whigs now."

"I'm glad to know that, at least, you're not a Tory," said Will. "I'd heard about your helping Brown escape to Fletchall's."

"Brown was an English gentleman tortured by a mob of drunken hoodlums," said John. "If he'd not been persecuted, he might not be harrying the Georgians."

"He's really gone whole-hog for the King now," said Wofford. "Fletchall's in prison, captured with a bunch of other Tories when Richardson came through here in the winter of 1775, but Brown's turned into an Indian-loving bushwhacker. Folks around here hate his guts."

"I'm afraid revenge has become an obsession with him," said John. "God help Chesley Bostick and his crowd if he ever gets his hands on them."

"Have you heard he's planning an attack on Georgia this spring?" Wofford asked. "Word is that Coffell will head for Florida to join Brown."

"Do you think there's anything to the rumor?" John asked. "Or will Coffell's crowd stay around the Upcountry, harassing the settlements while Brown attacks Savannah?"

"Coffell needs arms for his men," said Wofford. "My guess is that he'll take them to Florida, so they'll be armed and paid by the King."

"They'll be bound to come near Augusta in any case," said John. "I'd better head back there tomorrow to warn the militia to be ready for them. I guess there's not much I could do on Saluda Mountain."

"It's been good seeing you," said Wofford. "I wish you could have brought Mary Anne and Johnny."

"It looks as though it will be a long time before we can make family visits," said John.

John carried the news back to Augusta that Coffell and his Tories would be heading for Florida from Ninety-Six. Augusta's ferries would be the obvious crossing points on the Savannah at this time of year when the river was swollen with spring rains.

As the Assembly was in session in Augusta again, the news caused a furor all over the state. Word was sent to the newly created Volunteers, and Bert's company of Continentals were alerted for instant service.

The middle of April, the Scofolites, as Coffell's Tories were called, swarmed down from the Carolina back country and across the river, stealing cattle and horses, robbing barns and farmhouses of food and clothing, guns and ammunition. Some Loyalist settlers, tired of being harassed by rebels and Indians, and now by Carolinians, pulled up stakes and joined the group in migration.

There were no reports of outrages in Augusta itself. The Continentals made a point of patrolling the area around Rae's Creek, so this time the Sheldon farm was not molested. Bert and Ben had finally built a high fence around the house and farm buildings to discourage marauders. Colonel Twiggs' and Colonel Few's militia companies covered the Savannah Road and the Sand Bar Ferry Road to keep the Tories away from the city after they had crossed. The Center Street ferry was kept on the south side of the river. Like a swarm of locusts, the Scofolites followed the course of least resistance and pushed on southward away from the town.

Afraid that Brown would launch an attack across the river after the Scofolites had joined his forces, John Houstoun, who was now governor, called up militia, Volunteers and Continentals in May for an expedition into Florida. As usual the different forces went their own ways, unable to cooperate.

The Continental company in which Bert served had marched out of Augusta with militia troops under General Andrew Williamson and were to join General Robert Howe's Continentals in an attack on the Loyalists' strongholds. At Fort Tonyn above Saint Augustine, they attacked in force and were able to drive Brown's Rangers out into the palmetto thickets. Bert saw the squire on the walk at the top of the palisade during the attack, directing his troops in their retreat, then following behind them into the forest.

"Did you see old Burnfoot?" called a Georgia trooper kneeling next to Bert to reload his musket as Bert was sighting into the brush. "He was limping where the Augusta boys burned his feet. I wish I could have got a good shot at him."

Bert said nothing. He wondered if he could have pulled the trigger if he'd been close enough for a shot at Brown.

They slept in the fort that night and the next, enjoying the Tory rations and a roof over their heads, waiting for Howe's Continentals before pressing on toward Saint Augustine. Finally word came that Howe's force had gone back to Savannah. The attack had been cancelled.

Slogging back through the swamps in the summer heat, the Upcountry militia cursed the snakes, ticks, and chiggers—and that son-of-a-bitch Howe. At Sunbury they were mustered out and told to get home however they could. There were no funds to pay them.

Bert, at least, had his horse. There were no oats or hay, but Moonshine could live off the grass by the wayside. Bert had to forage in corn fields and gardens by night and shoot coon and possum for meat. One day he and three companions shot an alligator and cooked gator steaks over a campfire. It was September before he reached the Indian village of New Savannah, in sight of the Augusta sand hills. Moonshine seemed to know he was almost home. Skinny and unshod, tired from the long campaign, he nevertheless pricked up his ears and broke into a trot. They forded Butler's Creek, and Bert let him have his head, then slowed him as his canter became a gallop. No use letting him kill himself this close to home. As the road from the Sand Bar Ferry crossed the Savannah Road, they slowed to a walk to allow a wagon to turn in front of them, then trotted into town.

Bert had forgotten how crowded Augusta could be. Carriages and wagons jammed Broad Street at the market place, making it hard to pick his way among the carts and stalls of the hucksters.

"Bert," a shrill voice called, and he looked down to see one of the little Merrills, Betsy, grown almost beyond recognition.

"Where've you been? We've missed you. Susan thought she'd see you when we came back from Charlestown, but you'd gone off in the army."

"I'm on my way home now," said Bert. "I've been down fighting the Tories in Florida since spring."

"Hello, Bert," said Kate, coming up beside the horse, with Lissy following close behind carrying a large string bag filled with fresh vegetables. "Susan still hasn't found a suitable man, even in Charlestown."

"Hush, chile," said Lissy. "Mr. Bert, don't you pay her no mind."

"Come see us and tell us about the war," called Betsy as Lissy shepherded them toward home.

Bert waved without answering. He had almost lost the sick feeling when he thought of Susan. He hated to start all over again.

When he reached the Sword and Thistle, Meg called from the porch. Hurrying down the front steps as he dismounted, she threw her arms around him and kissed his cheek.

"Whisht," she laughed, pulling away and gazing into his face. "You do look like a swamp rat. I wouldn't have known you under all that beard if I hadn't recognized Moonshine."

"We're both of us pretty disreputable looking," Bert answered. "I haven't had these clothes off in weeks. I can't wait to get home to a hot bath."

"Your father was in yesterday," Meg said. "He and your mother have been worried about you."

"Are they all right?" Bert was almost afraid to ask.

"Everything is fine at the farm. Get along. I was going to ask you in for an ale, but I know you're anxious to be home."

*　*　*

September and October passed without an attack of any sort. In November the British finally decided to move their operations to the South. Intelligence sources claimed that South Carolina and Georgia were full of Tories just waiting to rise and join the forces of the King. Word came through the grapevine that three thousand British, Loyalists, and Hessians were preparing to sail from New York to conquer Georgia, then move north through South Carolina to Virginia.

John Stanley, riding out to the Sword and Thistle one morning in November, found the tap room in an uproar. The captain of a coastwise trading ship on the way from Savannah to the North Carolina capes had spotted a British fleet of warships and troop transports opposite Charlestown headed south. Putting into Charlestown, he had given the alarm, then piled on sail for Savannah.

Bert Sheldon was at the bar talking to Jamie and Angus.

"You were down there with Houstoun," Angus said to Bert. "What kind of troop concentration was there in Florida? Could they attack Savannah?"

"Hell," said Bert, "I was so far back in the swamps, I didn't see much but palmettos and alligators. We fought more mosquitoes than British. General Howe finally ordered us back to Savannah."

"General Howe's a damned fool," said Angus. "God help Savannah if he's in command of its defense."

John Stanley came up to the bar and took the tankard Jamie filled for him. "What's this about Florida?" he asked.

"George Galphin got word from some of his Creeks that a land army of a hundred British Regulars and three hundred Indians and Scofolites has crossed the border under the command of Lieutenant Colonel Mark Prevost, and Lieutenant Colonel Fuser has sailed with five hundred men for Sunbury. They're supposed to combine their forces there and march on Savannah to attack by land while Campbell attacks by sea."

"Lieutenant Colonel Sir Archibald Campbell?" John asked.

"Right, laddie," said Angus. "That's the word that's come through from New York. And a braw Scotsman he is, too."

"We'll be having the Assembly back in Augusta then," said Meg, who had come up with a tray of empty tankards. "They've hardly been back in Savannah long enough to sit."

"Like rats from a sinking ship," said Angus.

"I'd best be sure the rooms are aired," said Meg. "When they take over the inns downtown, we get the leftovers."

The news had been accurate. By the end of November word came that General James Screven had been killed trying to drive Prevost back from Medway. The Georgia militia moved back to a position on the Ogeechee River and prepared to stop him there. Prevost waited for Fuser's forces from Sunbury, and when they were late arriving, burned the Medway meeting house, then retreated into Florida, burning and plundering as he went. Fuser and his five hundred Tories arrived in Sunbury, where colonel John McIntosh defended a fort with two hundred Georgians. Ordered by Fuser to surrender, McIntosh answered, "Come and take it!" Without Prevost's forces to help him, Fuser declined the challenge and sailed away down the coast to Saint Simon's Island.

At the Sword and Thistle, the whisky flowed free. Angus's stock of real Scotch whisky was hidden where no one would ever find it, but his first barrel of malt whisky from Rae's Creek had now aged for four years.

"To as brave a Scot as ever raised a claymore," said Angus, raising his glass.

"To Colonel John McIntosh," answered the crowd at the bar.

This afternoon John Dooly and Elijah Clark had stopped in on their way home, and John Twiggs and William Few had ridden out to the Sword and Thistle with them. Downtown inns were so crowded that it was hard to talk, and the Sword and Thistle now served as many Whigs as Tories.

Accepting the whisky and joining in the toast, Twiggs drained his glass. "I didn't know you were such a patriot," he said to Angus as he set the glass on the bar.

"I'm proud of a lad who would risk his life rather than submit to tyranny," said Angus. "It was not far from there I lost my leg fighting against the Spanish."

"It's going to take a lot of stubborn lads to keep the Bloodybacks from taking over Georgia," said Few.

"I hear Howe has only six hundred troops to defend Savannah," Twiggs said.

"If he plays his cards right, that should be enough," said Angus. "I remember that the city is nearly surrounded by marshes and swamps. If he guards the places you can get through without bogging down, he can hold off the whole British Army."

"Didn't you say Howe was a fool?" Jamie asked.

"Aye, laddie, and Lieutenant Colonel Archibald Campbell most assuredly is not."

"Then we'd best be ready for an attack on Augusta and Wilkes County by spring," said Elijah Clark. "There are more Tories than patriots along the Savannah Road."

"They tell me the Savannah merchants are only lukewarm patriots," said Dooly. "They talk a lot about liberty, but they'll talk out of the other side of their mouths if they think they can save their property."

"The same thing can be said of the merchants of Augusta," said Dooly, "or anywhere else."

"I'll be damned if I'll give in to them," said William Few. "My militia can outshoot any bloody Regulars. I'm not going to let any Tory lovers keep me from mowing down the Bloodybacks."

"You're damn tootin'," said Clark. "We could stand off the whole British army in the New Purchase with your men and mine, Dooly."

"We'd better round up our militia and get out of town," said Twiggs. "You don't know who to trust in town."

"We can sure slow them down," said Few. "Your men and my brother Benjamin's can make it mighty hot for them as they come up country if only Augusta will protect herself."

"Our only hope in the city is the fortified farms around the edge," said John, "and they won't stand up against artillery. They're built for Indian warfare."

"It's a pity we've let the old fort fall to ruin," said Twiggs. "We never thought we'd have to fight other Englishmen here."

"Maybe Howe will hold firm," said John.

"Pray God he will," said Twiggs, "but I'm not waiting to see. Come on, Will, drink up and let's get on into town and round up the men." He and Few drained their tankards and went out to the hitching rail.

Clark and Dooly followed them out, tightening their loosened girths and trotting out the Cherokee Road toward Wilkes.

BRITISH
TAKEOVER

It was another month before the British were ready to move on
Savannah, but Campbell used the time well by sending spies to learn
the strengths and weaknesses of the city's defenses. Her best protection
was being surrounded by almost impassable swamps and marshes laced
with trails known only to local hunters and fishermen.

Howe had deployed some of his six hundred troops to guard the
main roads across the marshes and felt that his forces could withstand
any assault by water along the riverfront.

The Georgia Continentals under Colonel Samuel Elbert were posted
along the road through the swamps near the Girardeau plantation. Bert
Sheldon, swatting mosquitoes and scratching chigger bites, waited for
the British to attack. On the other side of the road, Colonel Isaac Huger's
South Carolinians sweated and cursed. A regiment of Georgia militia
waited at ease across the road.

Suddenly hell broke loose from all directions. Campbell had learned
from an escaped slave of a secret path through the marshes and had
moved around to flank the rebel defenders. On the right Turnbull's New
York (Tory) Volunteers and Sir James Baird's Light Infantry struck
Huger's Carolinians, while Campbell made a frontal charge with the rest
of his troops against the Georgia militia. The South Carolinians, surprised
and overwhelmed, broke and fled through Savannah with the Georgia
militia following close behind. Campbell and Baird followed, over-
whelming them in the streets of the city as they tried to rally and form
defensive positions in the squares. The whole corps was killed, wounded,
or captured.

Meanwhile Elbert's Georgia Continentals had fought to maintain their
position along the left side of the road. Bert himself had accounted for
six red-coated infantrymen. The poor bastards lay in the middle of the

road with the Georgia militiamen who had been mowed down and all the rest of the dead and wounded.

When the militia had broken, the bulk of the British troops had followed them down the road to town. Elbert and his men retreated into the swamp sniping at the redcoats who followed, then dropped their arms and dove into Musgrove Creek. Those who couldn't swim were captured by the British or drowned in the black, muddy water. Bert was one of the lucky ones who made it to the far shore and gathered with Elbert to start for Cherokee Hill about eight miles up river. Unarmed, the shivering Georgians slogged through the snake-infested swamps. The hill would be defensible, and they could slip across on the ferry into Carolina if the British came in pursuit. One of the Continentals whose home was in Savannah had hunted deer and gators in these swamps and knew the Indian paths.

Bert had gone ahead with the Savannah man to scout the way to the highway. There was little chance that the British would be on the road so soon after the capture of the city, but the two men picked their way carefully through the undergrowth, before venturing onto the road. As the Savannahan parted the moss hanging from a big oak by the roadside, he ducked back, his finger to his lips, then eased ahead to peer out once more. Bert followed carefully keeping a screen of moss and leaves in front of him.

A band of foot soldiers and two wagons, led by several men on horseback, were advancing along the highway. As they came near, Bert recognized General Howe in a mud-spattered uniform. One of his officers had a bandage around his head, and several of the soldiers had arms in slings or limped on bandaged legs.

"Better not make any noise," said Bert as his companion started forward. "We're liable to be shot." They could hear the rest of Elbert's men following their trail through the forest.

"Sir, General Howe and about twenty officers and men have just passed on the road," Bert reported as Elbert came striding up.

"Damn and blast his yellow hide," one of the Continentals said. "He must have sneaked away and left the rest of his army."

"I guess we did the same thing," said Elbert. "No sense in being captured. We need good officers."

"But not a stupid dolt like Howe," said a lieutenant, "Begging your pardon for criticizing a senior officer."

"Let's get on and find out what happened in Savannah," said Colonel Elbert. "Form up, and we'll march in."

Covered with mud and with no weapons but the sticks they had picked up in the swamp to guard against snakes, the Georgia Continentals marched toward Cherokee Hill.

General Howe had posted a sentry, who barred their way with rifle at ready, but when he recognized the muddy uniforms, he gave a whoop that brought Howe's group running.

"Thank God!" said General Howe, hurrying forward. "How are you?"

"We're cold and wet and damned near drowned," said Elbert, "but we're still alive."

"We'll bivouac here on the hill tonight," said Howe, "and cross on the ferry to the Carolina shore tomorrow."

"Leave Georgia?" Elbert asked.

"Savannah has fallen," said Howe. "The rest of Georgia is indefensible."

"Have you forgotten the Upcountry Georgia militia?" Elbert asked. "There are plenty of back countrymen who would dispute your assumption."

"My orders to you," said Howe, "and to all the Georgia militia, are to leave Georgia and regroup under my command in South Carolina."

"General, sir, I'll carry your orders to the militia," said Elbert, "but I wouldn't count on them any time soon."

Elbert's men stayed with Howe long enough to dry their clothes, obtain muskets from the wagons, and fill their empty stomachs by his camp fires. Before daybreak they moved out on the road to Augusta.

Bert rode straight home to let his parents know he was safe. Roused by the barking of the dogs, Ben went into the cold moonlit night to unbar the gate. The visitor was obviously known to the dogs, as their tails wagged frantically and they filled the night with bays of greeting. When Bert rode into the yard, Ben was too happy to speak. He grabbed him about the shoulders and hugged him, his eyes brimming with tears. The dogs raced in circles, trying to get into the act, whining and yipping ecstatically.

Mary, having stirred the fire and added a log, came out with her heavy woolen cloak over her nightgown. Like Ben she clung silently to her son, her head against his chest, then walked into the cabin with his arm around her waist.

"I've a good venison stew in the pot," she said. "It should be hot in no time."

"That's the best greeting I ever heard," said Bert. "I'm so hungry I could eat a deer, horns and all."

Mary swung the pot over the fire and went to the cupboard for a bowl and spoon. Bert stood with his back to the fire and rubbed his hands together. Finally he eased himself into the rocking chair, his boots stuck out toward the fire.

Mary knelt beside his feet and pulled at his boots.

"It will take Pa to get them off," Bert said. "I've worn them so long my feet are glued into them."

Bert turned the chair around, and Ben backed up to him taking one boot between his legs while Bert pushed with his other foot against his father's buttocks to strip the tight boot from his leg.

"Are you all right?" his mother asked anxiously. "We'd heard so many were killed and wounded."

"I was lucky," said Bert, "but I'm so all fired mad I'm ready to blow up and bust. General Howe is a stupid, blockheaded coward! He should be hanged for the murder of all those men, and now he wants to abandon all of Georgia to the enemy."

Ben and Mary sat on the settle and listened silently.

"Any half-way commander could have kept the British out in the marshes until they rotted with fever, but General Howe let them slip in the back way, then ran away to Carolina."

"You'd best watch your tongue, son," said his father. "Don't let anyone else hear you criticizing your commanding officer."

"God help me and all of the troops under him," said Bert. "We didn't know he was such a coward. And now he's given Colonel Elbert orders for all the rest of the Georgia militia to follow him to South Carolina."

"He'll have to obey orders," said Ben.

"Elbert plans to give the orders to Colonel Twiggs," said Bert, "but tell him what happened in Savannah. Twiggs can make up his mind what to do. Americans are free to do what they think best."

"Little as I believe in war," said Ben, "I know that an army has to obey orders."

"Elbert will give them the orders," said Bert again. "But if I know Twiggs and Few and Clark and Dooly, they won't quit and go to Carolina."

Bert was right. The militia commanders refused to run away. They had already mustered their troops and were ready to fight the British before Campbell began his march along the river from the coast. The Georgia forces were pitifully small, though fiercely patriotic. Most of the settlers around Augusta, however, were more interested in living peacefully than in fighting. Knowing that Savannah had fallen, they decided to be neutral and throw themselves on the mercy of the conquerors.

The Merrill household was a beehive of activity with Mindy and Lissy running up and downstairs carrying bundles of clothing and Saul carrying the silver, china, and some of the best pieces of English mahogany to the wagon in the stable yard.

"But I don't want to leave Augusta," moaned Kate as she tied the top of Dusty's basket down to keep her and her latest litter of kittens from escaping under the porch.

"Don't be silly, darling," said Jocelyn, as she checked through a hamper full of little girls' dresses, then fastened the strap. "We'll go down to stay with Grandmama on the plantation until this is all over, then we'll come back to Augusta."

"But I thought we were English. Why do we have to be afraid of the English troops?"

"Any time an army takes over a city, there are soldiers who get drunk and treat people badly, specially ladies and little girls. Daddy wants us all to be with Grandmama where we'll be safe, and you can ride your pony and fish on the river bank."

"But what about Francie Sheldon and the Seymour girls? They're staying here."

"We'll all pray that they will be safe," said Jocelyn, helping Kate into her hooded traveling cape.

Susan, in the next room, was braiding Betsy's hair. "Keep still," she fussed, aiming a slap at Betsy's bottom as she gripped the fat braid. "We've got to hurry. Daddy thinks the army will be here in the next few days."

"But why don't we stay and fight?" Betsy asked. "And why do the English want to fight us, anyhow?"

"Lord knows," said Susan. "I bet there are some nice young officers in Colonel Campbell's command. Before all this fight about tea and liberty and stamps, I remember that they used to have wonderful parties at the fort in Charlestown. I was too young to go then, and now I'm on the wrong side of the war."

"Come on, girls!" Jocelyn called. "Saul has the carriage ready, and the wagon is packed."

The Merrills were not the only family to leave town, but there was no general exodus. The Georgia Assembly was to have met in Savannah in January. Many of the Savannah members had been captured in the attack. Assemblymen from the rest of the state straggled into Augusta and set up shop in Matthew Hobson's house where they elected an executive committee to be in charge of the government until the regular Assembly was able to meet again. William Glascock was elected Revolutionary President of the state, and plans were made for the Assembly's evacuation in case of attack.

Since the old fort was beyond repair, the committee decided to take possession of Grierson's fort for the defense of the city.

James Grierson was furious, but unable to resist the will of the majority. His name was placed on a list of suspected Tories who "refused to defend the state in her present distress."

"Damned ragtag ruffians," he said to Angus as he sat at the breakfast table at the Sword and Thistle. "They have no more right to take over my property than they had to oust me from command and take over my militia."

"Easy, mon," said Angus, looking around at the other breakfasters. "You'll do best to bide your time and keep your own counsel. And I'd not benefit if someone tells the Committee I'm harboring Tories."

"You're right," said Grierson, "but it sticks in my craw to sit here and listen to them beating the drums and drilling in my own stockade just up the road."

"At least you can watch what they are doing and report any pilferage."

"They're digging ditches and stocking the larder for a siege, but I doubt they will stand up to the King's Regulars," said Grierson.

"God help us here at the Sword and Thistle," said Angus, "if they try to make a stand. We'll be blasted to hell by the cannon."

Reports and rumors flowed into Augusta with every traveler. It was learned that Brigadier General Prevost had moved his garrison from Saint Augustine to Savannah and taken command of all British forces in Georgia to release Lieutenant Colonel Campbell for an assault on Augusta. Thomas Brown's Rangers would be part of Campbell's army.

On January 2, 1779, the British occupied the Salzburger town of Ebenezer, above Savannah, and on January twenty-fourth began the march to Augusta.

Bert Sheldon was with Elbert's Continentals, whose ranks had been refilled with Georgians ready to fight, now that their homes were in danger. The regiment was bivouacked near McBean's trading post.

When Campbell's army neared the Burke County jail, Thomas Brown learned from his scouts that a group of Loyalists were imprisoned there. Twiggs and the Few brothers, whose militia companies were in Burke, saw Brown split away from the main body of British troops and head toward the jail to release the prisoners. Taking advantage of his isolation, the rebel militia attacked the Rangers at the jailhouse, killing five and wounding Brown himself. Brown limped back with his dead and wounded to join Campbell's army camped on Edward Telfair's plantation, while the rebel militia went to join Elbert's Continentals at McBean Creek.

The next day Campbell's army circled around the rebel camp, outflanking the hastily built fortifications and forcing the Continentals to leave without their breakfast, still cooking on camp fires, and retreat toward Augusta to Henderson's fort.

The cause seemed hopeless. Elbert, Twiggs, and the Fews stopped long enough to water their horses and feed their troops. When Campbell began lobbing artillery shells into Henderson's fort, they withdrew to Augusta to regroup with the forces of General Andrew Williamson, who had been sent from South Carolina to defend the city.

The night that Williamson's Carolina militia arrived at Fort Grierson, John Stanley rode out to the Sword and Thistle knowing it would be the first stop for thirsty Carolina militiamen. He had hardly got through the door before he heard a warwhoop from one of the tables near the bar, and Will Wofford came charging through the crowd to pound him on the back.

"I was afraid you'd gone off with Twiggs and Few and that bunch of Georgia Crackers," said Will. "Now you can join a good Carolina outfit with your old friends."

John grinned and, putting his arm around Wofford's shoulders, led him up to the bar. "Angus," he asked, "do you think you could find a little something special for an old friend of mine? Will and I went all through the Regulator troubles together."

"Aye, laddie, we'll scare up something better than the hogwash I serve to strangers," said Angus. "We're fond of John around here and happy to serve his friends," he said to Will.

"Thank you," said Wofford, "We've been missing him in Ninety-Six."

John introduced Jamie Stratfield to his friend. "Will's folks were from Maryland, too," John said as the men shook hands across the bar.

"I've heard about you, sir," said Jamie, "and of the good muskets you're turning out in your forge."

"I left the works in good hands," said Wofford, "and came off to fight the Bloodybacks. It takes South Carolinians to keep the enemy out of Georgia."

"I don't know," said Jamie grinning, "I understand Twiggs and Elbert beat hell out of Brown's Rangers the other day. A man from Burke County was in here a few minutes ago."

"Did he say Campbell had been stopped?" Wofford asked.

"The last thing he had heard Campbell was camped at Telfair's plantation while Brown licked his wounds."

"Then he'll be knocking at our door any time," said Angus, who had returned with two glasses of amber liquid. "The Campbells may not have arrived on time at the battle of the Cheviot, but I've never known a Campbell who couldn't lick his weight in wildcats once he got started."

"Come, John," said Wofford, "and talk to Williamson and the boys," and to Angus, "I thank you for this nectar of the gods."

"Made in my own still," said Angus. "Nothing's too good for John Stanley's friends."

John and Will carried their drinks to the table where General Andrew Williamson sat with three other officers in militia uniform. Williamson gave John a hearty handshake. "You remember Andrew Pickens here, John? He's in command of the Regiment of Ninety-Six."

"Sir, I'm glad to see you again," John said to Pickens.

"I've been trying to recruit John for our company," said Wofford.

"We need every good man we can get," said Williamson. "The people of Richmond County haven't flocked to our assistance."

"There are over two hundred Richmond militiamen out there on the road from Savannah trying to stop Campbell before he gets here," said John. "And Elbert has a lot of Richmond County men in his Continentals, too. They're none of them anxious to have Brown turned loose here after the way they treated him."

"Surely an English commander wouldn't allow his men to harass the townspeople," said Williamson. "Brown is an officer and a gentleman, and so is his commander, Archibald Campbell."

"I hope you're right," said John. "In any case, most of the hell raisers who tarred and feathered him have taken to their heels."

"They must have," said Williamson. "I've found few males of fighting age in town. The older men seem to think Campbell would be preferable to the Georgia Assembly to keep the peace and protect their womenfolk."

"It's an odd sort of war," said Wofford.

"Come to think of it," said John, "I'd a damn sight rather trust Mary Anne and Johnny to the British than to the likes of Chesley Bostick or George Wells."

"I hope you won't have to rely on British chivalry," said Williamson, "but I'm afraid you'll have little choice. Augusta has no defense against artillery. If Campbell can circle through the swamps to the sand hill, he can blow the city to blazes. Our militia forces will not be able to stop him before he can bring his artillery to bear."

The clatter of hoofs from the direction of town sent the officers hurrying out onto the porch in time to see Colonel John Twiggs and Colonel Samuel Elbert approaching at the head of a column of mounted militiamen.

"They'll be headed for Fort Grierson," said Williamson. "Let's be on our way boys."

Sending a young lieutenant to settle the bill, Williamson, Wofford, and the rest of the officers retrieved their horses, then forded the gully and galloped off beside the militia column toward Grierson's fort.

John Stanley carried his glass to the bar where Angus still stood with Jamie.

"They want me to join them," said John. "I've ridden with many of them before. They're my people."

"It's a hard decision to make, lad," said Angus.

"I'll have to talk to Mary Anne," said John. "I don't like to leave her here with young Johnny, though I can't believe Thomas Brown would let her be harmed, even if I'm a member of the rebel army."

"If Campbell shells the city, God only knows what will be left of any of us," said Jamie, "but you won't be able to protect them from cannon balls by staying here."

"I don't want to be caught in the city and made to fight for the King against my friends," said John. "In Savannah the British conscripted all the able-bodied men and made the older men swear an oath not to fight against the king."

As the din of hoofbeats and the roll of drums sounded from Fort Grierson, John swung onto his horse and started toward the Merrill house.

"Stop for me on the way back," Jamie called. "I can't sit here doing nothing. I'll join Williamson's militia if he'll have me."

Williamson and his officers arrived at Fort Grierson just after Elbert and Twiggs. The soldiers were sent to feed and water the horses, then drew rations from the commissary to cook over company fires, outside the palisade. The officers gathered in the great room of Grierson's trading post for a council of war.

"My intelligence reports that there are over one thousand men in Campbell's army," said Williamson. "He has a battalion of Highlanders, Turnbull's Tory Volunteers, and Brown's Rangers, who, with Innes's South Carolina Royalists, are acting as scouts and skirmishers. Most important, he has a detachment of Royal Artillery.

"These forces are spread all the hell over the land around Henderson's fort and up onto the heights. That's only a twelve-mile march from town," said Elbert. "All that's stopping them now is the swamps."

"There's not a defensible position between here and Henderson's," said Williamson. "Thank God for the swamps to slow down the artillery. Once they drag the guns across the swamps, the town will be at their mercy."

"Is there any hope of help from Carolina?" Elbert asked.

"I received a dispatch only today," said Williamson. "General Howe has been reprimanded and Benjamin Lincoln put in command of the southern sector. Lincoln's promised to send Colonel Mark Ashe up from Port Royal with artillery, but that's not going to do us a damned bit of good now."

"We've only got four little cannons here at Grierson," said Twiggs.

"What about the guns from the old fort?" Pickens suggested.

"They're rusted so the touch-holes are closed," said Twiggs. "We tried to use one to fire a salute a few years ago, and it blew up."

"My God," said Elbert. "No artillery and outnumbered three to one."

"Do you think we could hold them off till Ashe comes with reinforcements?" William Few asked.

"We have only Fort Grierson that might possibly be defended," Williamson answered.

"What is your plan, sir?" Elbert asked.

"That we move out and allow Campbell to take the city," said Williamson. "He is a gentleman and will honor the customs of war. The women and children will be spared, and the city kept intact. If we make a stand, we will all probably be killed or captured. If we move across the river now, we can retake the city when we have reinforcements."

There were murmurs of dissent, but no one could come up with a workable plan for defense. Twiggs and Few were determined to keep their militia in Georgia.

"We can scare up enough able-bodied men in the Purchase to keep the Lobsterbacks off our lands," said Elijah Clark.

"I don't plan to let my family be massacred," John Dooly agreed. "It's all very well to say Campbell will protect the women in the city, but the Tories in the backwoods will be on a rampage with Royal troops so near. It's my Tory neighbors I fear more than the troops."

"I'm with you," said Twiggs. "We can keep the soldiers busy if they try to leave Augusta."

"I'll depend on your doing it," said Williamson. "You Georgia militiamen can retreat to Wilkes County, and I suggest you escort President Glascock and what's left of the Assembly with you."

"They can set up shop at Heard's Fort," said Clark.

"Then make plans to leave as soon as you can gather the refugees," Williamson advised. "And you may use your own judgment in carrying on the defense of liberty. Elbert and his Continentals will cross to Carolina with me tonight, as will Wofford and Pickens. We'll set up communications as soon as we are able."

As the meeting adjourned and the General left the room, he found John and Jamie waiting in the anteroom.

"Sir," said John saluting, "we've come to volunteer for duty with the forces from Ninety-Six."

"Will Wofford told me you might join us," said Williamson. "It will be good to ride with you again."

"Thank you, sir," said John. "And this is my friend James Stratfield. He served in the King's Rangers at Fort James. He's been helping manage the inn since he married Margaret MacLeod. You met him there today."

"I remember," said Williamson. Looking keenly at Jamie's face and seeming to be satisfied, he said, "You may be of more use to me if you stay in Augusta."

"Sir?" Jamie queried.

"The Sword and Thistle is known to be a favorite of Loyalists as well as patriots. If the British forces take Augusta, they'll most likely make this fort their headquarters, and it's near enough to the inn that the officers and men will be there in their off-duty hours. I suggest that you develop some sort of disability, a broken leg perhaps, and stay on to help your wife and her uncle at the inn."

"Are you asking me to spy for you?" Jamie asked.

"That is putting it very bluntly, but yes. You will be paid as a lieutenant in the Continental army, detached for intelligence operations. When I set up a line of communication, your contact will show you a flint spearhead, which he will claim is Cherokee. It will be Creek, and you will tell him so."

Jamie was thinking fast. Did he want to be a spy? He would be derided as an able-bodied man malingering to keep from serving in the army. But he would be able to stay with Meg and be there when their second child was born. She and Angus really needed his help now that she was heavy and clumsy again.

Williamson was waiting for his answer, while several officers stood nearby to speak to him.

"Sir, I'll consider it a privilege to serve you, and my country," said Jamie.

With a twitch of one eyelid, Williamson raised his voice. "I'm sorry we can't use invalids," he said, loud enough to be heard by the waiting officers. "When you feel you are ready for full duty, apply to me in Ninety-Six."

John Stanley shook Jamie's hand as he turned to go and whispered, "Take care of Mary Anne and Johnny for me."

The next day, January thirty-first, the British army of General Campbell marched into Augusta with bagpipes skirling, drums rolling, and the kilts of the Highlanders whipping in the cold breeze from the river. Brass was polished to a dazzling shine and crossbelts claypiped to snowy whiteness, boots blacked and spit-polished to perfection.

In spite of themselves, the Augustans who lined the streets could not help cheering with tears in their eyes. After all, they were Scots and Englishmen for generations back into the past. Their hearts beat faster to the tune of the pipes and pride of ancestry that had lain dormant through their years in the wilderness and quickened at the sight of the disciplined troops in scarlet coats.

At the corner of Center and Broad Streets, Mary Anne stood with Johnny and the two black servants Joseph had left to keep house for them. The little boy marched in place in time to the drums, lifting his knees high and pushing on an imaginary set of pipes.

Lord God, why do I feel like cheering? Mary Anne thought. Next week they may be shooting at John and Will Wofford and Andy Williamson.

Lieutenant Colonel Archibald Campbell and his staff passed, mounted on blooded horses, followed by the Highlanders of Fraser's 71st Regiment, then the New York Loyalist Volunteers led by Colonel George Turnbull, followed by the guns and caissons of the Royal Artillery drawn by matched black horses curried to a splendid sheen, their harness buckles shining in the sun. Escorting them into town were the South Carolina Royalist regiment of Colonel Alexander Innes in Tory green and, at the end of the column, Lieutenant Colonel Thomas Brown and his East Florida Rangers dressed in the buckskins of frontiersmen and carrying long rifles. Brown himself was mounted on a fine bay stallion. At the end of their column was a company of Creek Indians.

As the Ranger company approached the corner where Mary Anne stood, Brown's face lighted in recognition, and he doffed his black hat with a jay-feather cockade.

Mary Anne curtsied but kept her eyes discreetly lowered. Brown might not be so friendly when he learned that John had joined Williamson's militia.

As Campbell and his staff approached Fort Grierson, Colonel Grierson, the Reverend Mr. Seymour, and a group of loyal Augustans were there to greet him. Campbell dismounted as the clergyman raised his hand in blessing, bowing his head for the short prayer. Then Colonel Grierson bad him welcome to Augusta and offered shelter and food for the King's troops.

Angus stood with Meg, Jamie, and young Angus on the porch of the inn, his eyes so clouded with tears that he could see only the scarlet of their coats as the pipers went swinging by. Meg wore her shawl of MacLeod tartan over her head and shoulders in the winter wind and cried unashamedly as she clung to Jamie's arm.

"They are magnificent," said Jamie. "They make our poor, ill-equipped militia look like beggars."

"Aye, lad," said Angus, "they make a mon proud to be a Scot. If the damned English had kept the Stuarts on the throne, we'd have had none of this frooferau."

The Highlanders had crossed the gully, and their officers pulled their horses up at the entrance to Fort Grierson to let the troops pass through the gate.

Thomas Brown's Rangers were halted beside the path to the Sword and Thistle as the artillery struggled to ford the swollen stream, the heavy gun carriages sinking into the mud and the horses floundering to keep their footing.

Brown saw the group on the porch and waved. "Angus! Jamie! Glad to see you! I'll be in for a dram and a talk as soon as we can set up camp. Your servant, Mrs. Stratfield." He doffed his hat and bowed to Meg, then squeezed his horse to move on.

"We'll not be overrun with soldiers," said Angus. "If the officers come to the Sword and Thistle, the men will find another place to drink their beer."

"It's just as well," said Meg. "The officers may get roaring drunk, but they aren't as apt to break furniture and smash glass."

Jamie said nothing. Officers in their cups were more likely to talk about plans and tactics. He had made a great show of falling from a ladder that morning and wrenching his leg and back. Now he walked with a limp.

As the last of the Indians crossed the gully, the crowd drifted back into the inn, where it took Angus and Jamie to keep the tankards filled and Meg to serve the tables.

Later in the afternoon, George Galphin came into the taproom, taking off his hat and heavy cloak, then backing up to the fire roaring in one of the fireplaces. Angus left the bar to Jamie and carried a tankard of ale to the fireplace. Holding the poker in the flames until it glowed, he thrust it into the ale and handed the steaming tankard to Galphin.

Galphin took a sip of the bubbling liquid, then waited for it to cool enough to drink. Moving over to the settle beside the hearth and stretching his legs out to the blaze, he motioned Angus to sit down beside him.

"Damn and blasted Lobsterbacks," he said when Angus had lowered himself to the bench. "They came into my plantation and stole ninety of my slaves. Broke into my office and went through my papers. Said I was stirring up rebellion among the Creeks."

"Were you?" Angus asked.

"Hell no," said Galphin. "I've tried to keep them from joining the Tories; I don't want them swarming over the settlements. But I haven't encouraged them to fight anyone. Most of them don't know one white face from another. Now Campbell's got my brother-in-law captive. I've got to eat crow to get him out of their hands."

"Why don't you write Campbell a letter?" Angus asked. "The state you're in, you might make matters worse if you confront him."

"I'd like to push his teeth down his lying throat," said Galphin.

"I'll bring you pen and paper in the back dining room," said Angus. "Desmond can carry the letter to him at the fort."

"I'd not send a black," said Galphin. "The bastards are liable to steal him and claim they're confiscating rebel property."

"Thomas Brown is coming in sometime today," said Angus. "I can give your letter to him."

"Would you send Jamie to me with the pen and paper and more ale?" Galphin asked as he rose and started toward the dining room. "I know your leg bothers you in this cold weather."

Surprised and touched by Galphin's thoughtfulness, Angus stumped over to the bar and took Jamie's place.

When Jamie entered the dining room, Galphin was seated at the table, his empty tankard before him and a small package wrapped in skins beside it.

"I know you're interested in Indian relics," he said as Jamie filled the tankard and took a quill pen and inkwell and a sheet of foolscap from a bureau against the wall.

Galphin opened the furry package and handed him a flint spearpoint. "I thought you might like to see this Cherokee point," he said.

Jamie's heartbeat quickened as the took the point and turned it over in his hand. The point was notched with obvious Creek markings.

"Don't you mean a Creek point?" Jamie asked.

Galphin looked at the window and door, then said in a low tone, "Williamson's heard from Ashe. He should be here with his artillery by the end of the month.

"I've a Creek nephew who is scouting with Brown's Rangers. He'll contact you with this spearhead some evening soon when he's fishing on the riverbank. Give him information if you have any. He speaks good English, though Brown doesn't know it, and has a sharp mind. He'll remember without having it in writing. I'll see that it gets to Williamson.

"Now, go back to the bar. We don't want to arouse suspicion."

Jamie limped into the tap room. There was no sense in letting Angus or Meg know anything about his work. If they didn't know, they would not be guilty of treason.

Galphin had hardly left the inn before a group of officers on horseback arrived, tied their mounts at the hitching rail, and stomped up the steps, their long cloaks gathered around them against the winter wind. Thomas Brown was with them, his buckskins embellished with Ranger insignia, his cloak the Tory green of a Colonial officer.

Angus went to the door to greet them, his peg leg thumping on the wide boards of the tap room. Brown shook his hand, then turned to the red-coated officers with him. "Colonel Campbell," he said, "MacLeod was a sergeant in the King's Highlanders at Bloody Marsh. His leg was lost in service to his King."

"I'm happy to know we've good Scots blood in Augusta," said the colonel.

"Aye, Colonel, we've mair Scottish names than English in the back country," said Angus. "No good Highland lad wants to settle in the lowlands."

"They'll all be given a chance to show their loyalty," said Campbell. "We'll start tomorrow to take their oaths of loyalty to their King."

Thomas Brown had seen Jamie at the bar and moved on to talk to him.

"Stratfield!" he exclaimed. "I'm glad to see you're with us. You and Stanley did a fine job for me at Brownsborough."

"Thank you, sir," said Jamie, neither confirming nor denying his loyalty.

"I owe a debt of gratitude to Stanley for his help in my time of trouble. Is he still in town?"

"No, sir," said Jamie. "He's joined the rebel regiment from Ninety-Six under his friend Andrew Williamson."

"The Devil he has!" Brown exclaimed. "I never thought Stanley would desert. And what of Joseph Merrill? I considered both of them my friends."

"The Merrills are in Charlestown," said Jamie. "They were afraid their house would be flattened by an artillery barrage or looted by soldiers."

"Campbell has given orders that there is to be no looting," said Brown.

"I'd be happier about Mary Anne Stanley and their son if she'd come out here to the inn," said Jamie. "They are staying at the Merrill house."

"The least I can do for Stanley is to see that his family is safe," said Brown. "I'll talk to Campbell about a guard for the Merrill house."

"Thank you, sir," said Jamie.

Angus had shown the officers to a table near the fire and was busy mulling the ale in their tankards. Brown brought a tankard from the bar to join their party.

The next morning Mary Anne answered a knock on the door to find a sergeant in the uniform of Fraser's Highlanders.

"Mrs. Stanley?" the sergeant inquired. "Ma'am, Colonel Campbell has sent me to guard the house so you and the wee lad will not be bothered." Johnny had come up behind her and was peeking out from behind her skirt.

"This is my son John," said Mary Anne.

The sergeant held out his hand. "My name is MacAlister," he said, solemnly shaking the little boy's hand.

"Thank you, Sergeant MacAlister," said Mary Anne. "Will you be staying here at the house at night?"

"Yes, ma'am," said MacAlister, blushing. "The colonel feels that would be best."

"Then I'll have Cindy make you a bed in the library. She can bring your meals there."

"Thank you, ma'am," said the sergeant. "I'll stand guard outside the door in the daytime so they'll know you are protected."

"My husband, as you must know, is with the South Carolina troops under Colonel Williamson," said Mary Anne. "It is very kind of the colonel to assure my safety."

"We're not here to fight women and children," said MacAlister. "I'll be taking my post now." Moving to the side of the front door, he stood at parade rest with his back to the wall of the house.

That night Mary Anne was glad of the Highlander's presence. Soldiers free to go to taverns and brothels for the first time since they had left Savannah kept the householders awake with loud laughter and bawdy songs, but worse, intermittent bursts of gunfire.

The next morning, Cindy brought Mary Anne's breakfast to her bedroom. "They're sayin' the rebels is sneakin' around outside town," said Cindy. "An' the Tory soldiers is raisin' sand in town."

"Was that the gunfire I heard last night?" Mary Anne asked.

"Good Lawd only knows," said Cindy. "Redcoats, they's tellin' black folks they can go free if they belong to rebels."

"Mr. John is what they call a rebel," said Mary Anne.

"Yes'm," said Cindy. "But I ain't leavin' to go with no Lobsterbacks. I'm a rebel, too, if you is."

"Thank you, Cindy," said Mary Anne. "Did you give Sergeant MacAlister some breakfast?"

"Yes'm. He's a fine gentleman," said Cindy. "Thanked me just like proper white folks."

"Of course he is," said Mary Anne. "When this is all over, people like MacAlister will be our friends again."

That night Mary Anne slept soundly, knowing that the sergeant was in the library downstairs. She was wakened by Cindy's screams and heavy steps pounding up the stair, then a shot and the sound of wood splintering under heavy blows.

The door of her bedroom burst open and a man in buckskins pushed into her room. Mary Anne pulled the bedclothes around herself like a cloak and slid out of the big bed, backing against the wall.

"Where's John Stanley?" the man asked looking at the empty bed. "We've come to free him from the redcoats."

"Lieutenant Stanley is with Colonel Williamson," said Mary Anne. "He left before the British troops came."

"Then the redcoat back there wasn't lying," said the man. "We heard he'd been taken prisoner and held in his home. We came to free him." He turned and pounded down the stairs, nearly knocking down Johnny who was coming from the nursery to find his mother.

"Let's get the hell out of here," the man in buckskins called out, and Mary Anne heard the clatter of boots down the front steps.

Cindy, collapsed in a heap on the floor, was moaning. "Dey done kill Mr. MacAlister!" she cried to Mary Anne. "Dey knocked me down when I gots in dey way."

Mary Anne hurried to the library and nearly fainted as she saw the grisly mess on the floor. MacAlister had been shot in the chest, then hacked with an Indian hatchet, his scalp partly peeled back as though the assailant had stopped in the middle of the operation.

Picking up Johnny, who had followed her and was sobbing wildly, she backed out into the hall. Cindy had pulled herself to her feet and seemed able to walk.

"Come into the parlor and take care of Johnny," Mary Anne said to her. "I have to run for help. The murderers must not get away."

Hurrying up the stairs, she pulled on her shoes and fastened a heavy cloak over her nightdress. Running down the steps, she turned toward Center Street.

Soldiers from one of the Broad Street taverns were walking toward the river bank, one of them holding his nose and squeaking like a bagpipe and the others singing the words to "MacCrimmon's Lament." Seeing the lady approaching, they stopped and stared through rum-reddened eyes.

"Oh, please help," Mary Anne cried. "They've killed Sergeant MacAlister and they're escaping."

One of the soldiers seemed to be almost sober as he snapped upright and said, "We'll help, ma'am. Where is the Sergeant? Which way did they go?"

"They shot him at our house," said Mary Anne. "I think they must have come in a boat from across the river."

The news seemed to have sobered the rest of the party, who scattered toward the river bank while their spokesman followed Mary Anne to the Merrill house.

Cindy was sitting in a rocking chair on the porch, singing softly to Johnny. When he saw his mother and the soldier, he began to sob again and held his arms up to her.

She squatted down beside the chair and hugged him, but said, "You will have to be a brave man and stay here with Cindy while I take this gentleman in the house. Mommy will be back as soon as she can."

She led the soldier to the library door and stood with her back to the wall, afraid she would be sick.

The soldier came out quietly and closed the door. His face was white and his eyes suspiciously red.

"Can you take the wee lad and go to a friend's house?" he asked. "The colonel will want to talk to you, I know, but that can wait. I'll have to report this to my commanding officer." He rubbed the cuff of his sleeve across his eyes.

Mary Anne wanted to comfort him but knew to leave him to his grief.

"I'll take Cindy and Johnny next door to the Martins. They'll take us in until things are straightened out here."

"Yes ma'am," said the soldier.

Still weak and shaky but determined not to let Johnny know, Mary Anne gathered up the things he would need and went back to the front porch. Cindy put a finger to her lips. "Poor little fella done cried hisself to sleep," she said.

"We're going to the Martins," said Mary Anne, taking the child into her arms. "Will you please carry these things there and ask Mrs. Martin if we can stay for the rest of the night? I'll bring Johnny."

Cindy tied the shawl that she had been using to cover the little boy around her shoulders, picked up the basket of his clothing and scurried down the steps. Mary Anne followed slowly, so as not to waken Johnny.

Elizabeth Martin met her on the road. "Cindy told us," she panted. "You're welcome to stay as long as you will. There's room for you and Johnny in the spare room, and Cindy can sleep on a pallet on the floor."

"Thank you," was all Mary Anne could say.

James Martin, fully dressed now, met them at the bottom of the steps and carefully took the boy from her so he wouldn't awaken.

"Who was it attacked you?" he asked.

"I'd never seen them before," Mary Anne answered. "They said they had come to rescue John. Someone had told them he was being held prisoner at the Merrill house."

They had started up the stairs to the bedroom when Johnny woke again and sobbed, "Mommy!"

"I'm right here," said Mary Anne. "We're going to stay the night with the Martins."

At the top of the stairs, she took him from Martin and carried him into the bedroom.

Mary Anne handed the still sobbing child to the black woman who gathered him to her ample bosom and sat down in the cane-bottomed rocking chair beside the bed. As she began to hum in time to the creak of the rockers, he put his thumb in his mouth and settled with a sigh. His mother tiptoed quietly out the door and down the stairs where the Martins waited in the front hall.

"Come in the parlor," said Elizabeth Martin. "James has poured you a good stiff drink of brandy. I want to see you drink it, then you can have a cup of hot milk to take up to bed."

"Do you feel like talking about it?" James Martin asked as she sipped the fiery liquid.

"I don't ever want to talk about it," said Mary Anne, "but I know I'll have to talk to Colonel Fraser in the morning."

"There's going to be a terrible reaction, I'm afraid," said Martin. "All Whigs will be punished for the murder."

"MacAlister was a good, kind man," said Mary Anne. "I don't think he cared a thing about politics. It was some horrible ruffians who murdered him." She put her hands over her face and bent her head till it almost touched her knees; a cold wave of nausea swept over her, leaving her trembling.

Elizabeth hurried to her side, but Mary Anne sat up and pushed her hair back from her face.

"I'm sorry," she said. "I had a pretty bad time with some of the same kind of Cracker outlaws once. I hate to think that John is fighting on the same side with them."

"Did you know the men?" Martin asked.

"No, I didn't really see but one. He was big, dirty, bearded, and he smelled horrible, as though he'd never bathed."

"That could describe half the men in Georgia," said Martin. "Did he have on any sort of uniform?"

"No. Just greasy buckskins and a coonskin hat. He had a homemade powderhorn and a hatchet . . ." With the last word she covered her face and reached for the brandy glass.

"There was a tomahawk on the floor in the library. The man who killed MacAlister must have dropped it when he picked up his gun to run. He'd been trying to scalp the sergeant."

"Thank God you're Brown's friend," said Martin. "We'd best send word to him in the morning, so you can tell him the story. Feeling is going to be high among the Scots. They don't forget."

"Surely they wouldn't blame Mary Anne," Elizabeth exclaimed.

"They might act first and think later," said James. "I don't think Mary Anne should be left alone. I'll try to get permission to take both of you and the children across the river to Martintown to stay with my mother and father."

"I'll ask Colonel Brown when I talk to him," said Mary Anne. "Maybe he can see that yours and the Merrills' houses are not ransacked while we are away."

The interview next morning was not as nerve-wracking as Mary Anne had feared. Colonel Fraser had already talked to Thomas Brown. The two officers arrived together to talk to Mary Anne. A captain and two enlisted men in scarlet uniforms and several in the Tory green of the Carolina Volunteers were milling around the Merrill house next door.

Brown introduced Colonel Fraser, then asked Mary Anne to tell them exactly what had happened and to describe the men.

"So they claimed to be sent to rescue your husband," Fraser said when she had finished.

"They wouldn't believe my nursemaid when she said he was gone, and the ruffian who burst into my bedroom said they had shot MacAlister for lying."

"Have you any idea where John Stanley might be?" Brown asked.

"He left here with Andrew Williamson and William Wofford to go to South Carolina," said Mary Anne. "I haven't heard from him."

"You know that his name will be placed on the list of rebels?" Brown asked.

"He knew that when he joined the militia," said Mary Anne. "He trusted British gentlemen to protect us. He didn't expect Whig partisans to act like savages."

"Do you plan to remain in Augusta?" Fraser asked.

"I hope to be allowed to go to the Martin's plantation in South

Carolina," said Mary Anne. "James Martin's parents live there. I would like permission for him to escort me and his wife and children to Martintown."

"I think that can be arranged," said Fraser. "I'd not like to think what might happen, now, if some of my troops have too much rum. It will be best if both of these houses are occupied by British officers."

"We'll be ready to leave before sundown," Mary Anne answered.

Word of MacAlister's murder reached the Sword and Thistle early in the morning when Desmond returned from picking up fresh eggs and butter from the market. Despite the surrender of the city, life was going on, and officers from Fort Grierson were crowding the inn for meals. Many of the market stalls in town were vacant, because Whigs had fled to Wilkes or across the river rather than live under British military rule. Most of the country people were still selling their produce regardless of politics. Hens kept laying and cows producing milk.

Jamie Stratfield had seen the hurried passing of Fraser and Brown with the detachment of Highlanders just after daybreak and knew something serious had happened. He met Desmond as he drove the wagon into the inn yard.

"From what all I hear," said Desmond, "Dey's been a soldier killed at the Merrill's house, and Miss Mary Anne's goin' with de Martins to get away from here. Dey say dey cut up de soldier in little pieces wit a axe."

"Who did?" Jamie asked. "Do they know who the murderer was?"

"De black girl at de Martins say it was a whole gang of cutthroats from over in Carolina. Rebel militia."

"Oh Lord," said Jamie. "And I promised John I'd take care of Mary Anne."

"Miss Mary Anne, she all right," said Desmond. "I asked special. She takin' Cindy and little Johnny to Martintown. The soldiers gonna let 'em go with Mr. Martin and his family."

"Keep your ears open, Desmond, when there are officers here. I'm afraid there's going to be hell to pay for this."

Colonel Brown stopped in the tavern on the way back to the fort. "I know you are a friend of the Stanleys," he said to Jamie. "What would cause a rumor that Stanley was being held prisoner here?"

"God knows," Jamie answered. "Maybe because he's not with the Georgia militia. He joined his old friends from Ninety-Six."

"I can't understand a man of his caliber deserting his King," said Brown. "We are going to have to approach every male in this territory and enlist them all in the King's militia. Low-life Crackers may not be much good as soldiers, but at least they won't be able to fight against us."

"I've heard that most of the Whigs have gone to the Purchase or across the river," said Jamie.

"Oh, yes," said Brown. "John Dooly and Elijah Clark are up in Wilkes County. They've sent their wives and families over to the Carolina side with the rest of the rebels.

"Campbell's going up into Wilkes with Fuser's Highlanders and Hamilton's North Carolina Loyalists to enlist the Crackers, or punish them if they refuse. It is a good thing to get the Highlanders out of Augusta. They're ready to shoot any Whig they see. MacAlister was a great favorite. I suggested him to guard Mrs. Stanley because he was trustworthy and personable, but never pushed above his station."

"It's a bloody shame," Jamie said. "Have they any idea who murdered him?"

"Renegade Crackers," said Brown. "But, believe me, they've stirred up the Scots. There will be no quarter now, when Highlanders fight against backwoodsmen."

"You say the Highland troops are in the Purchase administering oaths of loyalty? What if someone refuses?"

"I'm afraid," said Brown, "that they may make it so very uncomfortable that he changes his mind. We're starting today to enlist the men of Augusta and the nearby settlements. They will be given the choice of swearing loyalty to the King and, if able-bodied, joining the King's militia or of leaving their lands and going into rebel territory."

Jamie tried to mask his feelings. What would he say when they asked him to swear his loyalty? He could feel the sweat forming on his upper lip and the palms of his hands. He picked up Brown's tankard to refill it from the keg on the bar.

"We've had trouble with that ruffian Few and his men, and renegades like the ones who killed MacAlister," Brown continued. "They have been hitting the Loyalist settlements, stealing horses and running off cattle. If the settlers all proclaim their loyalty, the rebels will have more than they can do to punish them all."

Jamie was sure that the Fews, Twiggs, and Dooly knew who was forced and who was really a Loyalist, but he held his peace.

"Campbell and Hamilton will capture all the little stockaded forts up in the wilderness where the rebel families have gotten together and holed up for protection. With Savannah and Augusta in our hands, it's just these little Cracker settlements that keep us from bringing all of Georgia under the King's rule."

"What's become of the rebel militia?" Jamie asked.

"They've given up and crossed into the Carolinas," said Brown. "They'll be no hindrance to Hamilton's loyal North Carolinians."

Jamie felt like telling Brown he'd better not write off Dooly and Clark and the Few brothers, but he kept his mouth shut. If it weren't for Meg, he'd forget this idea of staying to gather information. He'd do a damn sight better job shooting at the enemy than serving them ale.

Brown left the inn without any mention of requiring an oath of loyalty from him. Perhaps he thought Angus and his son-in-law could never be disloyal to their King.

The information about Campbell and Hamilton's move into Wilkes could be important. He'd seen no sign of an Indian on the river bank, but picking up a pail of slops in the kitchen, he headed in that direction. He never emptied slops, but the British had no way of knowing that.

As he rounded the corner of the barn, he saw that a dugout canoe was tied to a clump of willows upriver from the inn. Reaching the bank, he saw an Indian begin to paddle toward him dragging a net full of fish.

"You want fish?" the Indian called to Jamie.

Jamie grasped the pail and climbed down the path that had been worn into the bank.

"What kind of fish?" Jamie asked.

"All fresh catfish," said the Indian. "Or would you buy Indian spear-head?" he asked, beaching the canoe near Jamie.

"If it's a Creek point," said Jamie. The Indian reached in a pouch at his waist and showed him the spearpoint Galphin had shown him.

"We could use the fish for dinner," said Jamie. "As for the spearhead," he lowered his voice, "tell our friend that Hamilton and Campbell have left with eighty men to attack the forts in Wilkes County, and that Mrs. Stanley has gone to Martintown."

"You can have all the fish for sixpence," said the Indian. "Will you need more tomorrow?"

"We'll have mussels from New Savannah tomorrow," said Jamie, "but you can bring me as many fish as you can catch the next day. Bring them early in the morning, so we can fry them for breakfast."

"I'll bring them just after sunup," said the Indian.

* * *

Five nights later, the forces of Andrew Pickens and John Dooly crossed the Savannah at Cowan's Ferry and surprised the Loyalists at Carr's fort. They had surrounded the fort and settled down to starve out the occupants, when a message was brought to Pickens by an Indian that Colonel James Boyd and eight hundred Loyalists were on the way from Ninety-Six, through the Long Canes, to join Campbell and Hamilton.

Breaking the siege of Carr's fort, Pickens sent Robert Anderson with a squadron of South Carolinians to harass the Loyalists as they tried to cross the river. John Stanley was waiting with Anderson's men at Cherokee Ford when the first raft load of Boyd's Loyalists started across. The river was so flooded by February storms, the ford was impassable.

"Let 'em get into the middle of the river, boys," Anderson said when some of his men raised their long rifles. "They'll be sitting ducks."

As the rafts approached the bank on the Georgia side, a volley rang out among the tall canes, cutting down a man at the pole of one raft and wounding others among the passengers. The current carried the first raft downriver with the others following. John and the men were so tangled in tall canes and mired in mud that they were unable to follow along the bank.

"Come on," Anderson shouted, "we'd better get back over to Carolina. The Tories are way the hell down the river by now."

On February tenth, Pickens' Carolina militia and Colonel John Dooly's Georgians recrossed the river into Georgia. Word had come to General Williamson that Boyd and his Tories were near the Broad River in Georgia where Colonel Elijah Clark was keeping track of them with his mounted militia. Combining forces on February fourteenth, with Pickens' Ninety-Six militia in the center, Dooly's infantry to the left, and Clark's cavalry to the right, they marched toward the Loyalist camp. Captain James McCall, sent on reconnaissance, came back with news that Boyd and his men were camped in a field by Kettle Creek with their horses turned out to graze and their foragers busy butchering cattle they had stolen from a farm nearby.

"They don't know we're in twenty miles of 'em." said McCall.

"Then let's catch 'em with their pants down," said Pickens.

A high rail fence ran obliquely toward the right of the camp. A canebrake covered the front and left sides. Pickens ordered John and the rest of the Ninety-Six contingent to the high ground beyond the fence. Dooly and Clark were to go through the canebrake and close in toward the center.

At Pickens' order to advance, the troops broke into the open. Pickets guarding the camp got off one volley of warning shots, then retreated. The Tories grabbed for their weapons and formed a line of battle with the fence at their back.

To John Stanley, on the hillside beyond the fence, the whole scene seemed artificial, like a scene from a play. It was too easy to sit on the hillside and sight along his rifle barrel at the men in green by the fence. The two lines had come together in places where green-clad Tories lunged with bayonets attached to their English muskets at frontiersman swinging rifle butts or stabbing and dodging with hunting knives or Indian axes.

He squeezed off a shot at a green uniform that knelt to sight at a man in buckskins and saw the Tory fall, his rifle firing harmlessly overhead. Then it was a matter of load and fire, load and fire, hoping his bullets were hitting green instead of buckskin targets.

Slowly the Loyalists were driven back from the fence toward Kettle Creek. John saw Colonel Boyd, the Tory Commander, fall. The field was strewn with green uniforms as the Tories forded the creek to form on a hill beyond. John and the rest of Pickens' regiment followed, wading through the swamp that lay between their position and the creek. Dooly's men closed from the other flank to surround the hill.

These North Carolina Tories knew as much about Indian fighting as the Georgia and South Carolina men and were not going to be caught on the hill top. As Pickens' men moved up the hill, the Tories charged down, then charged again. When they saw that the South Carolinians were about to gain the top, they turned and fled into the swamps and canebrakes. Most of them were captured by the triumphant rebels and confined in a roped-off corral guarded by men from the three rebel regiments.

John walked with Andrew Pickens around the improvised hospital compound. They had both known many of the men on both sides, fighting beside them against Indians and outlaws in the backwoods. Pickens found Boyd near death and squatted down beside him. The Tory colonel opened his eyes and focused on Pickens' face.

"I'm sorry it had to be this way," said Pickens. "German George isn't worth giving a good American life for. We'll do everything in our power to save you."

Boyd closed his eyes, then opened them again. "I can think of no greater glory than dying for my King," he said. "All I ask is that two of my men be left with me until I die, then allowed to bury me." He reached into the opened bosom of his blouse. "In the name of our friendship, please see that my wife gets this brooch. She'll know what it means."

Pickens took the brooch and tucked it under his own shirt. "I promise to do my best to find her," he said touching Boyd gently on the shoulder, then moving on.

The whole bloody battle had taken only an hour. The sun was just beginning to warm the frost-covered ground as the rebel troops began to dig trenches for the dead. By noon they were on their way, the wounded of both armies carried on litters, the captured Tories marching in a group with hands tied behind them.

"It's a terrible thing to herd Carolinians like a bunch of cattle," said Pickens, riding at the head of his regiment with John a pace or two behind, on his left. "But these bloody sons of bitches have raised havoc all over the countryside on the way here. They've robbed and burned like outlaws. I'm not going to hang them myself, but I'd like to bet the court in Ninety-Six will see they swing."

"Reminds me of the Regulator days," said John. "And I'd not be surprised to find some of these ruffians rode with Govey Black and his boys."

That night they bivouacked near the river and crossed over the next day to leave the prisoners in Ninety-Six and join Williamson, across the river, facing Augusta.

Word of Boyd's defeat reached Augusta just as Lieutenant Colonel Archibald Campbell was preparing to leave the town. He was overdue for a leave of absence to see his family in Scotland and didn't trust the militiamen recruited from the area to defend the city against Georgians and South Carolinians. He had tried unsuccessfully to dislodge Andrew Williamson's men from their camp across the river, and now Pickens and Dooly were marching to join them, charged up by the victory at Kettle Creek. The British marched out of Augusta as they had marched in, with drums beating and pipes skirling.

Marching toward Savannah, they were joined by North Carolina Tories who had escaped the rebel attack at Kettle Creek and by General Augustine Prevost's Florida Loyalists. The combined forces should be strong enough to meet any rebel attack. Campbell felt safe in turning his command over to Lieutenant Colonel Mark Prevost, the general's brother, and leaving for Scotland.

Campbell's troops were hardly out of sight of Augusta before the Georgians and Carolinians of Williamson's command began to cross the river. After only two weeks, the city was once again in rebel hands.

John Stanley, crossing on the ferry with Pickens and Dooly, wore the insignia of a captain in the South Carolina Militia.

Williamson had gone ahead to Fort Grierson, where he found that Campbell had left a large store of British supplies. As his staff gathered in the main room of the trading post, Williamson finished a dispatch to Governor Rutledge of South Carolina.

"I've recommended that the Georgia Assembly return to Augusta," he said when he joined his officers. "The backwoodsmen need to know that Georgia is part of the United States. I've learned that eleven hundred men from Richmond County joined Campbell's Loyalist militia."

"You can't blame them too much for trying to save their skins and protect their families when the governor and council had left them," said one of the officers.

"Lily-livered cowards," said Elijah Clark. "The people in Burke and Wilkes weren't so ready to turn their coats."

"They weren't so close to the Redcoats," said Williamson. "We'll have to give the turncoats a chance to come back over to our side, and give them a government to keep them there."

"You're going to have a helluva time protecting them from the men who've had their homes robbed and burned by Tories," said John Dooly.

"My orders are to keep the peace," said Williamson. "When I receive other orders from Governor Rutledge, I'll act upon them. Meanwhile you are to see that your men cause no disturbances among the civilian population."

The Georgia officers exchanged looks but made no further comment.

"Is that understood?" Williamson asked.

"Yes, sir," they answered.

There was less conflict than they had expected. Most of the homes that had been taken over by Loyalist sympathizers were emptied before the rebel troops returned. Others were returned to their owners in an orderly manner. The few arguments were settled by the militia, with Tories given the choice of leaving or going to jail.

The general ordered nine of the most prominent Tories brought to the fort and held in the guard house to shield them from attack. The Reverend James Seymour, James Grierson, Martin Weatherford, William Manson, Andrew McLean, and four others were kept in protective custody to wait for civil government to be organized. Whig families began to return to the city from hiding in the wilderness and on outlying farms.

John Stanley asked Colonel Pickens' permission to go to Martintown to bring Mary Anne and Johnny back to Augusta.

"I've talked to James Martin," said John. "You remember, he joined Dooly's regiment after his wife and children went to stay with his parents."

"The more good, stable families we have in Augusta," said Pickens, "the more chance we'll have of keeping peace. You have my permission to bring both families back here. I'll talk to Dooly about a pass for Martin."

The Merrill and the Martin houses were still in good condition. In fact, John found wine and cheese and other delicacies left in the larder by the British officers in their hurried departure. He had heard that Joseph Merrill had joined the Carolina forces in Charlestown and that Jocelyn and the children had moved into her mother's house on Tradd Street. He and Mary Anne could take care of the house on The Bay until the Merrills returned.

Mary Sheldon went to Fort Grierson as soon as she heard about Mr. Seymour's imprisonment. During the two weeks of British occupation, the rector had vouched for Mary and Ben, even though their son was a member of the Continental forces. Colonel Campbell had given them a pass so that Ben could ride into town to the market with vegetables and to the inn to deliver the whisky which was in great demand by the British officers.

John saw Mary talking to the sentry as he was leaving his meeting with Colonel Pickens. "Can I be of any help?" he asked returning the sentry's salute.

"Oh, Mr. Stanley, I'm so glad to see you," said Mary. "Mr. Seymour was so kind to us when the British were here. I'd like to help him, if I can. I'm bringing fresh vegetables and eggs to Mrs. Seymour and the children if I can get permission."

"I'll talk to Colonel Pickens," John said. "Let this lady wait for me on the bench," he told the sentry.

A few minutes later he returned, pass in hand, to walk with Mary to the wagon where young Benjy was arguing with a group of militiamen who were trying to barter for his produce.

"I'll bring more to town tomorrow," said Mary as she climbed onto the wagon seat. "These are for a lady at the other end of town." She let the brake off the wagon, clucked to the horses, and started into town.

A week later, as Augustans had just settled down to everyday living, the city was once more flooded with troops. General Ashe and his North Carolinians had finally arrived in pursuit of the British. Crossing from South Carolina, they camped overnight on the Common, then left at daybreak by the Savannah Road to pursue Campbell's army, now under Prevost's command.

By the third of March, they were camped on Brier Creek, waiting for General Lincoln's troops from Purrysburg to join them. General Williamson had ordered Pickens' militia from Ninety-Six to follow Ashe to back him up in an attack. John had had to leave Mary Anne in the Merrill house again to take to the field.

Pickens' South Carolinians were three or four miles from Ashe's camp when hell broke loose ahead of them. Prevost, learning of Lincoln's plan to join Ashe, had doubled back to attack before the North Carolinians could be reinforced.

Ashe had set up camp on a neck between Briar Creek and the river, and had sent out scouting parties in all directions to locate the enemy, leaving only eight hundred men in camp to repair harness, clean equipment, and make ready for battle when their reinforcements should arrive.

At four o'clock in the afternoon, Prevost opened fire with his artillery and charged the center of the hastily assembled North Carolina line. Within five minutes, the line had broken and the North Carolinians were fleeing for their lives, leaving their horses, artillery, and provisions behind. With water on three sides of them, they piled into the creek or the Savannah River, trying desperately to swim or drag themselves through the mud and quicksand of the swamp. Over four hundred were killed, wounded, or captured. Prevost lost only sixteen men.

As the men of the 71st Highlanders tore into the crumbling rebel lines, one of them shouted, "Remember poor MacAlister!" In the Highlander lines, no prisoners were taken. Warfare had ceased to be fought by civilized rules.

Pickens' militia, arriving too late, decided that discretion was more practical than hopeless valor and hurried off to join General Lincoln's forces near Savannah.

Mary Anne first heard of the defeat three days later, when one of Ashe's soldiers made his way to the Savannah Road and was picked up by a farmer driving his wagon to Augusta. All he could tell the authorities was that the whole army had been killed or drowned.

James Seymour, who had been released from custody and was free to make calls in the parish, hurried to the Merrill house as soon as he heard the news.

"We've had sad news of a battle," he said when Mary Anne invited him into the parlor, "but do not listen to rumors. They should have an official report soon at Fort Grierson. Colonel Williamson has promised to let me know the true state of affairs."

Mary Anne felt a hot wave wash over her, then cold, her arms prickling as though stuck with a hundred pins.

"Has there been any word of Pickens' men?" she asked when she was able to swallow the lump in her throat.

"No word except the story of a man who swam the creek and hid in some swamps until he could crawl to safety. I talked to him in the dispensary at the fort where he's being treated for pneumonia. He could tell me nothing of Pickens, because he hadn't seen the South Carolina militia."

"I know John must be safe," Mary Anne said.

"Keep that thought," said the Rector, "and pray to God to keep him that way."

"Always," said Mary Anne.

"I find that the Twenty-third Psalm gives me strength. Will you say it with me?"

Bowing their heads they repeated, "The Lord is my Shepherd; I shall not want . . ."

Ending with, "Surely goodness and mercy shall follow me all the days of my life, and I shall dwell in the house of the Lord forever," Mary Anne felt tears rolling down her cheeks, and Mr. Seymour pulled out a kerchief and loudly blew his nose.

"Remember, too," he said, "that it is important to be able to say 'Thy will be done,' and to mean it."

As he stood up to leave, Mary Anne held out her hand. "Thank you. I've missed my friend Charles Woodmason, who helped me in some bad times. You give me the courage to keep my chin up."

The next day, General Williamson received a dispatch from General Lincoln in Purrysburg describing the humiliating defeat and the loss of a whole corps of the American army. With Ashe's army destroyed, the Georgia and South Carolina back country would again be vulnerable to attack. Pickens' regiment had been spared but would be needed to protect the frontier from Tories and Indians.

James Seymour carried the good news about Pickens to Mary Anne, as soon as General Williamson told him. Though criticized by many of the radical Whigs for familiarity with an acknowledged Loyalist, Williamson realized that Seymour was doing his best to keep the peace between churchgoers of both sides.

At the Sword and Thistle, Jamie had heard about the defeat before the official dispatch arrived and had already told Williamson, who, however, had pretended ignorance when the messenger came. No use breaking Stratfield's cover. He might still be useful. All sorts of information surfaced in the taproom. People had grown used to seeing Jamie with his exaggerated limp, and did not question his absence from militia duty.

A few days later, Jamie had other alarming news. Having spotted the canoe and Indian fisherman, he set out for the river carrying the usual bucket of slops as an excuse. Galphin's messenger was seated on a log, but stood as Jamie broke through the undergrowth, holding his hand up in greeting.

"Word has come to the tribes of the death of John Stuart in Florida. Colonel Thomas Brown has been made superintendent over all the tribes in the Southeast and has sent orders for eight hundred Creeks to assemble with David Taitt and Alexander McGillivray to march to Augusta.

"When do they plan to attack?" Jamie asked.

"They are gathering now in the Creek Nation."

"Thank you for your help," said Jamie.

The Indian raised his hand in farewell and Jamie moved out of the thicket carrying the empty bucket. A few minutes later with darkness beginning to fall, the canoe was out on the river with the fishing net trailing over the stern.

Jamie passed the word to Colonel Williamson an hour later during the officer's evening visit to the tavern for a mug of ale. By the next morning, a dispatch had reached Andrew Pickens in Ninety-Six. Two days later, Pickens met with John Dooly, Benjamin Few, and LeRoy Hammond at Fort Grierson to plan a campaign. John Stanley was able to spend two nights at the Merrill house while the commanders made their plans.

Two days after the conference, Pickens and a combined force of mounted Georgia militia started for Fulsom's Fort on the Ogeechee River where the Creeks were known to be gathering on their way to Colonel Brown's camp. Although warned in time to leave their camp, the Indians were pursued and cut down by the cavalry. Not one Creek reached Brown's rendezvous. Augusta was once more spared an Indian attack.

Savannah was still in British hands, and Governor Wright, once more installed in office, claimed Georgia for the Crown. Upcountry Georgians were determined to prove him a liar by soon calling the full Assembly into session in Augusta. Life under rebel government would proceed as usual.

Mary Anne Stanley still went to Saint Paul's Church on Sunday. The familiar words of Morning Prayer took her back to her childhood in Charlestown and to Woodmason's outdoor services in the backwoods. There was something reassuring about the old words promising continuity in these times of stress. James Seymour, though a Tory, was respected as a minister, and though no longer called the Church of England, Saint Paul's was still a familiar source of faith and comfort to its members, most of whom were conservatives, but not necessarily Loyalists.

One beautiful Sunday in March, with dogwoods in bloom on the hillsides and wisteria filling the air with its grapey perfume, the church was well filled with people of varying political views, glad to put on spring clothes and meet with their neighbors. As the rector mounted the high pulpit for his sermon, everyone waited expectantly, knowing that he had blasted the rebels in the early days and counted disloyalty to the King almost as blasphemy to God. Although they knew he was still loyal, they had found he was tempering his criticism of American patriots.

The lesson for the day was from the eighth chapter of Hosea: "They have sown the wind, and they shall reap the whirlwind."

Looking over the congregation, Seymour said, "The world doesn't really change. All we need in this world is to love God and our neighbor. If everyone in this world practiced the two great commandments, there would never be war and hate and murder.

"Whether we are ruled by the King of England or free to form our own government should not be as important as how we treat our neighbors. If we sow seeds of kindness and understanding, never giving our neighbors a reason to hate us, we will reap a crop of good friends, and our days will be happy. But if we sow seeds of strife, feel envy and jealousy of our neighbors' belongings, if we resent their opinions and try to force our ideas upon them, we will only make enemies, and we will make ourselves unhappy.

"The controversy that is causing this war should be a matter of government against government, not neighbor against neighbor. We are letting our petty likes and dislikes, our envies and jealousies, control our lives. Every day we hear of families being attacked and driven from their homes, their belongings stolen. More often than not, their politics are not the reason for their persecution, but the greed and vengefulness of those who call themselves neighbors.

"We have transgressed against the covenant of the Lord and trespassed against his law. With war raging around us, it is difficult to remember to love your neighbor as yourself. But if we let ourselves fall victim to greed and vengefulness, we will be sowing the wind, as Hosea has written. We will reap the whirlwind. God save us from ourselves."

Turning to face the altar, he bowed his head, saying, "And now, to God, the Father, Son, and Holy Ghost be ascribed all might, majesty, power, and dominion, henceforth and forever more. Amen."

After the final hymn and the benediction, people were still stunned by the reminder of atrocities that had been committed. Out in front of the church, they stood in groups, reliving the happenings of the past weeks.

"Did you hear about the MacInnes family out on Spirit Creek? They were burned out when the British held the city because their son was in Few's militia."

"That's nothing. Whig neighbors stole the Goodings' cattle and pigs and moved into their house last week, saying the Goodings were Tories."

"It's getting so you can't go to bed at night, for fear someone will set your house afire."

"With Burnfoot Brown in the Creek Nation and outlaws taking this chance to rob and burn outlying farms, something has got to be done."

The "something," it was agreed, should be to get back some sort of government that could be depended upon. With the Assembly returning, maybe Augusta would finally have law and order.

·XXII·

SAVANNAH DISASTER

General Lincoln, sitting in Purrysburg with five thousand men to protect Charlestown from attack by the British in Savannah, decided it was time to start a spring campaign through upper Georgia. Augusta could be made safe for a stable government by neutralizing Upcountry Tories.

Leaving General Moultrie with only twelve hundred men at Purrysburg, he marched up the Carolina side of the river to Silver Bluff, and sent word for Moultrie to send him more men and artillery. He had hardly crossed the river into Augusta when word came that General Prevost was marching from Savannah to attack Charlestown with all the Tory forces available.

John Stanley, serving with the South Carolina troops in Lincoln's army, had one night at home with Mary Anne. Bert Sheldon, still in Elbert's Continentals, had only a day to spend with his mother and father on Rae's Creek before reporting to his regiment. Lincoln turned around and hurried the whole American army back toward Charlestown, arriving in time to force Prevost to break his siege and retreat to John's Island.

John was with Pickens when the militia from Ninety-Six attacked the rear guard of Loyalist troops near Stono Ferry. Caught in a fierce hand-to-hand battle with Campbell's Highlanders, he suddenly found himself facing a glowering, sandy-haired giant, with his bayonet leveled. As John swung his empty rifle at the Scotsman's head, he saw the point of the bayonet approaching, just in time to dodge to one side. The blade caught him in the hip, rather than in the gut. Another of Pickens' men swung a rifle and caught the Scotsman in the head, slamming him down. John sank to the ground, the bayonet still in his hip. Everything went black.

He woke in a wagon. On both sides of him wounded men moaned

or cried out as the wagon bounced along a rutted road. Too weak from loss of blood to move, he lay and watched the Spanish moss sway and dance in the wind, as the wagon passed under arching oaks. Was he a captive? Was this a British wagon? He could see a gray-haired black man sitting on the wagon seat. There was no telling where he was going.

When the wagon slowed, then stopped while the driver pulled a fallen limb from the road, John called, "Uncle! Where are we?"

The old man came around and looked over the side of the wagon. John tried to sit up, but found he could only lift his head.

"You lay quiet, massa, or you'll start de bleedin' agin," he said.

"Where are you taking me?" John asked.

"To Charlestown, I reckon. General Lincoln send word he gonna pay for wounded men brought to camp. My massa say go pick 'em up and take 'um in."

"Are we near Black Cypress Plantation, uncle?" John asked.

"Dat Miz Seabright place on de Ashley Riva?" the old man asked. "Yassuh, bout a mile or two."

"Could you take me there, instead?" John asked. "I'll be glad to pay anything you want."

"Massa say go to Charlestown," said the man.

"Mrs. Seabright is my wife's grandmother," John said. "She can take care of me and save the surgeons the trouble."

One of the wounded men rolled his head toward the old man and opened pain-filled eyes. "For God's sake get us somewhere soon. I need water."

"We's near enough Black Cypress. We gonna get you water dere," said the old man, making up his mind.

It was another twenty minutes before they passed through the gates and started along the driveway through the swamp. The huge black oak trees with their silver beards meeting overhead were a protective covering against the outside world.

Anne Seabright had heard the noise of distant battle since daybreak. Warned of the British army nearby, she had refused to flee to the city, even after the boom of artillery and the sound of rifle fire carried across the swamps.

"I've lived to be eighty years old, and I'll be damned if I'll go scurrying into town at the sound of gunfire," she had insisted. "Give me my pistols and leave me alone," she told her butler Isaiah. "Go hide in the swamp so the British won't steal you and sell you in the islands. I can still shoot straight enough to take any British soldiers with me to hell."

"But Miss Anne, your son gon' have my hide, sure nuff. He sent word to bring you into town."

"I'd rather have the British here at Black Cypress than have to live with my daughter-in-law," Anne said. "You take your orders from me, not from my son."

"Yes'm," said Isaiah. "Would you like to go down to the summerhouse and sit by the river? The sun's warm there now."

Anne smiled and nodded her head. "Thank you, Isaiah. Ask Rebecca to bring me that case from my bedside table. The one with my dueling pistols. And I think it's late enough to have a cup of rum and lime."

Picking up the goldheaded cane her son Archibald had given her for Christmas, she walked through the gardens toward the river.

She was still sitting in the sunshine, sipping her grog, her pistols primed and loaded on the table beside her, when the wagon creaked up the driveway.

Isaiah, running down the path to the river, called, "Miss Anne, Miss Anne, they done brought Mr. John Stanley in a wagon with two other sojers. Dey's in bad shape, all covered with blood."

"Have John carried into the green guest room and the other two men put in the office. One can be on the couch there, and Rebecca can make a pallet on the floor for the other. And bring Dr. Rob's bag."

"Miss Anne, don't you think you ought to send them all to Charlestown?"

"I'll take care of them right here," said Anne. "I've had plenty of chance to learn how to doctor since Robin died. I bet I know more than most of those young bloodletters in the army."

"Yes'm," said Isaiah. "You want I should carry these pistols up to de house?"

Anne put them carefully back in the case and handed it to Isaiah, then turned and trudged up the oystershell path. By the time she reached the front hall, Isaiah was supervising the transfer of the last of the wounded soldiers by four strong young blacks.

"I give de driver sumpin' for his trouble, ma'am," Isaiah said. "I took it from de box in de office."

"Thank you, Isaiah. Is John Stanley in the guest room?"

"Yes'm," said Isaiah. "He got a pow'ful big wound in he hip. He done loss a heap o' blood. Becky's up dere wif im."

Anne picked up her skirts with one hand and held the rail with the other as she hurried up the stairs. Being old was pesky when you wanted to run.

John was conscious, but looking very pale when she went into the room. Rebecca had cut his uniform trousers away, but had left the cloth which someone had wadded into the wound to stem the blood.

"Look over on the side table and bring me a bottle of brandy," Anne said. Turning to John, "I'm going to give you a good slug to drink, then I'm going to pour some into your hip. It's going to burn like nothing you ever felt before, but it's an old trick I learned from a ship's surgeon years ago. It will stop putrefaction if anything will."

"I'd trust you to cut off my leg and sew it to my head, Gran, if you said I needed it done," John said weakly.

Anne held the glass of brandy to his lips as Rebecca raised his head from the pillow. The fiery liquid made him choke but brought color to his face. As she carefully removed the cloth from his wound, the blood flowed scarlet onto the towel that had been placed under him. The bayonet had stabbed through the fleshy side of the hip, been deflected by the hipbone, then dragged down, cutting the muscle in the cheek of his buttocks.

"You must have been doing some fancy dodging," said Anne. "I hope you had a chance to get the man who did this."

"One of my friends split his head open with a rifle butt," John said. "He was a big, hardheaded Scotsman. I don't think he was killed."

"Just as well," said Anne. "You two may lift a glass together when this mess is over.

"Now bite down on that piece of wood Becky's holding. And don't be afraid to yell if you feel like it."

When Isaiah held him down on the bed and Anne poured brandy into the wound, John screamed in spite of himself, then fainted dead away. Anne pressed clean bandages on the wound and bound them around his leg and waist in a figure eight. If God was merciful, the wound would heal without infection.

Jamie Stratfield came with the news about John when Mary Anne had nearly given up hope. Jamie seemed to get news sooner at the tavern than anyone else in town. She packed that same night to go to Charlestown. General Lincoln had returned to Charlestown, and General Prevost, to Savannah after the terrible battle near Stono Ferry. With both armies licking their wounds, it would be reasonably safe for her to travel with one of George Galphin's wagon trains. She could close the Merrill house and take Johnny and the two black servants with her.

Ten days later, she was at Black Cypress.

* * *

With the lull in fighting, Augustans could breathe freely again. Militiamen headed for their farms to help their wives and children weed the cornfields and potato patches. On long, hot summer days it was all a man could do to get the chores done. Nobody was ready to fight. In Augusta Richard Howley and George Wells had taken charge of what was left of the Assembly and, with the help of John Dooly, struggled to keep enough militiamen on duty to control lawlessness. In outlying districts there were still reports of settlers fighting in the name of liberty or loyalty.

In July a contingent of regular Continentals from Virginia arrived in Augusta, and General Lachlan McIntosh was ordered by General Washington to command them. One morning McIntosh came striding up to the bar at the Sword and Thistle. Banging on the counter, he shouted, "By the Eternal! Can't a mon get a drink around here?"

When Angus hurried into the taproom, the general grabbed him around the shoulders in a bear hug then stepped back and looked at the pegs behind the bar.

"Dommed if you don't still have my tankard there," he chuckled. "Have you any decent drink for a fellow Scot?"

"I'm afraid real Scotch whisky is a thing of the past," said Angus, "but I've some barley malt liquor of my own making that's popular."

"Well what are ye waitin' for?" McIntosh asked. "And please join me."

It was early for Angus, who seldom imbibed before nightfall, but he would not insult the general. After he poured a good portion from a bottle under the bar into McIntosh's tankard and a splash into his own, they clicked tankards and drank.

"There's nothing wrong with this whisky that a little peat smoke couldn't fix," said McIntosh. "Tell me who of our old friends is in Augusta. I came into Fort Grierson last night, and I haven't had a chance to get into town."

"Most of the lads from the trading days have gone," said Angus. "When it came time to fish or cut bait, the old traders chose to gang wi' the King."

"What about McLean? Did "Macaroni" leave, too?"

"Nay, he's one lad who wouldn't leave, though he's a King's man at heart."

"A canny Scot," said McIntosh. "Business before politics. I'll have to call on him and see if he'll have an old friend as a house guest. Fort Grierson's too crowded with troops."

"If you stay wi' McLean, ye'll not be popular wi' Richard Howley and George Wells and that crowd."

"To hell with Howley," said McIntosh. "I'll bide where I please." Slapping a coin on the counter, he strode out the door and down the steps to the hitching rail.

The presence of Regulars in town had a soothing effect on combatants. The Assembly finally was able to entice its members to come out of hiding. By the end of July, the old legislature had gathered in Matthew Hobson's house to form a new government.

With many of the new members still missing, it was decided to elect a Supreme Executive Council of nine of those present to carry on the duties of government until the end of the emergency. The Council, in turn, elected John Wereat their president. Wereat immediately appointed General Lachlan McIntosh to command Georgia's troops and then set about trying to controvert Button Gwinnett's liberal Constitution of Georgia.

The disgruntled liberal element under the leadership of George Walton and George Wells called a meeting to form a government of their own, calling themselves the General Assembly of Georgia. With the two groups at loggerheads, little progress was made.

General McIntosh had more to worry about than political squabbling. Late in August, he received a dispatch from General Lincoln in Charlestown that an attack on the British in Savannah was being planned by the French fleet and was to be coordinated with a land attack by the Continental forces.

"God help us!" the General exploded at the meeting of his military leaders at Fort Grierson. "These damnable combined operations never work. We'll sit in the Savannah swamps and get eaten alive by sand flies and mosquitoes while we wait for the Frenchies, then have to turn around and come back. Meanwhile Augusta will be wide open for Burnfoot Brown and his Indians to come in and take the town."

"Does this mean we have orders to call up the militia?" Dooly asked.

"Better now than wait for orders. If they get caught up in the autumn harvest, we'll never get them assembled," said McIntosh. "I'll have orders ready today to send to all regular and militia units to assemble by next week. Our destination should remain secret. We hope to surprise Prevost in Savannah."

Bert Sheldon had been home on leave since the battle of Stono Creek, where he had been luckier than John Stanley. A wound in his upper arm had been enough to send him home, and he had been able to help Ben keep the weeds out of the corn and barley. Now that the grain was almost ready to harvest, there were rumors of another campaign.

One day in early September, when Augusta finally caught a breath of cool air from the north, Bert finished cutting wood for the kitchen fire and saddled Moonshine for a trip to town.

The sunlight on the road had lost its deep summer gold and shone thinner and whiter on the dusty weeds by the roadside. Summer would return in a day or two, but for now, men could stretch their muscles without drowning in sweat. In the Indian nations, it would be a signal to prepare for the warpath.

Moonshine pranced and bucked a little, just to show he felt the excitement of the weather change. Bert let him work out his kinks, then, when he had settled down, gave him his head to gallop along the dusty wagon track frightening rabbits and chipmunks into the ditch at the side of the road.

As he reached Fort Grierson, Bert could see that troops had begun to gather. Tents had been pitched in the field behind the palisaded fort, and horsemen and men on foot were milling around the gate. Riding up to the gate and dismounting, he found that it was manned, for a change, by a sentry who challenged him and asked his business.

"Sergeant Bert Sheldon of Elbert's Continentals," he said, then, indicating the sling still on his arm, asked, "What's going on? I'm home on leave, but I'm not too bad off to fight if there's anything brewing."

"You'd better report to the Officer of the Day," said the sentry. "They're calling up the militia, and that Polish general is due here any time with his forces. We're playing hell trying to assign bivouac areas."

"I knew General McIntosh was here with the Virginia Continentals, but I haven't seen any Georgia Continentals since Stono."

"I reckon they're still in Charlestown with Lincoln," said the sentry.

"Thanks," said Bert. "I'll not bother the Officer of the Day." Mounting once more, he rode on to the Sword and Thistle. Jamie always knew what was going on.

Jamie called to him from the bar; his eyes were bloodshot, but his haggard face was split by a wide grin.

"Come drink the health of my new daughter," he said, bringing out a jug from under the bar.

"Congratulations! Make it ale and I'll join you," said Bert. "My head wouldn't stand anything stronger this early. How's Meg?"

"She's sound asleep now. The baby was born at seven-thirty this morning. We're going to call her Jean after Meg's mother.

"You're a lucky man," said Bert. Maybe some day he'd have a wife to come home to. In his dreams, she looked like Susan.

"What do you hear from General Lincoln?" he asked Jamie.

"The word I get from the customers is that he's still in Charlestown. But that Pole, General Count Casimir Pulaski, has been ordered down from the Georgia mountains to join General McIntosh."

"Do they expect an attack here?" Bert asked. "Is Brown sending his Creeks on the warpath?"

"God knows," said Jamie. "I hear, though, that Brown's down in Savannah. I do know they've called up the militia all over Georgia and South Carolina."

"I'd better head back to my regiment in Charlestown," said Bert. "This arm's well enough to shoot. If I can shoot partridge, I can certainly shoot Redcoats."

Jamie looked down at his leg. He hated this crippled act. Meg was the only one who knew it was an act, Angus too, perhaps, although he never let on.

"I've tried to get back in," he said, "but they won't take me with this gimpy leg. I don't know what difference it would make on a horse, but General Williamson gave orders that I was not fit for duty."

"I'm glad you're here," said Bert. "I feel safer for Ma and Pa, knowing you are."

Bert started next day for Charlestown. A wagoner carrying corn to Lincoln's army had stopped him as he left the tavern and offered him a ride, for a small fee.

"I can use an extra gun goin' down to the coast," said the wagoner, "and you can spell me some at drivin'. My brother was goin' but he's down with the flux."

After arranging with the wagoner to meet early next morning, Bert took Moonshine back to the farm. Sergeants of infantry went into battle on foot and he didn't want to risk stabling Moonshine in Charlestown.

Pulaski stayed in Augusta only long enough to refit his troops with rations and ammunition before hurrying to the seacoast. Word had come that the French fleet under Count d'Estaing had landed troops at Beaulieu, near Savannah, and had called for the British to surrender the city. Pulaski would join General Lincoln, who was marching from Charlestown to coordinate his attack with that of d'Estaing.

General Augustine Prevost, the British commander, set to work to strengthen Savannah's defenses. General Lincoln did not have time to assemble his army and move on the city when the French landed. Now while the French fought mosquitoes in the marshes of Beaulieu and Lincoln was hurrying his army toward Savannah, Prevost had time to call in Tory militia from South Georgia and Florida and build thirteen redoubts in a semicircle around the city. Finally he ordered eight hundred troops under General Maitland to come to his aid from Beaufort and asked the French for a twenty-four hour truce to give the reinforcements time to arrive.

Lincoln arrived with his army of Georgia and South Carolina Continentals joined by McIntosh's militia brigade; all were ready and eager to attack. But d'Estaing, having foolishly agreed to the truce, allowed Maitland's troops to entrench with Prevost's men.

Bert was with the Georgia Continentals in Lincoln's main body of troops preparing to storm the center of the Spring Hill redoubt, while the French troops would attack on the right. Posted to the left, were Merrill in Huger's brigade and Stanley in Williamson's brigade, also waiting to attack the redoubt under Huger's command.

At five in the morning of October ninth, a bugle sounded the charge, and Count Pulaski's cavalry swarmed toward Spring Hill, clearing the enemy from the base of the hill. He was followed by the light troops of John Laurens, who stormed the fort on the left, while Francis Marion's Carolinians stormed the redoubt. One of Marion's sergeants, William Jasper, who had saved the Carolina flag in the battle of Fort Moultrie, scaled the ramparts and carried the regimental colors to the top of the parapet, but the fire of Thomas Brown's Rangers, who were defending the redoubt, caught and killed him.

Stanley and Merrill, advancing to the left with Huger's infantry, found themselves slipping in the dark and sinking in mud up to their knees in a flooded rice field. As daylight grew stronger, they struggled to dry ground and formed for the attack, but met a blast of artillery from the guns of the redoubt.

John and the other Ninety-Six men dropped to the ground and began crawling, Indian style, toward the hill. The light troops from Charlestown, charging up the slope, were met by cannon and musket fire, and had to retreat. John caught sight of Joseph Merrill, saber flashing in the pink light of dawn, as he fell with the dead and wounded, his head severed from his shoulders by a cannon ball.

John's wound was throbbing as though it had opened again, but he crawled on, stopping to load and fire his rifle at green uniforms on top of the redoubt.

Before he had covered the ground to the base of the redoubt, he heard a bugle sound retreat. All around him, tired men began backing toward the woods at the edge of the rice field. John slung his rifle over his shoulder and joined the withdrawal.

In the center of the hill, Bert Sheldon had been in the thick of battle for almost an hour, moving forward in a crouch, dropping and firing at the enemy on the rampart, then moving forward again. He had gained the base of the redoubt and had seen at least two green uniforms drop as he fired. Now, with the sound of retreat and the sun beginning to warm the sand on the hill, he moved back over the ground he had fought to gain.

By afternoon, the Continentals had assembled once more at Beaulieu with heavy hearts. At roll call that night, there was no answer to every fourth name. John reported Merrill's death to General Huger and went to look for Bert Sheldon among the Georgia Continentals.

Bert and four other Augusta men were sitting by the company campfire, drinking their double issue of rum.

"Lieutenant Stanley," Bert called. "I'll share my grog with you. Come join us."

"Thanks, Bert, but I'm already dizzy from my own ration. Glad to see you alive and kicking."

"Have you heard anything about where we're going now?" Bert asked.

"They tell me the French are talking about leaving before they're caught by the British fleet or a hurricane. They suffered eight hundred killed or wounded, and d'Estaing himself was wounded twice, leading his men."

"I've heard General Pulaski died," said Bert.

"And Joseph Merrill, Susan's father, was killed. I saw it myself."

"Oh no," said Bert. "I thought the Charlestown troops got off light. Poor Susan."

"We'll probably be heading for Charlestown," said John. "Mrs. Merrill and the girls are staying in the city."

"Do you think they'd want to see me?" Bert asked.

"It wouldn't hurt to try," said John. "They're staying with Joseph's mother on Tradd Street."

"When I can get to town, I'll go to Tradd Street," Bert said.

"I'm leaving," said John. "The surgeons are busy, but I need a new bandage for this hip." He limped away.

Bert was able to get a pass into town the day after the troops reached the Charlestown area. Colonel Elbert had grown to like the young sergeant from Augusta and knew he was not a hell raiser. When Bert explained his mission, Elbert sent his own condolences in a note to be delivered by his sergeant.

The Merrill house was near Mary Anne's family home on Tradd Street.

A narrow, three-storied brick building with galleries overlooking a walled garden at the side, it had a narrow front set flush with the street. As Bert climbed the front steps and lifted the big brass knocker engraved with a coat of arms, his heart sank. What did you say to a girl whose father had been killed or to a widow whose husband had died for his country?

A grey-haired butler in a long-tailed black coat and knee breeches opened the door.

"I'd like to see Mrs. Merrill or Miss Susan," said Bert. "Would you please tell them Sergeant Bert Sheldon is calling?"

The butler showed him into the front parlor and turned to go upstairs. Bert looked around the room, feeling like a country bumpkin. Family portraits, ladies in satins and laces with glittering diamonds and pearls draped over throats and bosoms and gentlemen in old-fashioned wigs and fancy waistcoats with billowing lace at neck and cuff, stared from the high walls. A dainty spinet stood in the corner, and soft, jewel-colored carpets covered the floor.

Susan and her mother came into the room together, dressed all in black. Jocelyn's eyes were bloodshot and rimmed with red, her skin pale and blotched. Susan, like her mother, showed signs of recent weeping but smiled at Bert as she hurried forward to take his hand.

"John Stanley told us you were here. I was afraid you'd been hurt in the fighting," she said.

"I've come to bring you a note from Colonel Elbert and to offer any help I can give," said Bert. "I'm so sorry about Captain Merrill." He turned to Jocelyn, "If I can run errands or be of any service to you, Mrs. Merrill, I'll do whatever I can."

"Thank you," said Jocelyn. "You are very kind. Everyone has been so helpful. I thank God for good friends."

"Will you be here long?" Susan asked.

"I have no way of knowing, but as long as I'm here, I hope you will call me if you need me. I'm with Elbert's Continentals."

"Bless you," said Jocelyn, "and all the other brave men who were at Spring Hill. I will remember your kindness."

Since there seemed to be nothing further to say, Bert bowed to them both, then turned and left the house. Now more than ever, he felt the contrast between Susan's way of life and his own.

* * *

Mary Anne waited for news at Black Cypress. Remembering all the times she had waited for John alone, praying for his safe return, she was thankful for Gran's company.

"Backwoodsmen will take care of themselves," said Gran, "and they'll kill more men with their rifles than the flashy dragoons with their cavalry charges and foolhardy chivalry."

"Andy Williamson is a smart commander," Mary Anne agreed. "He has sense enough to know when to take cover and how to advance without risking his men."

"I worry more for the young blades like Jocelyn's Joseph. They've been reared on tales of knights and dragons. They'll not last long against artillery."

"How do you know so much about battles?" Mary Anne asked. "It's a comfort to be able to talk to you. Mother tries to divert my mind from war when I try to talk to her about it."

"Damned silly females," said Anne. "I can't stand their gossip and talk of fashion with the world burning around them."

"It's funny. I missed my Charlestown friends when we lived in the mountains, but when I came back before Johnny was born, I was bored with them. I've liked Augusta. There's still enough of the frontier left there to be interesting."

"I'm afraid you're a throwback to your grandmother," Anne said. "Some day I'll tell you about my life before I married your Grandfather Seabright."

They had been sitting in the summerhouse in the October sunshine, watching the breeze sway the Spanish moss and the fish make circles in the water as they jumped for low-flying insects.

A clatter of hoofs on the driveway brought them both to their feet. John rode into the back driveway and threw his reins to the little black boy who had run from the stable.

Mary Anne picked up her skirts to run up the hill, calling, "John, we're down here."

They met on the path and Anne slowed her footsteps to give them a chance to be alone.

When they finally turned and met her, John put an arm around both women and started for the house.

"We couldn't run them out," he said to Anne. "The French got there too early, and we got there too late. Prevost had time to build earthworks all around the city and bring in reinforcements. We had the hell beaten out of us, and we outnumbered them almost three to one."

"Thank God you came home," said Mary Anne. "That's all I care about now.

John stopped and held both of them tighter. "But Joseph Merrill didn't," he said. "He was killed in a saber charge against a redoubt defended by artillery."

"They were about one hundred years behind the times," said Anne. "Poor Joseph was a romanticist."

"I'll go to Jocelyn," said Mary Anne.

"You'll do no such thing," said Anne. "You'll stay here with your husband. You can go tomorrow. Jocelyn has her mother and Susan."

John looked thankfully at Anne. "I stopped on Tradd Street before I came here," he said. "I saw him die. I wanted Jocelyn to know he died gallantly and didn't suffer."

"If I know Charlestown, she'll have more company than she can use," said Anne. "Charlestown people have always rallied around in time of trouble."

"Joseph was the only man lost by the Charlestown Dragoons," said John. "They retreated at the first artillery blast."

They were at the top of the garden when Johnny, fresh from his nap, tore out of the door and into his father's arms.

"I knew you'd be back safe!" he cried. "I kept telling Mommy and Gran!"

"I was sure you'd take care of them while I was away," said John, hugging him and lifting him to his shoulder.

"Tell me about the battle," Johnny begged. "Were you in the middle of it? Did you shoot a lot of Tories?"

"I'll tell you all about it when I've had a chance to rest and eat some of Sally's good cooking."

"Sally's making shrimp gumbo and fried pork chops," said Johnny. "She told me so before my nap."

"Then let me take my nap now, and we'll eat supper together." He set the child down on the terrace, then turned to Anne. "I think he can stay up to eat with us tonight, don't you?"

Johnny, satisfied with the break in routine, went off with his nurse to help Henry pull in the crab traps.

John and Mary Anne climbed the stairs to the room that Gran always kept ready for them. In the canopy bed that had seemed so big and empty with John away, they forgot about war and death and the troubles of the world.

·XXIII·

FALL OF
CHARLESTOWN

With the defeat of the Americans at Savannah, all of southern Georgia was acknowledged as British land. Augusta, as the seat of the rebel state government, was highly vulnerable to attack. The Georgia Continentals stayed at Beaulieu only long enough to regroup and count their losses, then they headed for home.

Bert sent a note to Susan by one of the South Carolina militiamen, telling her he'd been ordered to the Upcountry and would not be able to return to Charlestown.

Marching into Augusta with Elbert's Continentals on October twentieth, he helped set up camp on the Common, then reported to headquarters tent to ask for a pass.

"Just keep in touch," said Elbert. "The more men who eat at home, the less we'll have to feed here."

"My father may be able to supply you with some corn and fresh vegetables," said Bert. "He should have had a good harvest."

"Bring what you can," said Elbert. "We'll pay when Congress sends funds. God alone knows when that will be."

"Yes, sir," said Bert, saluting. "Does that mean I can stay at home till we get orders to move out?"

"That's right, Sergeant. As long as you make formations."

"Thank you, sir," said Bert, saluting again and hurrying out of the tent.

Ben and Mary were expecting him. Jamie had heard that Bert had survived the attack on Savannah and had told Ben only two days after the battle when he was delivering squash and turnips to the inn. Yesterday Jamie had sent word by one of John Rae's slaves that Elbert's Continentals were camped south of McBean's plantation.

Mary had soaked a ham from the smokehouse and baked it slowly, studding it with cloves and basting it with cane syrup. There were fresh squash, yams, and turnip greens and a pie made with apples from North Georgia. Bert ate until he could hardly move.

"Do you think they'll hit us here any time soon?" Ben asked, when they had moved to the settles by the fireplace.

"I don't know," said Bert. "The rumor is that they'll probably hit Charlestown first to cut off supplies and give them a port farther north. They may send Brown and his Tories and Indians to make life miserable, though."

"Does that mean you'll be here for Christmas?" Francie asked. "We have a goose to fatten for Christmas dinner."

"I'm feeding her plenty of corn every day," said Benjy, "and there's a holly tree up the hill that's full of berries. They're beginning to turn red."

"Pray God we'll all be together to enjoy them," said Mary.

At the Sword and Thistle, Jamie and Meg were kept busy with militia companies coming to Fort Grierson to be released.

Fox's tavern in town was filled to capacity with members of both factions of state government. Mr. Fox spent his time cooling arguments and easing out drunken customers before they resorted to fist or gun fights.

John Wereat's Supreme Executive Council still struggled to hold power over what remained of rebel-held Georgia, while George Walton, Richard Howley, and George Wells claimed the constitutional right to call the General Assembly and elect Walton governor. Wereat appealed desperately to the Continental Congress for funds to pay the Continental troops and ordered all county treasurers to bring funds to Augusta to pay the state militia. When no funds were forthcoming, he had to give permission for the troops to collect their pay by plundering known Tories.

The result was a return to bloody strife in the outlying areas, with Tories fighting back and hoping for help from the British government in Savannah, in the form of Loyalist or Indian allies.

Wereat's Supreme Council had set the date for a meeting of the Assembly in January, but Walton now claimed his legislature, which was already formed, held legitimate power.

In early November, General Lachlan McIntosh returned to Augusta, having distinguished himself as a leader at Savannah, where his troops were able to retreat in good order and avoid a total rout. As soon as he had arranged for the furlough of his militiamen, he headed for the Sword and Thistle and joined Angus at the bar.

"Welcome, General," said Angus. "I've been expecting you for days. I hear your lads made the battle hot for Brown and his Tories."

"Damned shame," said McIntosh. "If those bloody French bastards hadn't waited to land until we got there, Prevost wouldn't have had time to build defenses. Prevost's a seasoned strategist, and he doesn't make many mistakes. We outnumbered them three to one, but you can't use green troops to charge an entrenched army with guns emplaced and expect them to take the enemy by storm.

"Did you have many losses?" Angus asked.

"Not as many as you'd expect. Our men stayed before the line for fifty-five minutes of hell, until Lincoln ordered the retreat. We lost two hundred and fifty Continentals, but only one militiaman. Some of the militiamen broke and ran, but the seasoned Indian fighters fought from cover or kept a low profile."

"They'll live to fight another day," said Angus.

McIntosh took a long draft of ale, then passed the tankard to Angus for a refill. "How are things here?" he asked. "Is Wereat still in charge?"

"Just barely, if you want the truth," said Angus. "Wells and Walton have formed a government of their own and are doing their best to overthrow the Council."

"Damn their eyes!" said McIntosh. "As if we don't have enough, fighting the British. I'll have to see what I can do to spike their guns."

"They're a tricky crowd, laddie. They'll stab you in the back if they have the chance."

"I'll keep my back to the wall and watch for their treachery," said McIntosh. "Wereat's a sensible man. They say Wells talked Walton into his radical ideas when they were imprisoned together in Savannah. We need a man like Wereat with his feet on the ground and a good head on his shoulders."

Finishing his ale, he left the inn and headed for town. When he returned late in the afternoon, his eyes flashed fire.

"Pour me a good strong glass of your Georgia ouisquebaugh," he called out. "That low-life Walton has gone to Charlestown to blackguard me to General Lincoln. Wereat heard he's trying to get Lincoln to back him for governor of Georgia."

"I've heard rumors," said Jamie. "That group is claiming you're a Tory, because you are a friend of Andrew McLean."

"Damn lying skunks," said McIntosh. "I've known Andy McLean all my life. I don't give a hoot about his politics. Besides, he's done nothing to aid the Tories."

"There are a lot of Georgians who've been robbed and burned for no reason except that they've tried to mind their own business. That's why they've been moving to Florida."

Two weeks later, George Walton returned to Augusta with instructions from General Lincoln to set up a government according to Button Gwinnett's constitution. On November twenty-fourth, by vote of a small number of Georgia voters, a General Assembly was formed. George Walton was elected Governor, and William Glascock, Speaker of the House. On November thirtieth, a letter was sent to the Congress of the United States, over the signature of William Glascock, stating that the people of Georgia were dissatisfied with Lachlan McIntosh as a military leader and asking that he be removed from Georgia.

McIntosh made a habit, now, of dropping into Fox's tavern to keep in touch with political news. One of the clerks of the General Assembly found him at the bar there and asked to speak to him outside.

As the two men walked out to Broad Street and turned west toward the woods, the clerk glanced up and down the road. "There's something I think you should know, General. Speaker Glascock has sent a letter to Congress asking for your removal from command of Georgia troops."

McIntosh stopped in his tracks, then turned toward town shaking his fist. "Why that damned sneaky bastard," he growled. "I thought he was the one decent individual in that herd of swine."

"I'm sorry sir." The clerk followed him as he stamped off toward town. McIntosh stopped and grasped the man by the arm. "Of course, lad, you don't know how grateful I am. And I'll not let on where I heard the news."

"Thank you, sir. There are more men in Georgia who would be proud to serve in your command than ever heard of William Glascock."

"If you'll excuse me, son, I'll have a talk with that conniving blackguard. Thank you from the bottom of my heart," and he strode off in the direction of Glascock's home.

The clerk hurried back to the bar and downed two quick drinks.

William Glascock, about to sit down to supper, answered a pounding on the front door and was grabbed by the lapels and pushed back into the hall.

"You sneaky, slimy son-of-a-bitch!" McIntosh roared. "What in unholy hell do you mean telling Congress I was unfit to command in Georgia?"

Glascock staggered back, his eyes bugged and his mouth agape. McIntosh loosed his hold and stood waiting.

"General McIntosh!" Glascock gasped. "I have no idea what you're talking about, sir!"

"I understand that a letter has gone to Congress over your signature, asking that I be relieved of my command."

"As God is my witness, sir," said Glascock, "if there is such a letter, it is a forgery."

"I can't reveal my source," said McIntosh, "but I'm confident such a letter was sent."

"Then I will not only do my best to find the forger," said Glascock, "but I will write to Congress assuring them that there is not a responsible citizen or officer in Georgia who would not be happy to serve with you. By heaven, General, we've all felt safer knowing you were back in Georgia."

McIntosh's face had lost its crimson tint, and his hands relaxed from fists. "God forgive me, mon. I should na' hae dooted ye," he said, the Scots' burr surfacing in his agitation.

"Can I offer you a drink?" Glascock asked.

"Thank you," said McIntosh, "but I'll be on my way. My apologies for bursting in on you that way."

"Of course, General," said Glascock. "I'm glad you brought this calumny to my attention."

True to his word, Glascock wrote his letter to Congress commending General McIntosh and made certain his position was well publicized in the General Assembly. Although no accusation was made, it was whispered throughout the state that Glascock's signature on the forged letter was very like the handwriting of Governor Walton.

As the cold winds blew down from the north into Georgia, and Christmas once more rolled around without any sign of attack, Upcountry Georgians prepared to celebrate, convinced that the British were going to concentrate on Charlestown and leave Augusta alone.

John and Mary Anne Stanley came back in time for Christmas.

As usual the Sword and Thistle was alight with Christmas cheer. The Stanleys rode out on horseback to celebrate Christmas Eve, arriving just as the wagon from Rae's Creek was unloading in the inn yard.

Francie was nearly sixteen, her freckles faded, her once pale hair falling in golden waves, her plump body slimmed in the right places, her eyes shining with excitement over the gifts to come. Benjy was thin and wiry like his father, but the muscles of his arms and shoulders were beginning to bulge from wielding an axe and carrying wood.

John and Bert pounded each other about the shoulders and congratulated themselves on their good health and good luck in getting home safely.

"We've just left Susan and her mother in Charlestown," said Mary Anne. "I tried to get them to come with us, but Jocelyn wants to be in Charlestown for Christmas. Being in mourning, they won't go to any of the parties, of course, but Joseph's mother was dreading Christmas alone."

"I'd feel much better if they were out of Charlestown," said Bert. "If the British don't attack Augusta, it stands to reason they're getting ready to hit Charlestown."

"Come on in the inn, where it's warm," said John as the women and children made their way toward the holly-hung door. "We can talk in front of the fire with a cup of Christmas cheer."

Settled on a bench beside the hearth, Bert brought up the subject again. "Colonel Elbert is keeping us on our toes," he said. "Most of the regiment have gone home for Christmas, but we've got to be back on duty after New Year's. General McIntosh thinks they're going to try to conquer the whole South, now that Washington's got them stopped up in New Jersey."

"Williamson's keeping enough of his militia together in Ninety-Six, so he can call up the rest in a hurry," said John. "We'll all be fighting in Charlestown, or I'll eat my hat."

"Do you think General Lincoln will try to hold the city?" Bert asked. "Seems to me they'll be sitting ducks down there on that point if the British Navy comes down from New York."

"The smart thing would be to move out and leave the city to them," said John. "That's what they did in Savannah, and the British didn't harm the civilians."

"I don't like to think of Susan and the little girls in a city full of soldiers without a man to protect them," said Bert.

Wingus, as he was still called, came out of the back room, followed by Jamie, pushing a wheelbarrow full of wrapped packages which had been gathered as the guests arrived. Meg followed, carrying little Jean wrapped in a red knitted blanket, in honor of the season.

"In any good Scot's home, we should wait to celebrate until New Year's," said Angus, "but we'll go the American way and open presents tonight. Then I suggest we tak' a cup o' kindness, for Auld Lang Syne. The good God only knows whether we'll all be together for Hogmanay."

On January first, a vote for a new General Assembly was taken throughout Upcountry Georgia. Many of the Low-Country conservatives were still in the hands of the British, and George Walton's group again dominated the new legislature. Walton was sent as a representative to the Continental Congress in Philadelphia, and Richard Howley was chosen as governor in his place.

Bert Sheldon stopped in at the Sword and Thistle one day in late January. "I'll say this for Walton and his crew," he said to Jamie, "they're trying to make a real capital city out of Augusta. They've got people working on the streets and cutting down trees on the vacant lots."

"They want to build up Augusta while the Savannah crowd's out of power," said Jamie. "I hear they're taking land from people and calling them Tories without any proof."

"At least they're getting things done," said Bert. "They've started building a jail for criminals and vagrants, so they'll have free labor, and they're talking about building a school."

"They'd do better to build a decent fort. We're living on borrowed time if the British take Charlestown."

"Do you really think they'll take Charlestown?" Bert asked.

"General McIntosh tells me he's had word that Sir Henry Clinton sailed from Sandy Hook, in New England, with enough ships and men to roll over the whole South," said Jamie.

"God help us," said Bert. "I wish Susan and her family would hurry up and come home."

"I guess Charlestown is home to Mrs. Merrill," said Jamie.

"Maybe we'll be ordered down there soon," said Bert. "I wish General Lincoln would get a move on."

On February first, Bert had his wish. Orders were received for all Georgia and South Carolina Continental troops to report for duty to defend Charlestown. The British fleet was standing off Tybee Island, landing troops. From the number of ships, there could well be ten thousand men. And they were unloading horses and artillery guns by the hundreds.

The new Georgia Assemblymen were in a turmoil. Governor Howley issued a proclamation urging all Georgians to stand firm to their duty and exert themselves in support and defense of the great and glorious independence of the United States. Then he hurried off to Philadelphia to join George Walton as a representative to Congress, leaving George Wells, President of the Executive Council, to act as governor. Four days later, opting for discretion as the better part of valor, Wells and the Executive Council hurried into Wilkes County to set up shop in Heard's Fort.

Before leaving for Philadelphia, Governor Howley had fired off an order to General Williamson at Ninety-Six to move his militia to Augusta, and he had ordered half of the Georgia militia to rendezvous with the Carolinians at Fort Grierson.

On the seventh of February, the British fleet pulled up anchor and left a force of about two thousand men in Savannah with orders to move toward Augusta, then change course toward Charlestown. For two days, as scouts on horseback galloped into town with news of the British army's progress, Augustans shook in their shoes. When, on the third day, word came that the army had turned away from the river and taken the road toward Charlestown, they gave a sigh of relief and waited for more news from the coast.

Clark, Dooly, Twiggs, and Bugg assembled their militiamen at Fort Grierson, then moved them out to the Common with Elbert's Continentals.

The second week in February, General Andrew Williamson arrived at Fort Grierson with the militia regiment from Ninety-Six. The rest of his brigade had been sent to Charlestown to help defend that city. Coming into the Sword and Thistle the next day, he met General McIntosh at the bar.

"By the Eternal," he said, signaling for ale, "that fort is as empty as last year's birdnest. There aren't enough muskets to go around, and the powder supply is down to a nubbin."

"What happened to your supplies in Ninety-Six?" McIntosh asked.

"Our troops came back from Savannah short of everything," said Williamson, "and damned glad to escape with their skins."

"Did you think the Georgia militia stopped to tidy up the battlefield at Spring Hill?" McIntosh asked. "Hell, Andy, we had our butts beaten as bad as you did. But it's good to see you here."

"We'll try to get some muskets and flints from Wofford," said Williamson, "if we can get a wagon train through to Fair Forest. Those Carolina wagoners aren't anxious to travel with the Tories cutting up again in the backwoods."

"They're raisin' sand here in Georgia, too." said McIntosh. "Knowing that Clinton's landing troops on the coast has brought a lot of Tories out of hibernation. They've kept my militia busy."

"Pickens and Marion have found the same thing in Carolina. I wish Lincoln would pull his troops out of the 'Holy City' and get 'em up into the hills where they could fight."

"Damn it all," said McIntosh. "Hasn't that old son-of-a-bitch any backbone at all? He's let the Low Country elite persuade him that Charlestown is sacred ground. He hasn't a chance on that little peninsula, once they have him surrounded on land and sea."

By February seventeenth, Augusta was shocked with news nearer home. Up at Heard's Fort in Wilkes County, Council President George Wells had been killed in a duel by James Jackson, a young friend of John Wereat. Stephen Heard, whose land was the temporary capital of Georgia, had been elected president of the Council.

More important to General McIntosh, however, was the news that George Walton in Philadelphia was once more trying to have him removed from his command of the Southern militia.

By now Colonel Elbert's Continentals were back from leave and, outfitted with new boots, muskets, and rations, were ready to march to defend Charlestown. Sergeant Bert Sheldon was sitting on a log, rubbing bear grease into a pair of new boots, when John Stanley walked toward him between the rows of tents.

"It looks like you'll be shooting Redcoats before I leave Augusta," he said to Bert.

"Rumor says we'll be marching out tomorrow," said Bert, "though orders haven't come through."

"Just between us," said John, "General McIntosh wants to get the hell down there before he's relieved of his command. Walton's been bad-mouthing him in Congress again."

"I'll be glad to get on the road," said Bert. "This town's so full of soldiers you can't turn around."

"They're keeping most of Williamson's militia here in Augusta," John said. "I'll keep an eye on your folks when you go."

"They should be safe enough," said Bert. "Everybody knows Pa's a Quaker now. He'd give up the farm before he'd fight. Only thing worries me is Francie. With all these soldiers around, I've asked Ma to keep her close to home. She's growing up too quick."

"Mary Anne and I'll ride out with Johnny. He thinks Benjy set the sun in the sky."

"Thanks," said Bert.

"If you ever get out near the Ashley River plantations," said John, "you'd be doing me a favor to drop in on Mary Anne's grandmother at Black Cypress. She's in her eighties but full of spunk. God only knows what she'd do if anyone tried to take over her home, Whig or Loyalist."

"I'm afraid I won't have much time for visiting," said Bert, "but I'll sure keep her in mind." He put down his second boot and stood up. They gripped hands.

"Take care," John said.

"They tell me the South Carolina boys call Charlestown the Holy City," said Bert. "We'll try to keep it that way."

The Continentals moved out the next morning to the sound of fife and drums. Clark and Twiggs led their men toward the Cherokee lands, leaving Dooly and Few to keep order in the area around Augusta. General Williamson left a cadre of militia at Fort Grierson and sent most of his unit home to get their farmland ready for spring planting. By setting up a network of messengers between Augusta and White Hall, his plantation near Ninety-Six, he was able to oversee his own spring plowing, leaving John at Fort Grierson as executive officer.

John now knew all about Jamie's role. Careful not to be seen too often at the Sword and Thistle, he was able to exchange small bits of information as he and Jamie chatted across the bar or to slip into the dining room with dispatches that could not go through regular military channels.

Mary Anne was enjoying having John at home. They had the Merrill's house to themselves, with only their two servants and Johnny. Mary Anne was pregnant again, looking forward to having a brother or sister for Johnny. The boy had moved so often from one household of relatives to another, that he had grown almost too quiet and self-effacing. He missed the Merrill children.

Jocelyn had written at Christmas that they wouldn't be back before spring, but as February drew to a close, news from Charlestown was bad. The British had blockaded the harbor and had landed troops on the coast, north and south of the city.

By the end of March, Sir Henry Clinton had a fortified line of posts across Charlestown Neck, from the Ashley to the Cooper, and had begun a series of earthworks for a protracted siege of the city. Governor Rutledge had been given emergency powers.

One morning late in April, John dropped into the Sword and Thistle with General Williamson. As the two men carried their drinks to the dining room, Jamie asked Angus to take over the bar and went to join them.

"I'll need your help again," Williamson said. "Is our Indian friend still available?"

"Yes, sir," said Jamie. "He'll come if I signal."

"Governor Rutledge has called in all the South Carolina militia to defend Charlestown," said Williamson. "I'd like to rush a letter to him offering to take my whole command out of Georgia."

"My God," said Jamie. "Excuse me, sir, but are you going to leave Augusta to be defended by this bunch of bickering bastards?"

"My duty is to South Carolina," said the general. "Not that I'm fond of the Low Country rice birds, but they need help from somewhere."

"God help us if Charlestown falls," said John. "The whole back country will be overrun by Redcoats and Indians."

"We'll have to fight like Indians," said Williamson. "Strike at their supply trains and hit their small detachments. We could make it very unpleasant for them."

"With the whole army bottled up in Charlestown," Jamie asked, "who will be left to fight?"

"There are plenty of men in the backwoods who won't come out to defend Charlestown but will fight like cornered coons for their home lands," said John.

"Will you get this letter on its way?" Williamson asked Jamie. "I want an answer as soon as possible so that I can get my men on the march."

A week later, Williamson received an answer from Governor Rutledge in Charlestown. General Williamson should not leave Augusta. He should keep three hundred men there and send the rest of his militia to Charlestown.

"Great jumping Jehosephat!" exclaimed the general. "Where does Rutledge think I'll get three hundred men? There aren't but two hundred militiamen, counting officers, and I've only about ninety independents who have joined from around here."

"Maybe we could pick up some recruits along the way," John suggested.

"Fat chance, with smallpox in Charlestown," said Williamson.

Two days later, John moved out with one hundred ninety militiamen to join Pickens at Ninety-Six, while Williamson remained in Augusta with ninety volunteers. The Georgia militia might obey his orders, or they might not.

As April became May, Augusta was more concerned with political wrangling than war with the English. Money was so scarce that people traded food for services, services for clothes and fuel. The have-nots were always ready to accuse those who had fine homes, rich farms and slaves of being Loyalists. Although Heard's Fort was still the nominal seat of government, much of the Council's business was conducted in Augusta taverns with Council members ready to head for the woods in case of danger.

By May ninth, the siege of Charlestown had dragged on for so long that the Governor of Georgia ordered General Williamson to take his militia to the aid of Charlestown. Williamson, receiving secret word of the state of affairs on the coast, dragged his feet and stayed where he was.

Three days later, General Lincoln surrendered Charlestown to the army of Sir Henry Clinton. Two thousand six hundred and fifty Continentals piled their arms and became prisoners, while three thousand and thirty-four militiamen were paroled and sent home. Although Governor John Rutledge and part of his Council had been persuaded to leave the city to keep at least a token government in exile, real political effectiveness was ended. Without an army, it was only a matter of time before South Carolina became a British colony again.

When official word of Charlestown's fall reached Augusta, the Georgia Council gathered long enough to order the governor to hold a meeting with General Williamson and the Georgia militia commanders and then to retire to the North Carolina mountains. Williamson and the commanders were given the choice of staying in Augusta or retreating to the mountains with Stephen Heard, who was still acting as governor while Howley was in Philadelphia.

Most of the Georgia commanders chose to go with Heard. Elijah Clark, Benjamin Few, and John Twiggs assembled their men and took to the hills. John Dooly, desperately ill with fever, went home to his wife and children, while his men chose either to join the other militia companies in the mountains or stay in Augusta.

General Williamson hurried to his Carolina plantation to meet with Pickens' men who had not been able to reach Charlestown before its surrender. Pickens himself, was not there at the time, but Williamson offered to lead the Carolinians to the mountains to join the Georgia militia and keep up the fight. Most of the men decided to stay in South Carolina and take parole. Williamson stayed with them. John Stanley returned to Augusta.

As soon as he had bathed and changed and eaten a huge breakfast with Mary Anne and Johnny, John rode out to the Sword and Thistle. The town seemed deserted after all the months of being jammed with troops. Now there was not a single uniform to be seen. Shops and taverns were open, but the people were subdued, hurrying on their errands as though afraid to be seen.

At the Sword and Thistle, the taproom was empty. John and Jamie took mugs of coffee to the back room.

"Have you had any news?" John asked. "General Williamson's staying at White Hall, and I've come back to be with Mary Anne and take parole when the British come."

"I had a message last night. Thomas Brown's Rangers have been ordered here from Savannah. They're marching up the Carolina side of the river, cleaning out the farms for rations as they come."

"When will they get here?"

"My messenger was about three days ahead of them when he came yesterday," said Jamie.

"So we'd better hide anything of value and wait," said John. "This should give the fence sitters time to dig up their Union Jacks and unfurl them."

"Their warning will have to come through other sources," said Jamie. "I can't have any glances turned in this direction. General Williamson will need me now, more than ever before."

"You're right," said John. "When I give my parole, I'll still be watched, so I'd better make my trips out here few and far between."

"And I'll have to drag my foot pitifully," said Jamie.

"I'll be getting back to Mary Anne, then. She couldn't understand why I had to come here when I had just got home."

"If I need to get in touch, I'll send Desmond with a bottle of whisky that he'll say you ordered." said Jamie.

·XXIV·

THOMAS BROWN
IN CONTROL

On the eighth of June, Thomas Brown crossed the river on the Sand Bar Ferry and led his troops through the town. Along the sides of Broad Street, people stood silently watching the soldiers in green and white, their brass buttons shining in the sunlight as they marched jauntily toward Fort Grierson.

Once more James Grierson stood at the gate, with the Reverend Mr. Seymour and a group of citizens who had remained quietly loyal during the years Augusta had been under Whig government. Grierson, in his old militia uniform, saluted Lieutenant Colonel Brown as he dismounted.

Brown saluted, then strode forward to shake Grierson's hand. "I thought you'd joined the rebels," he said. "Glad to see you're still a King's man."

"I've tried to be a good citizen of Georgia," said Grierson. "I've served as a civilian, but I've never borne arms against the King."

"We'll see that all good citizens take an oath of allegiance to the King," said Brown.

"There are many Augustans who will be glad to serve their King once more," said Mr. Seymour. "Many families have continued to come to church, even though their husbands and sons were serving with the rebel army."

"They will all have a chance to take the oath," said Brown. "If they refuse, they may have their property confiscated and be escorted out of town."

Brown gave his officers orders to break ranks and set up camp in the field behind the fort, then moved into the office with Grierson.

"I'll depend on you as liaison with the people of Augusta," said Brown.

"We'll have to sort out the sheep from the goats as soon as possible."

"We should have no trouble from the townspeople," said Grierson. "The rabblerousers all left town when they heard your troops were on the way."

"We don't need their families here, either," said Brown. "Unless the man of the family has taken the oath not to bear arms against the King, I want the family out of town."

"Yes, sir," said Grierson.

As a colonel of Royal militia, he should rank Brown, but the commanding officer of the King's Rangers was in complete control. Grierson knew he'd be hated by the townspeople as Brown's henchman, but perhaps he could keep tempers from bursting into flame and save punishments.

Mary Anne and John watched the Rangers' triumphal entry from the corner of Broad and Center. Two of the Martin children from next door were watching with the black nurse maid.

"How is Mrs. Martin?" Mary Anne asked the black woman, "and the new baby?"

"Miz Martin, she still weak, but she mostly jus' worried about Cunnel Martin. He an' he brother gone with Elijah Clark to de mountains. Dey say dey die befo' dey take de oaf."

"I wouldn't say that too loud, Auntie," said John. "These soldiers wouldn't take kindly to anyone who feels that way."

"Yessah," said the black woman. "I reckon dey ain't as pretty as dey looks. Best I take de chillun back and see 'bout de baby." She turned back toward the river, and John and Mary Anne followed her as far as the Merrill house.

"Are you sure you want to take the oath?" Mary Anne asked.

"I don't want to," said John, "but I want even less to leave you alone or to drag you off into the country and take a chance on your losing this baby.

"Clinton has promised that our property will not be damaged or our families molested if we take the oath."

"I feel like a traitor," said Mary Anne. "It isn't fair for me to keep you here."

"Maybe we can both help by staying here. Brown may listen to me if I intercede for some of our friends. All I have to do is promise not to bear arms. I won't have to fight for the King."

They were sitting on the porch in the late afternoon, when two soldiers came to the door.

"Are you ready to give your oath?" one of them asked John as the other wrote his name on the list.

John nodded.

"Then go immediately to the Common and join the rest of the men," said the soldier, wheeling and hurrying down the steps toward the Martin's house. When the butler told them that Colonel Martin was not at home, his name was written on another list.

"Is the colonel in the rebel army?" the spokesman asked.

"Yessuh," said the butler. "Miz Martin, she still in bed from havin' a baby."

"You tell her we are taking over this house for the King's officers," said the man in green. "She must be out of town by sunrise tomorrow."

As the men left the house, they spoke to an officer who was standing in the road. The officer called to a detachment of men carrying muskets with bayonets attached. Moving into the back yard of the Martin house, they began to lead horses out of their stalls, pricking the stable boy with a bayonet when he protested.

Mary Anne hurried next door to her friend's bedroom. The nursemaid was moaning and shaking. Her mistress lay on the big bed, holding the new baby, while a five- and a six-year-old tried to climb up the side of the big bed. In the nursery the four-year-old twins were howling and shaking the sides of their cribs.

Mary Anne took the black woman firmly by the shoulders and shook her until she stopped her noise.

"I'm sorry, Auntie," she said, "but you have to be quiet."

The two youngsters shut their mouths, eyes wide and brimming with tears when the source of their discipline was disciplined. The twins, straining to hear what was going on in their mother's room, stopped their racket.

"Now Auntie," said Mary Anne, "you get the twins in here, while I help Mrs. Martin. You are all going to be good soldiers like Colonel Martin, and do as you are told."

"Thank God for your help," said the distraught mother, still holding her baby to her breast. "I can't make head nor tail of what Sophie is saying except the soldiers are going to kill us all and burn down the house."

"It's not quite that bad," said Mary Anne, "but they do say families of men serving in the American army have to leave Augusta. I'm afraid, too, they're confiscating the horses."

"What will we do?" the mother asked. "We could go to Martintown to James' mother again if we had the horses to pull the carriage."

"John is taking parole," said Mary Anne. "They may not take our horses, at least for now, but I'm afraid I saw them wheeling your carriage out of your carriage house.

"I'll get our man to hitch one of our horses to the wagon in the Merrill's stable and load it with hay. You can ride in that."

As the nursemaid came back from the nursery, "Auntie, you see if you can find the stable boy. He can drive you to South Carolina."

Elizabeth Martin turned back the covers and sat on the side of the bed. Mary Anne picked up the sleeping baby and held it to her shoulder. "Can you dress yourself?" she asked.

"I can certainly try," said Elizabeth. "Sophie has kept me in bed since the baby came, and I was glad for a rest. Now I'm weak and dizzy, but I've stopped bleeding."

Mary Anne laid the baby gently in its cradle as the nurse came back, her eyes like saucers.

"Missy," said the nurse, "de butler an de stable boy bofe are gone. Sojers say dey been confiscated to work for de King."

"Then we'll have to do without them," said Mary Anne.

Now that she was up and on her feet, Elizabeth seemed to gain assurance. "We'll need food for the trip in case we get stopped on the way," she said. "Sophie, you get the children's clothes packed. Just stuff them in pillowcases, and the children can sleep on them in the wagon. I'll do the same with mine. Be sure to put in something warm, if we have to travel at night."

"How we gonna drive without no driver?" Sophie asked.

"Didn't you ever help drive the wagon on the farm when you were a girl?" her mistress asked.

"Yes'm," she answered, "but my pappy always dere, loadin' de wagon as we went down de rows."

"Then you can drive us tonight, and I'll be there to tell you how."

Mary Anne smiled and patted her friend's shoulder. "You'll make it," she said. "I'll go down and get the cook to load a bag with provisions."

By the time she reached the kitchen, there was no sign of a cook. The larder was stripped clean, as was the storeroom in the lean-too behind the kitchen. Hurrying next door to her own kitchen, she found Cindy sitting in front of the door, a rolling pin in her hand.

"Jonah tole me dey shouldn' bother no houses what took de oaf, but I ain' takin' no chances," she said.

"You're a brave girl," said Mary Anne, putting her arm around the black girl and giving her a hug. "Your mother would be proud of you."

"Yes'm," said Cindy.

"I need food for Mrs. Martin to take with her. The soldiers are making her leave Augusta tonight. Would you fix a bundle for them while I see about the wagon and horses?"

"Yes'm," said Cindy. "You sendin' Jonah wif de wagon?"

"No," said Mary Anne. "We're going to keep Jonah close to home. The soldiers are liable to steal anybody with a black skin, no matter whom he belongs to. Cook and both men from the Martins have disappeared."

"I seen 'em take de boy from de stable, but I reckon Isaac got clean away."

"I hope so," said Mary Anne. "I'd hate to see him sold and sent to the sugar islands."

"No, ma'am," said Cindy. "You tell Jonah to watch hisse'f when you go to de stable."

"I certainly will," said Mary Anne.

The sun had dipped below the horizon and torches were lighted in the street before the wagon was ready to roll. John had finally come home from the Common, where he had had to wait in line with all the men in town to take his oath. He helped load the clothes and provisions for the Martins.

When Mary Anne told him that the mother and children were ready, he drove to the front of the house where they waited. As they climbed in, the nursemaid helped them settle in the hay, with Elizabeth propped on the clothing-filled pillowcases, the baby fretting in her arms.

"I can't leave town on my parole," said John, "but I can get this team on the ferry for you."

They moved toward the line of wagons on Center Street waiting to cross to the Carolina side. As they passed a clump of trees and underbrush between the street and the river, John heard a hiss, and slowed the wagon almost to a stop.

"I'm in de bushes," said Jonah. "If'n I can hide in de hay till we get acrost, I can drive 'em to Martintown."

"Good man," said John, stopping the wagon and walking back as though to check the wheel. The light from the soldiers' torches hardly reached this section of road. In a moment Jonah had stepped on the wheel and slithered over the side into the hay.

As the wagon joined the others on the ferry road, a man stepped up beside the horses. "Surely you aren't leaving us, Mr. Stanley," said Mr. Fox. "I saw you taking the oath this afternoon as I was waiting to do the same."

"No," said John. "I'm only helping Mrs. Martin get her wagon on the ferry. The poor lady has an infant only ten days old."

"It's at times like this I'm thankful to be a bachelor," said Mr. Fox. Then, walking back to the side of the wagon, he doffed his hat and reached into the inner pocket of his coat. "My dear lady," he said, "please accept this in the spirit in which it is meant. You may need it." He slipped a flask of fine French brandy into her hand then hurried away.

·XXV·

ESCAPE FROM
THE LOW COUNTRY

As Brown marched into Augusta, the people of Charlestown were beginning to settle into a melancholy state of peace. Captured prisoners filled the Watch House and the prison ships in the harbor. General Clinton had taken over Brewton House as headquarters, and the men of his staff were quartered in the homes of Charlestown families nearby.

Jocelyn Merrill, her girls, and mother now occupied three small rooms in the attic of their house on Tradd Street, the remainder having been commandeered by two British Dragoon colonels and three young subalterns. The servants had been kept on in their quarters behind the house, and it was understood that as long as meals were served, rooms kept clean, and beds changed regularly, the family would be given shelter and protection. Jocelyn was now running an officers' boarding house.

The men of the American militia regiments had been paroled and sent back to their farms, with the promise that they would stay out of the war. The Continentals, however, as professional soldiers, were imprisoned. Sergeant Bert Sheldon was sent with Elbert's men to a ship anchored in the Ashley River. Locked into the hold of a troopship that had been disabled during the attack, he and other Upcountry soldiers sweltered in the stench of dirty bodies and unemptied slops, with scant foul food to eat and only a short time each day to exercise on the open deck. By the end of the first week, he was determined to escape or die in the attempt.

He had been careful to be quiet and obedient and avoid any special notice by his jailers. Some of the other country boys showing too much independent spirit had been shackled together with leg irons and put on starvation rations. Bert bided his time and kept his own counsel.

Finally early one morning, he and his mates were taken up on deck for exercise to find the river dense with a pea-soup fog. Thanking the Lord for hours of swimming to while away the hot days at Fort James, he suddenly broke from the line and dove into the swirling mists of the river.

He had never dived from such a height before, and he had never learned to cut the water sharply, the way Jamie did. Landing flat, knocking his breath away, and painfully wrenching his back, he turned over and lay on top of the water, kicking his feet and gasping for breath. From the deck above him he could hear shouts and running footsteps, and in a moment there was a flash and the bang of a musket shot. He dove under, willing his arms and legs to push him toward the shore.

His heavy boots made swimming almost impossible. Kicking up to the surface, he somehow managed to float long enough to get rid of them. Thanks to the blessed fog, the musketballs were hitting at some distance.

The tide was coming in, and he let the current carry him up the river, swimming in the direction he supposed the shore to be. The shots had ceased, but when he stopped swimming to float and rest, he heard the creak of block and tackle as a boat was lowered. He had no idea how far he was from the shore, but he swam with all his might away from the sound.

Suddenly ahead of him, the fog thinned for an instant, and he could see a bearded monster reaching into the water. At the same time, he bumped into a cypress knee. Cautiously putting his feet down, he touched a riverbed covered with sharp pointed shells. The heavy woolen socks his mother had knitted were still on his feet and kept the shells from cutting too deeply as he waded to the bank. A great, gnarled oak tree formed a cave over his head with silvery gray moss curtaining the entrance from the river.

From the direction of the ship, he could hear a splash of oars as the boat pulled toward the riverbank.

"We'll never find 'im in this bloody fog," he heard a searcher say. "Moight as well look for a ruddy needle in a haystack."

"It's good to be off the damned stinkin' hulk," said another voice. "Let the poor blighter go, if 'e 'asn't already drowned. We don't 'ave to brike our arms rowin' up an' down the bleedin' river."

"Right," said the other voice. "Rest on your oars, mytes. We'll drift up the river for a bit until the tide changes, and let it carry us back."

Bert crouched near the tree trunk until the sound of their voices grew faint, then he moved away from the river. The sun was beginning to cut through the blanket of gray, and he found himself in an undergrowth of palmetto and scrub oak, like the swamps he had fought through near Savannah. He felt vulnerable without his boots, knowing how rattlesnakes thrived in this sort of land.

Beyond the dense growth of the river bank, he found a deer path and followed it until it crossed a larger path that showed tracks of human feet. Cautiously he followed this until it came out in a big grassy clearing sloping down to a dock on the river. Stepping to the edge of the clearing, he looked away from the river and could see a timbered house, built in the old-fashioned way he had seen in pictures of England.

Barking the alarm, a large black dog of indeterminate ancestry suddenly charged down a center path flanked by azalea bushes. Behind him came a gray-haired black man carrying a musket.

"All right, I sees you. Come outa dere," said the man as the dog reached the edge of the lawn and began circling him, growling and baring its teeth.

"Call off your dog," Bert said. "I mean you no harm."

The man whistled, and the dog backed off keeping an eye on Bert, then came to heel as the man reached the end of the garden.

Bert still wore the tattered remnants of his Continental breeches, but had no other identification.

"Did you done swim in from de prison ship?" the black man asked. "I heard 'em shootin' at somethin' a while back."

"Can you help me?" Bert asked.

"Come up to de house," said the man. "We ask Miz Seabright can we help you."

As they walked toward the house, Bert could see a woman standing on the terrace, shading her eyes with her hand against the morning sun coming through the fog. It wasn't until they reached the hedge that circled the terrace that he realized she was old. Although her hair was snow white and her skin mapped with wrinkles, she stood straight and slim as a girl.

"Who do we have here?" the old lady asked.

Bert stepped forward and bowed. "I'm Bert Sheldon, ma'am, late of Colonel Elbert's Georgia Continental Regiment."

The old lady held out her hand. "And I'm Anne Seabright of Black Cypress plantation. Welcome."

Bert took the hand, which gripped his as a man's might, then stared in amazement. "Mrs. Seabright. Are you Mary Anne Stanley's grandmother? John told me you lived here."

The black man seemed nervous, looking around in all directions, and Anne Seabright turned toward the house motioning for Bert to follow.

"I gather from your wet clothes that you are the one they were shooting at from the prison hulk. We'd better get you out of sight."

"Are there British soldiers here?" Bert asked, hurrying into the hall beside her.

"Not at the moment," said Anne, "but they could come at any time. They've already cleaned out the stables and the smokehouse, and they keep my gardener busy picking beans and squash."

The black man had gone to the dining room and now came back with a decanter and two glasses on a silver tray.

"Sit on the oak settle over by the fireplace," said Anne Seabright. "You can't hurt it with your wet clothes. We'll put some life into you with a shot of brandy, and then you can bathe and get into something dry. John Stanley keeps hunting clothes in the guest room."

Bert sat gratefully on the settle and took a glass from the butler's tray. As the fiery drink warmed him to the soles of his sockshod feet, he finally began to relax.

* * *

On Tradd Street, Jocelyn Merrill was desolate and inconsolable, but so far she had been able to avoid their compulsory house guests. As the recent widow of a rebel officer, she was allowed to grieve in the attic in peace.

Susan was a different matter. Colonel Throckmorten of the King's Dragoons had a roving eye and a penchant for pretty young girls. Susan had been able to slip away from his busy hands when other officers arrived on the scene, but it was only a matter of time before he cornered her when no one else was around.

Mindy and Saul were kept busy waiting on the officers, and Susan had to do many errands for her mother and grandmother. Not wanting to disturb her mother, she said nothing about the colonel but tried to take the two little girls along when she left the attic.

One morning the two children came running up the stairs in tears with Mindy close behind them.

"Miz Merrill, I don't want to grieve you, but Miss Susan gone."

"We were going for a walk," Kate chimed in, "and that nasty old colonel was waiting at the park in a carriage."

"I seen it, ma'am," said Mindy. "I was comin' from de market."

"He grabbed Suzy and tried to pull her in the carriage," said Betsy, "and Suzy hit him in the stomach and scratched his eyes out."

"Yes'm, she's right," said Mindy. "But it didn't put his eyes out. He let Miss Susan go, and she run off into de lane behin' de blacksmith shop."

"We went back there to look for her, but she was gone," said Kate.

Jocelyn sat up on the day bed where she had been lying and put an arm around each little girl. Poor children. She'd not been much of a mother lately.

"Thank heavens she managed to get away," she said. "Don't you girls worry. We'll find her."

"It ain't safe for her to be roamin' de streets," said Mindy. "Dey's sojers everywhere."

Jocelyn looked Mindy in the eye, then down at the girls and shook her head.

"Susan can fight any soldier," said Kate. "She grabs us and shakes us when we're bad, and she's strong."

"Of course she is," said Jocelyn. "Mindy, you go down and ask Saul to come up here, and I'll give the girls some of the sweet biscuits Mrs. Manigault sent me."

By the time Saul came upstairs, Jocelyn had convinced the girls that Susan was safe, and had quieted her mother-in-law's fears. Her own grief would have to be pushed aside. She would have to enter the world again, like it or not.

Saul had learned about Susan from Mindy and had questioned Ambrose, the stable boy the colonel had "requisitioned" from the Seabrights down the street.

"Miss Susan all right," he said as he bobbed his head to Jocelyn. "She done tole de blacksmith she need help, an' he see she get to Miss Anne down at Black Cypress. He a frien' of Ambrose."

Jocelyn's eyes filled with tears, but not of grief, for a change. "Thank you, Saul," she said. "I don't know what I'd ever do without you and Mindy."

"Yes'm," said Saul.

"We'd all be lost in Charlestown without the colored people."

Saul was embarrassed. This was something you didn't talk about.

"Miss Susan gonna be all right," he said again. "I'd best be gettin' back to de colonel. He was mad as fire bout de scratches on he face, but he say he run into a low-hanging branch."

Susan sat in the blacksmith's shop waiting for a wagon. Ambrose had brought her a cloak with a hood and a message from her mother telling her to stay at Black Cypress as long as Cousin Anne could keep her. It reassured her that the colonel was too embarrassed to admit what had happened, but it was better for her to stay away.

Cousin Archibald Seabright had arranged for a wagon to be sent across Ashley Ferry to Black Cypress to pick up a load of vegetables and fresh crabs and shrimp for the officers' mess. The driver was to take along a seamstress to help his mother at the plantation. The wagon was passed by the sentry at the ferry landing with only a glance at the signature.

It was so dark by the time they arrived at Black Cypress that the driver would have missed the turn had he not known the way. Bats wheeled and dove among the streamers of moss, and a screech owl screamed in alarm at the sound of wagon wheels.

They were still a hundred yards from the house when the dogs began to bark. Bert and Anne Seabright had just finished supper and were on the terrace behind the house watching the moon rise over the river.

"I don't think the British would come searching in a wagon," said Anne after Isaiah called the dogs to heel and they could hear the sound of wagon wheels on the oystershell drive. "You'd better go in the office, though, and be ready to hide in the cupboard I showed you."

They hurried into the back hall, Bert ducking through the first door on his right and Anne going on to the front door.

Isaiah hurried down to the driveway with a lantern as he recognized the wagon and driver.

"George, man, what you doin out heah aft nightfall?" he called to the driver. "Ain't you 'fraid de sojers'll shoot you?"

"Mistuh Archie gib me a pass," said the driver. "I'm bringin' Miss Susan Merrill, oney she sposed to be a dressmaker."

Susan had scrambled down from the other side of the wagon and ran up the steps and into Anne Seabright's arms.

"Oh, Cousin Anne!" she exclaimed. "Can I stay at Black Cypress? I'm in terrible trouble in Charlestown."

"You know you can," said Anne, leading her into the house.

"Isaiah, you see that George gets some of the leftover supper at the quarters and beds down in the men's cabin after he takes care of the horses. And bring Miss Susan some of that shrimp and rice from supper."

"Yes'm," said Isaiah, hoping the cook hadn't already taken it to the quarters for her children.

"I want to hear all about it," Anne said as Susan sank into a cushioned chair, "but I have to tell my other visitor that the coast is clear," and she hurried from the room.

When Bert followed Anne into the parlor, Susan couldn't believe her eyes. Bert walked toward her as if in a daze, and Susan rose from the chair to meet him. Before they met, both stopped as though suddenly remembering Anne, and Susan reached both hands to grasp Bert's hands and hold them.

"How did you get here?" Susan asked, as Bert said "Susan, what are you doing here?"

They laughed and dropped their hands, then turned to Anne.

"It's obvious you don't need to be introduced," said Anne.

"Bert lives near Augusta," Susan said. "We have known each other for years."

"Then you can tell us both about your trouble in Charlestown."

"It really is terrible trouble, Cousin Anne," Susan said. "There is the most odious, lecherous colonel quartered at our house. I was trying to avoid him, because he wouldn't keep his hands off me." Bert's hands doubled into fists.

"This morning I was taking the girls for a walk when he drove up in a carriage and asked me to ride. When I refused, he tried to drag me into the carriage."

"That b---bounder!" said Bert, remembering to be polite. "I'd like to get my hands on him."

"Well, I did get my hands on him," said Susan. "I hit him in the stomach and scratched his face until I had blood on my nails. He let me go, and I ran into the lane behind the blacksmith shop. The blacksmith sent word to Mother and hid me until Cousin Archie could send George with the wagon."

Anne chuckled. "Good for you. I couldn't have done better myself." Susan looked surprised.

"I learned to take care of myself when I was young, too," said Anne. "I was afraid this younger generation of females were lacking in spirit."

"She should never have had to fight a British officer. I thought they were supposed to be gentlemen," said Bert.

"There are bad apples in every barrel," said Anne. "And I'm glad you had sense enough not to be fooled by the uniform, Suzy."

"I don't think he'll make trouble this time," said Susan. "It would make him look foolish. But I want to stay out of his way."

"You may have the other guest room for as long as you like," said Anne. "It will be like old times having a houseful of young people."

"I'll be leaving as soon as I can," said Bert. "General Williamson will need all the men he can find to defend Augusta."

"Mary Anne and John are there," said Anne. "Maybe Susan would be safer with them."

Bert looked at Anne in surprise. "Do you think it would be proper for Susan to travel with me?"

"Proper, fiddlesticks," said Anne. "She'd be a lot safer than she would be in Charlestown with all the English gentlemen on the prowl. I judge you to be a man of honor."

Bert colored crimson. "Oh, yes, ma'am," he stuttered. "I would guard her honor with my life. I was afraid of what people would say."

"We'd best dress her in boy's clothes," said Anne. "She can be your little brother. From what she says of her scrap with the colonel, she seems to be able to take care of herself."

Susan's eyes were dancing. "I've always thought it would be fun to be a boy."

"We'll get Josie to cut down one of John Stanley's old fishing outfits. "He'll be surprised when you both arrive in his clothes."

The next day was spent fitting out the two of them for the journey. Anne cut Susan's hair in a tousled bob. I'm a wicked old woman she said to herself as she watched Bert's eyes following Susan in the made-over trousers. But they'll make a good match some day or I'll eat my hat.

The next morning early, Bert and Susan left Black Cypress leading a bony spavined mule.

"The army has requisitioned all our horses except the team to pull the wagon and carry seafood and vegetables for the mess," Anne told Bert. "You wouldn't get far riding a decent horse. That mule's a lot stronger than he looks, and nobody will try to take him from you."

Tied to the worn saddle was a blanket roll, while a fletch of bacon, a sack of corn meal, and jug of cider swung from thongs on either side.

Bert and Susan wore sun-bleached shirts and trousers of homespun cotton and moccasin boots. On their heads were wide-brimmed hats woven from palmetto fronds by the slaves at Black Cypress for workers in the fields.

Their story, in case they were stopped by British troops, was that their parents had died the day before of smallpox. They had buried them in the swamp by their shack and were headed up the country to claim new land.

Even the bravest soldier was afraid of smallpox, and the country around Charlestown was now infested with it. No one wanted to go near a man who had been exposed.

They took the well-traveled road that had been used by drovers and fur traders for almost a hundred years. The first day they were stopped several times and questioned by soldiers in the green uniform of Loyalist militia, but at the mention of smallpox, were sent hurriedly on their way. By noon with the sun boring down through the heavy cotton shirt, Susan felt dizzy and lightheaded, her feet like leaden weights.

"We'll stop under that oak tree for lunch," said Bert, "and we can water the mule at the creek."

Cook had packed them a lunch of cornbread and ham, careful at Anne's instruction, not to give them any fancy food to arouse suspicion if their saddle bags were searched. Susan sat on a fallen oak trunk and wolfed down the food, tipping up the cider jug then passing it to Bert.

"You don't seem tired at all," she said, picking up the hat she had discarded in the shade to fan herself and scare away the gnats that were swarming around her sweat-soaked head.

"I've done so much walking in swamp country in the last few months, I don't even know I'm moving," said Bert. "Would you like to ride a while? We can pretend you're feeling sick if anyone wants to know why a country boy is riding while his big brother walks. Then they'll really avoid us."

"I feel sorry for the mule," said Susan. "He looks as though he's on his last legs."

"Don't worry about that mule," said Bert as he watched it foraging in the undergrowth. "This is probably the easiest day of his life."

Untying the halter rope from the willow sapling, he swung it over the mule's neck to make a rein. He stripped a willow switch for a whip and handed it to Susan after he had given her a leg up.

It felt good to be astride the saddle. Men were lucky not to have to wear billowing skirts and ride sidesaddle. Bert adjusted the stirrups and smacked the mule on the rump to start him along the road. Susan squeezed his sides and dug in her heels, enjoying the way the mule stepped out to her command.

The sun was creeping down behind the live oaks lining the trail when they reached a drovers' inn with a yard filled with milling cattle. Their story of smallpox would not do here, so Bert told the innkeeper that his little brother had run away to join the army but he had caught him in Charlestown. Now he was taking him back home to Georgia.

The only space for two was in a big bed with two other men, but Bert picked an outside spot for Susan and lay awake beside her, afraid he might reveal his feelings in his sleep. Susan slept peacefully, worn out by her unaccustomed exercise.

At breakfast Bert talked to a wagoner who had arrived late the night before from Augusta on his way to Charlestown with a load of hides. He said that Thomas Brown had taken the city without a shot fired.

Susan turned to Bert with terror in her eyes. "Oh, what do you think has happened to John and Mary Anne?"

Bert shook his head and put his finger to his lips. The wagoner continued with his story.

"They say as how Brown's been made head of Injun Affairs for the whole South. Augusta'll be overrun with Injuns again, an' they say trade's gonna boom for trappers. That's how come I'm hightailin' it down to Charlestown to sell these hides before the price goes down."

"What's happened to the militia?" asked Bert.

"It's all busted up. They say John Dooly and General Williamson offered to lead them up to the mountains where they could come back down and fight, but most of 'em voted to split up an' go back home. Elijah Clark's up in the Ceded Lands, an' I hear he's gatherin' up strays who still want to fight."

Bert and Susan finished breakfast and left to load the mule. Susan filled the jug with fresh water from the well in the inn yard and tied it to the saddle once more. They would talk when they got out of earshot.

"I don't want to go back to Augusta," Susan said as they moved out on the road. "I've had enough of British soldiers."

"I'd trust Colonel Brown to keep them under control," said Bert, "but I wouldn't want to be Wells or Bostick or any of the radicals who burned his feet. Colonel Campbell was pretty fair when he was there last year. I think Brown will be, too."

"I thought you planned to go on and fight," said Susan.

"I do," Bert sounded annoyed. "But I'm going to get you to John Stanley first. I promised Mrs. Seabright I would. And you sure as hell can't join the army with me."

Susan was enjoying the freedom of a boy's life and didn't want to relinquish it. "Couldn't I be a drummer boy or something?"

"Not bloody likely," said Bert. "We'll go up above town and cross at Hammond's Ferry. If we cross late in the evening, maybe I can get to Pa's farm without being stopped. They can see that you get to the Stanley's safely."

"Do you think John's taken the oath?"

"I don't know, but I think Mary Anne will be there and safe. Colonel Brown owes John for helping him, and he's a man of honor."

It would be two more days before they could hope to reach Augusta. They spent another night at a crowded inn. This time Bert was able to get a single cot for his sick brother and space for himself in a big bed with two other men. He worried about the language and crude jokes Susan was exposed to, but they were safe.

The next day, as the road turned north toward Ninety-Six, they turned off toward the Savannah River on a less-traveled trail. Although they had been in constant fear of being stopped and questioned on the main road, the presence of wagons and pack trains had protected them from robbery. With Susan's rough clothes and now sunburned and freckled skin, she was the image of a skinny cracker lad. Bert, however, obviously old and fit enough to be in the army, was happy to trade the busy road for the forest path.

The country had changed from moss-hung swampland to sandy pine forest. Although the sun shone hot on their heads and backs, the air had lost the steamy, fetid feel of the Low Country.

For two hours they walked single file with Bert scouting the trail and leading the mule. Suddenly the mule stopped and pricked his long ears forward. He started to open his mouth to bray, but Susan flung her arms around his head and held his mouth closed. Bert motioned to her to pull the mule into the undergrowth, then stepped behind a tree farther along the trail with his hunting knife held low pointing upward.

In a moment, a Creek Indian appeared on the trail with his hand raised in the sign of peace.

Bert stepped warily from behind his tree, returning the sign.

"You need not fear to bring the mule out on the path," said the Indian. "I have heard your footsteps and have watched you from that hickory tree since before you crossed the creek back there."

"I bid you good day then," said Bert, "and we'll be on our way."

"If you are going to Augusta, know you that it is now in the hands of Colonel Brown's Florida Rangers?" the Indian asked, looking Bert up and down.

"I've heard as much," said Bert. "I hope to take this lad to his relatives in Augusta. His parents died of smallpox."

"You will be wise to take the western ferry," said the Indian. "The soldiers in town might notice this lad's shape, as I have."

Bert's hands reached instinctively for his knife, but the Indian caught his wrist in an iron grip.

"I have no wish to harm either one of you. May I suggest, though, that you go the Sword and Thistle Inn if you need help?"

Giving the peace sign once more, he moved up the path they had just traveled.

"Now who in tarnation was he?" Bert exclaimed. "He speaks English as well as any white man."

"He certainly saw through my disguise," said Susan. "I hope the soldiers don't."

"Nobody else has," said Bert, "and we'll avoid soldiers. I hope we get to the ferry so late that the guard will be sleepy."

Darkness fell long before they could reach the ferry, and there was no moon. The weather that had held till then now broke. Thunder rumbled in the west and lightning flashed through the pine branches.

"We'd better find some kind of shelter in a hurry," said Bert. "It's going to pour." He remembered a sand bank they had passed a short way back with a huge oak tree growing from the top, its roots reaching down through the bank. He took the mule's rope and jogged back along the trail. Tying the mule to a small pine, he used his hands and his knife to dig out a hole among the roots; then, unstrapping the blanket roll from the saddle he pegged two blanket corners to the ground on top of the bank and the other two to the ground below.

Raindrops were beginning to splash on the leaves around them when they crawled into the shelter. As they leaned against the tree roots, their legs stretched out in the sand and pine straw, lightning flashed through the tree tops and rain lashed the branches around them. A blinding light flashing around the edges of the blanket tent and an earsplitting crash of thunder drove Susan terrified into Bert's arms, her head burried in his shoulder. An earth-shaking crash told them that a tree had fallen nearby.

The wildness of the night seemed to have entered their blood. Bert wrapped her into a protective embrace that became less protective and more demanding as she turned her face up to his kisses. Thunder, lightning, and howling wind built to a crescendo as they satisfied the hunger that had been building in their hearts over the years.

Bert woke once in the night to find the rain had stopped. God forgive me. What have I done? he thought. Then, as Susan cuddled closer murmuring in her sleep, he kissed her tousled hair and fell asleep once more.

They woke to a red sunrise through the pine trees. The mule had stuck his head in the tent, trying to chew his way into the bag of meal.

Bert was afraid to move, afraid to look Susan in the face.

"How can you ever forgive me?" he asked finally, as she sat up and stretched. "I promised Mrs. Seabright I'd guard your honor with my life."

Susan leaned down and kissed him on the nose, then on the lips as his arms came around her again. Finally, struggling out of his arms, she rearranged her shirt and pushed aside the soggy blanket tent.

"If I know Cousin Anne," said Susan, "she'd say 'Honor, fiddlesticks. Love knows best.'"

"We'll be married as soon as we get to Augusta," said Bert.

"What about Mother?" said Susan. "She's always wanted me to be married in Saint Philip's Church with a long white dress."

"The fortunes of war," said Bert, grinning. "We'll talk to Mr. Seymour."

"But you're an escaped prisoner," said Susan. "Mr. Seymour's a Tory."

"He's a clergyman and pledged to keep secrets," said Bert.

They trudged up the bank toward the highroad. To the left, toward town, they could see the English flag fluttering above Fort Grierson. Bert turned toward his father's farm, swatting the mule to hurry him along. Susan strode beside him swinging her arms like a boy.

*　*　*

Having received a bottle of whisky from the Sword and Thistle the day before, John Stanley had come to see what Jamie wanted. Jamie sent him to the stable where Bert Sheldon was playing mumblety-peg with Desmond.

"I thought you'd never get here," said Bert, grasping John's hand.

"What in tarnation are you doing here?" John exclaimed. "I heard you were a prisoner in Charlestown."

"Now I'm an escaped prisoner," said Bert. "I'll be hanged if they catch me."

"Then why, in God's name, did you come to Augusta?" John asked.

"I've brought Susan Merrill with me," said Bert. "She lit into a British colonel when he tried to drag her into his carriage. She scratched him up pretty bad."

"You mean you two came alone all the way from Charlestown through the Tory patrols?"

"No problem with Tories," said Bert. "We said she was my little brother and our folks had died of smallpox. You should have seen 'em back off."

"Does her mother know she came with you?"

"She does by now. It was Mrs. Seabright's idea to dress her up like a boy and she gave us a mule."

"I'd better get word to Gran that you two arrived safely." said John.

"To Charlestown?" Bert sounded surprised.

"There are ways," said John. "But where is Susan?"

"She's with my folks," said Bert. "I didn't want her with me if I got caught coming to town. But I need you to do me a favor. We want to get married."

"Married?" John exclaimed.

Bert looked him squarely in the eye. "Since the trip I think we need to be married before I leave. I was hoping you could talk to Mr. Seymour.

John shook his head in disbelief. "You mean you want me to talk a Tory clergyman into marrying a fugitive rebel prisoner to a young girl without her parents' consent?"

"She's twenty years old now," said Bert, "and Mary Anne's her cousin. She can stand in her mother's place. Mrs. Seabright trusted me with Susan. I broke that trust, but I want to make things right."

John smiled. "If it hadn't been for Anne Seabright, Mary Anne and I would never have married. She's a wily old Cupid."

"Will you help us then?"

"I'll talk to Mr. Seymour," said John. "But you'd better stay out of town."

"I hoped he'd come out to Rae's Creek," said Bert. "You and Mary Anne can come out beforehand. We don't want it to look like a gathering."

"Susan had better come to live with us after the wedding," said John. "It makes sense for her to be staying in her family's house. You'd better keep the marriage secret so she won't be known as the wife of a fugitive."

"Jamie tells me you've taken parole."

"So have Dooly and most of the other militia officers. Elijah Clark, Benjamin Few, and John Jones have gotten together some of their men up in Wilkes County and refuse to lay down their arms. Most of the men around Augusta, though, were too worried about their families. Clinton has promised that if we don't take up arms against the King, we won't be called on to join the Loyalist militia. They're hard on the families of patriots. Our next door neighbor, whose husband is with Clark, was thrown out of her house in the night with a ten-day-old baby and four other children."

"Do you think Susan and Mary Anne will be safe?"

"They have been very courteous to us," said John. "In fact as soon as order was restored here, Brown gave notice he would hang anyone who plundered or disturbed peaceable citizens whatever their politics."

"I don't trust 'em," said Bert. "They won't take kindly to an escaped prisoner. I'm going to leave as soon as we're married and join Clark or Pickens."

"Pickens and Williamson have taken parole," said John. "Williamson did his best to keep his troops together to fight, but most of them were ready to go home and get the crops in."

"I'll be damned if I'll take a chance on hanging," said Bert.

Two nights later, Bert rode Moonshine on little used paths up into the Ceded Lands toward Heard's Fort. Susan rode home with John and Mary Anne.

·XXVI·

SIEGE OF MacKAY'S FORT

Shortly after Susan's return, the family was sitting on the front porch after supper listening to the frogs and katydids and waiting for a breeze from the river, when Thomas Brown came to call.

"Miss Merrill," he exclaimed, "what a pleasant surprise."

"We're so happy to have her here with us," said Mary Anne. "She has come to stay for the summer away from the Low Country fever. Her mother wanted her out of the city, now that Charlestown's filled with soldiers."

"A wise decision," said Brown, turning to Susan. "You have grown to be such a beautiful woman that it must be a sore temptation to poor homesick English lads to try to make your acquaintance."

"You're very kind," said Susan, knowing that her face was still sunburned and freckled. "We had several officers quartered in our home and not all of them were gentlemen."

"I'm sorry," said Brown. "But if you ever have any trouble with men in Augusta, I hope you will report it to me immediately."

"Thank you," said Susan.

"They have been very courteous," said Mary Anne.

"I want Augusta to be the trading capital of the South once more," said Brown. "I hope my men will be able to keep the peace. Once the Indians find that they are welcome as they used to be, I hope they'll flock in with their hides and pelts."

"Augusta people will be glad for the trade," said John. "I'm afraid, though, that the settlers will make trouble for you. The Indians in this area have taken advantage of the war, and have killed and plundered without investigating people's politics."

"I plan to put a stop to that," said Brown. "My Creeks have made peace with the tribes this side of the Mississippi, and I have friends among the Cherokees from the days when John Stuart was in charge."

"The farmers who have had their homes burned and their families tortured are not going to welcome them back," said John. "To a lot of backwoodsmen, the only good Indian is a dead Indian."

"Then, by God, they can pick up their belongings and leave," said Brown. "I'll not have trade disrupted because of a few Crackers."

Mary Anne reached over in the dark and squeezed John's hand, shaking her head when he looked at her.

"Do you plan to have Indian conferences here again?" Mary Anne asked.

Brown relaxed and turned to her. "I certainly do. General Clinton is establishing a series of forts with Augusta at its western end. We'll be able to send pack trains through to Georgetown on the coast, with protection of Loyalist troops all the way. The Indians can bring hides and pelts to Augusta as they used to without fear of attack."

"Then South Carolina has surrendered?" Mary Anne asked.

"All but a few partisan bands in the swamps," said Brown, "and Georgia, too, except for the Crackers up in the Ceded Lands."

"I wouldn't be too sure," said John, stung by his arrogance.

"Many of them like you will see their mistake and return to the King's protection, or be hanged as traitors."

Mary Anne could see Susan's hands gripping the chair arms and quickly brought the conversation back to the Indian trade. Their lives depended upon staying in Thomas Brown's good graces.

As June became July, Indians began to drift into town, and Brown made sure that they were well treated and their requests granted when possible. A company of Rangers was sent to Fort Rutledge in the Cherokee country that had been taken over by rebel partisans. When the Rangers captured the fort, Brown ordered all squatters illegally living in the area to be chased out of Indian lands.

Word came of scalpings and burnings throughout the Upcountry, even in the land that had been ceded and legally settled. Settlers gathered in the strongest palisaded fort in their neighborhood, and the paroled rebels who defended their families against attack were denounced for taking up arms. Farms were vandalized and families ravaged by other settlers in the name of loyalty to the King. Colonel John Dooly, who had given his parole, was killed by a band of ruffians calling themselves loyalists, as he lay delirious with fever.

In Augusta the fur trade was flourishing once more. Colonel Brown had been ordered by Governor Wright, once more in office in Savannah, to rebuild fortifications that had deteriorated. Intent upon establishing trade, Brown delayed building a new fort while he rebuilt warehouses and reinstated trading licenses. Instead of punishing vandalism in the country, he ignored it in hopes the rebellious troublemakers would grow discouraged and leave, without the use of military force.

John had given Bert a coded note for Elijah Clark from someone at Ninety-Six, warning him that a company of Loyalist Rangers were being dispatched to upper South Carolina to harass rebel settlers. Clark had sent word around the countryside to men in his old command to rendezvous at Freeman's Fort for a long campaign in the Carolinas.

On the night of June eleventh, one hundred and forty armed mountain men crossed the river above Petersburgh into the upper Ninety-Six District of South Carolina. Bert had been sent ahead as a scout and was walking Moonshine cautiously around a thicket when the horse suddenly shied and nearly threw him. As he gathered the reins and leaned over to reassure Moonshine, an Indian stepped from behind a tree.

"Well I'll be damned," said Bert as the Indian gave the peace sign. "You sure do show up in strange places."

The Indian nodded without smiling and held out a buckskin pouch. "Give this to Colonel Clark," he said. "The Loyalists have moved in force into this country. The dispatch will give the details." With no further conversation, he turned and faded into the forest.

Hurrying back toward the column of troops, Bert found Colonel Clark and handed him the dispatch. "An Indian gave me this," he said. "He says the Tories are ahead of us in force."

Clark signaled a halt, then ordered the company to disperse and form again on a wooded hill where they would be hidden and could make a stand if attacked.

"According to intelligence I have received," he told the men when they had reassembled, "there is a force of three or four hundred Tories and British Regulars scouting this area. Our only retreat would be across the North Carolina border, and that is dangerous country full of Tories and outlaws. We could well be cut off without aid."

"Does the Colonel suggest we retreat now?" Lieutenant John Freeman asked.

"It's up to you men," said Clark. "You are volunteers. I'd rather know now, if you have any idea of leaving me."

"Damned if I'll turn around now," said Colonel John Jones, who had brought his Burke County Georgians to join the Wilkes men in the Carolina campaign.

"You Burke County people haven't had as much trouble with Indians and Tories," said a man from Wilkes. "I don't like leaving my wife to protect herself and the children. We'd be damned fools to go against three times our number and Regulars, too."

"Let's put it to a vote," said Clark. "How many Wilkes men will follow me against the enemy?"

Bert and one or two others raised their hands.

"Who'll follow me?" Jones shouted.

All but three Burke County men raised their hands.

Jones smiled. "Then you other men can come with us if you like. And John Freeman will be my second in command."

Clark and his men turned back toward the river, and Jones, guided by a Carolina man, started toward the headwaters of the Saluda River with a company of thirty-five men, including Bert Sheldon.

As a mixed group of frontier volunteers, the men were not in uniform. Butternut shirts and breeches were matched and mismatched with buckskins. Some wore coonskin caps and some wore broadbrimmed wool hats to keep off the sun.

"If we meet any Tories, we'll pretend to be Tory volunteers," said Jones. "Most of these Upcountry people don't give a damn one way or the other, but they'll be more likely to help Tories with the King's militia in the neighborhood."

As they neared the Saluda River, a settler told them that a party of rebels had surprised a Loyalist force up the road a piece and had defeated them, taking a lot of prisoners. He asked if Jones' men planned to join the band of Tories who were going after them. Jones asked the settler for directions to the meeting place.

About eleven o'clock that night, they approached a clearing where the Tories were said to be camped. Leaving horses and baggage guarded by twelve men, the other twenty-three crept forward. Bert, reconnoitering on the left flank, was amazed to find the whole Tory company asleep without posting sentinels.

Suddenly one of the Tories' horses nickered and bumped into his neighbor, causing the other horses to mill in the rope corral. Four of the sleeping men sprang from their blankets, reaching for their guns. The others were wakening more slowly. In a hail of bullets from the dark woods, one fell dead and three wounded. Before guns could be reloaded for another volley, one of the Tories screamed, "Quarter, for God's sake!" and stood with both hands in the air.

The thirty-two remaining were rounded up, stripped of weapons, then made to promise to go home and live in peace. The Georgia men were given a chance to swap their guns for any of the Tory rifles they wanted, and the remaining guns were destroyed. Each man took one of the enemy's horses on a lead line, and they continued their march toward Earl's Fort on the Pacolet River near the North Carolina border.

By the time they reached the Pacolet, Bert was so tired he could hardly stay in the saddle. Leading a strange horse through rough, wooded country for three days and trying to control his own mount was enough to weary anyone. They'd been afraid to stop except to water the horses and gobble a cold meal, knowing that the Tories would have raised the alarm.

As they followed the path along the river to the ford, they were suddenly hailed from the woods, uphill from the river.

"Halt! Who goes there?"

Weary almost to helplessness, Jones' men turned their horses from the path and snatched their guns from their saddles, prepared to fight.

"Who are you?" Colonel Jones called into the dusky woods along the river bank.

"McDowell's North Carolina militia," came the answer.

"Thank God," said Colonel Jones, dismounting and walking out onto the path with hands raised. "We're John J. Jones' volunteers from Burke County, Georgia, and we're all-fired happy to meet up with you people."

Colonel McDowell strode from the protective woods, hand outstretched.

"You must be the Americans we were looking for," said Jones. "We met up with a Tory band gathered to punish you for stomping on a bunch of Loyalists near the Saluda."

"How did you come out of it?" McDowell asked.

"Well, my men have a lot of new guns," said Jones, "and we've got an extra horse for every man."

McDowell laughed and pounded Jones on the back. "Hell, you don't have no more'n a handful of soljers. We shoulda stayed and took 'em ourselves!"

Jones nearly crumpled under the blow, too tired to stand. "I think I'll sit a spell," he said. "We've been on the march without sleep for three days and nights."

"There's clear water for the horses below the ford," said McDowell, "and my men can share rations for tonight. We're camped in the woods about twenty yards upriver."

The Georgia men were already untacking their horses, carrying the saddles and bedrolls to the woods. Bert led Moonshine and the Tory horse to drink, then found a spot under a big tulip poplar for his saddle. Tying the horses to the picket line, he left enough rope for them to reach the grass and weeds, thinking he could scare up some oats and corn later.

The North Carolinians had been at the ford only a few hours but had built fires and stewed a cow from a nearby Tory farm with potatoes and onions from the garden. McDowell sat with Jones and Freeman as they cleaned their bowls and went back for more stew.

"We're not far from Fort Prince," said McDowell. "We'll have to douse the fires before sunset. Colonel Alexander Innes is in command of the regiment of British Dragoons and Tory Regulars there, and I'd hate to have him see our fires and come to investigate."

Bert had overheard the Colonel's conversation and went around the Georgia camp to instruct the men before settling down for the night. He'd kept the rank of sergeant when he joined Colonel Jones and was responsible for his men, though some were twice his age.

As soon as darkness fell, the camp became silent except for an occasional snore. The thirty-five Georgians were too tired to move farther into the woods and camped near the ford, their horses picketed deeper in the woods. Over the ridge, beyond them, McDowell's three hundred North Carolinians spread out in the cove.

Toward midnight, scouts from a troop of seventy dragoons from Fort Prince crept up on the sleeping Georgians and returned to report that thirty-five rebels were camped near the ford; but they had not discovered McDowell's camp over the ridge. Dragoon Captain Dunlap decided to make camp for the night and attack in the morning.

Bert Sheldon slept like the dead until four in the morning when he was roused by the sentry who had stood the midnight watch. After going to the river bank and splashing his face with cold water out of the mountains, he found a spot on a knoll overlooking the ford shielded by low-growing limbs of a dogwood tree. With his rifle ready beside him, he leaned against the tree trunk and listened to the night sounds that reached him above the chuckle of the rock-strewn river. When the birds began to stir and call with the first light of dawn, he felt a shaking of the ground under his feet. The river noise covered the sound of hoofs but peering out of his hiding place, he saw a nightmare. Trotting their horses into the shallow ford on the other side of the river was a column of British Dragoons that filled the path as far as he could see. Grabbing his rifle and firing a shot into the oncoming horsemen, he hurried back toward camp.

As the British bugler sounded the charge, the Georgians scrambled for their guns. Bert knelt in the underbrush at the edge of camp and reloaded his rifle, fired at one of the redcoated cavalrymen and saw him fall from his horse.

By now the camp was a shambles. Horsemen with sabres drawn had slashed through the dismounted Georgians in the clearing. Colonel Jones had ordered his men to take cover, forcing some of the dragoons to dismount and fight among the trees. Bert saw him engage a big British subaltern in a sword fight but was afraid to shoot the redcoat for fear of hitting the colonel. When Jones fell with blood streaming from his face and shoulders, Bert saw the British officer also sink to the ground.

Lieutenant Freeman rallied the men to retreat toward the North Carolina camp, and Bert called one of the Georgia soldiers to help him carry the colonel into the woods where they could bind his wound.

Roused by the gunfire, the North Carolinians suddenly advanced on the right of the beleaguered Georgians, mounted and ready to fight the dragoons on equal terms. Finding themselves hopelessly outnumbered, the British cavalry fled across the river leaving their subaltern on the ground. McDowell quickly organized a pursuit party under command of Captain Edward Hampton, whose South Carolina militia was riding with McDowell.

Bert and thirteen other Georgians under Lieutenant Freeman rode out with thirty-eight North Carolinians, all mounted on the best horses in the combined camps. The sun still hadn't risen above the treetops when they galloped out on the path to Fort Prince. Two hours and fifteen miles later, they came upon the British Dragoons watering their horses and eating breakfast beside a stream.

Charging into the clearing with their guns blazing, the Americans killed eight of the dragoons at first fire and several others as they were trying to mount. The frantic British, both on foot and on horseback, took to the woods, but Hampton's detachment followed them, firing as they went, to within three hundred yards of Fort Prince, Knowing that the fort was garrisoned with three hundred troops, Hampton gave the order to return to camp.

The victorious expedition rode back to McDowell's camp at two o'clock in the afternoon to the cheers of waiting comrades. Thirty-five horses wearing dragoon saddles and bridles accompanied wagons loaded with British provisions.

McDowell's forces broke camp, crossed the river and headed for Saluda Gap and the North Carolina mountain settlements. Swathed in bandages, Colonel John Jones was well enough to travel. Two of his men had been killed and six badly wounded in the fight at the ford. Carrying the wounded men in one of the captured wagons, Lieutenant Freeman and his remaining twenty-eight men escorted them back across the Savannah River to the Ceded Lands of Georgia.

Word of the fight at the ford reached Augusta by way of Ninety-Six. Someone serving in British headquarters there was sending news to the Sword and Thistle before it could reach Fort Grierson through military channels. Messengers in the Upcountry kept rebel forces informed of the movements of all British troops in the area. No one but Jamie Stratfield and one Indian runner knew who was sending the messages.

Elijah Clark was at Heard's Fort when he heard the news carried by a black slave from Augusta. Hurrying to see Stephen Heard, who was still acting as governor in exile, he asked for help in getting the lukewarm militia out to fight. Members of the Council in hiding with Heard allocated money which they hoped to get from the Continental Congress to pay the militia. They also spread word about a new act of the British government requiring all American parolees to serve in British regiments. Maybe the farmers would choose to serve in their own militia rather than be drafted by the British.

In a few weeks, Clark was ready to move back across the Savannah with a full regiment of Georgia militia. Colonel John Jones, though badly scarred, was back in the saddle and led his Burke County men to join Clark's at the Dark Corner boundary between North and South Carolina. There they met Captain James McCall with twenty men from Pickens' old regiment. The three commanders trained their troops in guerilla tactics, foraged in the countryside for supplies from Tory settlements, and dashed down to strike British supply trains bound for Fort Prince and Ninety-Six.

Clark and his men had been notified that an ammunition train was on the way from Fort Motte to Ninety-Six. Before an engagement, Clark always chose a strategic spot to which he could retreat and make a stand. On August tenth, he was preparing to strike the wagon train when Colonel Innes, with a force of over three hundred Tory cavalry, suddenly appeared riding at full gallop. Clark ordered his men to retreat to Wofford's Iron Works and deploy on ground well suited to defense. Innes spent the rest of the day trying to draw them out on open ground, then withdrew during the night. Clark returned to his base camp. Both leaders claimed victory, but Clark had succeeded in keeping the British on edge, unable to claim total control over the Carolinas and Georgia.

A week later, Clark received a note by messenger that Innes planned to attack him the next morning with a force of three hundred and fifty crack troops. Clark, meanwhile, had been joined by the troops of Shelby, Branham, and Williams from north of the border. Stationing his own troop of a hundred Georgians four miles north of Musgrove's mill in a position handpicked for its advantage, he held the North Carolina troops in reserve, hidden behind a fence to the right and left of an open field.

Innes advanced to within fifty paces of Clark before his flankers discovered the size of the rebel reserve. As Clark advanced down the center of the lane, Innes ordered his dragoons to charge, to force the Americans to fight a British-style battle on open ground. When the dragoons and Loyalist militiamen were fired on by the North Carolinians from behind the fences on either side, they closed in on the center, crowding the Regulars who had no room to form a battle line. Confused and catching rifle fire from three directions, the British fell in heaps with seven officers out of nine killed or wounded. Finally the British second in command called a close-order retreat for the four miles to Musgrove's Mill, with the Americans hot on their heels.

When the Americans withdrew and counted their casualties, it was found that four had been killed. The British had lost sixty-three killed and one hundred sixty wounded or taken prisoner.

Clark and Jones led their militia back across the river to Georgia after dividing the British supplies with the North Carolinians.

While the Georgia and North Carolina militia had been wreaking havoc on the western borderlands, the Continental Congress, against General Washington's wishes, had put General Horatio Gates, the hero of Saratoga, in command of all the American troops in the southern sector. Washington had wanted General Nathanael Greene in the job, knowing that Gates was a bungler whose victory at Saratoga was due to the brilliant strategy of Benedict Arnold.

Through Gates' stubbornness and stupidity, the Continental forces were completely routed near Camden, South Carolina, losing more than seven hundred killed or taken prisoner. Gates fled at top speed toward Charlotte, and General Thomas Sumter, asleep from exhaustion under a wagon, was so nearly captured that he had to jump on his horse bareback without hat, boots or coat and ride off with what was left of his command to disperse through the backwoods and return home.

Thomas Brown, in Augusta, was intent on keeping the peace so that the trade in hides could once again pour gold into the English treasury. Setting up a courthouse in Brownsborough on his old estate, he mediated any disputes between landholders in the area and meted out justice to outlaws and disturbers of the King's peace. Those who defied his regulations were thrown in jail or hanged. Indians were welcomed and given privileges to encourage their trade.

Robert MacKay's fortified trading post on the edge of town was well known to the Indians and convenient to the traders' path. Since MacKay's two stepsons were known to be in the rebel militia, Brown moved out MacKay's widow and took over the whole compound as a storehouse for Indian trading goods.

Meg was furious. "How could he do such a thing?" she asked Jamie as they cleared the tables at the Sword and Thistle. "I heard one of the soldiers say they had put Mary's belongings in a wagon and told her to leave town."

"The families of militiamen have no rights now," said Jamie. "Their property can be confiscated at the will of the army."

"But Robert MacKay was Thomas Brown's friend!" said Meg. "I've served them many a time when they drank together here."

"Robert's dead and his stepsons are fighting the Crown. Brown has become so embittered he won't let friendship stand in the way of what he considers his duty."

"Poor Mary," said Meg. "What will she do? Can't we take her in here?"

"She's gone to Moore's Bluff to stay with the Galphins."

"I wish we could pack up and leave," said Meg. "This isn't the Augusta we loved."

"Who knows?" said Jamie. "They say Cornwallis is being kept so busy by Francis Marion in the eastern swamps that the Upcountry militia may be able to take over, and make Augusta capital of Georgia again."

Angus had come up behind them and touched Jamie on the shoulder. "Have you had any news of an attack here?"

"Where would I get any such news?" Jamie asked. "No one has mentioned it in the tap room."

Up in the Ceded Lands, Elijah Clark was doing his best to recruit men for just such an attack. Rebel settlements were now being pillaged and stock stolen without fear of punishment. Men who had been happy to remain neutral were now ready to fight.

On September sixteenth, a month after their victory at Musgrove's mill, Clark and almost six hundred determined backwoodsmen rendez-voused and moved into the Augusta area by the three main roads. Lieutenant Colonel James McCall's division, many of them Carolinians from Ninety-Six who had been paroled with Pickens, circled the town and entered by the Sand Bar Ferry Road. Major Samuel Taylor's division came down the Cherokee Road, and Clark with the main body advanced toward the center of town on the Savannah Road.

Surprise was complete. Taylor's division found a group of Indians camped near Hawk's Creek, who fired and retreated toward MacKay's post. There a company of King's Rangers were billeted under the command of Captain Andrew Johnston, the son of Augusta's popular doctor who had been forced to move to Florida.

As the Indians retreated up the road toward MacKay's, they kept up a steady fire, killing and wounding several of Taylor's men. When they came near the trading post, Johnston's men covered their retreat into the house killing several horses and wounding more of Taylor's men. The Georgians retreated to the woods across the road, dragging their wounded with them, to wait for reinforcements.

At Fort Grierson, Brown, hearing Taylor's shots, sent Colonel Grierson and his Loyalist militia to reinforce Lieutenant Johnston's Rangers, while he led the main body of Rangers west to stop Taylor.

Clark and McCall, finding Augusta unguarded on the south and east, took over the partially rebuilt fort at the Center Street ferry without firing a shot then marched on to Fort Grierson. Finding it nearly deserted, they set a guard and hurried to join Taylor's men at MacKay's.

MacKay's white stone house would withstand almost any attack except from heavy artillery. Behind the house was a palisaded yard containing the office and storage sheds of the Indian trade. Set on top of a hill, the house overlooked the river with the wooded bluff of the river bank behind it. The river acted as a moat, forcing attack to be made from the front.

The Creek Indians Taylor had chased from Hawk's Creek had taken a position in the woods by the river to protect the house from flank attacks. Some of the men from McCall's Georgia regiment had dashed into the stable and storage shed near the house but found that enemy bullets could penetrate through the wide cracks between the boards. As Bert and his men arrived on the scene, McCall's men were running bent over, back to the main body of troops, taking cover with them behind the wall that had once protected Mary's flower garden.

The attack on the town had started early in the morning. By eleven o'clock, Brown and his troops, taking the river path, had joined Johnston's men in MacKay's fort, and the August sun was beating down on the men behind the wall. Through the rest of the day, militiamen from Wilkes and Burke and Ninety-Six kept up desultory rifle fire, taking a turn behind the cover of the wall then crawling back to the trees along the road to cool off and refill their cartridge bags.

Bert and his men took a turn as the sun was sinking low over the river. When darkness fell, another squad relieved Bert and his men, who crawled along the wall to the woods, then joined the rest of the Georgia militia in camp on the other side of the road.

Under cover of darkness, Brown's Rangers were busy all night long. Still in control of the river bank, Brown sent three messengers by different routes to Colonel Cruger at Ninety-Six, asking for help. With the river shallow in the August drought, they were able to swim their horses the short distance to the bank on the Carolina side.

The Tories dug earthworks close to the house, and the holes between the weatherboards and the ceilings of the storerooms were filled with dirt. Boards were taken from Mary's hardwood floors to nail over the smashed windows.

At daybreak Bert awakened in the camp across the road to the sound of whips and shouts and the creak of wheels as two cannons that James Grierson had mounted on his fort during his trading days were dragged in a wagon to the road opposite MacKay's fort.

"How in tarnation do they expect to shoot those things?" one of the countrymen asked Bert.

"I've seen them shoot the kind on wheels outside Savannah," said Bert, "but I don't know how they aimed them, or how they put in the powder and wadding and all that."

"Somebody told me there's a Captain Martin from across the river in Carolina who knows about artillery," said another man.

"That must be Bill Martin," said Bert. "His brother used to live here in Augusta."

They watched as the guns were dragged to the wall, and Captain Martin gave orders how to mount them, braced with stones at an angle he hoped would be effective.

A cheer rose as the first gun was filled with powder, wadding, and the ball and a long match touched to the hole in the top of its barrel. Sparks flew from the touch hole, and the muzzle shot flames as the ball lofted into the air. When it fell short of the target the cheer turned to a groan, but became a cheer again as the second gun belched smoke.

Taking orders from Captain Martin, the gunners kept their heads below the wall as much as possible. When one of the shots struck the chimney, however, they were all so excited they jumped to their feet, pounding Captain Martin on the back and tossing their hats in the air. Martin's hat remained on his head with a bullet hole through it as he fell beside the gun. Brown's Rangers were woodsmen and had dropped Martin as they would a deer in the Florida swamps.

With no one to direct them, the cannoneers gave up and finally scurried back to the woods for their rifles. Volley after volley of rifle and musket fire from the frustrated rebels splattered the boarded windows of the house.

When the sun finally went down again, there was little sign of damage. Under cover of darkness, Clark's men went among the dead and wounded beyond the wall, carrying those who were still alive back to the camp.

While the rebels were using the darkness to collect their casualties, fifty Cherokee Indians paddled canoes quietly across the river to join the Creeks along the river bank, willing to associate with their sworn enemies to help Colonel Brown keep Augusta safe for the Indian trade.

That night Colonel Clark gave Bert leave to ride out to Rae's Creek. Ben and Mary had kept word of Bert's escape and his marriage to Susan from everyone outside the family since Brown was confiscating property of the families of rebel soldiers. As long as Bert was thought to be a prisoner and Ben known to be a practicing Quaker, they would be reasonably safe from their Tory neighbors. Francie and Benjy, outside hoeing in the garden, ran to greet him with the dogs barking ecstatically at their heels. The family talked until almost dawn, when Bert had to saddle up and ride back to MacKay's.

"You'd better see that your valuables are well hidden and be ready to ride out," said Bert. "If we can't take Brown's Rangers before Cruger hears about this attack and sends help, we'll have to leave Augusta."

"You're right, Son," said Ben. "The Tories are going to be so furious they'll go after anybody who won't fight on their side."

Bert arrived back at camp before daybreak, sleepy but satisfied about his family's safety for the time being. Reporting to Colonel Clark, he found his unit preparing for an assault on the woods back of the house and compound.

"One of my scouts was reconnoitering the river bank and found Cherokee canoes hidden under the bluff and the woods crawling with Indians," said Clark. "We'll have to clear them out of there before they know we're on to them.

The mounted militia burst from the woods and crossed the road at a gallop, jumping the fence and charging across the garden and field, sweeping by the house and yard, rifles blazing as they neared the woods. The sun, rising behind them, shone in the eyes of the Indians and the Rangers in the house. Horses and men fell as their fire was answered from the woods and the windows of the house, but those who made it rode under cover of the trees, shooting at close range the dusky forms gathered there; then breaking through to the sandy bluff, they turned, reloaded, and drove back through the woods once more.

Seeing the horsemen return, those Indians who could run scattered out of the woods toward the opened gate of the palisade. Rangers stationed along the palisade with rifles covered their retreat.

Clark stopped his men at the edge of the woods and gave the order to turn by the right flank and circle around through the woods to the road. A detachment was left on guard among the trees. He had lost some men and horses, but the enemy was now contained within the house and yard with no access to water. The MacKays had been so near the river they had never dug a well.

Bert rode back to camp with Clark, unhurt except for a bruised leg where Moonshine had forced his way between two trees, driving Bert's right leg against the tree trunk. When he had downed his ration of grog and lost the excitement of the charge, he lay down on his blanket and slept until mess call for the midday meal.

By the third day of the siege, the heat and stench of rotting flesh was becoming unendurable to the troops surrounding the house.

Bloated carcasses of horses and men lay in the scorching August sun. With all the windows and doors boarded and the house crowded with sweating humans, Brown and his men must be suffering terribly.

Clark called Bert to him late in the morning when the sun had really begun to burn down from a cloudless sky with no sign of ease.

"Sergeant Sheldon," Clark said, "you know this place. I'm going to send you in under a white flag to ask for surrender. I want you to keep your eyes open and report to me on the conditions there."

"Yes, sir," said Bert.

"You will give a note to Lieutenant Colonel Brown in person, if possible, and wait for an answer."

"I'll do my best, sir," said Bert.

He put on a clean shirt from his saddle bag and rubbed the mud from his boots, glad he had let Benjy polish them while he was home. They were scratched, but the shine came up again with a little rubbing. Mary had trimmed his hair and beard, and had given him the buckskin vest she had made while he was away. He didn't want the Tories to see how shabby most of the militia were.

He was allowed to go into the house to give a note to the colonel. Brown lay on a couch in the hall that ran through the center of the house, stripped to the waist, his legs swathed in bandages.

Bert saluted smartly and held out the surrender note.

Brown sat up against his pillows and looked at Bert with pain-filled eyes. "My God, It's the Sheldon lad," he said. "I thought you were in prison in Charlestown."

"No, sir," said Bert. "I have the honor of serving with Colonel Elijah Clark."

"A dubious honor," said Brown, taking the note and breaking the seal, then holding it close to his eyes to read in the dim light.

"Write this down," he said to a man in green sitting at the desk beside his couch, " 'I have no intention of surrendering my command' and let me sign it."

Bert took the proffered note and saluting smartly once more, turned on his heel.

Clark was waiting with his staff grouped around him. "Damned stubborn bastard," he said when he had read the note, but there was a hint of admiration in his tone. "What sort of shape are they in?"

"The place stinks like a pigsty," said Bert. "Colonel Brown was wounded in both legs and couldn't stand. His bandages were showing fresh blood. Some of his officers had bandages, too. I didn't see Captain Andy Johnston. He may be dead or badly wounded. All of 'em, officers and men alike, looked like scarecrows with their skin pulled tight on their bones. Brown's aide was in uniform, but I think he put it on for my benefit. Most of them were stripped down to their trousers and they all had three-day beards."

"How bloody awful," said Clark sarcastically. "Those spit-and-polish gentlemen without shaving water."

The men gathered around him chuckled.

"They'll be drinkin' their own piss before they're through," said one of the backwoodsmen.

"I wouldn't be surprised if they already were," said Bert, "their faces looked so sour." The soldiers laughed again.

That afternoon another note was sent in asking for surrender and threatening to hold Brown responsible if it was necessary to destroy the house. Brown again declined, saying he would defend himself to the last.

"The man's either crazy or he knows something we don't," said Clark. "McCall, why don't you send one of your Carolina boys out to see if there's any sign of a relief party from Ninety-Six."

"We'd better get the hell out of here if there is," said one of his sergeants. "We've been losing recruits for the last two days. Most of the Burke County boys have gone home to visit their families, and a lot of the others have hightailed it off with sacks full of looted trading goods from Fort Grierson."

"Damn and blast their hide," said Clark. "If I ever catch 'em, they'll be sorry."

"Yes, sir," said the sergeant, "but that ain't goin' to do us much good now."

A short time later, McCall's man returned to camp. He had started to cross the river at Hammond's Ferry when he was hailed by an Indian in a canoe with a note for Colonel Clark. The troops from Ninety-Six were less than a day's march behind him.

Clark read the note, then turned to his officers.

"We'll be ready to march at dawn," he said. "This may be a trick, so we'll wait to see who they are and how many. See that your badly wounded are taken to houses in town where they may be cared for. Those able to ride will go with us if we have to retreat."

At dawn the next day, the militia was ready to march. By eight o'clock, the back countrymen were swearing lustily and swatting gnats and mosquitoes, as the horses milled about tacked and anxious to move out. Suddenly, across the river, green-clad troops crowded the river bank as far as the Georgians could see.

"Let's get the hell out of here!" Clark yelled to his men.

A small rear guard of crack riflemen was left on the hill behind the deserted camp to fire at the British as they crossed the river and to keep Brown's men from leaving MacKay's in pursuit. Those who had been left to guard the river bank were already on their way at a gallop to join the main body of Georgians as they headed up the Cherokee Road toward the Ceded Lands. Finally as the last of the militiamen disappeared up the road, the rear guard of riflemen mounted and galloped after them.

At Little River, Clark dispersed his troops to their homes loaded with provisions garnered from Fort Grierson. He would expect them to be ready to assemble again when he called.

·XXVII·

STRUGGLE
IN THE
UPCOUNTRY

At the Sword and Thistle, the rooms were crowded with wounded, both Tory and rebel. In the early hours of waiting for Cruger's troops to arrive, Clark had paroled all the Tory prisoners, including a surgeon who was sent to help the wounded as they were carried into town in wagons. Some were carried to homes of Augustans who had taken the oath not to fight against the King.

Mary Anne and John Stanley had taken in seven badly wounded men who were unable to ride with Clark to the Ceded Lands and one fifteen year old who had refused to leave his wounded seventeen-year-old brother. Mary Anne had made pallets on the floor of the porch so the men could lie in the breeze from the river that carried away the odors of putrefaction.

As the morning sun began to make life miserable for them, Mary Anne brought the Bass brothers a cool glass of grape juice.

"Ma'am, I wish you'd make my brother take off and save hisself," said the wounded boy. "I'm going to be all right with you to take care of me."

Mary Anne smiled at both of them. "You're lucky to have a brother who cares for you that much. I'm sure Colonel Brown will let you take parole."

"That's the trouble," said the younger brother. "He done took parole when they caught him at Charlestown. After they tried to make him join the Tory militia last month, he figured they'd broken their bargain and he run off to join Clark."

Mary Anne felt sick. Cornwallis had given orders that any soldier breaking parole should be hanged. But surely Thomas Brown would be merciful.

"Do you know Sergeant Bert Sheldon?" Susan asked as she joined Mary Anne with a plate of sweet biscuits.

"Yes, ma'am," the brothers answered together. "He's one of the best noncoms in the regiment."

Susan beamed and persuaded both to have more of the biscuits while Mary Anne moved on to the next patient.

Late that afternoon as the brothers were dozing, a patrol in green uniforms came stamping up the front steps. "We're looking for traitors who violated parole and fought with Clark's rebels," they said.

"We have desperately ill men here," John Stanley said, meeting them at the top of the steps. "They should not be disturbed."

"And who are you?" one of the troopers asked. "Are you one of the damned rebels?"

"I am Lieutenant John Stanley, late of Pickens' South Carolina militia. I gave my parole when Lieutenant Colonel Brown occupied the city, and I have kept it."

"Then why are you sheltering dangerous traitors?" the man snarled.

"These men are certainly not dangerous to anyone," said John. "They are too ill to move. If you speak to Colonel Brown, I'm sure he will agree."

The trooper conferred with his comrades in a low voice, then turned back to John. "We'll be back later. How many are you hiding?"

"You see them here. There are seven in all."

The trooper looked around the wide porch counting, then nodded. "They'd better be here when we come back." he said.

"I wouldn't think of moving them," said John.

As the soldiers left, Susan and Mary Anne hurried up. They had heard the conversation as had the wounded men.

"I'll see if I can talk to Brown," said John. "Ask Jonah to saddle my horse while I get my boots and coat on."

Two hours later he came back crestfallen. Brown had refused to see him after keeping him waiting in the hot sun at the door of the MacKay house. The lieutenant to whom he had talked had cited Cornwallis' order and had sent two guards back with him to be sure the wounded men would not be moved.

The next morning the seven men, including the Bass brothers, were collected in a wagon. John followed the wagon on horseback to MacKay's, unable to help but hoping to persuade Brown to have mercy. He was stopped at the road and made to remain with the crowd gathered at the wall while the wagon was driven to the front of the house behind another wagonload of prisoners.

A scaffold had been built over the front steps, and Brown's couch had been moved into the doorway. Those prisoners able to be put on a horse were mounted one at a time, their hands tied behind them, and led up to the front steps where they were blindfolded and a noose put around their necks. To a roll of drums, the horse was whipped into a gallop, and the prisoner left hanging from the scaffold.

In all thirteen men were hanged, and the Bass brothers were among them.

John stopped at the Sword and Thistle, so sick he could hardly stand. Jamie met him at the door and led him into the back room.

"I know," he said. "They took three of our wounded. I'd like to throttle their wounded Tories in their beds except that the poor buggers had nothing to do with the order."

"Has Brown gone mad?" John asked.

"Let me pour you a drink," said Jamie. "I guess he is a little mad. From what I can gather in the tap room, his wounds are festering and he is in a high fever. He's had a streak of madness ever since they tarred and feathered him."

"It must have preyed on his mind until it has warped it completely," said John.

"Cruger's officers who have been in here feel he's completely justified by Cornwallis' orders to hang anyone breaking parole."

"God help us!" John exclaimed. "After this, I'm afraid I'm ready to break mine."

"Can you imagine how I feel, looked upon by men on both sides as a crippled coward?" Jamie asked. Only John knew his secret. John had never heard him speak this way, and Jamie quickly changed the subject.

"If you really mean that about breaking parole, I suggest you get yourself and your household out immediately. Cruger's planning to strike in Burke and Wilkes, so Carolina should be pretty clear of troops for the next week or so except in Ninety-Six."

"I hate to take Mary Anne and Johnny away now that she's carrying another baby," said John, "but if we can get up to the North Carolina mountains with Clark's people, the Tories seem to be kept under control there by Shelby, McDowell, and Sevier.

"What about Susan?" Jamie asked.

"She'll go, too, of course," said John.

"I sent word to the Sheldons several days ago," said Jamie, "and they are already on their way. Bert was recognized when he delivered a note to Brown."

"But Ben Sheldon's a Quaker."

"Brown has given orders that all families of men in the rebel army be turned out and their property confiscated," said Jamie.

That night, while soldiers were celebrating in the taverns and officers were regarrisoning Fort Grierson and preparing for a full-fledged campaign into the Ceded Lands, the Stanleys slipped out of town by way of the road to the Sand Bar Ferry. John and Susan rode on horseback while Mary Anne and Johnny rode in the wagon with the two black servants. With friends in the backwoods all along the way, they should be able to make it to the mountains safely in a week or so.

At the Sword and Thistle, on the surface at least, life went back to normal. Soldiers from Fort Grierson filled the taproom while officers gathered in the back dining room. Jamie continued to serve them at table while Angus was busy at the bar.

Colonel Cruger and his men were not in Augusta long enough to become familiar with the Sword and Thistle. Leaving Lieutenant Colonel Brown to convalesce and to oversee the clearing up of rubble in the city, Cruger set off to round up the rabble who had almost captured the town. By the time they reached Little River, Clark had already crossed the Broad and was on the way to North Carolina with a small band of men who had not gone back to their homes in the Ceded Lands. Many of those who had gone home had packed up their families and joined him on the way to the Watauga Settlement in the mountains while others were pledged to meet in April at Dennis' Mill on Little River where Clark and his men would rendezvous for a spring campaign.

The Stanleys headed up through the Ninety-Six district, avoiding the town. John was still under parole, and they were safe until it was broken. They found Andrew Pickens living peacefully on his farm with his family and spent three days there, resting and catching up on news of friends.

Andrew Williamson had gone over to the British and was stationed in Cruger's headquarters at Ninety-Six. Most of Pickens' men had taken parole when he did, but after Cruger tried to draft them for the King's forces, many had joined partisan bands under McDowell and Davie fighting in the Upcountry.

John told Pickens about Brown's hanging wounded prisoners and of his own determination to join Clark's militia.

"I've not quite come to that point yet," said Pickens. "I've given my word, and the British have left me alone. But if my family or property are hurt in any way, by Heaven, I'll be away to the hills in a minute."

John had decided not to go back to his home on Saluda Mountain. The rugged country around Saluda Gap was still a haven for outlaws and renegades from both armies. He'd take his family to Watauga, then join Clark.

"Word is going around," said Pickens, "that Cornwallis has ordered Patrick Ferguson to cut off Clark before he gets to the mountains."

"He'll have a hell of a time catching him," said John. "Clark's moving fast. He won't tarry to fight local Tories."

"The last I heard," said Pickens, "Ferguson was in Gilbert Town, below the mountains."

"If Clark has any sense, he'll head straight for the hills up the Pacolet River and through Saluda Gap," said John. "I think I'll go that way."

"Davie and McDowell were up there in the Broad River area," said Pickens, "but Ferguson beat their butts near Gilbert Town, and they've gone back over the mountains. You'll get no help from them."

"Clark's people are trail wise and many are mountaineers," said John. "Ferguson won't tackle mountain men on their own home ground. They'll be in the Watauga Settlement by now."

John decided to take the wagon road west along the Saluda River. Mary Anne seemed to be having an easy pregnancy. She and Susan took turns in the wagon with Johnny and the two black servants and riding Star ahead of them with John.

They caught up with Clark and his party in a valley near the French Broad. Francie, out picking blackberries, was first to spot them. Dropping her basket, she ran after the wagon, calling to Johnny who was looking from the hole in the back of the wagon cover. Mary Anne stuck her head out, then called to Jonah to stop the horses.

By the time Bert Sheldon returned to his family wagon from scouting for Colonel Clark, he found the Stanley wagon parked nearby. Susan had seen him tie his horse to a sapling on the edge of the clearing, and ran into his arms. All through the excitement of meeting the Stanleys again, she held tight to his arm, and finally pulled him off toward the woods. As soon as they were out of sight of the wagons, Bert gathered her in his arms again, holding her close as she buried her head in his shoulder then turning her face up, brushing her hair out of her eyes, kissing her until she finally struggled for air.

"I've missed you so," he said.

"I've been afraid you might be wounded or taken prisoner," Susan said, putting her arms up around his neck and pressing close to him again.

"It damned near killed me to be so close to you in Augusta and not be able to see you," he murmured, kissing her again and again.

As they finally walked hand in hand back to the wagons, Bert squeezed her hand and let it go. "I have to make my report to Colonel Clark," he said, "but I know a cave on the other side of the river where no one can find us. We'll go there after the camp has settled down for the night." He leaned down to kiss her once more before they left the shelter of the woods.

Sitting by the fire after a good supper of ham and sweet potatoes from the Stanley's wagon, Ben and Mary Sheldon told John and Mary Anne about the trip with Clark from Augusta. For five days they had traveled as fast as they could, starting before sunrise and stopping long after sundown. All along the way, wagons and family groups on foot entered the road from side paths in the woods. When they reached Clark's forces camped in the Long Canes and started into the foothills, there were four hundred women and children and three hundred men, with only the food that they had been able to pack in their hurried departure.

"Colonel Clark made jokes about Moses and the children of Israel," said Bert as he put down the jug John had passed him. "He sure as hell would have given anything for a shower of manna from heaven."

"You can't believe how wonderful this ham tastes," said Mary Sheldon. "We haven't had meat in a week and very little meal."

"Andrew Pickens stuffed our wagon with meat from his smokehouse and meal from his grist mill," said John.

"Well, don't go talking about it too loud," said Ben. "You're liable to tempt some of our hungry neighbors to attack our wagon."

"I'll share what I can," said Mary Anne. "I don't want to be greedy."

"Game should be more plentiful once we get to the mountains," said John. "The farms are stripped bare all over the Upcountry."

When the fire was put out and the two families bedded down in and under the wagons, Bert and Susan made their way quietly to the cave across the river. As on their first night of love, they lay on the pine-needle covered earth, this time with the peaceful song of the river accompanying their lovemaking.

On the eleventh day of the trek, they reached the Watauga River, on the north side of the mountains and were welcomed by the people of the Over Mountain community. By this time many were nearly starved, their feet blistered and torn by rocks and briers. As soon as they filled up on food and good corn whiskey, they would have to start building cabins. Winter came early in the high country, and the men would soon have to leave with Colonel Clark to fight.

One crisp, autumn-hued day in October, a boy rode into camp with news of a great victory at King's Mountain, across the state line in South Carolina. He said that before Ferguson left Gilbert Town to chase Clark, he had sent a note to Colonel Isaac Shelby to be relayed to all Over Mountain: they'd better quit opposing the King or he'd march his army over the mountains, hang their leaders, and lay their country waste with fire and sword.

His threat backfired. Instead of being frightened, Shelby grabbed his rifle and ammunition and headed over the mountains. Most of the mountain men were at home to harvest crops, distill corn, and wait for spring. Their leaders had gathered at a race track near Colonel John Sevier's place on the Nolichucky River, and they were furious when Shelby gave them the message from Ferguson. The horses, instead of being raced around the track, were sent in all directions carrying messengers. "Let's catch Ferguson before he can get reinforcements and show him he can't scare mountain men."

As soon as Colonel William Campbell of Virginia received the message, he started out with his Upper Holston mountaineer regiment; McDowell's militiamen who had retreated to the mountains with him were called up to fight; Sevier and Shelby rallied the men from the Clinch-Nolichucky area. They all met on September twenty-sixth at Sycamore Shoals on the Watauga River, where the Reverend Samuel Doak preached to them about Gideon's battle with the Midianites and sent them off with the rallying cry: "The Sword of Gideon!"

Hurrying down from the mountains, eating the cold rations packed in their saddlebags and washing them down with creek water or corn liquor, they arrived at Quaker Meadows, Colonel McDowell's farm on the Catawba, where they stopped to eat and drink deeply of the colonel's bounty. They were joined here by Benjamin Cleveland's men from Wilkes and Surry counties. Colonel William Campbell was elected to command the whole expedition, and the mountaineers swarmed down toward Gilbert Town.

Ferguson, meanwhile had learned of their march and had turned back from his pursuit of Clark's cavalcade. Hurriedly sending messengers from Gilbert Town to Cruger and Cornwallis for help, he began retreating toward Cornwallis' camp at Charlotte Town. At King's Mountain, learning that they were gaining on him, he decided to take cover on the ridge of the hill and await reinforcements.

When the mountain men found him there, they surrounded the hill and closed in a circle, Indian style, shooting from the cover of the woods at anyone putting his head above the ridge while they climbed. The Tories and their Scottish commander were unable to flee. Colonel Ferguson was killed with one hundred eighteen others. One hundred twenty-three Tories were wounded and six hundred sixty-four captured. The mountain men lost twenty-eight killed and sixty-two wounded.

A cheer went up from the crowd around the camp fire as the boy finished his account.

"Hot damn," said Elijah Clark, beating Bert on the back. "They finally showed the bloody bastards that they can't push backwoodsmen around."

"I wish we'd gotten the message," said Bert. "I'd have liked to have been there."

"We'll be getting back down there soon," said Clark. "This will make the Bloody Backs think hard before they come to the mountains. Our people should be safe here."

That night jugs, hidden under wagon frames and buried in the woods, appeared as if by magic, and fiddles played for dancing. Bert and Susan crept away from the fire to the nearly finished Sheldon cabin. It had been such a short month with so little time to be alone.

The next week was spent making the cabins liveable and preparing food, clothing, and ammunition for Clark's militia. Word had come that Colonel Twiggs and Colonel William Few had mustered their Georgia militia from the Ceded Lands and were operating with General Sumter's Carolinians to keep Cruger and Tarleton busy in the Upcountry, while Marion harried Cornwallis' supply lines from Charlestown. The tide seemed to be turning for the Americans. It was time Elijah Clark's militia left the mountains and joined the fight. Hearing that Sumter was on the Tyger River, Clark's men marched out of the mountains to join him.

As they rode through the country between the Pacolet and the Tyger, they lived off the land. Tory farmers were forced to give up arms, ammunition, and livestock or were beaten for resisting. Whig farmers fed them royally on corn, pumpkins, yams, and meat and cracklin's from newly slaughtered hogs. It was from one of these Whig farmers that they learned of Sumter's fight with Major Wemyss at Fish Dam Ford on the Broad River.

"Tarleton sent Wemyss and part of the Sixty-Third Regiment after Sumter, while he went after Marion on the Pee Dee," the farmer told the men gathered around a campfire in his meadow. "They came upon Sumter's camp unawares on a night march, and Sumter's sentries shot hell out of the advance guard. Major Wemyss was shot from his horse, wounded in arm and leg, and his lieutenant ordered a charge in the dark—right into General Sumter's tent."

"How'd he get away?" one of Clark's men asked. "Bare arsed like the time they caught him at Fishing Creek?"

"How'd you guess?" chuckled the farmer. "This time he didn't have a horse handy and he had to jump a rail fence in his nightshirt and run barefoot through a brier patch, but he got away."

"What happened to his company?" Clark asked.

"Colonel Taylor rallied the militia while the British were regrouping and led a flank attack on the left. He got pushed back to the river, but his men on the right flank shot hell out of the enemy from the woods, and they were all able to get out in order, leaving twenty-five British wounded and seven dead."

"How about Sumter's casualties?"

"Four dead and fourteen wounded," said the farmer. "General Sumter crawled out of the hole in the riverbank where he'd been freezing, collected his clothes, and left with them"

"Have you heard where Tarleton is now?" Clark asked.

"Word is," the farmer answered, "that he's left off chasing Marion in the swamps and brought the rest of the Sixty-Third, artillery and all, to catch old Gamecock Sumter. The Georgia boys under Twiggs, Candler, and Jackson joined Sumter last week. They're camped at Hawkins' mill, on the Tyger.

"Then we'll be getting on in that direction early in the morning," said Clark.

They rode into Sumter's camp at nightfall. When Twiggs' militiamen from Augusta saw the Wilkes County men, they jumped up from the campfires and ran whooping and hollering and pulling them from their horses to beat them on the back.

"Damned if you didn't finally get some sense," one of the Georgia men said to John. "I heard you'd knuckled down to old Burnfoot."

"Hell, man," said another Richmond County man, "half of Augusta stayed put. I didn't leave myself until Brown hanged my friends."

"We're glad to have you, Stanley," said Colonel Twiggs. "As I remember you were with Pickens' militia at Charlestown."

"Yes, sir. Most of my friends were with the militia from Ninety-Six."

"I see you've kept your rank as lieutenant."

"Yes, sir. I was a lieutenant in the old militia company at Fort James, and Colonel Clark took me in as a volunteer at that rank."

"We can use every man who wants to fight," said Twiggs.

The next morning Clark called his officers and noncoms to a briefing. A raiding party from Sumter's command had caught a large detachment of Tarleton's dragoons and MacArthur's Highlanders bathing in the Broad River and had peppered them with musket fire.

"I'll bet General Sumter was tickled to hear they'd been caught with their arses bare, too," said Bert Sheldon.

"Don't you say nothin' about that to Sumter's men," said Clark. "They're sensitive."

"No, sir," said Bert.

"Sumter expects Tarleton to come looking for us," said Clark. "He's decided to make a stand at Blackstock's farm where we can command the hillside with the river behind us."

"What's the strength of Tarleton's command?" John asked.

"There are MacArthur's Highlanders, Tarleton's Dragoons, and the mounted infantry of the Sixty-Third Regiment, plus a detachment of Royal Artillery."

"Wheeew!" said Bert Sheldon, "all those Regulars against a bunch of militia!"

"It'll give us a chance to show what militia can do," said Clark.

On November twentieth the combined militia forces were camped, as planned, at Blackstock's farm overlooking the Tyger River. The log farmhouse and outbuildings along the top of the hill were strongly built. The barn and smokehouse had spaces between the logs that sharpshooters could use as loopholes to cover an open field sloping down to a creek that would have to be crossed by anyone attacking from the front. The rear of the land dropped off sharply to the river, and, on the left, a heavy rail fence with brush growing along its lower bars ran down the hill toward the creek. On the right along the ridge, the tangle of pine and hardwood trees was almost impenetrable.

Sumter put his command post on the wooded hill to the right, and sent Colonel Henry Hampton's riflemen to occupy the house and barns. Colonel Twiggs and one hundred Georgia riflemen were stationed along the creek on the left, backed up by Clark's and Few's four hundred Georgia militiamen in the wooded area beyond. The South Carolina militia were on the hillside below Sumter's command post.

Tarleton was determined to catch the Gamecock before he could retreat across the river. Leaving his infantry and artillery to follow, he hurried his dragoons toward the Tyger with his mounted infantry and the mounted infantry of the Sixty-Third, not realizing he was leading two hundred seventy British regulars against a thousand militiamen.

As Tarleton's legion came into view along the road to the farm and took position in the woods beyond the road, Tarleton dismounted the men of the Sixty-Third and ordered an attack with fixed bayonets on Twiggs' militia across the creek. The rebel forces, with few bayonets, were known for shooting once and retreating after firing their one-shot muzzle loaders.

Bert had no bayonet but had a Cherokee tomahawk handy in case he needed it. With his rifle primed and ready to fire, he advanced with the rest of the militia into the open field, feeling naked as he ran down the hill toward the creek. The militia wasn't used to British-style fights in the open. At the bottom of the hill, the unit halted, aimed, and sent a volley crashing toward the advancing British.

The red line didn't falter, but kept coming with bayonets fixed. Bert reached for his powder horn to reload but saw he was too late. Grabbing his rifle by the still-hot barrel, he swung at the head of a big redcoat infantryman and felt the jolt as it smashed into his skull. Then he saw a bayonet leveled at his chest coming a mile a minute, backed up by a mass of red and white. Dodging sideways, he avoided the blade, and the Britisher sprawled over the soldier on the ground.

Bert reached for his tomahawk as he saw the man start to rise. The blade was sharp enough to spill brains all over the grass. "What the hell," he muttered, turning the blade and striking with the flat of the axe, putting the man to sleep with a chance to wake and fight again.

While Bert was cracking skulls on the creek bank, the attack had passed through and over the Georgia riflemen's position, and men of the Sixty-Third were chasing the demoralized militia up the hill toward the farm house.

As the redcoated infantrymen neared the farm buildings, Hampton's sharpshooters opened fire, killing British Major Money and two of his lieutenants and slowing the red line that was advancing toward the fleeing Georgians.

Across the road at the edge of the woods, Tarleton's Dragoons sat in their saddles watching the infantry battle. Suddenly gunfire erupted on their right and horsemen began to fall from their saddles, horses rearing and kicking in pain. Under Sumter's orders, Colonel Lacy's South Carolinians had sneaked around through the woods and blasted the Dragoons pointblank with buckshot. Though twenty of the horsemen went down, the Dragoons rallied and drove Lacy's men off into the woods with their sabers.

Men were moaning around Bert, and he could see one of his victims beginning to stir. Crawling off toward the right, away from the British position, he slowly made his way toward the woods, then dodging between the trees, circled up and around toward the back of the farmhouse.

John Stanley had been in the thick of the retreat up the hill. With men running desperately all around him, there was nothing he could do to stop them, but perhaps, if he could reach the barn, he could add his rifle to the ones that were mowing down the British infantrymen.

As he rounded the smokehouse, he dodged behind the building and pounded on the door. One of the Carolinians, seeing his buckskins through a chink in the logs, opened the door and let him slide inside. Now he moved to a spot between the sharpshooters and began to clean and reload his gun.

Suddenly the man beside him gave a shout, "I'll be ding-dong damned if the sons of bitches aren't going to charge."

The riflemen crowded to the front of the smokehouse as bugles sounded from the bottom of the hill and Colonel Banastre Tarleton galloped out of the woods at the head of his green uniformed Dragoons, jumping the creek with the sun glinting on the silver blade of his saber. Behind him horses thundered over open ground with their riders forward and low in the saddle, charging up the hill into the range of the sharpshooters on their right and the rifles of the Carolina militia in front of Sumter's command post in the woods on their left.

"That damned crazy bastard," said one of Hampton's men. "Doesn't he know any better than to order a cavalry charge against an established infantry position? This is slaughter."

And so it was. As the cavalrymen barreled across the road near the farm buildings, there was such intense fire from three directions that the road was blocked by fallen men and horses, the wounded men unable to avoid the crossfire and the hoofs of wounded horses.

Finally realizing that his position was hopeless, Tarleton ordered a general retreat. As the cavalry and the survivors of the Sixty-Third Infantry retreated, they passed the woods in which General Sumter and some of his staff were watching from horseback. Spotting the officers' gold epaulets, some men of the Sixty-Third turned and fired a volley. One of Sumter's officers fell dead, and the general, took five buckshots in his shoulders and spine. Riding erect in his saddle to the command post, he dismounted and turned the command over to the officer next in rank, Colonel Twiggs of Augusta, before he let the surgeon dress his wounds.

Twiggs had the general placed on a litter slung between two horses. The three rebels killed in the battle were hurriedly buried, and the three other wounded were carried with the troops as they rode slowly up the country to the Broad River.

John Stanley and Bert Sheldon, riding together ahead of their unit, spurred their horses down the river bank and into the shallow, rock-strewn water of the ford to let their horses drink.

"Do you think we'll get a chance to go home now?" Bert asked.

"Where's home?" John wanted to know.

"Where Susan and Ma and Pa are. Up in the mountains, of course."

"We'll have to see what Colonel Twiggs says."

"We beat hell out of them, didn't we?" Bert gloated.

"When the colonel had all their dead and wounded collected," John answered, "one of the surgeons told me they lost ninety-two dead and over a hundred wounded."

"I guess our boys could run faster than theirs," said Bert. "Did you see those men of the Sixty-Third plowing up the hill when they had bullets whizzing into them from all sides?" That's real guts."

"It's damn foolishness," said John. "We'll be able to fight again. They won't. We don't have enough men to be able to lose 'em to show we're brave."

They had reached a clearing beyond the river where men were dismounting, loosening their girths, and letting their horses graze. Colonel Twiggs and Colonel Clark stood with Majors James Jackson from Richmond County and James McCall and Henry Hampton from South Carolina. Bert and John joined the group tending to their horses.

"Lieutenant Stanley," Clark called, "you know these people around Ninety-Six. Do you think it would be worthwhile going that way to recruit more for our militia?"

"Yes, sir," said John. "Colonel Pickens' men took the oath last year, but when I talked to him in September he told me most of them were ready to break parole. Cruger's been forcing them into his Loyalist militia and taking it out on their families if they refuse."

"What about Pickens?"

"He said they've left him alone, and he's given his word of honor."

"Let's go," said Elijah Clark.

"I'd like to go in that direction to check on my family," said James McCall.

"Pickens told me Colonel Williamson's been hard on the families of men in our militia."

"Let's go and persuade them all to join us," said Clark.

Twiggs, Jackson, and Hampton decided to move their militia toward Charlotte Town, where General Greene was expected at any moment to replace General Gates.

"I'd like to meet the new commander," said Twiggs, "and let him know we've still got some men ready to fight in the Upcountry."

"God help us if he's anything like Gates," said Clark.

"From what I hear, he's a real soldier's soldier," said Twiggs, "and he's brought Dan Morgan out of retirement as second in command."

"Hot damn," said Clark. "They say Morgan was the one who really won at Saratoga. He's an old Indian fighter."

"If anybody can get along with the Upcountry militia, he can," said James McCall.

"While you go and make up to Greene and Morgan," said Clark, "we'll nip at the Tories in Ninety-Six and see if we can't talk some of Pickens' old troops into joining us."

After a few days rest, Twiggs and his troops rode east while John and Bert, with McCall's and Clark's militias, rode westward across the Enoree and Reedy rivers, staying north of the strong Tory settlements. Somewhere below Pearis' fort, they met Colonel Benjamin Few with a force of Georgia volunteers who'd left their families to come from the Over Mountain settlement. Fear of Tory raids there had lessened, because people in the mountains stayed home by the fire when winter set in.

John and Bert searched the newcomers for a familiar face and found a man who had built his cabin near the Sheldons.

"Your folks are snug as can be," he told Bert. "Miz Stanley and the little boy are living with them. Ben and your brother have promised to keep my family supplied with game. Benjy liked to bust to come with us, but your pa says he's too young."

"Dern tootin' he is," said Bert. "I'm counting on him to take care of Susan and Ma and Francie. Pa's religion wouldn't let him fight unless they're damn near killed."

"Your pa's been more help in time of sickness or trouble than anyone," said the man. "We all respect his religion."

"Has my wife been all right?" John asked.

"Fit as a fiddle. Looks like you'll have a little mountaineer, come spring."

"It's a comfort she'll have Mary and Ben and Susan," said John.

Passing well north of the fort at Ninety-Six, the combined Georgia forces, now under command of Colonel Few, pitched camp in the Long Canes area, sending foraging parties out into the countryside.

John took Bert and a squad of men with him through the hilly farmland, splitting them into pairs so they could walk up to farmhouses without scaring families. All of them were dressed in battered buckskins or linsey-woolsey, and there was no way of telling whether they were rebel or Tory.

John had young Jim Pollard with him as he approached a farm gate on Norris Creek. "Halloo the house," he called as the dogs began to bark.

A young woman came to the door carrying a long rifle, a toddler pulling her skirts. "Who aire ya, an' what's yer business?" she called, leveling the gun at them.

"John Stanley and Jim Pollard, and we're looking for food."

"Jest stay where ye aire," the girl called. "We ain't got enough food for ourselves since the sojers come an' robbed the house an' drove off the stock."

"What soldiers?" John shouted across the farmyard.

"From Ninety-Six," the girl yelled. "Took my brother with 'em, too, to fight for the King."

"We were hoping we could get your husband to join Clark's militia," said John.

"My husband was killed at Charlestown in Pickens' regiment," said the girl.

"Can we do anything to help you?"

"Jest get outa here an' leave us alone," she answered, keeping her gun level. "I want nothin' to do with fightin' and killin'."

They had the same sort of welcome at most of the farms. Two men, however, filled their saddlebags with bacon and corn meal and rode back with them to camp.

"Them damn stinkin' Tories come an' drove off my young heifer jest as she was ready to give milk," said one farmer. "My wife can't suckle the baby no more, an' we sure needed that cow. I'd like to see them all in hell."

"What about your wife. Can she take care of the farm?"

"My pa's crippled with rheumatism, but he's there to help her."

In the next few days, the combined forces of Few and Clark grew to five hundred men. When farms were found to belong to Tories, they were stripped of food, horses, and clothing that could be used by the militia. If the owners put up a fight, their houses were put to the torch.

It didn't take long for Colonel Cruger to react. Hoping to take the rebels by surprise, he sent a force from Ninety-Six to surprise the militia's camp in Long Canes by night; but before the force had come within three miles of camp, a messenger from Ninety-Six alerted Colonel Clark to call out his men. Colonel Few sent Clark's and McCall's militia to attack the enemy while he rallied his forces to back them up.

John and Bert rode out with Clark. As the eastern sky turned red with the rising sun, it revealed the Tory militia advancing across a frost-covered field.

John and Bert took positions at the edge of the wood, and waited until the Loyalists were within range to loose a volley into the massed troops.

Since there was no sign of Few's four hundred reserve militiamen, Clark sent a messenger urging him to hurry while rebels held their ground. Firing and loading and firing again, they advanced, and the Loyalist militia began to give way, turning back into the Regulars and taking a position behind them. One of their parting shots caught Elijah Clark in the shoulder, causing him to fall unconscious from his saddle. Bert jumped from his horse and helped make a litter from his blanket and the rifle of another militiaman, to carry Clark off the field.

Cruger's men, many of whom had been drafted against their will, refused to resume the attack, and by the time the Regulars could be brought into line, Clark's men had carried him to safety. When the Regulars charged through the woods, John saw Major McCall flinch and drop his reins, shot in the arm. An instant later, McCall's horse reared and fell dead on top of him. All about was a jumble of horses and riders with British infantry charging in among them, jabbing bayonets into horses' bellies or into wounded soldiers on the ground. When he saw that McCall was conscious and had struggled from under his horse, John jumped down and helped the major into his saddle, swinging up behind him as the rebels began to give way. As the only officer left standing, John called the militiamen to him and they retreated in good order.

When they finally arrived back at the camp, they found Few's reserves mounted and ready to retreat. The weary, wounded men of Clark's and McCall's militia looked at Few in disbelief and disgust. He had sent them to face an enemy that outnumbered them four to one, while he withheld four hundred fresh reserves!

With Colonel Clark in a sling between two horses and six other wounded men, including Major McCall, sitting their horses with difficulty, they rode off toward the North Carolina mountains, leaving fourteen of their number dead.

December arrived in Augusta with none of the joyful expectation of Christmas in years past. A sullen peace reigned in the town where most of the rebel militiamen's families had been run out of their homes, and neighbor accused neighbor of sympathy with the cause of liberty in hope of confiscating land or household goods of the accused.

Even the Tory soldiers at the forts were in low spirits. During Clark's attack in September, the rebels had taken the supplies from Fort Grierson, including all the Loyalist militia uniforms that were not on the soldiers' backs.

Colonel Brown had fired off letter after letter to Governor Wright in Savannah, asking for more supplies, but the wagon trains and boats were being stopped by rebel militia patrols and their provisions confiscated. Instead of the smart green-clad troops who had captured the town in September, Brown's men were now a motley crew in patched trousers and mismatched blouses, their brass buttons replaced by bone ones.

The food supply was almost as bad. Farms in the countryside for miles around had been raided so often that the few remaining farmers had as little to eat as the townspeople.

At the Sword and Thistle, though food was scarce, Meg managed to keep a supply. Since most of the officers and men from Fort Grierson depended on the inn's kitchen to supplement their meager ration, Desmond's vegetable garden and the smokehouse were kept under careful surveillance. Anyone creeping among the cabbages and onions was likely to be hauled before Colonel Grierson. Soldiers from Fort Cornwallis, the new stronghold built beside Saint Paul's at the other end of town, were given the cold shoulder by Grierson's men and encouraged to patronize Fox's.

When Jamie heard militiamen in the taproom brag about Tarleton's victory at Blackstock's farm where General Sumter had been killed and about the deaths of Elijah Clark and James McCall at Long Canes Creek, he had a hard time keeping a straight face. Word had come to him by his Indian messenger that Clark and McCall were safe in the mountains, and he knew that Tarleton had lost more than ninety killed and one hundred wounded at Blackstock's, while Sumter had lost only a few men and had been carried home to the High Hills of Santee to recover from his wound.

Meg felt sorry for the soldiers as Christmas drew near. Even those who were loyal to the King were human and homesick. Many of them had been forced to join the militia under threat of harm to their families and were not allowed any leave for fear they'd not return. They would all have Christmas goose and a wassail bowl at the Sword and Thistle, no matter what their politics. Christmas Eve, however, would be quiet, with the inn closed. Remembering past Christmases with the Sheldons and Stanleys and Merrills, Meg couldn't bear to have the Tories take over the inn that night.

When the Reverend Mr. Seymour held Christmas service at Saint Paul's, in the shadow of the new fort, the church was jammed with men from both forts. Meg, Jamie, young Angus, and even Presbyterian Angus MacLeod took communion, praying for old friends and better times to come.

Shortly after New Year's came news of a crushing defeat that shook the Loyalist militiamen and sent them to the Sword and Thistle to drown their sorrows. General Morgan had licked Tarleton on open terrain at the Cowpens in Upcountry South Carolina with a force of Americans about the same size as the British. In addition to Continental Dragoons led by Colonel William Washington of Virginia and Continental Infantry from Delaware and Maryland, Morgan had used the mounted riflemen of Georgia and South Carolina in a classic, set battle and they had measured up. McCall and his men were there; so were Elijah Clark's men, now under the command of James Jackson and John Cunningham, and the Ninety-Six militia under the command of Andrew Pickens, who had finally broken parole when his family home had been ransacked by Tories.

James Grierson came into the Sword and Thistle the day the news of Tarleton's defeat reached Augusta. Angus drew him a tankard of cider.

"My God, Angus, where is this all going to end? Tarleton is a son-of-a-bitch the way he's been slaughtering prisoners, but he's a British Regular and knows his tactics. He's let a bunch of colonials beat hell out of seasoned British Regulars."

"Maybe, if the British Regulars hadn't slaughtered prisoners and ransacked the homes of civilians, those colonials wouldn't have been out there fighting," said Angus.

"It has made me ashamed, old friend," said Grierson. "I've always been proud to be a British subject, and I've tried to keep my militia from harming civilians. I can't help thinking lately of a sermon of Mr. Seymour's: 'If you sow the wind, you will reap the whirlwind.'"

Angus refilled their tankards. "I'd say yon gale was roaring around us," he said. "M'Lord Cornwallis has no one now in the backcountry to protect his flank, and we're sitting out here on the frontier in the middle of a swarm of angry backwoodsmen."

"God help us," said Grierson.

"Amen," said Angus. "I hae ma doobts that Cornwallis will hurry west to our aid."

The news of Cowpens seemed to boost the morale of the rebels. All through Georgia and South Carolina, despite the bitter January weather, raiding parties attacked supply lines and Tory detachments whenever they found them. Captain James MacKay and Captain Stephen Johnston had a camp deep in the swamp near Matthews Bluff on the river between Savannah and Augusta. Sallying forth with a few militiamen, they attacked supply boats when they tied up for the night and confiscated clothes and provisions meant for Augusta.

Thomas Brown was furious. Sending out one detachment after another to spend weeks futilely skirmishing in the swamps, he became more and more frustrated. Tory militiamen, afraid of being caught and slaughtered by the rebels, deserted and fled to the Indian country by the dozens.

MacKay's own force was growing, and South Carolina militia under Colonel William Harden had been sent to reinforce him. When Brown led a strong force of Rangers and Indians against this combined rebel force, his charge against the outnumbered Americans resulted in seven of his Rangers being killed and many more wounded. Harden and MacKay, with few casualties, left the field in good order and vanished into the swamp.

·XX̄VIII·

FORT
CORNWALLIS

As the winds of March blew along the Savannah bringing a touch
of spring, word came that Lord Cornwallis had decided to withdraw
his army to Virginia to fight General Washington. James Grierson, as he
usually did when troubled, dropped in the Sword and Thistle to talk to
Angus.

"I'm afraid this is the beginning of the end," he said dolefully. "He's
left Lord Rawdon in Charlestown to try to protect the whole South
without enough men and with unprotected supply lines through hundreds
of miles of enemy territory."

"Here in Augusta, we're way out on the end of the cow's tail," said
Angus, "and that's a fact. We've had a hard enough time all along, getting
supplies. Now we'll have to wear skins like the Indians or weave our
own cloth if the rebels take the Carolina forts."

"God help us," said Grierson. "This General Greene has been losing
battles and coming out ahead by retreating with his army intact. He'd
be smart to use Francis Marion and Sumter and young Henry Lee of
Virginia to harass the supply lines until he's starved out the Upcountry
forts. I don't see any way he can be stopped."

"I understand Colonel Pickens has joined the rebels," Angus said.
"They say John Stanley is back with Pickens' militia."

"One of the worst things about this war is the loss of old friendships,"
said Grierson. "I had hoped the lad would keep parole."

"He told me before he left that Colonel Brown's execution of those
wounded prisoners changed his mind."

"That was an unfortunate incident," said Grierson. "Lord Cornwallis
had given the order, you know, to hang anyone breaking his parole."

"Hell," said Angus, "half of the rebel army has broken parole."

"Yes," said Grierson, "but we were all pretty bitter then. Young Andrew

Johnston had been killed, and everyone at MacKay's was nearly dead of thirst and starvation. There were some terrible things done for vengeance."

"Terrible things are still done here every day," said Angus.

"God help us if the rebels ever take Augusta," said Grierson. "They have reason to hate us."

By the middle of April, it was obvious that General Greene was using the strategy Grierson had predicted. One by one the forts were attacked. Fort Watson on the Santee, guarding the British supply line from Charlestown, fell to Lee and Marion while Greene was keeping Lord Rawdon busy near Camden. Though Greene was finally forced to retreat, Lord Rawdon found that the whole countryside had been aroused by the successful raids of Marion, Lee, Sumter, Pickens, McCall, and Clark and were swarming out of their settlements to join the partisan bands.

Deciding that discretion was more sensible than valor, Rawdon moved out of Camden toward Charlestown and sent word to the commander at Fort Granby to abandon it and retreat to Orangeburg. He ordered Colonel John Harris Cruger to abandon Ninety-Six and reinforce Brown at Augusta. Both messengers were captured, and the orders never reached either fort.

By May tenth, the British fort at Orangeburg and Forts Motte and Granby had all fallen, their men made prisoners and their cannons and supplies taken by the Patriots. In the back country, only Ninety-Six and Augusta remained under British control. The rest of the British army in the South was concentrated in Charlestown and Savannah.

Thomas Brown knew that he would have to withstand another siege. This time, however, he had at least one modern, well-built fort with artillery to defend it. One noonday early in May, he stopped in at the Sword and Thistle on his way to Fort Grierson.

"Colonel Grierson and some of his officers are in the back room," said Angus as he filled his tankard. "Mayhap you'd like to join them for lunch."

"Tired of soldiers' fare at the fort, eh?" Brown asked. "I haven't tasted any of your good food for quite some time. Thank you," and he carried his cider on into the private dining room.

"Greetings," said Brown. "Amanda is the only cook I know who can take the gamey tang out of deer meat."

"Have you any word of the supplies from Savannah?" Grierson asked. "It's hard enough to keep men from deserting without having to feed them on meager rations."

"With Pickens stirring up trouble between here and Ninety-Six, Hammond and Jackson along the river between here and Savannah, and Clark up in the Ceded Lands, it's going to take a strong escort to get any supplies through."

"I thought Clark was out of it," said Grierson.

"He was. He had one hell of a shoulder wound and a case of smallpox to boot. But my Indian scouts tell me he's back from the mountains and has brought a hundred men with him."

"Good Lord," exclaimed a young subaltern, "do you think they'll attack us here?"

"I believe they're waiting for reinforcements from General Greene."

"Can we hold out against them?" asked another officer.

"We are certainly going to try," said Brown. "I've sent messengers to Ninety-Six and to Savannah. With luck, they'll get through and bring aid."

"God help us if the rebels take over," said the subaltern. "They will be bent on revenge."

"We'd better pray there are Continental Regulars in command," said Grierson. "I understand Greene has given orders that prisoners are to be treated according to the customs of civilized warfare. Perhaps they will hold the militia down."

"The militiamen around this part of the country don't know what civilized warfare is," said Brown. "I'd rather be taken by Indians."

As the hot weather set in in earnest by the middle of May, word came to Brown that a shipment of Indian presents from the crown had come through to Galphin's fort with a strong guard, but there was no sign of reinforcements.

Rebel communications were better. Word had gone out about Brown's lack of rations the day he lunched at the inn. Early one morning, Jamie asked Angus and Meg to come to the kitchen behind the inn separately so that anyone watching would think they were just getting more food.

"Don't ask any questions," he said to the two black servants and the family. "I want each of you to find time to pack your clothes and valuables in as small a bundle as possible and slip them into the wagon under the hay. Go at different times."

"I'll not leave the inn," said Angus. "All my life's work is represented in this inn."

"I'm depending on you to take care of Meg and Young Angus," said Jamie. "Let us just say that it will not be possible to stay here at the inn."

"Won't you be coming with us?" Meg asked trying to cover her fear.

"I have things that I must do here tonight. I'll come as soon as I can."

"But where are we going?" Young Angus asked.

"Desmond will drive Amanda to the farm on Rae's Creek late this afternoon 'to pick peaches from Ben Sheldon's tree,' if he's asked. The soldiers are used to his going there. The rest of you will be hidden under the hay. Instead of coming back, you'll cross the river at Hammond's ferry. I've arranged for the guards to be friends of mine who want to see you safely out of town. And there will be more friends to help you on your way to the Sheldons in the mountains."

"But where are you going?" Meg asked.

"The less you know, the less you can tell if you're stopped," asked Jamie. "I wouldn't ask you to leave if I didn't know it's absolutely necessary."

Angus stared at him for a moment, then shook his head. "But what of the inn?" he asked. "The soldiers will be coming in tonight for a drink or supper."

"I'll serve them" said Jamie.

"Nay, I think not," said Angus. "I have had a long and happy life, and I have the right to do as I want with what's left of it. Meg and the young ones will be safer without me. No one will be suspicious of a woman and children traveling in a wagon."

"We have been too friendly here with the Loyalists," said Jamie. "The rebels might shoot you first and ask questions later."

"And what of you?" Angus asked.

"Let's just say I can duck faster," said Jamie.

"Sorry," said Angus. "Ye'll just have to put up with my company."

That afternoon the wagon left the inn yard while the inn was full of soldiers. Jamie told them that his son was ill with a fever and that Meg was caring for him upstairs. Amanda had left supper ready in the kitchen, so Jamie could serve the tables while Angus tended bar. The officers, busy preparing for a possible attack, were all at the fort.

After the tables were cleared and the candles snuffed for the night, Jamie slipped down to the tree on the river bank to find a message that his family had arrived safely at Martins' plantation. With it was an official dispatch informing him that Colonel Henry Lee was on his way from Fort Granby with three troops of cavalry to aid Clark and Pickens in an attack on Augusta.

As Jamie came into the darkened inn, Angus was waiting at the back door. "Do you have news, lad?" he asked.

"The wagon went through with no trouble," said Jamie as he threw the papers in the fire and stirred it to make them burn. "They're at Martin's plantation across the river. But I have to leave right away. I may not be back tonight or ever."

"Will you be joining Meg?"

"No. I can't tell you more, except that the town will be attacked in the next few days. You'd do well to leave the inn and go out to Rae's Creek."

"Nay, lad, I've lived through many battles. Whoever wins will want food and drink, and their politics are no concern of mine."

"Meg will never forgive me if you are hurt."

"Meg knows I'm a stubborn Scot. She'll not blame you."

"Fort Grierson may be bombarded. The inn's too close for comfort."

"I'll duck out if I hear the cannon's roar, never fear. But I'll be here to stop any foot soldiers, from either side, from stealing my whisky."

Jamie put his arm around Angus's shoulders, then turned and went back into the night.

Before dawn, he was on the road to Fort Granby on a horse that had been waiting for him at a farm across the river. Under his buckskin hunting shirt he had a commission in the Carolina militia and insignia to put on his hat as soon as he was safely in rebel territory.

He had ridden only five or six miles when the sound of many horses coming at a fast trot made him duck in the pine trees at the side of the road. The morning sun shining in his eyes made it hard to see the riders until they were almost abreast of his hiding place, but as soon as he recognized the Continental uniforms, he spurred his horse out of the underbrush and rode to the head of the column.

"Lieutenant James Stratfield, South Carolina militia, sir."

"Captain Ferdinand O'Neal of Virginia Light Dragoons," said the captain, after giving the command to walk.

"Sir, I've come from Augusta where I've been serving as an undercover intelligence agent. I can show credentials if you need them. I thought Colonel Lee should know that a large shipment of ammunition and rum, among other supplies, had arrived at Galphin's fort below Augusta for the Indian trade. The fort is just a stockade around a house and trading post, but it's garrisoned by two companies of Brown's Florida Rangers."

"I thank you, Lieutenant, and I would like to see your papers," said O'Neal.

"Yes, sir," said Jamie. "I'm afraid I'll have to dismount, as they're in my boot."

"Column halt," ordered O'Neal. "Dismount and water your horses at the stream."

The troopers swung from their mounts. Jamie sat on a log and one of the dragoons backed up to him and took his right boot between his legs. When the boot came off, Jamie took it and removed a paper from a pocket sewn in the side.

Captain O'Neal unfolded and read the paper, then reached out to shake Jamie's hand. "I'd wondered about the information we were receiving from Augusta," he said.

"I don't plan to go back in hiding," said Jamie. "I'd like permission to ride with you."

"We'll be reporting back to Colonel Lee," said O'Neal. "He may want you to join the militia under his command."

When they met the rest of the legion in a mile or so, Lee was overjoyed. "You and your men are great providers," he said, clapping O'Neal on the back. "I sent you to forage for food for our men, and you bring word of enough provisions for the whole army."

"Yes, sir," said O'Neal, "and from what Stratfield says, they're just waiting to be picked off."

"You know the country," Lee said turning to Jamie. "I'd like to take Captain Rudolph's cavalry and a cannon and some infantry and take over that fort. We'll send the rest of the dragoons on to meet Clark and Pickens as planned."

"I think we can reach Galphin's by back trails without alerting the Rangers there," Jamie said. "They'll be expecting you to join Clark and Pickens west of town. They know you're on your way."

"Can you show me those back trails?"

"Yes, sir. I surveyed some of the land for George Galphin."

"Then turn up your hat brim, put on a cockade, and ride with us," said Colonel Lee.

"Yes, sir," said Jamie. "You don't know how glad I am to show my colors after all that time as a cripple." He hurried to his horse with no sign of a limp.

By having every other cavalryman carry a foot soldier behind his saddle, then switching them to the fresher horses, they were able to make good time, arriving at Galphin's on May twenty-first.

From the pine barren which surrounded the trading center, Lee planned his attack. Dismounting some of his militia, he sent them to the opposite side of the fort with orders to draw the enemy out.

The Rangers discovered their presence when the militia fired a volley into the palisade. Seeing their militia insignia and guessing them to be likely to retreat before a bayonet charge, the Loyalists swarmed out of the fort to take them before they could escape. Captain Rudolph and his mounted militia backed up by the regular infantry and a troop of dragoons charged the fort, sweeping through the gate and taking the few men left within the stockade as prisoners.

As soon as the fort was breached, the horsemen returned to the fray in front, helping capture the men who had been lured out by the militia.

The Tories found themselves surrounded in the open field and though some of them made a dash for the woods, most of them surrendered. A few who fled were shot down, while the several who made it into the woods were tracked down by Rudolph's horsemen.

Jamie, riding along a path looking for fugitives, came upon two Rangers hiding in a willow thicket whom he remembered as customers at the inn. Young boys of sixteen or seventeen, they were in this war for the pay which helped supplement their parents' farm income. Pretending he didn't see them, he turned his horse and trotted back toward the fort, hoping not to get a bullet in his back.

At Fort Galphin, the troops were jubilant. Prisoners were loading wagons full of supplies to be sent to General Greene's army in eastern Carolina. Fearing the effects of rum on triumphant soldiers, Colonel Lee would not allow the casks to be broached.

While Lee and Rudolph were taking Fort Galphin with no losses, Major Eaton was leading the rest of Lee's Legion to meet General Andrew Pickens and his Carolinians at the Cherokee Ponds, six miles from Augusta. They were joined there by Elijah Clark and his Georgia militia and mountain volunteers.

John Stanley who had been with Clark's men since the refugee trip to the mountains, was greeted by old friends from Pickens' brigade as they set up camp to the west of town.

"The damned Tories are still holding Ninety-Six," said one of the Carolinians. "Let's get the scrap over here, so we can go back home and kick them out of there."

When Lee and his men rode in with the supplies, they were cheered by the soldiers sitting around campfires. The rum ration was finally passed around to the troops.

Bert Sheldon saw Jamie dismount and walk over to claim his share. "What are you doing in uniform?" he called, walking over and slapping him on the back, "and where's your limp?"

"It left me all of a sudden when I had to get word to Colonel Lee about the supplies at Galphin's,"

"What about Meg and Angus and the children?"

"Meg, young Angus and Jean are safe at Martin's plantation. Angus, the old curmudgeon, wouldn't leave the inn. He seemed to think he could take care of himself and his hoard of whisky."

"The old warhorse," said Bert fondly.

When Major Joseph Eggleston, commander of Lee's cavalry, came into camp after reconnoitering the two forts in town, he reported that Thomas Brown had refused an order to surrender. Brown and his Rangers and Indians were holding Fort Cornwallis while Colonel Grierson and the Loyalist militia occupied Fort Grierson.

Lee briefed his officers at a council of war and asked for any knowledge they might have of the fortifications.

"It would seem," said Lee, "that Fort Grierson should be easier to take than Cornwallis. After all, I understand it is only a fortified trading post like Galphin's."

"Yes, sir," said Jamie, "but there has been so much plunder and rapine on both sides that the militiamen are afraid for their lives. They may fight in desperation rather than surrender."

"What about armaments?" Lee asked.

"Most of their artillery has been moved to Fort Cornwallis. They have been so anxious to make Cornwallis strong that they have nearly stripped Grierson. I would expect Brown to send a force to protect a retreat of the garrison from Fort Grierson to Fort Cornwallis."

"Then we'll stop him before he starts," said Lee. "Pickens, I suggest that you and Clark attack Fort Grierson from the north on the Cherokee Road. Eaton and Jackson will attack through the swamp from the southeast, and I'll take my infantry and artillery to the south to support Eaton and watch for Brown to come out of Fort Cornwallis. Eggleston will take the cavalry into the woods behind me to attack Brown's flank and force him back into Fort Cornwallis if he comes out.

Pickens and Clark took their men around through the swamp so as not to have to cross Campbell's Gully in sight of the fort. Swarming out of the woods, they kept the Tory riflemen on the stockade so busy that men with scaling ladders were able to get under the shadow of the stockade.

Colonel Grierson, knowing the fort would be overwhelmed, opened the gate so his men could make a rush for the gully where they would be protected by the high bank until they got to the river and could swim the half mile downriver to Fort Cornwallis. A few of them made it. Thirty were killed and forty-five wounded. Some who surrendered were slaughtered by Clark's men to avenge their families in the Ceded Lands.

When the fort was nearly emptied, Colonel Grierson surrendered to Andrew Pickens and was confined to his quarters under parole. Later, his body was found shot through the heart. No one admitted to knowing anything about it.

Lee's Regulars had kept Brown from going to the aid of Grierson's militia. Brown had brought out of Fort Cornwallis a large force of Rangers and two cannons which were aimed at Lee's position. Lee's one field gun lobbed cannon balls in answer to Brown's cannonade. Although no one was hurt on either side, Brown soon returned to the fort dragging the guns behind him.

"It's a damn good thing Colonel Lee captured those Indian stores," said Bert Sheldon to another sergeant as they helped set up headquarters in captured Fort Grierson. "Clark cleaned out all the Tory stores here last summer, and it doesn't look as though they'd gotten many replacements."

"That means Brown's going to be hungry at Cornwallis," said his friend. "We should be able to starve him out in a hurry."

"Don't be too sure," said Bert, "Clark had him treed at MacKay's last summer, and he lasted till help came from Ninety-Six."

"From what I hear, they're too busy fighting at Ninety-Six to give Brown any help now."

Jamie, still with Rudolph's cavalry unit, asked for permission to check the Sword and Thistle across the gully from Fort Grierson. Burial details were still gathering Tory bodies from the gully as he rode into the inn yard. The inn seemed deserted.

"Angus," he shouted as he pushed open the unlatched back door. There was no answer. Benches were knocked over, tables pushed around, and the cider cask and whisky jug were missing from the bar. Someone had taken an axe to the floor of the storage room behind the bar and had left a gaping hole. At the front door was one of Angus' crutches, but no sign of Angus.

Jamie took the front steps two at a time on the way down to the gully. "Have any of you found a man with a peg leg?" he asked the burial patrol.

"No, sir," said one of the men. "We've found a few with their legs damned near shot off though."

"What about the wounded? Where were they taken?"

"I reckon they went to the fort we just captured. These was all dead as doornails," the man said pointing to the wagon loaded with bodies.

Jamie went back to the inn and searched all the rooms. Most of them had been looted of anything portable, though there was no sign of a struggle. The kitchen, barn, and smokehouse were the same. Hurrying down to the river bank, he found militiamen searching the brush for more dead or wounded. At the willow thicket, he waited for two of the soldiers to move on, then reached into his hidden cache.

The note was from Ninety-Six in the usual handwriting. "Greene approaching here with one thousand men. Cruger stripping fort of Loyalist militia to save rations for siege." As usual it was unsigned. Through force of habit, Jamie tore it in small pieces and threw them in the river, then hurried back to report the news to Colonel Lee.

When Jamie reported to Lee, preparations were already being made for a siege.

"So we won't have to worry about Cruger," said Lee. "I've ordered my troops to confiscate any shovels and picks they can find on the farms around here, and there were a bunch among the Indian supplies. They're going to gripe like hell, but we're going to have to dig trenches around Fort Cornwallis clear to the riverbanks on both sides. The river's low enough for men to move along under the bank without being shot. We've got to keep Brown from getting supplies by boat."

Jamie said, "Sir, may I have permission to question some of the prisoners from Fort Grierson? My wife's uncle has been taken forcibly from the inn. Some of the prisoners may know what happened to him."

"Good idea, Lieutenant," said Lee. "Maybe you can learn something from them about the armament at Fort Cornwallis while you're at it."

"Yes, sir. I'll try," Jamie answered as Lee scribbled permission and signed his name.

The Tory prisoners were under close guard at Fort Grierson. Pickens was taking no chances on vengeful Georgia militiamen's eliminating any of them. Jamie found several good customers of the inn sitting in the guardroom.

"What are they going to do with us?" a boy of seventeen asked. "I didn't never want to be in their danged army."

"You'll be kept as prisoners of war and treated honorably," said Jamie.

"Was they bein' honorable when they shot the colonel?" a man with his arm in a sling called from the bench by the wall. Jamie recognized him as Zeke Simpson, a Richmond County farmer.

"We're all sick about that," said Jamie. "Colonel Pickens has ordered a search for the murderer."

"Fat chance they'll find him," said Zeke. "Those bastards from the Ceded Lands was shootin' wounded and prisoners."

"That's why Colonel Pickens has you under close guard. I bet there isn't a man among you who hasn't taken rebel property in the name of the King."

"I thought you was one of us," said the boy who had met him at the door. "What are you doin' with a rebel cockade on your hat?"

"He left town and jined the rebels to save his skin," said Zeke. "That's why they took old Angus."

"What do you know about Angus?" Jamie walked toward him.

"One of Brown's Rangers saw you riding with the rebels at Galphin's," said the man. "Brown had old Angus taken to Fort Cornwallis for questioning, and they didn't bring him back to the inn. Some of the boys went through there to see was there any rebel property they could confiscate.'

"Well, he'll be back by tomorrow," said Jamie. "Colonel Lee's going to walk right in and take over Fort Cornwallis."

"He'll have one hell of a time doin' it," said Zeke. "Brown's got cannon mounted on the walls, and the middle of the fort's filled with sand so the rebel cannon balls will just sink it. He's got the prisoners penned up by the magazines, so if a rebel ball sets the powder off, it's gonna kill their kinfolks."

"Don't seem fair to me to take it out on those old folks," said the seventeen-year-old. "They was mean enough, draggin' them around behind horses and dang near killin' 'em, just because their sons were fightin' the Tories. It warn't the old men"

"Reckon' ole Angus is with 'em now," said Zeke.

"Those yellow-bellied bastards!" Jamie exclaimed. "Angus didn't give a damn about politics. He never considered himself anything but a Scotsman."

"I guess old Alexander felt the same way, but his sons didn't. They're both rebel officers. Grierson sent his men out to the country to pick up their father—he's seventy years old—and they made him walk into town forty miles an' whipped him when he tried to climb up into the cart," said the boy.

"We been talkin' about that," said Zeke. "We reckon it was one of the Alexanders' shot Grierson."

Jamie kept his mouth shut but vowed he'd take care of anyone who hurt Angus.

"I guess Colonel Lee will just have to starve them out of the fort," he said.

"Brown's ready for that," said Zeke. "We've all been on short rations so he could squirrel away food for a siege at Fort Cornwallis, and he's takin' no chances of drinkin' his own piss this time. They've got a well inside the fort."

"All I'm worried about is Angus," said Jamie.

"You shoulda thought of that when you joined the rebels," said Zeke. "They must be hard up when they take cripples."

"A game leg doesn't keep me from riding," said Jamie.

Colonel Andrew Pickens stopped him outside the guardhouse. "Did you get anything out of them?" he asked.

"My wife's uncle, Angus MacLeod, is a prisoner at Fort Cornwallis,"

Jamie answered. "God knows, I hope they haven't tortured him. He didn't know I was helping the rebels."

"What about Cornwallis?"

"Brown's expecting a siege. He can hold out indefinitely. He's got the prisoners penned in the bastion beside the magazine."

"Then we'll have to avoid that corner of the fort," said Pickens. "With only one six-pounder, we wouldn't be able to do much damage anyhow. I'll get the word to Colonel Lee. I'm headed out to his bivouac now."

"I'll go with you," said Jamie. "Have you had any word from Ninety-Six?"

"Only that Greene has laid siege to the fort. One of my men got word from his neighbor that General Williamson left the fort before the attack and went back to his plantation at Whitehall. Damned son of a bitch was hand in glove with Cruger, and now he's going to pretend to be neutral."

Jamie said nothing.

"Next thing you know, he'll be trying to get back in the militia."

Jamie could appreciate his concern. If Williamson returned to the militia as a general, he would outrank Pickens. And no one but Governor Laurens knew of Williamson's intelligence activities; most Carolinians thought he was a traitor.

"Maybe he'll stay out of things," said Jamie.

"We'd do damn well to confiscate his land and property as a Tory," said Pickens.

As they rode toward his position across the Common they could hear sporadic musket fire from Fort Cornwallis and from Lee's troops. They found Lee talking to the crew of the six-pounder. "See if you can clear out those buildings on the edge of the Common between us and the fort," said Lee. "We want a clear view of what Brown is doing and a clear field if we decide to charge."

"Yes, sir," said the artilleryman lowering the angle of the gun.

As they rode up, Lee greeted Pickens and asked, "What have you to report?"

"We've a whole hell of a lot of wounded Tories at Fort Grierson," said Pickens. "We haven't enough medical supplies for our own, much less theirs."

"Have you any suggestions?"

"I'd like to send a flag to Brown with a request for medical supplies," said Pickens.

"It's a good idea," said Lee, "but after the contemptuous way he treated Eggleston, I'd hate to subject our flag to insult."

"Eggleston was asking for surrender," Pickens answered. "Brown thought he was dealing with Clark's militia and you know what he thinks of Clark."

"That's right, sir," said Jamie. "Colonel Brown has reason to hate Clark's men. He would probably welcome a chance to help his own wounded."

"You sound as though you know him," said Lee.

"Yes, sir. I did some work for him a few years ago. He will act as an officer and gentleman when he finds he is dealing with gentlemen."

"I'm surprised," said Lee. "He has been painted as a barbaric monster."

"Harry," said Pickens, "A mob of these same Georgia Crackers tarred and feathered him and burned his feet with pitch pine because he didn't agree with their politics back in '75."

"Sir," said Jamie, "they were planning to kill him. Some of my friends helped him escape."

"Would he listen to you?" Lee asked Pickens.

"I believe if you sent a letter with your signature, he'd respect it," Pickens answered.

"We'll both sign it," said Lee.

Brown's answer was cordial and thanked Colonel Lee for his interest in the wounded soldiers. Medical supplies were sent with the messenger.

Meanwhile every shovel and pick was put to use digging entrenchments. Starting at the river bank on the left side of the fort, men began digging round the clock in shifts, keeping their heads below ground level to be safe from musket fire and angling their trench toward the wall of the fort.

The six-pounder was doing very little damage. The log walls of the fort were thick and solid, and the barracks and storehouse were at the farthest edges so they were almost impossible to reach with cannon fire. Saint Paul's Church beside the fort, however, was a pile of splintered boards.

"It looks as though we're going to have to do what we did at Fort Watson," said Lee as he and Pickens inspected the fortifications. "Build a Maham tower."

"What is tarnation is a Maham tower?" Pickens asked.

"When we were attacking Fort Watson," said Lee, "one of Marion's men, Hezekiah Maham, had the idea of building a siege tower high enough to see into the fort. Our men could shoot from behind a shield pierced with holes at the top of the tower. We'd asked General Greene for a field gun to put on the tower, but the fort surrendered before it arrived."

"You'll be lucky if you can get Brown to surrender," said Jamie. "Clark damned near starved them to death at MacKay's and he wouldn't give up."

"But he knew Cruger was coming to his aid. Now Cruger's penned up at Ninety-Six, and Brown knows it."

"I'm with you," said Pickens. "Anything's worth trying to hurry this thing up. My men are ready to go home. Their militia time is up and they may desert."

"Damn their militia time," said Lee. "Can't you talk them into staying on?"

"I'll try," said Pickens. "They're a good lot of lads, but the heat and gnats are getting to them, and they don't like digging ditches."

"What soldier does?" Lee asked. "But you can set them to work tearing down Fort Grierson instead. They can drag those logs back to help build the tower. We'll stack them behind one of the houses west of the fort so they can start the tower with the houses as a shield."

The next few days were filled with the sound of pick and shovel and axe and hammer, as the earthworks inched closer to the fort and the base of the tower began to take shape behind the houses. The work continued at night but was often interrupted by the attacks of Brown's Rangers, who sallied out under cover of darkness to disrupt the work parties. When Jamie questioned prisoners taken on these sorties, they refused to comment on conditions in the fort but reassured him about the safety of the elderly prisoners. Angus, it seemed, had made friends with the guards, and one of them had replaced his lost crutch.

As the tower grew, Brown erected a platform in the corner of the fort opposite it and mounted two heavy artillery pieces on the deck. Even with these canon firing at the tower, construction continued until June second when the tower was high enough to overlook the fort. The six-pounder was dragged up a ramp at the back and aimed through an embrasure cut in the log barrier at the top.

When the six-pounder began to fire down into the artillery crews of the fort, it was only a matter of time before both Tory guns were silenced. Brown had his guns dismounted and the platform removed. That same noon, while the officers were at dinner, an orderly came in to tell Colonel Lee that an old Scottish sergeant had come from the fort to desert to the American side. Jamie pricked up his ears, but the man's name was unknown to him. He was taken to Colonel Lee's office for questioning and Jamie asked, "What made you decide to desert?"

"I've no use for German George," said the Scot. "'Tis Charles Stuart whom I would serve."

"You've picked a strange time to make up your mind to that," said Jamie.

"Nay, lad, I do feel that I can now be of help to the American colonel.

• 294 •

With his big tower and his cannon, he can blow up the whole fort if he knows where the powder is stored."

"Do you propose to tell us?" Lee asked.

"I can show you just how to sight your cannon," said the Scot.

Jamie thought about Angus and the other prisoners held next to the magazine. There was something odd about this whole episode.

"Sir," said Jamie, "I suggest you put this man in the guardhouse. I'm sure your gunners don't need his help."

"I had just come to the same conclusion," said Lee, calling the orderly to take the man away.

"Now what do you think that was all about?" Lee asked.

"It might be an attempt to blow up your tower. We'd best keep a close watch on the buildings around it."

All but two of the houses near the fort were set afire that evening by Tory infiltrators. Only the house nearest the tower and the Merrill's house were left standing.

John Stanley came upon Jamie as he stood looking at the Merrill house. "Do you suppose Brown spared that house because the Merrills helped him escape?" he asked.

"Not bloody likely," said Jamie. "I'm trying to get some sort of grip on his reasoning."

"Why would he leave a house so close to the fort?" John asked. "It would be an ideal place from which to launch an attack."

"You've got it," said Jamie. "That's just what Lee's planning to do. Brown must have figured that out and hidden someone there to stop the attack."

Lee agreed with Jamie's reasoning when he was consulted and ordered the house searched from top to bottom. Nothing, however, was found.

"We'll wait until nine o'clock tomorrow morning and launch an attack in broad daylight," Lee decided.

Meanwhile, seeing activity in the house, Brown decided that Lee had stationed sharpshooters upstairs to cover the attack and filled the lower floor with assault troops just as he himself would have done in similar circumstances. He gave the signal to ignite a bomb hidden in the ground under the house and blew the empty house sky high.

Before the cannon was raised to the top of the tower, Colonel Thomas Brown had been asked again and again to surrender. He had replied that it was his duty and inclination to defend the fort to the last extremity. Now, on June third, he was asked again, and again he refused.

With the Tory artillery useless and the rebel cannon able to fire from the tower into any part of the fort, Brown's men dug tunnels in the ground to protect themselves as they moved from one part of the fort to another. Lee and Pickens decided to attack the next day, and made scaling ladders during the night.

On the morning of June fourth, as the combined forces of Lee, Pickens and Clark assembled and waited in the trenches surrounding the fort, the gate of the fort opened, and an officer in the green uniform of the King's Rangers rode out with a white flag and handed one of Pickens' officers a letter addressed to his commander and Colonel Lee.

Talk in the trenches went from a buzz to a roar. Militia officers had trouble keeping their men in line while the letter was being carried to the commanders. Lee broke the seal, motioning to Pickens to read with him. Men standing around them craned their necks to see.

"Lieutenant Colonel Brown has offered to surrender under certain conditions," said Lee. He motioned for quiet as a cheer went up. "General Pickens and I will have to review his conditions and discuss them with the staff before answering. Meanwhile you may stand at ease."

A groan went up from the men, but they remained in ranks as the two commanders and their staff walked back to field headquarters.

"He's asked for a day's delay," said Lee. "Would you believe it's because today's the King's birthday?"

The staff officers looked at each other in amazement, then burst out laughing.

"I guess if you've been fighting for seven years as he has, and had your feet burned because you wouldn't renounce the King, the old bastard's birthday is important. But I can't see how German George is worth the trouble," said Pickens.

"His other terms," said Lee, "are that parole be granted to all members of the garrison, who would also be allowed to carry their arms to Savannah. Officers would be permitted to keep their horses and personal property."

"Why that cheeky son-of-a-bitch," said Elijah Clark, "he'll be damned lucky if we don't hang him."

"After all," said Lee, "the British gave those terms to the American troops when they surrendered at Charlestown."

"You're right, Harry," said Andrew Pickens, "but Brown's had three other chances to surrender, and we've lost a lot of men while he decided."

"We can let them go to Savannah all right," said Lee. "Good riddance. But we can't let them have their arms. Officers' swords and horses are all right, if they can prove they own them."

"What about Brown's sword?" Pickens asked. "Doesn't he have to surrender that?"

"Of course," said Lee. "That stands for the surrender of the whole outfit. We'll send it to General Washington."

"I won't vouch for my men if they turn all those bastards loose," said Elijah Clark. "There are too many who've sworn to kill the ones who have raped their sisters and killed their brothers."

"We'll have to send a strong escort with them all the way down the country," said Lee.

"Clark's men are more used to dealing with outlaws and Indians," said Andrew Pickens. "I think I can depend on my men to abide by the customs of war."

"We'd better not take any chances with Brown and his officers," said Lee. "The men blame the leaders for hangings and torture. They'd better be paroled and sent straight to Savannah. Brown can surrender his sword inside the fort, and we'll spirit all the officers out to a boat on the river while the enlisted men are laying down their arms."

"We'll be leaving to join Greene," said Pickens. "Maybe we'd better take the rest of the Tories to Ninety-Six with us and let them go down through South Carolina and cross the Savannah near the coast."

"They're more likely to get there safely," said Clark.

That night Brown and his officers dined with Lee and his staff in one of the few houses left standing in the town. Troops from both sides were able to eat in peace around their own cooking fires.

The next morning on June 5, 1781, Brown surrendered the fort to Captain Rudolph, who was to command a Continental garrison there. The Union Jack was hauled down and the new Stars and Stripes rose to the top of the flagpole. The Loyalist troops marched out of the gate and laid their muskets and sidearms in a pile. One by one they took an oath not to fight any more. A detachment of Continentals marched into the fort to take formal possession. With Lee's permission, Jamie Stratfield accompanied them.

As the last of the Rangers marched out, a group of men in tattered buckskins were led through the gate by Angus MacLeod. When he saw Jamie waiting beside the gate, he waved his crutch, then came swinging across the ground.

"Ach, mon, it's glad I am to see you," he laughed as Jamie grasped his shoulders.

"Here I've been worrying myself silly about you," said Jamie, "and you're in better health than I am."

"I'm sure you're no better fed," said Angus. "There was plenty of food in the fort for a long siege."

Angus waved his crutch at a tall, sandy-haired Ranger who was waiting to take his oath. "I'll see you in the morning, laddie," he called. "That's Roderick MacLeod," he said to Jamie. "Would you believe the Good Lord sent my own cousin's son to be a guard at Fort Cornwallis? It was Roddy that found this crutch for me in the medical supplies."

"I had visions of you lying in chains, tortured and starving."

"Nay, laddie, ye must remember that Squire Brown was always well fed at the inn. He had no reason to punish me."

"It's as well you were in the fort and not at the inn," he told Angus. "There's not much left of it but a pile of rubble."

"Aye," said Angus. "Roddy saw it blown to blazes when Brown was cannonading that infernal tower. He said the artillerymen must have sighted too high and demolished the inn before they brought the cannon to bear on the tower."

They had reached the end of the Common. Houses that had stood between Lee's artillery and the fort were ruined, but Fox's Tavern had not been in the direct line of fire. One of its chimneys had fallen and there were holes in the roof, but Mr. Fox had carried tables and benches out to the lawn and was already serving. He waved Jamie and Angus to join him.

"You must share my good luck," he said to Angus. "Your drinks will be on the house here until you can rebuild."

"I'll not be rebuilding," said Angus, "but thank you for your sympathy and hospitality."

"You're not giving up," Jamie exclaimed.

"Nay, laddie, but Augusta will never be the same again. I do na' like to leave you and Meg and the boy, but I've made up my mind to gang back to the Highlands. Alexander MacLeod, Roddy's father, has a tavern in Inverary and a distillery in the hills nearby. He and I grew up there together before I joined the King's Highlanders. I'm gangin' wi' Roddy tomorrow when the Rangers leave for Savannah to be sent back to England."

"Meg will be sad," said Jamie.

"Nay, lad. She has you and Wee Angus, and you both ha' youth. I'd be a fool to turn down this chance at my age."

"Bless you, and I know you'll prosper," said Jamie. "But it's hard to have you go."

Mr. Fox, who had gone to serve other customers, now returned to the table.

"I'm planning to build a bigger and better inn," Fox said. "There is a rumor that Augusta will be capital of the state again, and we'll need an elegant place for government parties. I'd be glad of your help, if you change your mind."

"Thank you, my friend, and all the luck in the world to you. But I can hardly wait to get out of the heat and mosquitoes and back to the cool mists of the Highlands."

The next morning, Lee's Legion marched out, followed by the enlisted men of the King's Rangers and their wagon train of supplies and belongings. Behind them was a long train of wagons filled with Tory families and their possessions. General Pickens' militia followed far enough behind to let the dust settle, but close enough to protect the wagons from vengeful rebels.

One of the first of the civilian wagons belonged to Mr. Seymour and was driven by Angus MacLeod. Before leaving, the rector had told Jamie that he felt he must take his family to the safety of Savannah.

"You've been a brave man to stay here as long as you have," said Jamie. "You'll have no pulpit with Saint Paul's destroyed. Will you go back to England?"

"God only knows," said Seymour. "If, in His wisdom, He allows me to, perhaps I will find a pulpit in Savannah or a congregation in Florida."

"Good luck to you all," cried Jamie as the team pulled the wagon into line. The Seymour family waved goodbye.

Turning back toward camp, Jamie fell in step with Bert who was going to tell John Stanley goodbye. They found John on the Common with Pickens' mounted militia, tightening his girth and preparing to mount. "Are you two going to the mountains with Clark?" he called.

"I've been transferred to Clark's militia," said Jamie. "We're going to bring the Georgia families back home."

"I'm stuck with Pickens' brigade," said John. "God grant this siege doesn't last too long at Ninety-Six."

"We'll take care of Mary Anne and Johnny," said Bert, "and we'll get word to you if you're a father."

"Get in touch with Williamson," Jamie said in a low voice. "I'll see that he gets a message."

Pickens' bugler sounded the command to mount, and John waved as he turned his horse into the column and started toward the ferry.

Before the Tories were well across the river, the Georgia militiamen were on their way to the Ceded Lands. Most had finished their duty so military discipline was forgotten as they rode up the Cherokee Road toward Wilkes County. Honeysuckle festooned the underbrush, filling the air with fragrance, and jays and mockingbirds sang and scolded in the pine trees.

Georgia was free of British soldiers, and families could go back to farms with a whole summer ahead to live and love and cultivate the soil in peace.

Jamie and Bert rode together.

"I'll go back to Rae's Creek with Pa," said Bert, "and help him repair the house and plant the crops. But once the family's settled, Susan and I'll be heading back to that land near Fort James."

"I'll have to see how Meg feels about building on Angus' land by the Gully," said Jamie. "I don't think she'll want another inn. Maybe we can sell that lot or swap it for one farther down the river beyond Center Street."

"Susan never had to do anything for herself at home," said Bert, "but I reckon she's had to learn, living in the mountains."

"Meg's always had to work," said Jamie. "I'd like to build her a house like the Merrills' and have Desmond and Amanda to keep it for her, if they're still around."

It should take a week to ten days to get across the mountains to Watauga, longer if the fords were flooded. All day the horses moved out, feeling the eagerness of their riders and sensing they were headed for familiar pastures and barns.

At night by the campfires, lonesome lovers and husbands poured out plans for the future, each intent only on his dreams. Some whose homes had been broken or loved ones killed, sat away from the fires, drinking themselves to sleep.

At Heard's Fort, they stopped long enough to refill their saddle bags and rest for the night. The next morning they had been on the trail only two hours when they met a boy on horseback hurrying toward the fort.

"Davey Gordon," called Elijah Clark, "What are you doing down here?"

"Howdy, Colonel Clark," said the boy. "I've gotta tell 'em at the fort that the wagons are comin' in!"

"What wagons?" Clark asked.

"We-uns all done left the mountains. We're comin' home."

A shout went up from the men and horses leaped forward to race up the trail, leaving an astonished Davey Gordon sawing his reins to keep his horse from bolting.

Jamie found Meg's wagon first, with Bert coming close behind. Meg, who was driving with young Angus by her side, handed the boy the reins and scrambled down into Jamie's arms.

Susan, who was riding Star beside the next wagon, swung out of the saddle and pulling the mare behind her, ran to Bert who was dismounting Moonshine. With reins tangling and horses pulling, Bert picked her up off the ground and kissed her soundly, holding her as though he would never let her go.

The wagon train had halted, and the road was filled with dogs barking, children screaming and hugging their fathers' legs as mothers and fathers embraced. Horses, pulling away from hands otherwise occupied, ran crashing through the brush.

When the first madness of meeting had quieted, Bert and Susan walked to the back of the wagon Benjy was driving to find Ben climbing out and Mary leaning down to kiss her eldest son.

Bert heard a squeal from the next wagon in line, and Francie jumped down to hug and kiss him.

"Mary Anne's in there with the new baby," Francie said when she'd caught her breath. "It's a little girl named Anne."

"The baby was born the week before we started across the mountains," Mary Sheldon said from the back of their wagon. "Mary Anne is still weak, but she's been able to suckle the child."

"I've been helping Lissy care for the baby and keeping Johnny and Angus out of trouble," said Francie. "They've gotten to be little devils."

Bert walked behind the third wagon. Mary Anne Stanley leaned out to hug him, and Lissy held up a pink-faced bundle wrapped in a knitted blanket.

Whips cracked and horses broke into a trot, drawing the wagons toward tomorrow.

Author's Epilogue

At the end of a novel, the story should come tidily to a close, with the characters' problems settled and their plans made for the future. In a historical novel, however, the reader is often left wondering what happened to the real people who formed a background for the fictional ones.

The Sword and Thistle was a figment of the author's imagination as were Angus, Meg, and Jamie. Fox's Tavern and Mr. Fox were real. The Sheldon family was fictional, although John Rae really owned the property which they farmed along what is now Washington Road, and Rae's Creek now runs through the Masters' course at the Augusta National. John and Mary Anne Stanley and the Merrills were my creation, too, and though Anne Bonny was a real person, her later life is unknown, and was fabricated as Anne Seabright in an earlier novel.

The men who met in the dining room of the inn, however, were very real, dynamic people who made events happen as they did in Georgia and the Carolinas. Of this group, few were left in Georgia after the war.

John Stuart, the Superintendent of Indian Affairs, died in Florida of a chest condition before the war was over. Edward Barnard, Robert MacKay, and John Rae all died of natural causes during the time of my story, and James Grierson was shot by a rebel militiaman after surrendering.

Thomas Brown was exchanged when he arrived in Savannah after the surrender of Fort Cornwallis. He became Indian Agent for British Florida, where he helped the Creeks during the turnover to Spain after the Treaty of Paris. He finally settled in the Bahamas with large grants of land and became a respected planter and statesman.

Lachlan McGillivray went back to Scotland. His half-Indian son Alexander led the Creeks in Florida in a continuing war with the United States for the next decade.

Martin Weatherford settled in Abaco in the Bahamas, near some of Thomas Brown's plantations there.

Andrew McLean married Catherine Chilcott, Mary MacKay's daughter by her first marriage, and also settled in the Bahamas.

The Reverend Mr. James Seymour, after the trek to Savannah with the Augusta Tories, moved to Florida where he was the only Church of England clergyman in the territory. After the Treaty of Paris, he was invited by the congregation of Saint Paul's to come back to Augusta as their rector. Instead, he sailed for England and died en route.

Doctor Andrew Johnston answered the pleas of his patients and returned to practice medicine in Augusta for the rest of his life.

George Galphin, who accepted the position of Indian Agent under the rebel government, helped keep peace among the Creeks and Cherokees until his death at the age of seventy-one at Moore's Bluff.

Lachlan McIntosh, who was captured at the surrender of Charlestown, was finally exchanged and moved with his family to Virginia until the end of the war. After the peace, he returned to Savannah and spent the rest of his life in near poverty, trying to regain his land and possessions that had been confiscated.

Many of Georgia's patriots returned to the Augusta area and prospered.

William Glascock served on the commission to settle the Florida border dispute with the Creeks, then settled near Augusta at The Mills, his country estate, where he was buried.

John Wereat also settled in Augusta after the fall of Fort Cornwallis and used his boats and slaves to take rice and provisions to people left destitute by the struggles. He was president of the convention that ratified the United States Constitution in Augusta in 1787 and later moved to Bryan County, where he died in 1794.

George Walton, captured at the battle of Savannah after he was shot from his horse, was exchanged and returned to Augusta. He lived and died there as a statesman, serving twice as Governor of Georgia, one term as a United States Senator and six terms as a United States Congressman. As a signer of the Declaration of Independence, he is buried under the Signers' Monument in front of the County Building in Augusta.

Andrew Williamson, who returned to his plantation near Ninety-Six when Brown took Augusta, has gone down in history as a coward, if not a downright traitor. One historian called him "the Arnold of the South." After the war, his property was on a list of Tory land to be confiscated. Evidently he had been too successful in covering his intelligence activities for the patriot cause.

His fight to prove his patriotism was ignored in most post-Revolutionary accounts. He was exonerated, however, by some very important patriots, including South Carolina Governor John Matthews, Patrick Calhoun, and General Nathaniel Greene, who wrote that he wanted the Legislature to know that Williamson was employed by John Laurens in "the business of intelligence" and "has faithfully served the Army; and he has given generally the best information we have had." His lands were not confiscated, and he died a respected citizen.

For starting me on the search for information about Andrew Williamson's activities, and for encouragement in the two years I spent among the rebels and Tories, I give my undying gratitude to Ed Cashin, Chairman of the Augusta College History Department. He seems to share my weakness for the bad guys in history. He was never too busy to stop, find papers he had written, and have them copied for me, or just chat about the idiosyncrasies of our mutual eighteenth century friends.

My accounts of most of the battles were taken from Henry Lumpkin's *From Savannah to Yorktown*. I tried not to quote directly, but often found his words too perfect to be able to paraphrase successfully.

I am thankful for my good friends Cathy, Eve, Anne, Alice, and Fritz who read and corrected my manuscript before I sent it to Sandlapper, for Jane Kelly and Virginia Ingram who helped me winnow the chaff from the final draft and for a husband who uncomplainingly ate and slept with all the old boys of Revolutionary Augusta for those two years.

Saluda, North Carolina
1988

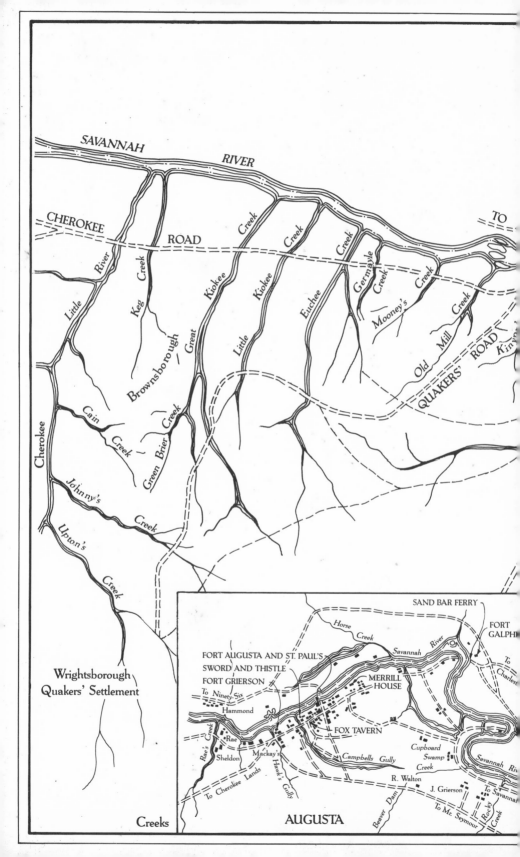

SAVANNAH RIVER

CHEROKEE ROAD

Little River

Keg Creek

Cain Creek

Johnny's Creek

Upton's Creek

Green Brier Creek

Brownsborough

Great Kiokee Creek

Little Kiokee Creek

Euchee Creek

Germaple Creek

Mooney's Creek

Old Mill Creek

QUAKERS' ROAD

Kinyo...

Cherokee

TO

Wrightsborough
Quakers' Settlement

Creeks

AUGUSTA

SAND BAR FERRY

FORT GALPH...

Horse Creek

Savannah River

FORT AUGUSTA AND ST. PAUL'S
SWORD AND THISTLE
FORT GRIERSON

To Ninety-Six

Hammond

Rae's Creek

Rae

Sheldon

Mackay's

Hawk's Gully

To Cherokee Lands

MERRILL HOUSE

FOX TAVERN

Campbells Gully

Creek

Cupboard Swamp

Savannah Riv...

R. Walton

Beaver Dam

J. Grierson

To Mr. Seymour

To Savannah

Rocky Creek

To Charlest...